THE
MAGICK of
MASTER
LILLY

Tobsha Learner

sphere

SPHERE

First published in Great Britain in 2018 by Sphere
This paperback edition published in 2018 by Sphere

1 3 5 7 9 10 8 6 4 2

A CIP catalogue record for this book is available from the British Library.

ISBN 978-0-7515-6213-2

Typeset in Garamond 3 by Hewer Text UK Ltd, Edinburgh
Printed and bound in Great Britain by Clays Ltd, Elcograf S.p.A.

Papers used by Sphere are from well-managed forests
and other responsible sources.

Sphere
An imprint of
Little, Brown Book Group
Carmelite House
50 Victoria Embankment
London EC4Y 0DZ

An Hachette UK Company
www.hachette.co.uk

www.littlebrown.co.uk

Assist me O glorious God, for my task is difficult, and thy servant is of little understanding! Few, nay none at all are the helps I expect from any man living (having hitherto had no assistance) but what thy pleasure is, by the universal Anima Mundi, to infuse into my obtuse intellective part that will I candidly deliver without deceit or fraud.

William Lilly 1647

For all those across the globe; the magical thinkers, the non-believers, the believers – there is magic in wonder!

Disclaimer

Dear Reader, this is a book written with great respect for William Lilly and all practitioners of astrology and the occult. However, although I have gone to great lengths to research and depict these years of the astrologer, this novel is a faction designed to attract a broader audience to the wondrous life and achievements of the great astrologer – having said that, there was a plethora of mystical secret societies during the English civil war, so who knows . . .

CHAPTER ONE

☊ ♀ ♛

August 1641

The Cottage, Hersham, Surrey.

If a Question be asked of marriage, behold the ascendant and
the Lord thereof, and the Moon, and the Planet from whom
the Moon is separated, and give those for the Significators
of the Querent; and the seventh house, and the Lord thereof,
and the Planets to whom the Moon applieth, for the Signifiers
of him or her concerning whom the Question is asked.

I should introduce myself to you, dear Reader. I am William
Lilly Esquire, of some thirty-nine years of age at the beginning
of this chronicle. At this time I resided in a large cottage in
Hersham, in the county of Surrey, and was in the midst of an
unhappy second marriage – but I shall elaborate on that later.
My religion, which in the era of my times defines a man, was
the reformed Protestant Church of England, although my
dealings in the world were more with the Papist than
Protestant. And in those days, with the great schism and
hatred between Catholic and Protestant growing by the day, I
did strive to be as flexible as a sailor steering a boat in a storm
and, in this way, keep both my life and my head.

My profession was that of Philomath, specialising in the
predictive craft of horary, although I secretly practised the
dexterity of the occult (the benign and learned form) as well as

performing as medic and herbalist to many of the local community. Horaries, Natal figures, seduction of reluctant lovers, the finding of lost things, and the location of errant husbands, were just some of my expertise and, as Physic and Astrologer, I was obliged to examine the urine of my clients for ailment, and so I was oft referred to as a piss prophet, to my chagrin.

We are all born with our Fates written like maps across the cosmos, but our faith and humanity give us choice. This is what I, William Lilly, believe: the Stars incline, they do not compel, and it is up to us mortals to know when to play our hand and when to fold.

I remember it was one of the last heady mornings of summer; the scent of lavender still floated over the hedgerow and the hay had not yet been cut from the stem. I had been in my chambers tending to a horary request in a half-hearted manner (it being a minor question of theft). For, dear Reader, lately my discontent had become a threatening rumble, the constant vexing of my peevish wife whittling my patience to a thin veneer. Plainly I craved adventure and the silence of the countryside, once a comfort, did now make me panic. My only escape was provided by my most munificent and ever-bountiful friend, William Pennington, who did oft summon me to London; the gentleman was my mainstay. Bold, very rich and eminent, he was a major patron of mine whom I had helped avoid charges of false paternity and several other ventures in which he was so sorely abused.

Nevertheless, here in the village my life was the slow shuffle of peasants and farmers who sought me out for such portentous events as predicting where stolen goods might be hidden, descriptions of potential spouses they are yet to meet, and the reading of men's Fates from the moles and other marks upon their bodies. Important for the 'small' man, but my talent hungered for greater challenges.

To my vexation, the pealing bells of London, the bustle and shrieking of the pedlar — even the acrid smell of the tanners — pricked at my dreams and crept into my waking day like haunting memories of opportunities lost. I yearned to have power; and the thirst to examine the *great* Questions all scholarly Astrologers wish for, the chance to give direction to the politick of the day, to save and direct powerful men to better ruling, surged up through my body like Desire, and I could quell it no longer.

The night before my restlessness had been ornamented by a dream — a vision. I confess that both my soul and conscience was plagued by this second sight of mine that oft plunged me into moral quandary and did haunt both my nights and days since I were a child. In this dream, I saw myself again in London, in mine own house upon the Strand. I were seated upon a throne, the feet of which were oozing blood, and my head did rest upon a beautiful peacock whose plumage was, most disturbingly, satin black, and what this portended I dared not imagine.

And so it was that morning I found myself at my desk, drawing up a figure, when a carriage of exquisite wood panels, pulled by horses of such breeding that it was no wonder to see the royal crest upon the cabin, rattled down the road. Staring out of the window I did hope King Charles himself might be passing through the hamlet to hunt — anything to break the tedium of this self-imposed exile. Then, to my astonishment, the coach arrived at my cottage. Convinced it must be a courier with some query he sought answer to — perhaps the tricky engagement of some by-blow to a daughter of a wealthy lord, or the outcome of an ill-advised foreign investment — I ran out to greet my city visitor.

The coachman jumped down to open the door of the carriage and I waited with trepidation as the embroidered shoe of a gentlewoman appeared upon the step, the rest of her personage following, her short cloak trimmed with fox thrown across her shoulders, the yellow silk of her dress billowing in the breeze. To both my horror and astonishment I saw that she wore a peacock feather in her cap, and that it was black as in my dream. Nevertheless, assuming she be royalty and no sorceress, I bowed low, my hand scraping the gravel of the path.

'You are Master William Lilly? The Astrologer and Adept?'

'I am, my lady, and you are from London, from the Court itself?'

Stepping forward she gave me her gloved hand, and I did glance down dumbly at such a fragile thing. I was now most conscious of Jane, my wife, at the window, the heat of her gaze setting the back of my doublet ablaze. Curse the jealousy of the woman, an emotion born not of love or the desire for marital congress but of sheer spite. Many are the days I rue the lust that blinded me, an Astrologer, to her true nature during our courtship.

Jane Rowley is my second wife, a union far less happy than my first marriage, Jane being of the temperament of both Mars and Saturn: that is to say, cold, phlegmatic, argumentative and unforgiving. In marrying her I gained a portion of five hundred pounds, but in truth she is spendthrift, with many poor relations forever seeking alms. I love money as my servant — I adore it not as my master, and believe me, William Lilly will be no slave to income or to the will of any man. Jane is also a Quaker, a fact I was not aware of when courting and, as such, disapproves of my astrology and craft. This is hypocrisy most unfair, for she is still content to live off the profits of my industry.

Thinking upon my irksome marriage, I kissed the perfumed gloved hand.

'My name is Magdalene, Lady de Morisset.' The aristocrat's lilting voice suggested a polished girlhood at the French Court.

'I am here on behalf of a certain painter who works for Queen Henrietta and who, having heard of your fame, seeks the advice of the stars.'

I prickled at the mention of the Queen's name. I was, after all, a Puritan and the Popish French royal was much vilified, amongst my ranks. But, dear Reader, I am a practical man, and pragmatism is the virtue of the survivor – and if that virtue be of many hues, so be it. Besides, there was a cast to this woman's features that suggested Venus in Taurus – a steadfast nature but also an adorer of luxury – she was not a beauty but boasted a comeliness a muse might have: strong in feature, green eyes set wide over a patrician nose and most intelligent mouth; I decided I would trust her.

I had by this time been living in Hersham for seven years. Before that, I lived and practised in London at a house on the Strand I did inherit from my first wife, the fortune of my first marriage having allowed me the education of the Philomath. I sought out the best of teachers, but I tell you at great risk of prosecution, my skill as a people's astrologer I had not learnt from Books, or any manuscript, but from a Cabal lodging in Astrology.

And so it came to be that, as a younger man, I began to make a living as both an Astrologer and Magician. I did learn a number of spells: how to summon angels, fairies and spirits, how to secure the hearts of the indifferent for the lovelorn, and suchlike.

More importantly I learnt how to manipulate outcomes, not just predict them.

Indeed, I was once employed by a doctor of Physic, a John Hegenius, to practise the use of talismans and dowsing rods, which I did with great effect in 1634. And I would have remained in the capital if it had not been for two incidents of magick and mystery.

The first was a search for a quantity of treasure that hath, in theory, been buried beneath the cloisters of Westminster Abbey.

I was called in, along with my partner in such magical matter, John Scott, and a gentleman called Davey Ramsey, to search with the use of divining rods the place whence this treasure could be unearthed. Followed by a disbelieving and jeering crowd we did accidently uncover a coffin, then, after moving into the Abbey Church itself, a severe wind of most unnatural description did blow up suddenly, terrifying both ourselves and our deriders, and thinking it unhappy spirits, we did flee.

The second event was the suicide of one of my Querents by the poison Ratsbane: a young pregnant woman of lowly status, made with child by an indifferent young Lord who wanted no part of the child and was forever avoiding the said woman. I had correctly predicted where she would encounter him at a theatre box at such and such a time, and that encounter had been successful, though again the young noble made himself unreachable, and again I had predicted where his abused lover would corner the rascal, but this time she did execute her threat and swallowed the Ratsbane at his feet. These events left me afeard and greatly afflicted with the melancholia; more pressingly, rumours of my occult practices had placed me in disfavour of the Old Bailey and Parliament, and I was finally driven out of my beloved London.

These days King Charles stomps upon the ordinary man in his arrogance and taxation has become intolerable. The Monarch wages a silent war upon both Puritan and his own peoples. The capital is much changed and a far more dangerous place than whence I left.

I stared upon the awaiting coach and the urbane woman before me. Could she be the conduit to the adventure I had been craving, a chance to influence greater destinies, a sign I should return to the great city?

After ordering my wife (who, now, sensing the possibility of a wealthy Querent, hovered like a gadfly) for ale and riddle-cakes and to make sure the horses were fed and watered I invited the noblewoman into the cottage.

Once in the privacy of my study, I questioned the mysterious visitor further.

'Who is this painter and what does he want of me?'

'What makes you so certain it is a he?'

'A man would know to send a woman as yourself as the messenger – he knows how to coat the bait with honey, a woman would just send her manservant.'

At which she laughed: a full-throated chuckle, not the least becoming to her sex, and I confess I was intrigued. I am of the growing belief that Woman in some ways might be the more powerful gender – swayed by my witnessing of such female visionaries and seers. After all, the power lies not in the strength of the vessel but in the essence God pours in it.

'My master is a mistress, and yet she is no mistress over me,' Lady de Morisset answered with a smile.

'You speak in riddles, like the Sphinx.'

'And you, sir, make your living speaking in such like pretty metaphor.'

'Based on the truth of the stars, and the stars live in Heaven, therefore I speak of a truth written by God himself.'

'You believe our lives are written out in the skies in such exactitude that we have no race to run, and not that victory is won by man's will alone?'

'Faith! I think thee an inquisitor who means to trick me into a declaration of allegiance for I can see from your employment and your garb you are a Royalist, and perhaps a Catholic, whereas I am obviously not?'

'The woman I carry the message for is a friend, and I am no woman's or no man's servant. My friend is indeed a great painter, an artist of our times despite her gender. Artemisia Gentileschi, the daughter of the late Orazio Gentileschi, and she is in

Greenwich in the employment of the King, finishing a great mural in the palace.'

'And it is she who wishes me to draw up a figure?'

'A horary for a particular occasion, but she will tell you more in person. You will escort me back to London this very eve.'

'I will? So, you are now my mistress and myself no longer a master of my own Fate?' I could not help but jest.

At which she cast her gaze about the room and I swear, dear Reader, in that moment it was as if I was viewing through her eyes – the drab comfort of the place, plain and a little worn in its function – the hearth and old iron spit, the heavy dark chairs and tables of an older time – one of solid purpose no more and no less. A half-played game of basset still lay upon the table, an indication of time idled away. A few books upon the shelves (my secret library being further within), the cat curled sleeping upon an embroidered stool, my wife's spinning wheel in the corner, some thread still upon it. And all I could perceive was the meagre ambition of my life spiralling into an anonymity that was surely a waste of my talent.

To my surprise, the gentlewoman took me by the arm and pulled me to the window.

'Master Lilly, what is the emblem painted on the side of the King's coach?'

'I see the royal coat of arms, a unicorn and a lion.'

'But there is something else painted upon the door, a beautiful youth with winged feet and a single golden lock falling from his forehead, waiting to be grasped as he races past. Caerus, the young god of opportunity.'

'I know of him and he has deceived me more than once,' I answered warily.

'This time he is true, Caerus only passes momentarily and if you do not grasp him he will escape this time for ever, Mr Lilly. Great talent doth not hide its light.'

'Tis untrusting times, and I have more friends in Parliament than in the King's Court.'

'Artemisia and one far, far higher in status will vouch for your safety. Pack your things: we leave within the hour.'

Again, it was a command, but this time I did not argue, so I bade her wait then retreated to my study, a wood-panelled chamber lined with my many books of both magick, astrology and studies of the occult, a collection that I am proud to say hath amongst it *The Works of Guido Bonatus*, Ptolemy's *Tetrabiblos* and even the *Commentary on Alcabitius* by Valentine Naibod. I had chased libraries of my peers, both in the occult and astrological worlds and the hunt paid dividends. Although, in the dark months before I was forced to leave London, I made it known that I had burnt these very same books, such was my terror of being branded a Wizard. Yet now the most dangerous of the tomes sat brazen on the shelves before me, like friends one could never betray.

At my desk I rolled out a blank scroll and, with the assist of a ruler and an abacus, calculated the auspices of the journey and the following day. How had my reputation – still in its infancy – reached the ear of an influential courtier? A man of law, perhaps, a whisper of a quandary solved, an auspicious time and place predicted correctly?

I finished the horary figure and studied the planetary symbols. The auspices for the journey were mainly favourable, although Mercury in Gemini, ill-aspected by Saturn, suggested caution in any communications or business transactions. Could this be the opportunity for adventure I craved? So, on balance, I instructed the maid to pack a trunk with some clothes and books. Then, despite the loud complaints from my wife, by the time the sun was shining over the thatch we had departed.

I watched Magdalene de Morisset against the velvet upholstery, the motion of the carriage making her coiffured hair and breasts shift against the silk in the most fetching way. I found myself wrestling with the Puritan within: such a woman is the very embodiment of original sin, displaying her assets with such obvious delight. But to my confusion the intensity of her intelligence seemed to me both a paradox and a counterbalance to all that glittering splendour and in this I could not dismiss her as a whore nor as a lesser being. It was most vexing. To distract myself from such temptation, I endeavoured to gaze out of the window.

'It has been over a year since I have visited the city.' I spoke lightly, conscious of our touching knees. 'My London patrons tell me it is much changed?'

'Like a clock that is uncomfortably wound, it gets tighter,' she answered obliquely.

'The King has made himself unpopular. It was a mistake to have dismissed Parliament in the first place, but then to rule for so long without one . . .'

'Eleven years. The King takes his duty most serious, sir, and we cannot forget he is the representative of God himself. Besides, he restored Parliament last year.'

'The so-called short Parliament – appointed in April, dissolved in May. Is it any wonder the people doubt that the King really hears them, never mind the guilds and merchants? A head needs a body, legs to walk and arms to hold. The King is the head, the army and navy his arms – but the rest is his People. The ship tax is deeply unpopular, the folk are frightened about a war in Ireland and of Scotland rising and they fear the Queen's French connections. They want England to be one faith. The King does himself no favours.' I was shocked at my own audacity; in truth, this noblewoman summoned the younger, braver and undoubtedly rasher man in me. Was it her beauty or her intelligence that emboldened me this way? I still do not know, but I knew now that my words did allow her to mark me for a traitor. Thankfully, she put her finger to her lip, warning me to say no more.

'The King is an uxorious husband and has all the hallmarks of an austere and religious man. His weakness, which he shares with the Queen, is arguably that of a zeal for the patronage of the arts, but is it so sinful to want Hampton Court to rival Paris in its high culture? Surely it is for the good of the nation to have such investment in such a heritage?' She leant forward and I could smell the scent of violets and her own musk. 'Artemisia herself is finishing a series of extraordinary panels started by her father for Her Majesty at Greenwich palace – an allegorical piece that will inspire all who gaze upon it, from peasant to earl. And it was her great friend and paramour, Nicholas Lanier, master of the King's music, himself a fine artist and musician, who bought van Dyck to Court, just as Lord Buckingham persuaded Rubens to grace us. I might add that Rubens' *Crucifixion of Christ* at Denmark House is the most inspirational depiction I have ever seen,' she concluded passionately, and I wondered if she herself was an artist.

'That it might be, nevertheless the starving cannot eat art.'

'But it is food for the soul.'

She slept whilst I gazed upon the passing fields and forest, reflecting upon the visit. Such a day, such an hour of significance that it made me examine the portentousness of the encounter. I stole a glance. Her hair was auburn, but in the sunlight that dappled the carriage as it moved forward it appeared blonde in parts, russet in others. Her hands anchored to long fingers, betraying sensitivity, her figure was slim and girl-like, yet there was a maturity. She looked, I wagered, like a woman whose hips had not borne a child. She appeared to be around twenty-eight years in age, against my own thirty-eight, and yet it was as if I had known her from an earlier time. So overpowering was this familiarity I decided that it was the sole reason I, a cautious man, had lowered my guard and spoken so bluntly, courting the politics of the scaffold by doing so. What manner of magick was this?

Just then, the coach came to a sudden stop, jolting me from my seat. Outside, the air was full of men shouting as Magdalene, thrown toward me, grasped my arm. 'What's this? Are we at the inn already?'

At this time there were large numbers of rogues and beggars lurking in the countryside, to the great terror of the traveller. Exploitation by the wealthy of both worker and peasant had made two Englands — one blind to the other. Sensing danger, I drew Magdalene from the window, indicating that she should keep silent.

I pulled the curtain aside: a group of men in the plain robes of the Puritan had blocked the path with an old wooden cart. There were four of them, two carrying hoes, the other two with swords on their hip. The coachman appeared to be trying to reason with them.

I immediately took off my purse, bidding Magdalene to do the same, then hid them between the cushions of the coach. A moment later the door was yanked open.

'Good sir and Madam, pray descend so that we may gauge the cut of your cloth.' The man, in his twenties, spoke with the local accent, and yet I did not recognise him. Hoping to protect my companion I climbed out first.

'We are unarmed and on an errand of a personal nature,' I declared, now wishing I had packed my dagger upon my person.

There were four of them, two younger and two older. Only one looked to have soldiering skills, the others had the cast of the farmer about them. It was an odd encounter, and they were not of the appearance of the usual highwaymen. Nevertheless, there were four of them and three of us, and although the coachman bore weapons I saw, with failing heart, he was restrained by one of the men.

'I am a local man and you have no business with this gentle-woman,' I urged as Magdalene stepped down, all eyes upon her.

'A local man, in a coach that hath the royal crest upon it?' The leader who addressed us spat upon the ground in disgust.

'A Surrey man and one of plain prayer, as you can see of my attire,' I insisted, hoping to draw their attention to myself and away from the young aristocrat, whose proud bearing I feared did her no favours.

'Then what are you doing with this Royalist whore?' The youngest, whose pockmarked face betrayed a mean and vicious nature, lurched forward. I flinched, fearing they meant to violate Magdalene, but she stood her ground and met their gaze with a defiance that, after a coiled moment, engendered embarrassment in the men like a tiny flame licking tinder.

'I am no man's whore, good sirs, but it is also true I am no man.' She spoke in a steady voice. 'So if you wish to assault me, pray do it knowing I am not the King's property, I am my own woman, with my own politick. Assault me and you assault all womanhood, but not the King. If you wish to take that burden upon your righteous shoulders I shall lie myself down upon the grassy knell yonder.'

Faith, I was impressed, she had the courage of a bull and the wit of a lawyer.

Now the men, shifty about their feet, looked abashed. Finally, the leader spoke.

'But the coach is of the palace?'

'She was sent to fetch me, and I, Brother, am both godly and straight.' Again, I stepped between the men and Magdalene, tugging on my white collar as an indication of my Puritan ways. 'I am Master William Lilly, of Hersham.'

'I've heard of thee. Thou art the Astrologer, a great predictor of happenings; you told my aunt where her favourite breeding ewe had gone wanderin',' the youngest piped up, his face broken by a greening smile.

'And did she find it?'

'Aye, she did. So now the King calls for thee — maybe he's lost some sheep?'

The others laughed, and again I felt the tide turning. If we were to travel safely on I had to act quickly and most cleverly.

'If he has, he is bringing forth the right man, but I fear he had lost a lot more than sheep these past years . . .' At this the air grew very tight indeed, our Fate dancing upon the whim of the moment. 'He hath made enemies of three goodly men in our Puritan leaders Prynne, Burton and Bastwick, and now courts a dangerous fortune. King Charles' stars and blessings are mixed indeed.'

There followed a short silence in which a cow bellowed in a nearby field, and a bumblebee, attracted to the yellow, danced before my lady's silk skirts.

Finally the leader pulled open the coach door. 'On your way, good sir and Madam,' and turning to the lad holding the coachman, 'Jack, let the coachman to his post.'

Greatly relieved, I helped Magdalene back into the carriage, but as I was about to ascend the leader pulled me toward him.

'Master Lilly, you tell the King he must stop bleeding the people. No more taxes, for army or ship — I have five children, two of which have died of hunger. We have no land of our own, yet each year the squire takes more and more. You tell him, Brother, the people must have a voice.'

And so, with these words resounding in my head, we continued toward London, that cornucopia of life and chance.

♊ ☿ 👂

CHAPTER TWO

Night, London

**The Sun: The Solar man: Prudent and of incomparable
Judgement: of great Majesty and Statelinesse,
Industrious to acquire great Honour and a large
Patrimony yet willingly departing therewith again;
the Solar man usually speaks deliberately . . .**

We arrived at the walls of the city just as much of London was
sleeping, except for the nightsoil men, and usual denizens of
those most dark hours who scurried about the streets — crimi-
nals, whores and all those who hath lost their souls in the bustle
of the waking day.

Driving over the cobbles, the overwhelming acrid smell of
the coal fires, the stink of animal dung, human sewage and the
tang of Mother Thames carried on the dank air — a familiar
stench hauling out of the depths of memory images of my city
life before. It was like returning to a woman you had forgotten you loved until you saw her again: such is the fickle nature
of men, for oft we know not what we desire until it is in front
of us.

I told myself: I am returned to the youth I was when, naïve
and wide-eyed, but blessed with a natural intelligence, the
son of a farmer who ended up in debtors' prison, and whose
mother had died only a year before, I did head toward the

house of my then sponsor and master, Master Wright, a salt merchant. Green about the brow, and full of hope at eighteen years of age, I had entered the metropolis dry-throated and heart pounding, keen to try my destiny against her hard-edged ambition.

The coach turned into the Strand and the Corner House I inherited came into view. How did I get my wealth, dear Reader? In death and matrimony, for oft Fortune hath a two-sided face.

I served the illiterate Mr Wright as a clerk for a number of years. His first wife, Margery, a goodly woman who first introduced me to the use of amulets in the warning-off of spirits and disease and then to astrology itself, was much neglected by her husband. She loved me as a friend as well as a servant, but sadly perished of a canker of the breast despite my fledging efforts as a medic. When Mr Wright himself died a natural death, his second wife – Ellen Whitehaire, a corpulent woman, plain of face and tongue and a good deal older than myself, and having married twice before to old men for profit, not love of heart or the pleasures of the bedchamber – wished to marry an honest man who would love her in every manner and she cared not if he were penniless.

Faith, I am not a calculating man, but I do believe in grasping the good goddess Fortune if she so favours thee. I was twenty-seven years old and handsome enough in my visage and of strong health, despite my propensity to intellectual reverie and melancholy (my Moon in Pisces, my Mercury in Taurus and my Mars in Virgo, both in plodding Earthy signs). More pertinently, my fellow servant in the household had made it clear to me that my mistress moaned my name in her bed and thus I was encouraged to pursue my suit. But the courage it took on the night I declared myself was Herculean indeed, for I risked as much by staying mute as I did pressing my suit.

On one hand, I knew my audacity could find me in the gutter, yet if I did not present my case such an opportunity might pass me by. How confronting my quandary, and how significant was such a chance to move out of servitude and into a respected and learned class in which I might pursue both education and my astrology!

That evening, well plied with drink, my comely but aged mistress spoke of how she wanted to marry a man of genuine emotion and good bedchamber play, an honest fellow who cared nought for her wealth, but where to find such a man? Thus challenged, I swallowed my stomach down, jittery with doubt and suchlike fears, and suggested I knew of such a creature. With a knowing glint in her eye my mistress asked who that might be? (A tease, I realised afterwards, but in my naivety thought her innocent of my advances.) Puffing my chest out with the brash confidence of a young man who knows nothing but is sure of everything, I declared him to be myself.

At first she argued I was too young, but I convinced her that what I lacked in wealth I could compensate in love and other such sturdy things a youth has to offer – that, and the caresses I bestowed upon her that night, swayed her – and so, dear Reader, I secured both my match and fortune.

We were left with an income more than both gentleman's and baronet, enabling us to live very pleasantly and to afford a servant and meat twice a week, and for myself to keep a couple of dogs.

It was both a good life and a good marriage. I would take breakfast at six, do all my study before noon, then after my meal to go out to meet friends or enjoy myself at the bowling green. Apart from the company of my loving wife and my astrological studies (the attendance of lectures two to three times a week) I occasionally angled, played a great deal of both basset and primero with friends but much of my time was spent down Little Britain, searching through the booksellers there for rare tomes of astrology and the occult, or at the tavern, drinking and conversing, or at my beloved church St Antholin's, attending religious lectures. An insatiable hunger had come upon me to consume the wisdom of all the ancient teachers of such practices and I sought out those in England who could apprentice me in the hermetic arts.

I had many masters, but my first teacher was the talented but unscrupulous Welshman, Mr John Evans, a drunkard, Astrologer and scholar of the black arts, a most fantastic debauch, but he was well-versed in the Nature of Spirits.

I will describe, for the benefit of the disbeliever, one such ceremony I did witness. For the fee of forty pounds John Evans did promise to summon the fearsome angel Salmon to retrieve a stolen title of deeds for a righteous gentlewoman. The ceremonial magick took a good fortnight of both ritual and invocation and when the ferocious Angel did appear (being of the nature of Mars) the winged spectre did destroy some of the dwelling of the thief who had been withholding the title from Mr Evans's client. Yet when the Angel returned the deed to the righteous gentlewoman, he did lay it upon the white cloth most gently before evaporating back into the ether. It were the most terrible and inspiring sight and, understandably, I was eager to take instruction from Mr Evans after such a display of expertise.

There was also an Alexander Hart, once a soldier and now aged; his speciality was to give auspicious times to gamble to the young noblemen addicted to the dice. He ended up upon the Pillory for cheating, but not before I purchased some of his excellent magick and astrology books to serve my study. And who can forget my drinking companion, the comedic William Pool? A middling Astrologer, who, after the death of the Justice who had accused him of theft, found the man's grave and excreted upon it leaving two verses:

Here lieth Sir Thomas Jay, Knight,
Who being dead, I upon his grave did shite.

Indeed, as the carriage pulled up outside my house on the Strand I reminded myself to again befriend the amusing Pool, a dabbler in Astrology, sometimes a gardener, sometimes a civil servant, sometimes a bricklayer – but always a wit and a man most apt at drolling, as such distractions are sorely needed in these dark times.

Perhaps it was the alluring woman sitting beside me, or perhaps the ever-presence of my unhappy second marriage that brought back memories of great affection, but it might surprise you to learn that notwithstanding the difference in age and fortune between myself and my first wife – I was twenty-five and she in her sixties – and despite the opposition from her dead husband's relatives, seeking to secure his substantial fortune and who thought me dishonourable, we truly loved each other and our adoration survived for six years until Ellen's natural and peaceful death in October 1633. It were a year later I did purchase the majority share of thirteen houses along the Strand and my material fortune was secured.

After promising I would to Greenwich Palace the next day, I took my leave of Magdalene de Morisset. Then, after Mrs Featherwaite, my steely cook and housekeeper, escorted me to my bedchamber (as welcoming if not a little dusty as it ever was) I collapsed upon my bed and fell into the arms of Morpheus, still dressed in my doublet and hose.

The next morning, after being woken the noisy shouting of my neighbours, I found myself sitting at the kitchen table, a chunk of bread and cheese before me, simple fare I very heartily enjoyed.

As I stared out of the window I remembered how, as a humble servant, I'd swept the street in front of the house for my master, and had hauled water up from the local well for both washing and drinking. How my own fortunes had improved – but outside, the city and its most dense atmosphere hath undergone a transformation and it felt ill to my senses.

With crumbles still in my beard I turned to Mrs Featherwaite to ask how she found her fellow city dwellers; her being the eyes and ears of the temper of the streets.

"Tis a tinderbox, my good master, with much discontent. As you 'ave 'eard, last May Day we had the 'prentices rise up – thousands of them there were, howling for the blood of the Papist Queen's mother, that Mary de' Medici, and Archbishop Laud, the snake. Horace, that's the baker's lad down the road, he ran with them, told me they got as far as Lambeth palace, joined by the dockhands and sailors they'd picked up down St George's fields but the Archbishop had run off – coward that he is – so they went on to the manor of Earl Arundel, and made a great racket and destruction there.' She swore like the Devil. 'It's Queen Mary of France and all her Papist family! Even the money men with their wares and businesses are angry at this Popish King with his Popish wife in league with the Popish Spanish and French. Why, good master, I 'ave 'eard from yonder across the road, wot she's heard from a maid serving down at Lady Cavendish's in Mayfair that her mistress and her master were both persuaded by Queen Mary herself to trot to Mass (and them sworn Protestants both!) on Sundays at Denmark House. It's a disgrace! Worse still, the servants were forced to accompany them, and so they all go, and now that poor maidservant, proper English and a good Protestant, is afeard for her soul and is probably heading straight to Hell all on the whim of a Queen!' Here she paused to kick the cat. 'King Charles is making an enemy of London and I blame the Scottish war and all the King's finery and fancy art. What good is that to us? And what's he buy that new palace – Wimbledon – for? He's got six palaces already.' And here she started counting on her fingers. 'Greenwich, Hampton Court, Nonesuch, Oatlands, Theobalds . . .' She faltered.

'Holdenby?' I added, eager to clarify our shared disapproval.

'And now bloody Wimbledon – a gift for that stuck-up Queen of his who 'as him wrapped around her little finger, or his little cock wrapped around hers. Not to mention that French mother-in-law – remember when the Queen's mother first came to London with her mob? What a procession, six carriages all sparkling with gold they were, acrobats, dwarfs, them Catholic monks, all them foreigners with their prancing and gilded ways, and us English expected to pay for it all with our taxes!'

At which I got up and pulled shut the window, worried that the neighbour might hear, but the good woman continued loudly indifferent to the possibility of an accusation of treason.

'And you know what else?' she exclaimed, 'the King never comes out of Whitehall to visit London proper. He never lets the lame or the poor touch his cloak or hand to be cured, as is their Christian right. He is always hiding in the palace, he has no interest in his people, many of us . . .' Then lowering her voice she glanced at the window as if there might be a spy behind it '. . . who was great supporters of those leaders of the people, Prynne, Burton and Bastwick, the great rebels of the Parliament, Godly men, Master Lilly, Godly, blessed men of God. Their humiliation is not forgotten, it were a crime to crop their ears. And when the guards rode the people's leaders through the streets to display their shame, those poor men mustered a great cheering from the people – they were heroes, not traitors – cheering in front of the royal guard despite the *royal* decree by his *Royal* Majesty. I'm telling yer, go east to Tower Hamlets, speak to them who are gathering both arms and training – there will be a people's army within the year.'

At that point, a young boy dressed in a coal-stained jerkin with a head of cropped red hair that made him look as if he'd just been rudely plucked from a field somehow, appeared at the kitchen door. I was about to shoo him away when Mrs Featherwaite pulled the lad to her ample bosom.

'Oh, Master Lilly, I've been meaning to tell yer, this is Simon Pure-in-heart Featherwaite, my nephew. In your absence I have appointed him kitchen boy. He is very useful, hardworking and handy with a ladle or spade.' She pulled me aside. 'And he takes his Bible very seriously. Costs you nothing 'cause his wage comes out of my pocket, given his mum died last year and all.'

I studied the lad, who already had the look of a fighter about him. And I did wonder whether it was the cudgel and not the ladle he had such skills in. It then occurred to me that he might be useful as a guard to the house in these troubled times, and if he had cunning — a spy. In turn Simon Pure-in-heart gazed back at me with eyes wide with ignorance and wonder.

'Me aunt says you are a great teller of fortunes and can magick up all manner of spirits, both good and evil?'

'I did not, Simon, and that is no way to address your master! He is Master Lilly to you, you understand?' His doting aunt cuffed him about the ears.

'Tell me, Simon Pure-in-heart, are you strong and fearless?' I asked, smiling to put the lad at ease.

The boy struck a pose. 'As strong and fearless as them guards at the Tower. I'll not let you down, Master Lilly.'

'He is employed, Mrs Featherwaite, and I'm sure I can afford an extra shilling a week.'

As mentioned, dear Reader, Mrs Featherwaite is the *vox populi* and I have always valued her as such and so her observations of London perturbed me greatly. She also had a most industrious tongue and I dare not tell her I had been summoned to the very Court she so belittled for fear the whole street might eventually know. Instead, I took careful note of her opinions, for they indicated the sway of the land and would serve my calculations.

I have always believed the politick of above influences the politick of below (I am naturally referring to astral and terrestrial bodies) but I also believe the flow of authority, like water heated by the Sun, also runs upwards and there is no harm in gathering as much information before drawing up a horary figure. A good Astrologer collects notes to exercise his genius and, as such, I can only recommend the cultivation of friendship amid the clerks at the Old Bailey as well as several individuals who drink regularly at the three most popular taverns of Westminster, aptly named Hell, Heaven and Purgatory (Hell having the best pickings as that most favoured by members of Parliament with several hidden exits for a quick getaway). Other fortuitous places of loosely shared information are the playhouses and brothels of the city. For, a good Philomath should always endeavour to get in the way of luck and, in that manner, ensure good fortune. But as I have mentioned before, I am also skilled in the ways of manipulating luck and circumstance itself, and these skills lie in ceremonial magick – something even the best spy in the kingdom cannot manufacture.

I finished my bread and cheese and pushed the plate away.

'Mrs Featherwaite, I will be back in practice as of the morrow. Please send out a crier to let the parishioners know. The usual charges – a horary, half-a-crown from them who can afford it, a shilling from the less well-pocketed, medical advice for those who seek it and any astrological predictions for love, objects lost, found or stolen negotiable at the same rates, and the poor I will see for free if they dare. Spread the word, Mrs Featherwaite, at church, the stocks and market – I know thy tongue is golden.'

*   *   *

That afternoon I took the boat to Greenwich, careful to place upon my head a wide-crowned hat, my personage wrapped up in a jacket with a high collar hiding my face for it would have been unwise to advertise my journey to my neighbours, or to my two servants. This city has always had the discretion of a drunk fishmonger's wife, but now, more than ever, men have taken to labelling their neighbours in a most unchristian and dangerous way. I think it be the great uncertainty of our times. It was as if the country is drawing a huge struggling breath only later to exhale through two nostrils — one for the Royalists and one for the Parliamentarians. *William Lilly*, I told myself, stepping into the dank wood of the barge, *you must watch your back for it is twice marked*.

And so, with this sensibility, I paid the boatman an extra shilling for his silence. As I watched the swans and other barges sail past I reflected that some might call me a trimmer, a man who swims backwards and forwards with the tide, with no strong loyalties of his own, but in those troubled times it seemed even more imperative to adopt the flexibility of a reed. For all men are born with a set of astral equations and all are God's creatures, no matter what their politicks, station or whatever evil or unfeeling aspect they care to adopt. Regardless of the qualities of their Nativities, the course of their lives is always a question of free will — Murderer or Saint.

King Charles was not exempt in this. I regarded him as manly and well-fitted for venial sports but he rarely frequented illicit beds. I had not heard of any children apart from those of the Queen's, and I heard he was extreme and sober in both his food and apparel. And yet he ruled not wisely.

And so, pondering such paradoxes, I arrived at Greenwich Docks, where in a blaze of colour and billowing silk Magdalene de Morisset was waiting to escort me to the palace. The lady had with her a palace guard and a small African page dressed in the same colours as herself, by which I took him to be a loyal servant, and indeed, the child did help me up upon the docks to greet the Lady.

'I trust you are well-rested, and settled in your house?' she asked, strangely formal, at which I guessed both the page and the guard in attendance were paid spies for others.

'I am, my lady, although I find London a changed city.'

'How so?'

'A storm cloud is gathering; men will soon be forced to declare themselves.'

'Well, perhaps betwixt the two of us we might have some influence as to whether and when that storm breaks.'

By this time we were walking through the narrow streets of Greenwich village, through the market stalls, past the town square and stocks, amid the curious gaze of several sailors busy in a game of bowls upon the green, and the iron gates of the Palace loomed before us before I had a chance to collect myself.

'You have the ear of the King?' I asked making sure my gaze was held steady before me, but trying nevertheless to stay my growing excitement, for, although I had patrons amongst the aristocracy, I had yet to visit the palace – Parliament, the Old Bailey and the tavern houses of Westminster being my more natural milieu.

'I have the ear of the Queen; I am one of her ladies of the bedchamber. You will find I will not disappoint,' Magdalene murmured back, surprising me with the innuendo of her comment. I glanced over to catch her page grinning cheekily up at me whilst my lady's face remained inscrutable.

The guards at the gates needed no instruction and it became obvious to me that Magdalene was more powerful than she had intimated, and again I wondered why she had felt so familiar to me.

'The artist is to be found in the House of Delight,' she told me, a description that could only intrigue as she led me through the gardens straight to a building with two curved stone steps, agreeably symmetrical, at the entrance. Well-pleased with the simple beauty of the place, more temple than dwelling, I paused admiringly.

'It was built by Inigo Jones and was begun for the King's mother, Queen Anne of Denmark, but only completed six years ago,' Magdalene told me proudly.

We stepped into the hallway, to encounter a sweeping white staircase curling upwards in a spiral with fantastical ornate iron railings. When I looked up it were as if I was looking into a great eye with sunlight radiating down from a central oval window set above.

'These are the Tulip stairs,' Magdalene whispered reverently, and indeed I felt as if I had stepped into a cathedral but one that worshipped the aesthetic.

Beyond lay the main hall which was full of scaffolding stretching to the ceiling, and there, surrounded by several assistants in smocks, was a woman lying on her back atop a platform as she painted the tip of the wing of an avenging angel, her hair tumbling over the edge of the wooden scaffolding giving the impression of a languid repose, yet there was an air of fierce industry about this reclining figure.

Dumbfounded, I counted nine half-finished panels of extraordinary beauty and allegory above the artist. I had not, until that point in my life, seen a woman, especially a gentle-woman, engaged in such profession, and I watched, fascinated, as this figure (so slight against the drama of her own creating) continued to paint, a cloud of concentration tapering into one sharp point, which was both her will and her craft. And as I observed the wonder of her intensity, the abandonment of protocol as if all that mattered was the conversation between her paintbrush and the story unfolding under its sable, I could not help but bring my own craft into play. An ascendant in Pisces, born in the hour of the Sun, I concluded, after a second glance at the dark mane of tumbling hair and the grandeur of her surrounds, with perhaps Venus also in the sign of the Lion, close to the ascendant as this was a woman clearly at ease with royalty – such was her passion.

'Signora Gentileschi, Mr William Lilly, the Astrologer, is arrived!'

Magdalene called loudly so that she might be heard. There was an exclamation in Italian before the artist leant over to one of her assistants straddling the scaffold behind her and spoke in the same tongue before sliding away from her position to allow him to continue her work.

Now a rounded face, which in a strange way mirrored the cherubic demeanours smiling down from the painted panels, appeared over the edge of the platform.

Artemisia stared down at me critically, as if to assess my intentions. Sighing, the artist abandoned her palette and began climbing down one of the narrow wooden ladders with a fearless dexterity that suggested this was commonplace for her.

Once she reached the bottom, I was able to observe the full extent of her personage. She was of short stature, and not as young as I had first thought, still comely to the eye, but somewhere around fifty years of age, I wagered, and of the dusk of the Mediterranean. There was a sharp intelligence to those black eyes, and a wryness to the full mouth. In short, a matron of pleasurable appearance.

'My lady . . .' I bowed, then indicated the painting above us. 'Your work is sublime and quite without comparison; even unfinished it astounds me. What is it called?'

To my surprise she glanced at Magdalene as if she did not understand my speech.

'The work was begun by the artist's late father, who died two years ago,' Magdalene answered for the artist. 'Signora Gentileschi is commissioned to complete it. It is, naturally, an allegory for the benevolence of His Majesty towards the arts.'

'Naturally,' I responded, practising a smile on my future patron, to no avail. A slow fear started creeping up through my liver and spleen: why now did I feel as if I were on trial when I was the invited party?

To add to my discomfort, Artemisia Gentileschi began walking about me, examining me like a farmer examines a horse at market (I was half expecting her to open my mouth and examine my teeth or tap my hindquarter). Finally, she turned to Magdalene and spoke in her native tongue.

'*Quindi questa è la stargazer, spero che egli è buono.*' While I, unable to comprehend apart from the words *stargazer* and *good*, stood feeling a little foolish, to my surprise Magdalene retorted in fluent Italian.

'*I migliori, apparentemente, e un pensatore indipendente, sarà una valutazione del destino il più critico.*'

Again, all I understood was the phrases 'independent thinker' and 'destiny most critical' and before I had a chance to query Magdalene the artist had replied, '*Sono lieto.*'

Again, I wondered whether that I was being led into some kind of political trap, like a fox offered a chicken to entice him to walk between steel jaws.

'Ask the good artist why she is not consulting Sir George Wharton, the King's own Astrologer? Surely he would be the more obvious candidate?' I held my voice steady against my growing anxieties.

Magdalene turned to translate, but before she had a chance to begin, the artist had retorted, again, in her native tongue, which only led to more suspicion on my behalf, her tone growing harsher.

'*Cerchiamo una obiettiva opinione. Capitano Wharton è un servo, l'uomo prima di me è un uomo libero.*'

'We seek an unbiased opinion. Captain Wharton is a *servant*, the man before me is a free man,' Magdalene translated.

The answer pleased me; it showed that although Artemisia was in the employment of the King, and although a Catholic (as are all her countrymen), she was also of an independent mind, and within that, I wager, she calculated the chance of a more honest reading from one such as myself. I bowed deeply.

'And I can assure you, you will receive the most objective of calculations for whatever event you so choose—'

'Enough!' A veiled lady emerged from a darkened doorway. Immediately my companions dropped to a deep curtsey; assuming this must be an individual of great authority I followed with a low bow.

The gentlewoman walked toward us, her skirts rustling across the marble tiles, the veil of delicate gossamer concealing her features hung to her waist which was encircled by a gold chain beaded with the largest pearls I had ever seen. I could not help but notice she was unaccompanied, yet I sensed others watching us most carefully.

I glanced over and saw two faces staring out from the shadows; one was that of a dwarf, a grotesque indeed, wearing the cap of a jester and a striped doublet. Towering above him was an older woman, as grand as the other, and by her dress and face I recognised to be the Queen's mother, Marie de' Medici. I feigned ignorance, and returned to look upon the Queen, but to be in the presence of the two most influential women at Court pricked at my vanity. I had to remind myself to stay wary of my tongue and not to prattle in a dangerous narcissism. I have Mercury in Taurus and Mars in Virgo, out of its term and face, causing my conceptions to be dull and my discourse defective, and it receives Mars by trine, making my gabbling more of a hindrance than advantage.

'Monsieur Lilly,' the voice imperious, Queen Henrietta held out a hand, bejewelled by most costly gems. My bowels turned to water.

'Your Majesty,' I managed to utter.

'Indeed,' came the reply and she lifted her veil to reveal her features set in an air of sobriety and nervousness. She was far uglier and far shorter than her portraits, her teeth protruding over her lip yet there was a grace to her movements. 'Your proclivity' (and here I took her to mean my politick) 'has not gone amiss in these parts. But, luckily for you, neither has your ability to predict and your particular skill in the horary.'

At which I found myself scraping even lower.

'I am here to serve, Your Majesty . . .'

'And you will,' she replied firmly then turned to the artist, 'Artemisia, I thank you for the ruse.'

''Tis my delight,' the artist replied in perfect English, then turned back to me. 'The mural is called *The Triumph of the Peace and the Arts*,' she informed me curtly, then ascended back up the ladder. As the state of both the Nation and the Court was precarious, the title struck me as being ironic.

'Artemisia is as good as her father and is a great heroine of our gender, sir, a woman who describes herself as having the soul of Caesar in a woman's heart. We should all live in her example; however, I fear I will have no choice in the matter,' the Queen elaborated.

'I am to venture then, Your Majesty, it is you who is my client?'

'I am your client, but not the subject.' At which she slipped her hand into a pocket and produced a square of paper of the finest parchment. She handed it to Magdalene who then handed it on to me. It bore the royal seal and I held it gingerly as if it were a powder keg.

'Monsieur Lilly, my husband has not knowledge of this meeting and I intend it to stay that way. You understand that if this encounter, or any of its imports, be made public in any manner whatsoever it will be the Tower and worse for you?'

'I understand, Your Majesty.'

'You may break the seal.'

Which I did, failing to hide my trembling fingers; inside was the exact time, date and location of the birth of His Majesty, King Charles the First.

'As you can see, this is the true information of my husband's Nativity. There is only one other who has such facts and that, understandably, is the Royal Astrologer, Captain Wharton. But I wager you are the superior practitioner.'

'You have placed your faith well.'

'Captain Wharton is blinded by love for his King, whereas I suspect that you are not. I am hiring the "clear eye". I wish you to draw up a figure on my husband's future in both Scotland and Ireland. The Scottish treaty concerns me, and I do not trust the Marquess of Montrose, James Graham, and now, of course, this rebellion in Ulster. It will not bode well for Charles.'

'Quite possibly, Your Majesty,' I interjected, perhaps a little too enthusiastically.

'A set of auspicious dates is your order, and fear not, you will be paid well. Madame de Morisset will be my representative in this case. Good day to you, sir.'

At which Queen Henrietta replaced her veil, then with another swish of her skirts disappeared down a corridor, followed by the footfalls of the Dowager Queen of France and the dwarf. Magdalene and I waited in silence, with just the soft whoosh of the paintbrushes above us, until the footsteps had faded.

'Her Majesty is a kind and brave lady in need of much comfort,' I finally spoke, a query as much as a statement.

'Her unpopularity eats at her heart, and say what they may, the love between the King and Queen is fidelitas incarnate, of body and soul.'

'Is this not unusual at Court?' I inquired wryly.

'Politics makes whores of most men. Except you, Master Lilly, which is why she has hired you and not the Royal Astrologer.'

'And yet I fear I will need to temper the aspects.'

'The message is more important. How it is delivered is in your hands.'

And with that ominous warning Magdalene escorted me out of the palace.

At the docks, she placed me with the same discreet boatman, and pressed her address upon me, telling me if I needed any assistance she was there to serve me.

'I am also myself an alchemist and amateur Philomath. It was my recommendation that brought you to the Queen, Master Lilly. You are not alone in this city; take faith, there are like souls whose practices mirror your own. We are watching you.'

'We? Do you mean a cabal?'

'Let's just say when the time is right, you will be approached.'

I studied her carefully. I had heard rumour of such a society, secret and buried deep within the influential power mongers of the elite, but I also knew it would be certain execution if such alliances were made public.

'The Queen was influenced with purpose?' I ventured.

'That I cannot confirm or deny, until then if you have any doubts or fears, I am both your servant and apprentice.'

At which my thoughts did wander in a most sinful way. The

dress and cape she wore did little to conceal the curves of her body, and I did wonder on the beauty of her nakedness. The barrenness of my marital bed and the nocturnal wrestling I had with my own carnal needs preyed upon me. Here was a woman I sensed could meet me equally in matters of philosophy and the occult, and (I am shamed to say) in the sensual arts. This was most transgressive and I could barely look at her for fear my lust would be achingly apparent.

As if guessing at the cause of my discomfort, she smiled and I did wonder if I could trust myself to be alone with her in any chamber.

CHAPTER THREE

The Corner House, the Strand

The Moon: She signifieth one of composed Manners, a
soft tender creature, a lover of all honest and ingenuous
Sciences, a Searcher of and Delighter in Novelties,
naturally propense to frit and shift his habitation . . .

That evening I carefully laid out my parchment, quills, ink, my
tables and books as well as my ruler. The first task I set myself
was to draw up the birth figure of his Majesty.

I found that the King arrived on this Earth when his ascendant was in Virgo at eleven degrees, making Mercury lord of the
geniture and the King born on the day of Mercury. His Mercury
was in Sagittarius in the fourth house, a placement that suggests
discretion and a reluctance to look beyond the walls of one's
own clan, family or enclosed world. This was not favourable —
an ill-placed Mercury can signify a troublesome wit, a quarrelsome tongue and pen pitted against every man, an individual
who wastes his estate and time in gossip and trying his conclusions to no purpose; a great liar, boaster, prattler, busybody and
false.

He was also born the hour of Jupiter, which was in the first
house and connected to his Sagittarius Sun in the fourth house.
This was his most extrovert placement — here lies his commitment to duty but again the degree was not advantageous. At

twenty degrees it indicated a most frugal mercenary individual – one who lives for gain no matter how wealthy, a coin-counter of unpleasant liverish disposition.

And so we have four planets; Sun, Mercury, Venus and Mars, all in Sagittarius and all in the fourth house! As the fourth house is an angular house, each of these planets gains accidental dignity (perhaps a saving grace) whilst Jupiter is in mutual reception by rulership with Mercury, forming another connection between the first and fourth houses. However, as I have explained above, Mercury is in its detriment. The fourth house placement shows that the King will risk everything to protect his family, his lineage and the court. He will call upon all his resources if these are threatened. It also suggests a conflict between his private world and the world beyond – in this case the Kingdom and his people. This is the negative; the positive is the angle which means he is a loyal character and attracts many a good fellow, but underneath this charming façade and seemingly straight arrow-talking, great secrets can lie.

The Sun falls in the sign of the Archer, suggesting unyielding willpower, and at eight degrees as you, dear Reader, most probably know, it is next to the star Antares – *the Scorpion's Heart* associated with being rash, heart-strong and obstinate. This star is violent and is said to denote a violent end – the King cannot take this current placement lightly – for this aspect proposes his status could change suddenly and most unpleasantly.

I noted this, searching for a metaphor with which I could convey the message whilst keeping my own head. The fourth house is the domain of family and the immediate private environ. That the Sun is in the fourth house also means the King's family is all unto him. This he values above England herself. For a man in his position, family before State could be considered a weakness, and surely reflects how much the Queen has control over her husband.

His Moon, the planet of movement and change, however, is in the sign of conciliation Libra. This is a most favourable placement for a Monarch, and could counterbalance the prominence of fire that I see races through his Natal figure like a renegade. It would suggest that King Charles will avoid violence, and would seek to maintain harmony. It is also a placement that gives him the ability, like the tuning fork of a harpsichord, if he so desires, to listen to the *vox populi* – to the fashions and discourse that flow and ebb through the ether. A placement he has ignored to date; if only there were a way to encourage him in such ability it could save both His Majesty and this country much grief.

Even so, this charming Moon is restrained: it is placed in the second house. Here is manifest the King's greed for luxury, his obsessiveness with statuary and painting as well as his fascination with possessions. As the King himself is austere in dress and behaviour, I warrant this aspect is expressed through his art collection, an expensive amusement he places above the welfare of his own subjects, and also in his choice of wife – for Henrietta has been a woman obsessed with the making of the English Court as luxurious (and some would say wasteful) in its lavish ornamentation as the French Court.

Just then, outside the window, a town crier reported another riot. Again, I debated whether the King even knew of the growing discontent amongst the apprentices, the most agitated of our young men – or of the number of good wealthy citizens broken by the Ship Tax, or the unhappiness over his insatiable appetite for Scotland and Ireland.

Upon hearing more shouting and the distant thud of cannon fire I instructed Mrs Featherwaite to double-bolt the doors then returned to my labours. It felt curiously powerful to be examining the intimacies of a King inside whilst outside his kingdom already rumbled in discontent, as if I could be the puppet master in the travesty of his rule.

And so we arrive at his Venus – and lo, again in the house of the Archer – so much fire! It does not bode well, but it could be worse – he could have all these planets in Aries, which would be most disastrous. I could not help thinking on my cankerous wife Jane at this point: how could as learned an Astrologer as myself have married such an ill-starred creature? I would like to say that love is blind, but in truth I have concluded that it is the loins that are truly blind as so many of my Querents would testify.

The Monarch's Venus in Sagittarius means he seeks constant change and new sensation, the aspect of a cocksman most active. However, yet again (Oh wondrous is Nature in its symmetry) this planet is also in the fourth house – the house of family and clan. The King will not wander far and will limit his affections and true face only to those nearest – his family and blood. Thereby is the reason behind his fidelity; however there is a darker seam to this Venus – her degree is twenty-three – which suggests a man of most colic and depressed nature, a sad man, perhaps even a man predisposed to taking his own life under certain circumstances. It also indicates that the Monarch should avoid any recreation on or in water as there is a greater vulnerability of fatal accident here.

Now I come to the warrior planet Mars again with the Archer. It was with some unease that I looked for its placement at the time of King Charles' birth. For Mars, if well-dignified in feats of War and Courage, is invincible, scorning any who should exceed him, subject to no reason, bold, confident, immovable, contentious, challenging all honour, valiants, and lovers of war. But ill-dignified Mars can become a prattler without modesty or honesty, a lover of slaughter and quarrels, murder, thievery, a promoter of sedition, frays and commotions, as wavering as the wind, a traitor of turbulent spirit, perjured, obscene, rash and inhumane. In such a man as the King, this placement is keystone to the monument of his destiny.

By the time I put down my ruler and quill I had been at the desk for six hours and it had passed the hour of midnight. My spirit depressed, I peeled off my doublet and hose and crept under my bedding where I hoped to sleep the coma of the exhausted.

It wasn't to be, for as soon as I closed my heavy eyes, a great vision came upon me. It was as if Magdalene herself visited me in the form of Lilith or some dangerous seductress who wished to bleed me both of my senses and seed, her naked form with those breasts and hips wound around me. Like a succubus, she crept into my bed and wrapped herself around my lips and over my face and mouth, binding me to immobility as much as I wished to shout out or wake myself. I was helpless, pinned to the mattress as if trapped by my very Fate. Then, as I gazed upwards, the heavens appeared and displayed in frank candour a cosmos I recognised as a manifestation of the skies at my own Nativity – the Sun in Taurus and there my Moon riding the Goat. Yet where celebration and familiarity should have reigned there was nothing but fear and foreboding. I could not move arm nor leg, I could not shout out, nor banish this oppressive panorama. It seemed to me all those opportunities I might have played over the past thirty-nine years, those golden cards – Jupiter's bounty, Venus's seductive allure, Mars' strategy — looked down and mocked me for wasting their great gifts.

Then, as I lay there transfixed, my seductress leant down and kissed me, her long hair falling about me like a veil. At which my senses seemed to return (within the confines of the vision) and I sat up. Smiling, the phantom spoke the following:

'Good William, thou art a greater adept than thou hast acknowledged; you are committing the sin of squandering celestial gifts. You must become a prophet for both England and the People, a warning bell for all those who will listen and they will. It is your moral duty to undertake this task, without fear and without partisan or prejudice. For, at the judgement hour, Man stands apart from politick no matter what standard he hath raised in his life. Warn the people of the disasters that are to follow, both from the hand of God and Man.'

As she spoke, she floated up toward the ceiling whilst a huge chasm opened beneath her. I watched in an abject fascination as a mist seemed to fill this void then manifested into two adjoining beings who I recognised to be the young twins of Gemini, the ruling sign for the great city of London itself. Behind this ensemble were the distant forms of masked men pitching wrapped corpses into huge ditches – plague workers ridding the city of the dead. Then a great Devil appeared and grabbed both twins by the ankles and, to my horror, began to feed them into a great raging fire.

I woke, my sheets drenched in sweat, and immediately rang for Mrs Featherwaite, thinking I might have a fever or, worse, the pestilence itself. This gift of premonition is itself like a disease, as oft I have no say nor control as to when it is upon me. It is almost an apoplexy, for it is all consuming of the Spirit. Thank the good Lord, Mrs Featherwaite then made a purge of camomile and nettles, which calmed my nerves, after which I began to draw up a horary for London itself using myself as the Querent.

My question – if my vision is to be truthful, when will this most disastrous bout of plague consume the city to be followed by a huge fire? I worked upon this horary for three hours without faltering in a fervour of great anxiety, aware of the implications of my findings. I finished at six in the morning, just as

Apollo began racing his chariot below the horizon and the sky was shrouding herself in a rose mantel. The vision still weighed heavily, more so as the plain evidence of the future disaster stared up from the page. My only solace was that it was in the distant future – 1665, by my calculations, so a number of years was to pass before London would be changed for ever.

I left the house and wound my way down to the banks of the Thames, thinking on the beauty of the wooden Tudor houses that leant in all natural manner across lane and street. The density of this haphazard architecture, born from man's necessity and community, had a pleasing anarchy; was this all to be destroyed?

I hurried past the Palace of Whitehall, and could see from the flags that the King was still resident at Greenwich, the palace gates barred and guarded against the populace. I was stopped by sheep being herded by farmers hurrying their flock down to Shepherd's Market for auction that morning, the startled animals pushing and shoving their way through the narrow lanes, some scrabbling over the back of others, eyes wide in terror as the shepherd dogs snap at their heels, the whistling of the farmers echoing through the streets, empty, except for rag pickers and the last of the night-soil collectors, the odd flower monger and town crier readying themselves for the day's work. I have always liked the early morning, when the day's events are still unfurling like the bud of a flower; this is the hour when Fate is most potent and, with foresight, uninfluenced by a man's distemper or joy. I then walked east. I confess, standing at the top of the London Bridge road, staring down the bridge itself with the high wooden houses built on either side (some of them seven stories), like a row of tall men crowded in upon each other, I did not feel my customary exhilaration, instead foreboding filled me like a sickness.

Hoping to dismiss the malady, I started across the bridge, the occupants of which were only now waking. The smell of freshly baked bread curling from behind the half-open doors of the bakeries, the sudden perfume of lilac grown beside a window to mask the stink of the gutter beneath, the rank familiar stench of the River drifting up from the water below — it was everything I both loved and hated about my adopted city.

I stopped at a break in the buildings and glanced across the water. The tide was out and the mud-covered bones of all kinds of refuse littered the foreshore. Looking down I could see the narrow ladders of the Three Cranes stairs leading to the grand, gabled houses on the north bank. Below winkle pickers and other scavengers worked their lonely way up the river beach, laundrywomen beat out their washing, fishing men hauled in the first catch, spirals of seagulls circled as the birds fought over scraps whilst the blackened skeletons of long-sunk boats, protruded from the sands, reminders of lost eras. Beyond that, Billingsgate, the wharves of the custom house then the Tower Wharf, the Tower looming up behind it, a grim monument to tyranny past and future, the Irongate stairs, a place where many a barge filled with the condemned had moored, all green metal, glinting in the rising sun.

Further down the riverbanks the shipbuilding yards of London Dock squatted in defiant industry. Straining my eyes, I could just see the Poplar shipyards through a distant mist, great half-built wooden hulls gaping incomplete, the glow of the smelting fires red smudges against the jutting chaos of enterprise, the billowing chimneys of the tanneries and factories, the pungent smell of smoked fish drifting down from a hidden fishworks.

In that moment the commerce of Man seemed like the frantic scrabbling of ants, a pointless struggle against the grindstone of Time; I felt my old malady of spirit returning, the Demon of a melancholy I feared I carried within me always, but what had brought it forth now? Perhaps, I told myself, this is the affliction of the prophet: to always have one's perception hauled into the epic, to see the headstrong foolishness of Humanity plough on blindly.

How much could I prevent? Was I seeing a future that had perhaps, in the way pouring glass can fold over itself invisibly, happened already? Did Time indeed run in a straight line? There were some Occultists and Philosophers who believed otherwise; I, myself, was undecided.

I turned back to the river. A vast number of cargo ships stretched across the water, waiting their time to unload at the docks, tall masks bare, their sails curled. I counted six abreast, spanning the whole width of the river, and wagered I could probably cross by foot by leaping from one deck to another. Their flags flapped feebly in the thin breeze telling of distant and not so distant lands: the Hanseatic Crest, the Flags of the Netherlands, Spain, France, Sweden and the East India company, London was the hub of trade – the Nexus of the merchant world, my world now.

Just then a pedlarwoman thrust her tray of cockles under my nose. To rid myself of her company I bought a bag, and ate them staring back at the old wooden city, still ringed by ancient Roman walls. In that moment sunlight caught the glass of the windows and the city looked as if it was ablaze. Again, my premonition swept through me and I staggered, catching myself on the edge of a horse trough then remembered Magdalene de Morisset's promise of help.

It was a large, fashionable brick house of a good width, built within the last ten years I wagered, the house of a prosperous merchant or aspiring courtier. Wondering about her husband

and the source of his good fortune, I removed my hat before lifting the door knocker: a brass dolphin of most elegant sweep. A maidservant answered, flustered with the morning's duties. It was then I remembered that it was still early; the church bells were yet to toll seven.

'Yes? Are you from Court? Is my Lady summoned?' she asked impertinently.

'Forgive the hour; a Mr William Lilly to call upon Lady de Morisset?'

'And does she know you, sir?' The girl looked not seventeen, and yet she had the authority of a thirty-year-old, and appeared as protective of her mistress as a young lioness. I liked her a little more for that despite her brisk manner.

'I have been placed in her charge by the Queen herself. So yes, I believe I have made Lady de Morisset's acquaintance,' I answered, now hesitant with doubt. Was I foolish to risk sharing my premonition? But before I had a chance to turn on my heels the maid had pulled me onto the doormat.

'In that case you'd better come in, but mind yer boots, thick with horse's dung they are.'

I looked down; indeed, in my daydream I must have trundled unwittingly through the debris of the morning's traffic.

'Lady Morisset! There's a gent to see you, a Mr William . . . Rose!' she yelled up the stairwell as I slipped off my boots to hand to her to clean.

'Lilly!' I corrected her.

'Lilly! I knew it were a flower!' she shouted to the floor above with the aplomb of a fisherman's wife.

I had taken a chair without my boots, the stockings upon my feet worn and sad in the corners, when Magdalene appeared at the top of the stairs, her stays visible over a linen smock, her hair loose down her back.

'Master Lilly, has there been a catastrophe? Something you

might have portended in his Majesty's nativity figure that is most pressing?'

I averted my gaze and stood in respect whilst attempting to hide my unclad feet. ''Tis true the Monarch, like the rest of us, was born with mixed blessings, but that is not why I am here.'

She ventured further down the stairs and peered at me curiously.

'You are in some distress of an internal nature?'

'Of a psychic nature, and, in truth, it was an instinct that led me here. But now I apologise for the intrusion.' I bowed, and backed away. 'As soon as my boots are returned to me, I take my leave.'

She climbed down a couple more stairs. 'You hast had a premonition?'

'A vision most violent and disturbing, but it would be blasphemy to talk of it to another . . .'

'Stay, sir, I will dress and be down shortly.'

Some time later Magdalene de Morisset joined me as a clock, deep in the bowels of the house, chimed eight of the hour.

'Is the master of the house not in attendance?'

'My husband is usually to be found in his country estate. The marriage was a fortuitous union for both our families – and in a manner for ourselves, for we allow each other freedoms others might not have.' I hid my embarrassment badly, for she smiled dryly. 'I fear you must think this most ungodly, Master Lilly?'

'I think the aristocrat lives a different morality to the rest of us.'

'Then I think him less of a hypocrite,' she retorted, that wit of hers a worthy opponent that only heightened my own very ungodly interest. 'We have a unique wedlock that precludes intimacy. Come, to my study; we will have more privacy there, for in these times it is not only walls that have ears . . .'

And after dismissing her servant, she hurried me through a narrow corridor then up stairs leading to the top of the dwelling. Eventually we arrived at a tapestry — a most wondrous depiction of the ancient Egyptian magician Hermes Trismegistus changing water into wine like Jesus himself — that she did lift to reveal an oak door. From a purse hanging off her belt, Magdalene produced a large brass key.

As the door swung open, it appeared as night within, and immediately a heavy scent of musk and incense interlaced with the smell of dried roses floated out, making me sneeze.

'You are very honoured, no man has entered this chamber before, just myself, my maid and some of my fellow Occultists, all of the fairer sex.'

'Then I am honoured indeed.' But still I faltered at the step, wondering what transgression or, perhaps even more disturbingly, commitment, might be unwittingly entailed by crossing over such a border.

'Are you frightened, Master Lilly, of a harmless Witches' coven?' she jested.

'I only wish not to give offence unintentionally.'

'This is my place of worship and I am inviting you in,' she replied whilst ushering me into the pitch-dark chamber. Then, after brushing against me, and with the habitual ease of someone who knew the room lit or unlit, she found a flint and ignited several candles.

It was of a curious octagonal shape. I was reminded of the egg-chambers of a beehive, and was convinced there must be a magical numerical reason behind the design. Each wall was lined with books and upon closer inspection a dedicated theme, indicated by a sign in Latin, handwritten in beautiful scroll, hung at the top of the shelves. Some were of an optimistic and beneficial nature — for example: *Of stars and their influence on terrestrial matters* and *Alchemy and potions* but there were other titles of a darker nature – *Manipulation and Magick, How to banish vampires, A meditation upon mermaids and their wiles* – but I also recognised books I myself had editions as well as the very rare almanack by Regiomontanus I have craved possession of some score years.

'Madam, you have a depth of intellect I had not calculated, and you are also a Latin scholar, I see?' I was much impressed.

'The servants do not speak nor read it, nor my husband who is of a more venal character, and I keep no scribe. My husband thinks these are gardening books. I have my detractors, and these are treacherous times.'

'I fear increasingly so. But Madam, your taste in the literature of the mystic arts is both excellent and rarefied. I have not met many women who are educated in such matters and have an understanding of Latin *and* Mathematics.'

'My childhood was unusual. I was one of two children but my brother died in infancy and my father, a nobleman at the French Court, had an interest in astrology; he brought me up with the freedoms and education that would have been due my brother.'

'And yourself?'

'I am interested in power, and if it is possible to glean information about future events or the nuances of fortune through such methodology I apply it, and certainly seek it for those I support.'

'Indeed; however, a certain political flexibility is required in dangerously polarised times,' I retorted diplomatically.

'Master Lilly, I am of the Court and am of aristocratic parentage; I must both protect and fight for the governance that should and will prevail.'

'Even if the morality of such governance is beyond redemption?'

'We have not arrived there yet.'

'No, indeed we have not. And I pray the King will take guidance before it is too late,' I answered, knowing the walls were solid and the servants far away.

I knew I had cornered her as far as I could, and so I stepped back, the air between us thickening: I trusted not any further proximity without a betrayal of desire. My hand reached for the curve of a globe of the zodiac cosmos and I took the opportunity to spin it – a pretentious gesture, but useful to keep busy those fingers that so wanted to play upon softer and far more responsive matter.

'In astrology, I sense we are the same animal, but I presume you are a conduit and not a practitioner?' I asked her, painfully aware of the whiteness of her bare neck.

At which she smiled, her own hand trailing over a crystal orb that sat on a central desk, the leather of which was covered with all kinds of apparatus, manuscript, and powders; in this I wager we were both making the love we wished to make upon each other upon inanimate objects.

I struggled not to be fascinated by her deft, caressing fingers.

'So, you really do wish me burnt at the stake?' she teased. I glanced down at the table, quickly assessing the calibre, illustrations and tone of the texts open before her – if she was *Witch* she was of the benign genus.

'If you were a sorceress, you are in good company,' I retorted. 'I have my own skills, I am a fine maker of Sigils, I have a good knowledge of ceremonial magick—'

'I do not doubt it.' Magdalene moved closer and my mouth dried in desire; now nervous, I prattled on.

'And I also learnt the art of divining. Indeed, I, with two others, divined for treasure in the cloisters of Westminster Abbey, and in doing so called up Demons, that, if I had not dismissed them would have blown the Abbey down, along with ourselves. Also, I have colleagues you might have heard of: the Dutchman John Hegenius . . .' (Faith, is she going to touch me now? If so I am undone!) '. . . with whom I have devised various divining rods, Sarah Skelhorn, the best crystal gazer in the kingdom . . .'

'I have had correspondence with the same Sarah,' she interjected.

'She is a most excellent seer, but you should also know that I also have consorted with Spirits, Angels and fairies . . .' (Lord, save me from temptation, her hand just brushed my knee) '. . . I once even encountered the Queen of the Fairies in my own Hurst wood. The friend I was with, a man of most rational countenance, when confronted with her appearance called out, *No more I beseech you!* His hair stood on end such was the sight of her most terrible and noble visage. Frightened his heart might give out, I bade the Queen to leave, and she did. I have had clients come to me begging to resort their rights to angel favours. A man called Gladwell, a friend of Sir Robert Holhorn—'

'He is a gentleman of my acquaintance.' She was so close I could feel the warmth of her skin.

'—hath had both speech and sight with the angels Uriel and Raphael but had misused them most carelessly, in trivial earthly matters, so that they no longer appear to assist or advise. Two hundred pounds he offered me for their recovery but I am not easily bought . . .' I was talking too much and too fast, throwing the words down between us like obstacles, for I feared if I stopped talking I might simply pull her toward me and run my lips across that long neck.

'But you no longer practise the art?'

'The horror of my experience at the Abbey taught me humility. It is one thing to summon spirits, quite another to place them firmly back into their own sphere.'

In lieu of an answer she poured out two goblets of wine. 'But you are here to talk of your vision?' She handed me one.

I drank, the images still lingering in the very muscle of my body like an ague. 'I saw the twins of Gemini being held upside down and fed into a great fire despite their screaming, people running to and fro throwing water upon this great fire which burnt on regardless — and in the land that stretched behind, a thousand deaths being gathered by the plague workers. After I did cast a horary most meticulously. I fear for London, I fear for this city I love.'

The words spoken, they appeared to form the very picture I had described, hanging in the room like the burning bush of Moses, indisputable and terrible. We both seemed to stare at this, at the very air, to the point I did wonder whether she too might have the second sight.

'Gemini is the sign on London's ascendant . . . you fear she will burn?' Magdalene finally ventured.

'She will burn, but not in war — something else, a great apocalypse. A fire following plague — plague like we have never witnessed.' I spoke from the very depths of my soul. There was a silence that broke with a soft plop of wax falling from a candle.

'When?'

'Not soon . . .' I did not want to voice the date, as if by doing so I would bring it into certain manifestation.

'When?' she insisted, her eyes catching the light; there was no doubt in my skill as a seer in her concentration, exhilarating for a man whose own wife doubted him so much.

'1665.' This was the first time I'd spoken the year out loud; it seemed far away and yet we both knew how fast the jester of Time somersaulted. He is a vicious clown who toys with everyone's lives.

'Then tell no one until you merit it be the right date, else it will not only be London burning,' she warned.

'It's a curse, this gift of prophecy. If one cannot change the future, is it worth foretelling it?' I ventured, a dilemma I oft wrestled with in the dark hours of both my mind and of the night, but had never dared shared. It was therefore of great comfort to me when, unperturbed, Magdalene replied as if such a quandry was natural.

'You answered yourself by describing it as a gift. It is a gift, God-given, and for reason, William Lilly. You are an exceptional man, living in exceptional times. You must make no concessions, and say your piece. This is your destiny. There will be other visions, there have been other visions — you and I both know it. You must make your astrology for the People. In these times they starve for guidance and so you must publish almanacks of your calculations which will be of profound influence.'

Faith, the woman had an ability to give voice to my own ambition, and it was water to a thirsty man to receive such encouragement.

'In confidence, I have been meditating upon such a path, but have received no support from my wife. She ridicules my labours and regards the study of astral matters as sinful.'

'Marriage is a labyrinth one must learn to navigate to secure happiness, and yet not be seen to do so. It is an art at which I have learnt to excel.' She moved closer.

'My first marriage was very happy,' I ventured, 'but in this second wife I fear my judgement was skewed by corporeal desire. From the very beginning it was apparent she was of an argumentative and peevish nature — with an ill-aspected Mars, Sun and Venus, and so it has proved.'

'And now?'

'Now I cannot stand the sight of her.'

'You should take a mistress,' Magdalene announced, her meaning clear, and yet I did not make my move, for the sport that was on offer terrified me in its complication. In short, she was a match, not some strumpet one could tumble and leave.

This would be an entanglement of heart, spirit and intellect. It would risk both life and equilibrium. And so I played a little.

'Indeed, but who would have me? Ours is the era of distrust, one might find oneself bedded for the sheer pleasure of one's information — for every wedded woman knows how easily a man's tongue is loosened after lovemaking.'

'And not just his tongue,' she jested, a knowing jibe that placed her between courtesan and whore. A worthy bedfellow no doubt — the observation rendered my hose a little tighter. Worst, I was sure she knew it and was now toying with me like a cat does a mouse. 'Everything is a trade, Master Lilly, surely you know that by now, and it is naïve to imagine otherwise.'

'And what of love?'

'A poem composed by knights to give purpose to their idle.'

'You are a hard woman, and most likely a harsher mistress,' I countered, wanting her more than ever.

'I choose to live in the bright sunlight in which everything is illuminated, and not in the half-light of illusion. Perhaps it is the unhappiness of my own marriage that has taught me this.'

'Perhaps . . . and perhaps it can be untaught?'

Now it was she who moved away, desire still a silvery spider web catching at our lips, eyes and clothes. 'What of the King's Natal figure? Has the Monarch the temperament to make war?' She shrugged, changing the topic; she was, dear Reader, as mercurial as a lawyer.

'If I were given this figure and did not know the man to whom it belonged, I would say yes, his sphere of interest is narrow and lies in the fourth house, within the family, Court and friends. He needs to look beyond and realise the full responsibility of his influence to survive. When the King was brought into this world, the Sun stood at eight degrees three minutes Sagittarius — conjunct Antares—'

'Which is a fixed star, most slow-moving and therefore most

influential as its shadow passes across the figure. Antares is malevolent in nature, this does not auger well . . .' she elaborated.

'Indeed, it indicates a rash person, destructive through his own obstinacy,' I observed. 'He will need good advisers to survive, and even more challenging, he will need to find the humility to listen to them.'

'You will persuade the Queen of this tomorrow. She is expecting you at midday.'

'I am obliged to present the King's proclivities in full. However, the commission was also to find favourable dates and this I have done – and I have been told you cannot see the sky or the stars from the Tower.'

'Henrietta respects you; she is no fool, you will keep your head.'

'But she is ambitious and, understandably terrified by these times, methinks.'

'I will protect you.'

'She is also fickle. Lady Hay is an example of this, in and out of favour at the Queen's whim.'

'You know Lady Hay?'

'Lady Hay?' I repeated the name as a stratagem for I needed to know who Magdalene's allies were and who were her enemies. 'I have not had the pleasure but we share friends amongst the Parliamentarians.'

'Lucy Hay has too many admirers for the Queen's taste – it is sensible to keep one's beauty low. This I have learnt for myself.' A statement which made me smile as I could not imagine how such a woman might present as invisible. 'But for you I shine,' she continued boldly, now pressing her body against mine. I remained rigid, my hands bolted to my sides. The transgression of taking her rendered me momentarily witless, my yard now hard in my hose. 'We would be good together, Master Lilly, the two of us. Two wise heads to the same Chimaera, of different faiths but one central belief, supporting different sides but with one idea — survival — fusing us back to back.'

I moved away, frightened of my own desire; thinking on how the messenger of my vision had manifested as the woman before me. Surely that was a warning?

'The Chimaera is a hybrid monster, so which of us is the lion and which the snake, Madam?' I countered making sure my cloak now concealed the front of my hose. She kissed me lightly on the lips.

'I can abide my time, and regardless of your qualms we are facing a dawn of much terror and need each other. What say you?' she asked, smiling.

'I say we have an understanding.' After which I quickly took my leave.

A mere street away I collapsed against a wall, my knees trembling, thanking the good Lord I had found the fortitude to resist my baser nature.

CHAPTER FOUR

♄ ♍ ♄

Whitehall Palace

Venus: She signifies a quiet manner not given to Law, Quarrel or Wrangling, not Vitious, Pleasant, Neat and Spruce, Loving Mirth in his words and actions, cleanly in apparel, rather Drinking much then Gluttonous, prone to Venery oft entangles in Love matters . . .

'And so, Master Astrologer, of the King's character?' Queen Henrietta sat forward in the high-backed carved wooden chair, thin lips pulled over those famously crooked teeth. Her favourite, the dwarf Jeffrey Hudson, sat at her feet, his enormous head (although fine-featured in the Latin way) staring up at me, the dachshund in his lap curiously only making the dwarf look smaller.

I swallowed and searched my mind for a palatable description with which to present my case.

We were alone, apart from her diminutive playmate, the Queen having dismissed both her guard and Magdalene who had escorted me into Whitehall. Much lay in the balance; my destiny, Charles's ability to play his hand successfully, nay, the future of the kingdom itself, but how to give voice to the truth of his ill-favoured birth? I decided to emphasise the fortunate aspects: after all, was I not there to give hope and perhaps some guidance?

'The King's Sun is in Sag-Sag-Sagittarius, a most noble and intellectually curious sign,' I stammered. I glanced up, saw her attentive face, so took encouragement. 'It is also placed in the fourth house, which, Your Majesty, is the house of family and of his most private and immediate domain . . .' Saying which I gestured, my hands sweeping in the luxurious surrounds of the chamber, the windows beyond embraced views of the massive courtyard and the green trim. As she smiled my stammering disappeared as I continued with greater enthusiasm.

'This is fortuitous,' I emphasised diplomatically. 'His ascendant is in Virgo, which makes him a cautious individual given to analysis; it also can make him modest in appearance – in short, the gracious simplicity in his attire would bear this out, the rising sign being the indication of how one appears to the external world.' I wanted to say there was also a heightened danger of the Monarch falling into being calculating, secretive, petty, and narrow in his regard, but stayed my tongue.

'And what about the placement of his Moon? Lady de Morisset has told me this is important?' the Queen tentatively asked.

'His Moon is in Libra, which can taper some of the less favourable aspects of the figure, Libra being the sign of the scales, the balancer; this enables the King to place his ear to the needs of his people if he so desires, it also indicates a need to create harmony . . .' I faltered as the Queen's face fell.

'You mean to say there are some aspects that are not favourable in the King's figure? He is the representative of God, surely He has bestowed nothing but blessings upon the King?' she insisted.

'God chooses to try even the most exalted of men. For what is life but the gaining of wisdom? King Charles, like all of us, has been born with a specific hand of cards; how he plays it is up to him.'

'Tell me of his challenges – and be brave, Master Lilly, for the sake of the kingdom.' She spoke with such genuine emotion that I forgave her Popish and imperial ways, for suddenly here was a simple woman who truly loved her husband and only wished for his safety and longevity.

Oh, foolish and trusting Philomath! I should have been wilier in my assessment of her character. Only then did it occur to me that a sensible man would have cast the Queen's own figure and therefore be armed with some foreknowledge of the obstinacy she was currently displaying. But I have displayed similar short-sightedness before, as the troubles of my second marriage can testify.

'The King has much fire in his figure, his Venus is also in the sign of the Archer, a difficult placing tempered only by the house – which is again the fourth house of family, clan, and private domain. The danger here is that he will become too inward-looking and represent his true nature only to those closest in blood. Not a bad thing, you might surmise, except for the degree – which indicates both colic and depression. Both his Mars and Mercury are also in Sagittarius and again in the fourth house. With Mars this means he will risk anything – and by that I mean *everything*, Your Majesty, to protect both his family and lineage. In a citizen this might be a fortuitous aspect, but in a Monarch there is a wider responsibility and a necessity to engage with the outside world – the kingdom and the needs of its citizens. But to have Mercury, the great communicator, also in the fourth house, again emphasises a tendency to look inward, to withhold when one should be expansive . . .' I paused, reluctant to give account of the most dangerous element in the Natal figure. However, the Queen, reading my expression, leant forward, fear playing behind those dark eyes.

'You are withholding, sir. I beg you share the worst — one needs to go to war with as many arms one may muster.'

'A wise sentiment, Your Majesty. The King's greatest challenge is the proximity of the fixed start Antares to his Sun. It is at eight degrees, and although this is a royal star, the placement *can*, and mark I use the word *can*, be the messenger of upheaval and violent change. He must learn to be as diplomatic as not to anger this star.'

I waited, holding her gaze, keeping my thoughts as politically neutral as possible, for she knew me to be of Puritan leanings, but truth is truth and a spade is a spade and it would have been a sin to have withheld such information from any Querent, royal or otherwise.

'Plainly, sir, is the end of his life described within the mathematical geometry upon that piece of paper?' She pointed to the figure now dangling from my trembling hand.

Time stretched in that magical way fear makes it; the puppy, still in the arms of its diminutive master, yawned, showing a pink tongue and tonsils, and the dwarf, glancing up, winked at me — to my disquiet.

I found myself wondering at my own death, confronted with the possibility of predicting another's, then the thought of the courage of Astronomer Giordano Bruno, executed for defending Copernicus, and the cruel way his executioners tied his tongue so that he could not address his last audience made me muster my own pluck.

'As I have noted, Luna is with Antares, a fixed star which is said to denote violent death and the King's own actions will decide his Fate. But I would say, as an Astrologer, it is essential His Majesty must go against his own rigid nature and be prepared to meet Parliament halfway, as well as listen to his people.'

What I could not tell Queen Henrietta was that the King's Mars approached Caput algol — an aspect which is said to denote beheading and might intimate exactly that; in which case King Charles' death would be the most violent for a Monarch in our own times.

'But remember, my most gracious Queen, as I have said many a time, the stars might incline but they do not compel. The King *can* save himself if he wishes it.'

The Queen took a sharp breath then adopted a false calm. 'You have the list of auspicious dates?'

I reached into my satchel and pulled out the manuscript.

'I took both the figures of the good cities of Ulster and of Aberdeen and arrived at a number of dates.' I moved to place the list in her hand, but she clicked her fingers and the dwarf reached up and snatched the manuscript from me. He tucked it into his waistcoat pocket with a flippant irreverence then sat back at the Queen's feet like a naughty but obedient dog.

I was about to protest but the Queen raised her hand. 'My husband was compelled by Parliament to sign the death warrant for the Earl of Strafford, who acted for him in Ireland, and yet the Irish rebellion was not in his control. The people now have the audacity to criticise the King's actions there and so propose that Parliament and not the Monarch be responsible for this country's defence?'

After which, I thought it prudent to nod my head most vigorously. Satisfied, she continued her rant. 'This is revolution and unacceptable. Is the King not the head of state, anointed by God? They marched against my good mother, Queen Marie, and tried to hunt down the good Archbishop Laud, then they forced my husband to sacrifice Strafford; I fear they will force him to sacrifice me, next.' The Queen studied me for signs of dissention. She was right, and most blunt about her own predicament, but short of suggesting she abandon her religion I could only give her advice on the King's strengths and not her own weaknesses, astral, political or otherwise.

'I am acutely aware of the King's dilemma . . .' I kept my tone firm, 'and as I said before, my calculations suggest he must tread lightly; the days I have marked favour diplomacy and he would be wise to use the information.'

'And *you* will be even wiser to forget this meeting took place, or that you ever met my own royal personage.'

I bowed, practically kissing the buckles upon my shoes.

'I will be for ever, my Queen, the guest you never had,' I quipped, hoping to introduce some brevity into the encounter. She did not smile.

'And the King's Nativity?' she requested. In silence, I handed the Natal figure to her then watched as she climbed out of her chair and walked over to a candle. Six hours of labour and much hard arithmetic went up in smoke, the flame and glowing embers eating into the parchment as if to extinguish the King himself. Luckily, I had taken the wise precaution to scribe a copy. A practice I suggest all aspiring Philomaths, spies, and general survivors would be wise to adopt.

A breeze blew in from a half-opened window scattering ash-flakes of blackened paper across the floor, the Queen oblivious, so intent was she upon seeing the manuscript burnt.

She finally spoke. 'You have my word I shall take note of your findings, but George Wharton, the Astrologer Royal, hath made many of the same observations, except for one notable exception, this doomed star Antares you speak of so grimly. However, his reading was infinitely more favourable . . .' *Because he is a paid monkey, Madam*, I was sorely tempted to retort but naturally could not. 'I thank you for your honesty and plain-speaking, I understand it is considered a virtue by men like you.' (By which the Queen meant Puritan.) 'In my world it is considered a great rudeness, but I have paid you for your truth. But perhaps one man's truth is not another's?' (Oh, how I loathed the French habit of philosophising to mask a point!)

'Now it is one you must forget if you are to keep your life . . . you understand, Master Lilly?'

At which I nodded and bowed again. When I straightened, the dwarf held out a purse of gold.

'Fifty shillings as agreed,' the Queen informed me as Jeffrey Hudson dropped the coinage into my hand; in actuality, the sum agreed had been sixty shilling. The hypocrisy of the Royal frugality has not gone amiss amongst the many guilds and craftsmen who serve both King and Queen which had not added to their popularity. But as they were notorious for not paying at all, who was I to quibble? Better ten shilling less than one head less, given a man will always have more shillings than heads.

'Lady de Morisset will show you out, you will find her spying at the door,' the Queen added wryly before dismissing me.

I shuffled out backwards, head bowed in submission, careful not to show the Monarch my back as is the custom, but verily, the Republican in me did prickle at the action.

After climbing off the barge at London Bridge, Magdalene and I walked through the streets. It was pleasant, that late summer morning. There was a breeze that swept away the stink of the city. To look upon the streets – the pedlars with their wares vending for business as the merchants raced west in hackney carriages, horses whipped and straining, whilst the poor and those seeking coin flowed in from the slums of the east, their wares carried across their shoulders or tucked under a thin arm wrapped in a ragged sleeve – one would think it a city still turning in seamless industry and not divided, that neighbour trusted neighbour and worship was not marked by ornament nor black collar.

And as our footsteps fell into unison I was aware of Magdalene's every movement despite my eye upon the gutters and glistening pebble stones. The wind was making a mockery of her red hair, the grace of her movement catching at my senses . . . We made an odd couple, her in her blue and scarlet Court finery and myself in the plain cloak, jerkin and shirt. But there was a pleasing symmetry to our intelligence that did bind us as a natural match. Desire is a terrible burden for the moral man. How I wanted to touch her, even then, in plain view in the street — a certain transgression against both law and the institute of marriage.

'You told the Queen the plain truth?' Magdalene ventured, the blue ribbons of her attire now whirligigs she could not control.

'I told her *a* truth; it will take a strong constitution and bravery to guide a King who, to date, seems bent on self-rule.'

'He is a good man.'

'But is he wise?' I countered, at which she stumbled and I reached out to steady her, my fingers touching her skin between sleeve and glove. The touch burnt like the stigmata. Momentarily she rested against me (for me an eternity) then resumed walking.

'Do you know the Calvinist Parliamentarian John Pym?' she asked, turning toward the impersonal whilst making light of a name that had begun to strike fear in Royalist hearts.

'Who doesn't? A godly man, he is the creator of a new law in Parliament, a man concerned with religious propriety, who fears a French invasion, who is the voice of some — some of whom are friends of mine,' I answered, knowing anything I said could be reported back to Court. But it was true I had friends amongst both the Levellers, the Anglicans and the Calvinists.

'He thinks Catholics should wear clothes that mark them, and that Papists be removed from London,' Magdalene retorted.

'They say that he was behind that vicious and false pamphlet "The Declaration of Fears and Jealousies" which was an assault upon our Queen. Pym thinks she is conspiring with the French and Spanish, and demands she rid her Court of Catholic servants.'

'The Queen is driving a wedge between her husband's subjects and their Lords. We cannot afford a Catholic aristocracy and a Protestant populace.'

'Indeed, I myself have been attacked walking to Mass.'

I did not know what to say; in truth I abhorred this violence growing amongst my fellow Englishmen but understood their alarm.

'It might be possible to avoid this burgeoning conflict. But only if the King learns some humility. Many have terror of Ireland, Spain, and France, all in allegiance with the Pope. Many fear the King will make this a Catholic country. The Queen plays a dangerous game and she will drag her husband down with her if she continues. You see how the ordinary man suffers; they ask themselves what god needs to be worshipped in images made from gold and silver? What god needs to be spoken to in Latin and be impenetrable to his flock? For the true God is surely carried just as easily in the soul of a milkmaid as a lord or knight? They ask themselves what King doesn't worship with his own people? They have seen the long war in Europe between Protestant and Catholic; they've seen how French Catholics prosecute their Huguenots,' I argued.

'The King looks to Europe for culture and guidance,' she snapped back.

'Are not the ways of his ancestors, or even the good Queen Elizabeth, enough?' I was thinking of my compatriots with such views. 'You must understand, dear lady, that without a Parliament preserved in its just rights the King would vanish to nothing.'

'And *just rights* include giving Parliament control over the army and taking it away from the King?'

'It is the *country* that requires defending from the Irish and the Scots, not the palace. Understand that, if anything, I have been more Cavalier than Roundhead, and so taken notice of, but increasingly I find my body and soul engaged in the cause of Parliament. But don't mistake me; I have great affection for His Majesty and unto monarchy which I love and approve beyond any government whatsoever.'

'You twist and turn with the wind, sir.'

'I am a realist, Madam. Human nature is not naturally divided into sides. Even the stars make us complex and fashion our natures with paradoxes, strengths, vulnerabilities, and contradictions. The King is a man, and I love him as such, but he is also Monarch and, I pray, will prove himself a just one.'

'A posy! A posy for the lovely lady!' A flower seller thrust a small bouquet of peonies and forget-me-nots toward me. I paid her a penny and pressed the flowers upon Magdalene, who tucked them into a buttonhole.

'Enough of this politicking. I have tickets to a new farce at the Cockpit this afternoon. It would beholden you to join me?' she asked.

'How so?'

'There is a gentleman, a powerful gentleman of much influence, who wishes to make your acquaintance in an "accidental" manner. He is kin to individuals like ourselves and wishes to get the measure of you.'

'With what intent?' I asked, intrigued.

'If your Craft and integrity prove to satisfy you will find out in time.'

I studied her, wondering if this man was of the secret guild she had alluded to that first time I visited the Queen.

'And all of this against the backdrop of a farce?' I jested, knowing how quickly farce can turn to tragedy.

'I have a private box, set back from prying eyes. They say the play is a parody of the times, in which two wealthy young heiresses and their beaux go travelling with a band of beggars in search of liberty and a new world. I think it will prove a distraction from our troubles.'

'Actually, such a theme might illuminate our troubles,' I replied taking her arm as we walked further along the riverbank.

'I care not. I fear theatre, too, will be taken away from us. Your friends, the Puritans, regard all such performance as sinful. They make much ado about the Queen's masque and such sports as playmaking. They whisper the Queen is a whore for acting in such pageants and I myself have acted in them. Tell me, good Master Lilly, you think me a whore?' she provoked.

'I think you have the heart of a woman but the courage of a man,' I replied carefully, for in faith, my flesh wished her whore there and then. She laughed at my answer.

'I hope not, for I have known some very cowardly men, and the most brave of women! If the Puritans had their way we would be bowed in black with covered heads and sobriety would rule the day. I fear in a year or so this will be a much-changed country.'

Later, after a lunch of oysters and ale, we found ourselves at the Cockpit theatre, although you, dear Reader, might know it as the Phoenix. Lady de Morisset's box was set to the left of the stage and so dimly lit it was possible to remain in shadow and out of clear view and of this I was thankful.

It had been years since I had attended a London theatre and I looked about me with curiosity, for I have always regarded such auditoriums as a mirror to society in its flux. Here I found the usual suspects: the pit below that was crowded by the penny stinkards, the standing yobs happy to escape their daily misery for a penny; whilst above us the rowdy young apprentices up in the gods jeered and jostled for a view, and mixed in between them the painted strumpets looking for a wealthy young blade or patron, some dressed as gypsies (a homage to the theme of the play, I presumed) their rouged lips and cheeks shiny in torchlight, fanning themselves with a drama that drew the reluctant eye (faith, I even saw a few of the older Puritans – not that there were many in plain collar there – looking furtively upon such promising sin). I glanced down at the bill of players Magdalene had handed me and was pleased to see an old client of mine – the actor Tobias Young – was in the leading role. I had helped him secure the affections of a wealthy widow with some horary and astrological guidance, and he had sworn to be forever in my debt.

'I know the lead actor; it would be most entertaining to visit him backstage after the play.'

'Then we will. See yonder,' she whispered, pointing to one fop wearing the most exaggerated lace collar, pleated-sleeved silk shirt and a waistcoat heavy in gold brocade, 'that is Monsieur Vindecot, he is of the Court, no doubt here to spy for the King, he always keeps an ear to the playhouses for discontent. Although he claims to be Huguenot, I know for fact he is Catholic.'

'If he's a spy he would have done better to have disguised himself – in this company he is as conspicuous as a black goat in a herd of sheep,' I noted.

'Or a whoremaster in a flock of nuns?' she joked. 'Unfortunately, far more dangerous; your actor friend would do well to heed him.'

She was interrupted by the arrival of two people; a tall man clad in a cape and a young girl, ornately dressed, perhaps ten years of age. Magdalene rose to her feet and I gleaned I must be in the presence of someone she both respected and perhaps feared. The man slipped his hood off, revealing a gaunt countenance framed by silver hair that fell to his shoulders, the top half of his face — his eyes, nose and brow — concealed by a half-mask, usually wore at carnival. Following Magdalene's cue, I stood too, but the man said nothing; instead he took a chair in the shadows of the box whilst the girl, white-blonde and pale as a Christmas ghost, stepped forward, holding out her hand imperiously.

'My master sends his greetings to you, Master Lilly.' It was disconcerting; she spoke with the authority of a far older woman, her eyes aglow with an ancient intelligence.

'And I to him.'

Behind her, the man gave the faintest of nods at which Magdalene resumed her seat and I followed. To my surprise, the girl then did sit upon my lap, with the simple grace of any child. This was a strange business indeed, and as she settled herself I noticed a bracelet upon her wrist strung with a number of magical amulets that I recognised being of great power. Faith, I did then I confess become nervous, sensing that I was in the presence of a Magus and perhaps a soul he had bewitched.

'He believes you to be a Philomath of considerable talent, but he has questions of you,' the girl told me.

At which Magdalene leant forward and whispered, 'Answer well and the door will be opened; this is a great opportunity indeed.'

Thus encouraged, I replied, 'I am ready.'

'If you had to choose an Angel to serve, which would it be, Nalvage or Illemese?'

Knowing that both these beings did spake to the great mystic John Dee and recited to him the famous Claves Angelicae, I answered with confidence, 'Both, for both are true servants of the Lord and have his tongue. Indeed, I do have a manuscript of their recitations, a rare edition with both John Dee and Kelley's own handwriting in the margins.'

The Magus nodded approval and his disciple continued, 'This is a good answer, Philomath, but tell me, if you were put to rack and pressed to betray your own brothers in magick, would your flesh prove weak?'

'Nay, for I am able to free my own soul and mind from this skin-and-bone gaol, and float, at will, far from mine own body. Thus I fear no torture nor pain and so am the most dependable of comrades.' Again, the girl looked to her master who appeared satisfied. She turned one last time to me.

'Now the final question: would you put the needs and protection of the Grand Council above your own politick and even the safety of thy family, in the way a soldier would die for his army and country?'

I thought carefully before answering; My Craft, ancient and benevolent, was already under attack from two fronts. Firstly, from the old superstitions and prejudice toward Cunning Folk and folk-magick. Secondarily from a new front – the nova scientia, a movement started in the Netherlands – a rationalist dissection of astrology and astronomy, godless and without Spirit. But could I die for such a cause? In my hesitation, Magdalene took my hand and I allowed her touch to put the words into my mouth.

'I would,' I found myself answering.

We were interrupted by the sound of the stage curtain rising to reveal the visage of a country lane.

'Watch your hours and days carefully, William Lilly, for you will know when we contact you,' the young girl warned me with a seriousness entirely at odds with her angelic youth. She then slipped off my lap and the two of them were gone. After which the actors entered the stage with a shout and it were as if our mysterious visitors had vanished like a strange dream.

The play was an amusing morality tale, the plot displaying the usual devices. A beggar who is born rich without knowing it, two young aristocratic girls who disguise themselves as vagabonds, their hapless suitors who follow – dear Reader, I'm sure you know all the ruses. One particularly unpopular character was a corrupt judge who, reflecting the ignorant bigotry of our times, constantly boasted how he pre-judged the cases that came before him solely upon the appearances of both victim and claimants. The lampooning and the hypocrisy of 'playing' at being poor as well as the arrogance of the young aristocrats' romanticism had the working poor up in the 'gods' booing as much laughing. How they hissed! I can only commend the playwright for hitting upon such a raw nerve.

I think it be a true mirror of the distance that is now between rich and poor in England. This is a dangerous schism, for even the squire should look to his tenants, else risk revolution. Happily, all the lovers in the play, as in many dramas but, alas, not life, ended marrying most unnaturally for love.

Sitting there in the artifice twilight, watching with hundreds of others as one animal, I wondered upon the quixotic symmetry of fiction compared to the mercurial realities of life and did think upon the Philomath as the lone watchman holding the lamp up high in a misty darkness to guide others. But my most recent encounter troubled me: was I soon to be of a great cabal of Occultists? What would this mean to both my freedom and safety?

We found Tobias Young just as his boy servant was helping him out of the vast padding that had been his stage girth.

'Why Henry,' here he cuffed the boy playfully, 'look smart,

here comes London's finest Adept, Mr William Lilly and with him a gentlewoman of most refined appearance. Milady.' The actor kissed my companion's hand then bowed low, which in a man of lesser grace and of less pleasing appearance might have looked ridiculous, given he was clad in nought but cotton breeches and a ridiculous bush of a wig with moustache to match.

'Tobias Young, Esquire, of the Beeston travelling company at your service.' He completed his introduction with a flourish.

'Lady de Morisset.' She retrieved her hand. 'I believe we might have met before, at Whitehall? The Queen favours you, does she not?'

Tobias glanced about him, then gestured for his servant to shut the door of his chamber.

'Occasionally Her Majesty has sought my advice on performance for her famous Masques,' he replied somewhat furtively. 'She is a good actor herself, but naturally, outside of Court, it is not to be seen to encourage the ladies to the stage – that would be considered a sin, would it not?' he continued in a deadpan voice, then glancing at me, said, 'Your friend is neither fish nor fowl; that is to say, he has a Puritan head but a Royalist heart. However, his member swings both ways,' he joked bawdily and to my intense embarrassment winked at Magdalene, 'in that it is to be found both in Parliament and Court. But his Puritan heart will tell you the stage belongs only to the male gender whether in skirts or breeches, and it would be against God to suggest otherwise.' He then called for his boy Henry to bring ale.

'Indeed, it would,' I answered sternly.

'And entirely unnecessary, considering how many pretty boys there are to be found,' Tobias further joked, pinching the long-suffering Henry on the bottom as the boy handed us all a goblet.

'Your performance was sublime, Tobias, I would not have recognised you,' I told him for wont of a compliment; in truth, I had thought the play shallow.

'I was aiming for the ridiculous, but sublime will do,' Tobias retorted. 'New work is always so difficult,' he explained to Magdalene. 'The first time a role is performed marks it in history so for ever more shall my character, Oldrents, be immortalised in a wig fit for a clown!' He pulled off the false hair and shook it vigorously, covering all of us in a descending cloud of white powder. 'Of course, who knows how much longer us actors will be in employment. Daily we are vilified, and accused of all kinds of extraordinary things – blasphemy, idol-worshipping, Papist spying, witchcraft, treacherous propaganda – I only wish my life was that exciting. 'Tis no matter.' Here he lifted his glass. 'To farce, life, and the ability to laugh, ridicule, and parody whoever we want, whenever we want!'

A dangerous toast, but as there were nought but his servant present we joined him, whilst Tobias, enjoying like most actors the luxury of a captive audience, continued his rant. Lurching over he threw his arm about my shoulders.

'Madam, you are in excellent company,' he told Magdalene. 'Make this gentleman your companion and your fortune will be made . . .'

'Now Tobias, I have told you before I do not tell fortunes—'

'I said *made*, not told, for indeed this Philomath, obscene in his modesty, can manipulate "coincidence" as well as any Prospero.'

'You speak of Time-Magick?' Magdalene asked Tobias, who turned back to me.

'Faith, she is a sorceress also? William, guard thy heart, she has witchcraft in her lips.'

'I am a simple Stargazer and a well-wisher to mathematics, no more, no less,' I protested.

'He is coy. Whatever the mystical geometry and calculus the good man has applied, it has made *my* fortune,' the actor retorted. 'The good widow, Agatha Quake, has consented to meet me again. And it is all because of you, my dear Astrologer.'

'All I've done is to place luck in your path: you still have to do the wooing.'

'Quite, but fear not – if there is one thing Tobias Young excels in, it is the wooing!' he declared, much to our amusement. 'I owe you, Master Lilly.'

'And one day I intend to collect, Mr Young,' I retorted wryly, for an actor's skill is very useful indeed, particularly in times where deception and disguise are needed and in truth Tobias did owe me five shillings, but I had calculated that to have debts outstanding to such a talented individual could only be an investment, and so it was to prove, but more of that later.

The actor turned to Magdalene. 'Agatha Quake is a shy creature, much sought after for both her fortune and her beauty; I noticed her only as a veiled woman who appeared in one of the upper galleries for the whole season of *Hamlet* in which, naturally, I had played the lead. Only when I pursued the matter with Master Lilly was I given the power to hurry Fate along and found the circumstances, place, and time which led to both of us satisfying our curiosities. But, alas, the widow remains suspicious of my motives.'

'I cannot think why,' I interjected, jesting. In response, Tobias drew himself up in mock outrage.

'My heart is pure, and when I give myself to a woman, it is in my entirety – even if it is only for a night. No one can accuse me of flippancy. No indeed, I am a man of most serious intent – depending on the role I am playing at the time. But this one I love. If not for her riches, then her face, for she is very fair and I am very poor.'

Magdalene glanced at me most puzzled, for the actor had a propensity to talk in riddles, particularly when he sensed it amused.

'Mr Young doesn't think before he speaks, he thinks as he speaks,' I explained. 'For the life of me I cannot decide whether it is a handicap or an attribute, but it *is* liberating.'

'And is another of my charms,' Tobias added, 'or so the good widow keeps telling me, but to more serious matters, William: you intend to stay in London?'

'It called me, I could resist no longer.'

'Then you walk the tightrope with the rest of us, friend. London is now a wasp's nest of spies, and no one dare even fart for fear of being reported. Yet we are all sailing by the same foul winds,' he concluded, and grabbing the flask from his boy he filled our cups again.

'Indeed, and all ships need a navigator in such a storm. Men like me are needed in these uncertain times. These will be interesting years and I mean to use them before they use me,' I replied before swigging my mead.

'One coin, two faces,' Tobias replied enigmatically, then flicked a farthing high up into the air, to catch it like a trickster in the palm of his hand. Covering the coin, he placed it on the table. 'But which face will our illustrious Astrologer show the world?'

When he lifted his hand, the coin was spinning. An hour later, much intoxicated and now with the names of three new potential actor clients scribbled in my notebook, I swear that coin was still spinning.

CHAPTER FIVE

The Corner House, The Strand

Mars: In feats of Warre and Courage invincible, scourning any should exceed him, subject to no Reason, Bold, Confident, Immovable, Contentious, challenging all Honour to themselves, Valiant, lovers of Warre and things pertaining thereunto, hazarding himself to all Perils ...

It was but days later when I had two most unusual visitors. It was a windy day, beset with rain and hail, and believing such weather can only bring chills and fever I had Mrs Featherwaite hang the parlour and the study with lavender pouches and scatter fresh rosemary under foot. But it was no respite for the creeping damp.

My first Querent for the day was a request for the recovery of stolen goods, a common query, and one that horary astrology is so perfectly fitted to.

I will educate the amateur Astrologer on the following rules: the ascendant will represent the place from which the object was stolen and the actual planet ruling the ascendant *the person robbed*, whilst the Moon and the planet ruling the second house – *the stolen object*. Two houses are important, the seventh which offers the description of the thief and the fourth house for its ruling planet will reveal where the object was concealed.

However, the chances of recovering the lost object are only good if the Moon was moving toward the ruler of the ascendant, or toward the planet ruling the twelfth house, or the planet ruling the house in which the Moon itself was placed. Otherwise the prospects are not hopeful for finding the lost object apart from one exception: if, at the time of the theft, the Moon was in the ascendant or in the second house.

In short, the Astrologer must look to the position of the Moon and the planet ruling the zodiac sign the Moon was in at the time of the theft.

In this particular figure, the gentleman had a gold watch stolen from his desk and wanted information as to whether it would be found or returned or information as to the location of the thief.

I took the details, carefully ascertaining the exact time of the theft, and date. I then opened my casebook and wrote:

Question: Gold watch stolen. Who stole it? Is it recoverable? 7th October, 1641, 2.30 p.m.

After some calculation I could see that Taurus ascended and, along with the ruler of the ascendant Venus, described my Querent – in both physicality and in mind (a corpulent silk merchant, much given to pleasure and drink). After mapping out the figure further I discovered that the messenger (or in this case intruder) Mercury fell into the seventh house and had no essential dignity, and in Partile conjunction of Saturn and Square of Venus (severe positioning, particularly the Square which is always an indication of hardship, trouble and sometimes the presence of just plain evil) I read this to be the thief himself. However, the Moon was in a feminine sign (Scorpio), applying to a feminine planet (Venus) – so I concluded my thief was a woman. Furthermore, a young woman not more than eighteen or twenty years of age (Mercury is always young) and perhaps already known to the questioner

as Venus is oft sympathetic to Taurus and the silk merchant's
Sun sign was Taurus. I asked him whether there had been any
young woman in the house that he had an intimate relationship with, other than his wife (he was well over forty). Judging
by the placement of Mercury, and because of Mercury's proximity to Saturn, a young woman of pox-marked appearance,
and possibly involvement with an immoral trade (courtesan
or whore, however I simply emphasised the word 'professional' to carry my meaning without giving offence) at the
time of the theft.

The merchant went very red (as is often the wont with the
stout, food-loving Taurus) then spluttered and huffed about,
before confessing he had brought a young woman into his house
(his wife being to country that day). After their congress he had
fallen asleep, but it had been a day later that he noticed the
watch had been taken.

If his memory served him well, she had been of seventeen
years or so, and indeed dark-faired with a pox-marked face;
other than that very pretty, he concluded, abashed, but where
to find the watch?

I consulted the planets and noticed that Mercury was in
conjunction with Jupiter, the ruler of the ninth house, the
planet of expansion in the house of the law courts. I suggested
she had already been detained on a former charge and he would
find her at the Old Bailey.

And so it came to pass, and again my Querent was most
pleased with both the result and my discretion! But the consultation, as successful as it was, did not vanquish my discontent,
a restlessness brought about through wrestling with a temptation to visit Magdalene de Morisset.

In a temper most foul I sat at my desk studying my books
and tables, thinking that the restriction Saturn hath placed
upon Mars might be worsening my irritation, when my

housekeeper did usher in the most peculiar couple: a preacher of some forty years or so, and although he wore the dress of a Jesuit, methinks there was decadence about his manner that did not fit with such a character, whilst his companion was even more bizarre. A young girl, not more than twenty, I guessed, but tall and unbecoming in her thinness. Her hair hung about her face, covering her eyes and prominent nose with a veil of lanky strands, her skin coarse, particularly about her chin, her garments an ill-fitted smock, and her large feet (which she did attempt to hide beneath her petticoats) squeezed into wooden clogs. She said not a word, and did avoid my gaze as if I were the Gorgon herself. But the priest was loquacious and jolly.

'Master Lilly, I wish to know the nature of my niece whom you see before you, a creature of great shyness but of rare talents. I believe if I equip you with her birth date and time you might be able to give me such an insight?'

'I can, but understand an individual can always transcend the natural gifts of his or her astrology through foresight and discipline,' I answered, thinking the poor creature indeed would need to do so to secure a husband.

'In that case, name your price, for I have a most generous benefactor, and the girl is dear to him.'

Encouraged, I doubled my normal fee, a sum the priest then insisted upon doubling again on the condition that he would be able to wait with the girl whilst I completed my calculations. Naturally I agreed, but it was most uncomfortable to be observed as I drew up her Nativity.

However, as I crouched over my desk it became more and more apparent that there was something very amiss about the young woman's figures. I noted that four moons ago Jupiter did enter the fifth house and most fruitful sign of Pisces and where the Moon resides. This placement and other aspects suggest the girl was with child. And yet she was thin as a stick.

'Are you sure these are the correct details of the birth?' I asked the priest tentatively, who was fanning himself with a small ivory fan.

'Most certainly; they are entirely accurate,' he reassured me. I glanced over at the girl, who was staring down at her feet. Was she a halfwit I did wonder, so out of the moment she did appear? I searched for a polite inquiry without giving insult to the girl's chastity.

'Did any event take place some four months ago? A significant event, involving good fortune or fecundity?' I carefully asked her uncle.

'My niece did come into some money she did win through a wager . . .'

'Then, and forgive me my audacity, for it is most strange, this figure appears to be that of a man – for if it were of a woman, she would be now with child or suffered some ailment of the womb.'

At which, to my total amazement, the priest burst out laughing, and the young woman (abandoning her bashfulness in an instance) herself roared in a deep baritone.

'Master Lilly, you are indeed a great Philomath, for in fact this is no woman, but Cullum Monroe, a young Occultist in fear for his life! And you have passed the first test of the Grand Council of Theurgy.'

At which the 'young lady' threw back her locks, and took my hand in the manliest of grasps.

'A great honour indeed to be "disrobed" by you, maestro! And now my Fate is entirely in your hands,' he concluded with the flourish of a young Chevalier.

I studied the two carefully. In truth, dear Reader, I have a distrust of the pampered scions of the aristocracy, and this nebulous creature had all of the hallmarks of the mollycoddled.

I was suspicious, and having revealed my craft to him, he now was compelled to reveal more of himself to me.

'How so?' I asked his guardian, who was already closing the door of my study so that we could not be overheard.

'The second part of this "audition" to test your loyalty to the Council is to shelter and secure this young man's passage to Europe, after which he can then fall under the protection of some of the great Magi of the Netherlands or perhaps Spain. We know you have good relations there with several eminent sages.'

'I do indeed. But tell me what was your crime,' I asked the youth, whose persona grew more confident by the moment, 'that you are fleeing the authorities?'

'I am accused of sorcery and of having murdered my uncle through the use of unnatural means,' he answered, his Scottish brogue now apparent.

'Is it true?'

'In some ways, yes and in some ways no. Although my family have sided with the Presbyterians and are at war with the King, I, myself, am a Royalist. And so, having heard and seen the Spirit world since a young age, I secretly studied the occult to understand that I was not mad, but gifted. When my father and his brother, both officers with the Scots, insisted that I join them in the fighting against the true King, I did conduct a Time-Magick ceremony during which my uncle, some twenty miles away on his estate, did drop dead with an apoplexy.'

'A powerful spell indeed.' I was cautious in my admiration.

'I did not intend to kill him, merely scare him into a paralysis that might deter him from going back into battle. He was a man over fifty.'

'But how were you found out?'

'My father's valet came upon me. I had created an effigy of my uncle and it were this that condemned me.'

'Master Lilly, the lad is just seventeen year of age, and has a great natural talent,' his guardian added.

'And you wish me to shelter him?'

'This is the last place Parliamentarian guards would think of searching. And we know you have good relations with many of the shipowners.'

''Tis true I have made several successful horaries on the fate of missing ships for the insurers; I could secure him a passage if he merited it.'

'The Council has already passed judgement and Cullum is under our protection: complete this task for us and your own appointment is guaranteed. What say you?' the 'priest' asked me.

I looked back at the youth, who now held my gaze without a flicker of fear or arrogance, and I could see, playing in his face, wisdom far beyond his years. But I was also swayed by something else I had noted in his Nativity – an aspect I chose not to share with the two of them – that in his twentieth year there was a great vulnerability that almost certainly portended an early death.

'Come to my door at midnight, in your true guise, and I will shelter thee.'

Cullum did return that very night, and for a short but memorable time we were as close as father and son, as well as master and apprentice.

CHAPTER SIX

Autumn 1641

The Corner House, The Strand

Mercury: Being well dignified, represents a man of a subtil and politick brain, intellect and cogitation; an excellent disputant or Logician, arguing with learning and discretion and using much eloquence in his speech, a searcher into all kinds of Mysteries and Learning . . .

In the mornings, Cullum would help me in the calculations of the stars then would draw up the figures for me. Whilst I executed the horaries, he would spend hours studying my books and manuscripts. In the evenings, after supping, I would shut my study door and we would debate subjects it would be both mortally dangerous to discuss with anyone else: the intricacies of summoning both Angel and Spirit, how to manipulate time and circumstance and establish concepts and ideas in an unsuspecting mind, how to both cause and prevent a haunting. These and many other magical complexities I pondered with the youth, both of us learning as much from each other as from the manuscripts opened before us.

A week later my wife Jane did arrive from the country in one of her fits of zeal, determined to both assist and thwart my business. Upon her arrival, she took umbrage with Mrs

Featherwaite on her management of the household, convinced the housekeeper was overpaying both the fishmonger and butcher. Jane was indeed a quarrelsome woman by nature and mistrustful by design and I am happy to report that on several occasions Cullum Monroe, a handsome lad in his true gender, proved himself to be the most efficient of diplomats and did ensure peace between the two women. For this alone it was worth having the youth in the house, although Jane had insisted we did charge him board — a farthing a week. Mrs Featherwaite liked Cullum well enough, but her nephew did not. Simon Featherwaite, now in full throttle of his new Roundhead fanaticism, was immediately suspicious of this curly haired educated youth not much older than himself, and that suspicion did make my disposition jittery; I knew it would take just a few words in a Puritan ear to set the Parliamentary guards upon us.

Meanwhile, my wanting grew in my flesh like a canker. No matter how many times I prayed or chastised myself, Magdalene hung in my dreams and waking sensibility like an insidious fragrance I could not wash myself free of.

I had not been summoned back to Court, nor had the Queen sent any messenger, and judging by the King's ongoing obstinacy in matters of both realm and law, I suspect she hath ignored the Nativity I drew up for him in its entirety. Finally driven mad through the lack of information and convincing myself this was why I had to see Magdalene, I told Jane I was to the White Hart Tavern that evening with my printer friend, Harry Pickles, then later to a game of bowls, and instructed Cullum to entertain her most thoroughly in my absence.

After leaving the house I turned left instead of right, toward Chancery Lane.

*   *   *

'Why, it's Master Tulip!' Rosie, Magdalene's maid, the same young girl who had greeted me last, exclaimed defiantly as she opened the door.

'Master *Lilly* – and I am an esteemed gentleman of trade,' I reminded her, unamused by her cheek.

'Oh, I knew it were a flower!' She turned to yell to the lady inside, 'Milady, 'tis the Philomath on a mission of most importance!'

'I said no such thing!'

'So, do you wish me to tell her it is a matter of little consequence?' Rosie retorted – forsooth, a Philosopher in the making!

'Nay, you have me there! Shall I wait in the parlour?'

'Indeed, 'tis good to stand away from the window. In these times 'tis best to keep one's friends unknown to others.' And again I marvelled at the intelligence of such a servant, reflecting that it would be most useful if Mrs Featherwaite had half the young girl's wit and caution.

A few moments later Magdalene joined me and, after ordering that honey mead and figs be brought, took me into her study.

'I was expecting a visit, but you are lucky to find me here, for I have been at Court until yesterday. I hear you have a new apprentice?'

I watched her warily, struggling with both my natural distrust of the Royalist but also my desire, which – now that she were actually in front of me, all curves and palatable light – taunted my senses.

'I like him well enough,' I answered, yearning a hot stone in my mouth.

'You do both the Council and humanity a great service if you are to prevent Cullum Monroe's arrest. But you will see in time just how powerful an Occultist he is, and yet, in his youthful innocence, barely knows it. The Scots would have lynched him, but the Council managed to smuggle him over the border. You must find him a passage, William, as soon as you can. I know the Presbyterians are pressing Parliament to take greater measures to find him. They want him hanged.'

'I plan to have him on a ship by the end of the month.'

'In the meanwhile, for your own safety, you must conceal him well.'

'You would not recognise the Cornish lad I have staying with me! Methinks Cullum is well gifted to disguise himself.'

At which she laughed. 'He doth make a pretty lass.' She stepped toward me. 'So why are you really here tonight, William? Is it just the need for discourse with a kindred spirit?' The heat of her arm was a burn across my skin as she leant forward to stir the coals.

'I am not entirely in control of my senses, Madam. What man is? But I confess I also crave news from Court. Has the Queen acted upon my advice?'

'She has suggested two dates to His Majesty that would be most favourable for discussion and meeting with Parliament. But I believe these were rejected by Parliament. I fear the Royal Astrologer, George Wharton, has more sway.'

'An arrogant popinjay, but well-meaning.' I was determined to remain diplomatic.

'Fear grows at the palace – I do not want a war, yet our world seems to be more divided by the day. I have missed you, only yesterday I was studying a grimoire by Trismegistus and imagined discussing it with you.'

She moved toward me, to place a fig in my hand, a most provocative gesture, and we both knew it. Yet I could not take her. Instead, with trembling fingers I peeled the fruit, whilst watching her bite into her own with the gusto of a whore. I'm ashamed to report I was most pinched at this moment, as the

Puritan fought the natural libertine. 'My wife has finally joined me in London,' I stammered.

'That must be of great comfort.' She smiled and I did not know whether to slap her or kiss her. I watched the juice travel down her chin and she watched me watching her.

'It is not. But I remain a pious man.'

'If piety is to deny Nature, and, as Nature is God, surely such piety is against God? You are a man: not priest or castrato. Some unions are not made at the altar but in the soul.'

'You are a wicked woman.' I was not jesting, but she laughed anyhow.

'But an honest one. Besides, it was you who came to me.'

'Indeed, and I respect thee greatly as a fellow intellect.' I would have stood, but my state of excitement was all too obvious so I remained seated, hoping it would pass.

'Yet it is apparent this is not just going to be a meeting of minds?'

A provocative question that did not help my tumescence! Averting my eyes I gazed upon my fig, uneaten upon its plate. Then, to my surprise, my joy and despair, she straddled my knees and loosening my hose freed me, my yard as eager as an enthusiastic puppy.

'What are you doing?' I could barely speak.

'The magick of natural pleasure, the wished for, yet unspoken,' she murmured, pushing away my protesting hands.

Transfixed both by shame and intense pleasure I looked on as she took the rest of her fig, crushed it in her hand, and rubbed it upon my member. Then, with a sly smile, sliding to the ground did take me into her mouth. Faith, she played me like a flute, her tongue circling about the tip then taking me deep into her throat, my knees trembling in such violent pleasure I did not know whether to weep or shout. But seeing her there on her knees, her hair now tumbling about her bare shoulders, I wanted her to know that this was not mere lust but an affection of far deeper consequences. And therefore I held myself back, then lifted her to her feet. After which I did also reach for my own uneaten fig, and also after crushing the juicy fruit betwixt my fingers, did myself drop to my knees, and under the wonderful tent of her dress, run my hands up those plump thighs, finding the soft folds of her sex and the bud of her hard. I gently rubbed the fig both against her and in her, then laying back onto the ground drew her fully down upon my face and lips, sucking, licking and pleasuring her until, protesting she could not take all the pleasure, she lay atop me and did take my member again into her mouth and so we played each other with such instinct and expertise it were as if we were one beast, a loop of continuous pleasure that flowed through both our bodies as one, until she reached her pinnacle shouting, her fingers curled tightly in my hair and I did follow.

Afterwards, spent and still lying undone upon the rug I did rationalise that, because I had not entered my lady, this was not full congress and therefore far less of a transgression against my marriage. This I did not share with Magdalene, but with her curled asleep against me, the scent of her still upon my face, I knew that, although I might have won the battle, I would lose the war. For, dear Reader, I did love her.

On the way home, in the lane outside I stopped to stare up at Venus, more luminous and glorious than I have seen her for many a night, and cursed myself for my sanctimonious hypocrisy.

The next day I asked Cullum to teach me the ceremony he did inflict upon his uncle, a John Dee incantation I was familiar with, but I did want to see the alteration the young man had made that had caused such havoc. I could barely wait for the evening. It had been a most auspicious day with five conjunctions and trines – the most interesting being Neptune conjunct Sun and a Jupiter trine Uranus and I knew the Moon would be entering the most powerful phase around midnight.

In the top room of my house – a loft room criss-crossed with roof beams in which I had installed Cullum's bed, and chosen for its distance from both my wife's room and the maid's – and with Dee's *Monas Hieroglyphica* beside us for reference, Cullum did draw out a chalk circle divided into twelve and did mark symbols of the occult and of astrology in each house.

And it was here that I could see that the youth had changed two of symbols within the circle and did point out his mistake.

'See here, Cullum, you have replaced the Hebrew word *Briah* with the Hebrew word *Assiah*, I think this must affect the summing of the angel. I believe you summoned Raziel instead of Ohrmazd.'

Cullum, on his knees studied the chalk inscription marked into the wood, then rocked back on his heels.

'You are right, Master Lilly, but it was this way I was taught by my nursemaid.'

'Methinks she planned for both your uncle and your own demise.'

'Perhaps . . . She was in my uncle's employment as a young woman, and there was rumour she was once with child by him but was forced to abandon the babe.'

'Grievances indeed, but now we have found the error we must learn. I have decided to send you to a man I much admire, an Augustinian Friar called Leonardo Ferrer who lives in Valencia, a most wondrous Astrologer. I have been in correspondence with him for several years and he is a great supporter of mine. He will teach you well, Cullum, do not squander such an opportunity, I beg you.'

Just then the windowpane began to rattle violently with an unnatural wind, and both of us took fright.

'Quickly, Cullum, rub the circle out for fear we have woken some Demon!'

And, grabbing his bed sheet we did erase the markings as fast as we could, but as I finished I thought I heard a creak on the stairs outside the door then as another gush of wind rattled the windows, thought nothing of it.

That night I did sleep in the same bed as my wife, a cold bag of complaints I thought to warm up. Was it guilt? Perhaps, although I had not lain with my wife for over two year, I did think of her fondly, then, and of her vulnerability should we be besieged by Demons, or beset by ill fortune. Precarious times are dangerous times and in those days my marriage was my only fortress. I was naïve . . .

In the morning I sent Simon with a message around to a client of mine – a shipping insurer by the name of Caleb Masson. It is common practice for Astrologers to offer such men advice on the paying out of insurance for vessels potentially lost at sea. Passages to far-away places such as Virginia (and there are many Puritans leaving to strike their fortunes in this most God-fearing colony) or to the Spice Islands and sugar plantations such as Barbados or Jamaica were greatly perilous, and it so happens this client of mine was indebted to me for such services.

I arranged to meet the shipping insurer at the Devil's Tavern at Wapping, a real stink hole set by the Thames, favoured by pirates and honest sailors alike, knowing that Caleb, once a smuggler before he found respectability, frequented the place in a strange nostalgia.

But it was useful for other reasons: no Parliamentarian spies nor Roundheads would dare to enter such an establishment.

That day was beset by fog and a chilly damp rising from the river pervaded the tavern like the cold fingers of an old whore. The spindly rigging of a Dutch schooner poked up through the mist and behind it the fainter shadow of a German trading ship, both moored nearby yet rendered ghost vessels in such dim light.

In the dingy alley beside the side of the tavern two cockerels with spurs flashing silver on their legs tore into each other, surrounded by all manner of men, both criminal and respectable, each urging on his wager. I was not surprised to find Caleb there, for is it not true, dear Reader, that all insurers are merely gamblers dressed up with a clean ruffle about their necks? To my relief, the cockerel he was championing fought back, and after Caleb pocketed his winnings we retired within.

Truly it were as foggy inside the tavern as it was outside — such was the thick smoke of the sailors' pipes and the foul smoke of the cheap candles smouldering above us. As a blind fiddler and one-legged flautist played a manic jig in the corner, customers were forced to shout about us.

I followed as Caleb pushed his way with a casual familiarity through men I would normally dared not turn my back to for fear of a knifing and found us a barrel with two sailors standing about it drinking.

'Do you not know who stands before ye, you great lumps of shuddering whale fat? Master Lilly, a great master of fortune who could curse thee with one look of his black eye!' Caleb growled at which the two men backed away. Grinning, he turned toward me. 'Works every time. But it is true thou art a great Wizard,' he told me, then shouted for ale.

As he did, I noticed a strumpet lolling against the top bar and she did notice me. With her red hair and arrogant manner there was something of Magdalene about her, and I did wonder should I not take her upstairs and exorcise my longing upon her. Caleb, seeing my distraction, did clap me on the back.

'They say when the balls are full the brain is empty, Lilly. Come back to me, man, you can take her afterwards!'

'I apologise – I am not myself of late.'

'So tell me, William, what's on offer? It must be a thing of great temptation for you to agree to meet in such a putrid watering hole as this?'

Before I had a chance to answer two tankards were slapped down before us, swilling over the top of the upside barrel.

'I have a trade to make,' I replied carefully knowing Caleb's weakness was greed, 'one that could be of great advantage to a shipping man.'

'Tell me more.'

'I have under my roof a young apprentice who seeks a passage to the Netherlands and then on to Cordova.'

'A youth? An unskilled, soft-handed youth is no advantage to any captain.'

'Oh, he has skills.'

'Methinks his only skill is escape – and I warrant there is more to his journey than just an interest in the exotic. At these times I am good with the merchants and the city. It hasn't always been so and I cannot afford the scandal.'

'But can you afford to lose a ship in a storm or have a wayward captain navigate onto the rocks through his ignorance of the stars?'

'You know I cannot.'

'My lad is capable of lulling a storm to sleep and he knows the stars as good as myself, perhaps even better.'

'Truly?'

'He is but seventeen years, but his knowledge of astral matters is astonishing.'

'Perhaps even supernatural?' Caleb grinned wryly, revealing two gold teeth and a row of blackened stumps. I chose not to answer, which was in itself an answer. 'Now I am interested,' the old sea dog concluded.

'His skills for the passage: that is the trade. One passage to Rotterdam, then secure him a journey to Cordova,' I bartered.

'Why Cordova? It is full of nothing but Jews and Witches.'

'That *is* why,' I replied in a manner that closed any further inquiry. Caleb, pressing his great circumference against the barrel in the habit of a captain steadying himself in high seas, studied me closely, squinting with his good eye.

'It is possible; my agent in the Netherlands has Spanish friends.' After emptying his tankard he belched loudly but, methought, thoughtfully. 'I would want more for this, Lilly, if you are not to give me coin.' His bloodshot eyes peered from under the two bushels of black hair that were his eyebrows — even drunk he was not a man to make light of a bargain.

'I will barter two horaries for your next two returning ships — and I will give you the grace of one year in which you can claim these horaries.'

'This I might be able to use. I have a schooner due in from the West Indies, yet she is two months late and the owners would have me pay out on it. You will sign on this trade?'

'I will.'

'Then we have ourselves a deal. What is the lad's name?'

'For now, we will call him Barnacle.'

The redheaded whore was now lolling nearby upon a stool, gazing brazenly at me. Caleb looked at me then her.

'Barnacle it is, I will send a boy to your premises with a letter of agreement with ships and dates of the passages he is to travel upon. And you will draw up a horary on my lost West Indian schooner. Now, for God's sake and the rest of us, go to her, William, and find thyself again!'

Caleb Masson kept his promise and within a day I received a letter of agreement, and in turn did cast the horary for his lost ship and did declare it was to return within a month but had suffered and survived several bad storms around the Horn of Africa, hence the delay. The news was greeted with enthusiasm, and Caleb did agree to hold off payment to the owners until the next full moon.

A week later I took Cullum down to the dock myself and did see him begin his passage to Amsterdam. I confess, dear Reader, I shall miss him greatly.

Later that day I did buy a puppy spaniel from a man to cheer my spirits up. I named him Copernicus.

CHAPTER SEVEN

The twenty-third day of
the month of October 1641

The Corner House, The Strand

Jupiter: Magnanimous, Faithfull, Bashfull, Aspiring
in an honourable way at high matters, in all his
actions a Lover of fair Dealing, desiring to benefit
all men, doing Glorious things, Honourable and
Religious, of sweet and affable Conversation . . .

This morning I was woken rudely by the town crier ringing his bell. 'Oyez! Oyez! Awake! Awake! Irish invasion threatens the shores of Mother England! And be afraid! Revolt in Ulster! The Irish Papists are murdering our good Protestants in the streets of Dublin and Ulster! Papist invasion afoot! Awake! Awake! And be afraid!'

At which I drew the bed sheet across my head, hoping to complete a particularly sweet dream in which I was the King of Sweden and all my subjects had wings. Instead, I was woken again by the terrible clatter of footsteps below, followed by the sound of Mrs Featherwaite scolding the new scullery maid and then the unmistakable rattle of pots and pans, another clatter of footsteps, and a banging on my bedroom door.

'Master Lilly! Calamity is upon us!' Mrs Featherwaite yelled on the other side of what I had regarded as a perfectly sound oak door until that moment. Reluctantly I pulled myself out of bed, narrowly missing the pisspot on the way, then opened the door in my nightshirt.

'For pity sake, Mrs Featherwaite, I was up with my calculations until dawn. You could not let me sleep?'

'Not unless you plan to be murdered in your bed by Irish Papists! They say they have invaded West Riding and are already in Halifax and will be here by sunset!' It was here that I noticed that the good woman was dressed in what appeared to be a flour sack, the front of which was stuffed with various knives. 'We must pack our bags and arm ourselves! Before the Queen invites the Spanish and the French in to finish poor England off!'

'Faith, woman, you are not making sense, the Papists are not upon us, and certainly will not be by nightfall.'

'But they are rebelling in Ireland! Catholics murdering good Protestants, and you know what happened in France and Germania? Well, it's begun here! John Pym warned us again and again, and what has King Charlie done about it? Upset the Scots who will now not defend us against the Irish, and all because his Papist wife has his balls! It's going to be up to us Londoners to defend the city. And I,' she waved a meat cleaver (a fine piece of steel purchased from Sheffield) 'intend to be ready!'

'I am sure, even if the rebellion in Ireland is raging fast, it would be a good month before the Irish could arrive here, and besides it would be Parliament's army who would defend us. And so, as honourable as your intentions are, my dear Mrs Featherwaite, I believe they are premature.'

'That might be the case, Master Lilly, but I shall take the precaution of hanging something over the door to declare us a Puritan household. There are many in this city who are afeard.

The maid Nancy from next door, she told Simon there's a mob roaming the city looking to burn Catholic houses and any Irish they find.'

'As you wish; I would not want a window smashed, such is the cost of glass. Now get thee to the kitchen and brew a big kettle of camomile and skullcap for both our nerves. I have clients at eight.'

After which I disarmed the woman and led her back toward the kitchen, annoyed that my sleep would have to wait.

My first caller of that morning was to be a gentleman Chevalier who had asked me to investigate the paternity of a bastard child he hath been accused of fathering to a maidservant of brief acquaintance, having heard of my great success with a similar case I executed for my patron William Pennington. I had prepared the horary and all other information beforehand and this I shall explain.

Full of outrage and scorn, my Querent had claimed it was impossible for him to be the father as he had been away fighting in Scotland at the time of conception, and he claimed, upon seeing the child, it was older than its mother suggested, and that he was the victim of fraud. In turn, I had asked him for a full description of the babe, any particular features that would mark it – its eye colour, proportions and so on – as well as the name and birth date of the young woman in question.

It transpired that the baby had reddish hair and rather large ears. I then did some investigation, asking legal associates of mine if they had heard the mother's name by way of court or the paupers' yard. It so happened a lawyer friend had seen her accused once before, when the very same woman had falsely claimed a gold chain had been stolen from her and she sought damages from the thief.

Through this I then discovered the villainous woman's previous employers and went to see them using a false name I had adopted before — Mr Sute, Esquire — under the pretext I was seeking recommendations for the maidservant. When I met the master of the house it was notable that he had red hair and ears of great protuberance. I waited until the mistress was out of the room then confronted him with the truth, saying a good friend had been accused of fathering a babe upon the poor girl, and yet, despite my friend being of swarthy complexion with black hair, as well as being out of the country during the supposed time of conception, the babe had red hair and remarkably large ears, similar to the good gentleman's own. I had thought to share this intelligence with his wife, but being a fair man I had waited until we were alone before beginning the discussion. Then, cutting to the quick, I asked the reason for the maidservant's dismissal, at which point the master of the house broke down and confessed all, promising to settle with the girl in the utmost haste.

I can assure you that 'Mr Sute' left most satisfied, and I was even happier with the result. I also prepared a figure of auspicious occasions for cock-fighting gambles for the same Chevalier client, as well as a prediction for the type of woman he would marry and an aphrodisiac he had requested for his flagging yard.

The client came at ten, dressed in much lace and frills and foppery such Papist men are given to. Naturally his Sun was in the sign of the Lion, as was his ascendant, and beside being of such fifth planet nature he was a jolly fellow and I liked him well enough for his good humour and his generosity with the coin.

As he was there, I noticed that he was of very high colour and limped badly on the right side, so I also took the precaution of selling him my remedy for gout as well as another remedy for piles which I will share with you, dear Reader: take Yarrow and

May butter and stamp them together and apply as may be suffered and you will find help. Indeed, the Chevalier was most appreciative of both cures. I then charged him a half-crown for the gambling dates, another three shillings for solving his paternity troubles, and a further three shillings for the remedies, and the good gentleman thought he was well served! Happiness all round. However, as I was escorting him out of the door we came upon my next client, a demure Puritan woman in mourning, who reeled back in horror that I should be entertaining such company.

I hurried the good Chevalier out before returning to explain myself. 'Madam, I turn no one from my door unless he be here in jest or ridicule or here with some evil intent. The people that seek my advice either astrological or medical are all good Christians and all equal in the eyes of God and therefore in my own. Once past this threshold . . .' and here I pointed to the last stone before my door, 'they are merely seekers of truth who are here in all humility and I am here to service them without judgement.'

'Even murdering Papists?' she asked in a loud Ulster accent. Just then I noticed my neighbour leaning from her balcony in curiosity at my visitors and knowing that in those times every house harboured a spy, I pulled my Querent into the house.

It was there that I learnt she was a widow of only a few days, having lost her husband in the Irish uprising, and was much afeard for her two young sons who were last seen in the company of their father. Now understanding her great hostility toward my Royalist client, I sat the Irishwoman down in my study. Shaking in the memory, and being a very honest person, she made a great conscience of what she spoke – of terror, looting, and rioting. I noted the particulars of both her husband and the two sons as well as the longitude and latitude of their last location in Ireland, whilst reassuring her that, although I might have Royalist clients, I myself was a good Protestant and she need not fear betrayal in any manner.

In truth, I saw tragedy in both sons' figures, but did not want to add to her sorrows; instead, I promised to glean as much information as I could, and report back to her in a month. I had not the heart to take payment, and the good widow was most grateful.

After she left I told Mrs Featherwaite the suggestion that perhaps the time had come to escort different clients to different entrances to the house: the Royalists to the front door, the Puritans to the side gate, and in this way avoid collisions of faith and sensibility. The housekeeper agreed only when I swapped the order around, quite rightly arguing that since most of our neighbours were Puritans it would be sensible to appear of like-minded faith – even (and she said this with ironic emphasis) if certain individuals within the household insisted on keeping with bad company.

I did not reply but made a note to ensure that Mrs Featherwaite should never learn of the truth of my relationship with Magdalene, even under the most benign of circumstances. Although the woman was an invaluable source of information and an even better assistant in the art of herbal remedies (so well had I trained her), the housekeeper was not above a little spying herself, as was most of London at that time, and I certainly did not trust Simon, her nephew, certain sure he was not above taking money happily from the Parliamentary guards for information.

By that evening of that busy day my mind was spinning with calculations and I wished to empty it of all thought, so I went to my local church, Saint Antholin's.

The pews were filled with men, women and children, all praying for deliverance from the Irish Papists whom they thought were upon us in a matter of days. At the front of the church the young men had gathered, ashen-faced, some with their jerkins bulging with sticks, knives, clubs, all manner of weapon barely hidden before the eyes of God, so determined were they to defend London from this looming invasion of Catholic murderers and rapists. In the pulpit a preacher I had not heard before, a tall thin man with a beak of a nose and a great mane of hair, held his audience in rapt horror. Throwing his arms about in expressive description he spoke of unborn babes being ripped from their dying mothers' wombs, wives raped before husbands, a young boy's eye gouged out and a cross carved into his forehead, all stories told by survivors of the Protestant massacre in Ulster. Then, in graphic adjective, he called the murdered martyrs to the true faith of England, and declaimed that as martyrs they deserved revenge and that, if the King would not defend England and the true home of God, then he personally would. At which a huge (and rather unchristian, I felt) shout of approval went up from those listening and a shiver cut through me.

Methought I saw the future in that great howl.

By the end of the sermon the preacher had half the men in the congregation waving their makeshift weapons in the air and then, with great clamour, they bundled out of the church ready to attack any innocent who vaguely resembled a Papist.

Afeard, I ran with them, amid the shouting and rowdy encouragement, thinking the distance between Man and Savage is far less than we like to envisage. Trailing behind the yelling mob I watched helplessly as they smashed the windows of those merchants rumoured to be Papists, the screaming wives and daughters of the unfortunate victims cowering behind the broken glass.

As the mob moved east, I hurried on ahead to Magdalene's house, anxious that she, a known Royalist, might be targeted.

*   *   *

The church bells were just pealing out ten of the hour when I arrived at the gate of the townhouse. The windows were darkened but in the distance I could already hear the cries of the approaching rabble. I was about to step through the gate, when the rattle of coach wheels upon the cobbles drew me back into the shadows.

I swung around, and in that instant threw myself behind a hedgerow as the coach pulled up outside the house.

From my hiding place I could see two gentlemen, both dressed in the fine clothes of the Court, one older and slightly more austere, in flowing cloak, a dagger in his belt, the other in the bright uniform of the Chevalier. They descended and began moving towards the gate in a grim silence. As the moonlight fell upon their features I recognised one as Magdalene's husband from the portrait I had seen in the landing of her house; the other, walking behind him, was Monsieur Vindecot, the French spy Magdalene herself had pointed out to me at the theatre. What were they doing this time of night? A husband naturally is entitled to visit his wife at any hour, but as for Monsieur Vindecot, a man who profits from the misfortunes of others, what was his business here?

I waited until her maid had welcomed them into the house and then, transfixed both by curiosity and fear, spied through the windows on the ground floor. Moments later I saw both Magdalene and her husband watch intently as Monsieur Vindecot explained something to them with great passion.

The intensity of the unheard conversation made me wonder fearfully whether we had been followed when we'd walked beside the river. Or perhaps noticed at the theatre? I could not imagine that even if we were that her husband would care; after all it was not uncommon for women, especially, to have an Astrologer or medic as an innocuous companion.

In truth, I had often marvelled at the trusting nature of these husbands who seemed to attribute the sensibility of eunuchs to such men – as if we were priests. And I had wondered whether this phenomena had not encouraged the exploitation of such blindness by great Astrologers such as the notorious Simon Forman, himself a great lover of the female, and my old rake friend, Captain Bubb. And so I studied Magdalene's husband with both guilt and some fascination. He was young, handsome, and an obvious effete. I could not envisage the two of them in any act of love nor lust, and in this I took some comfort.

Just then Rosie, her maid, appeared at the back door of the dwelling, a pail of night soil in her hand. I waited until she had emptied it in the gutter then approached her.

'Rosie! 'Tis I, Master Lilly!'

Startled, she stumbled back.

'What mischief brings you here, to lurk in the shadows?'

'I need you to give your mistress a message, privately, away from the ears of her husband.'

'What's in it for me?' The maid had gathered her wits with admirable swiftness; such is the acumen of the ruthless survivor. I pressed a farthing into her palm.

'Tell her the Scottish lad is now safely to Holland.'

'Are you sure that is it? No undying declarations of love or less noble inclinations – or does the Lilly lack a stem? The husband will be away by the morning, and my mistress is a woman in need.'

'You mistake me,' I stuttered. Were my sentiments so obvious?

'I think not.'

'Just the simple message will suffice.' And after a nod from her she slipped back into the house whilst I returned home by way of the back lanes. Later I found respite from my fears through a very strong sleeping remedy I made myself. Even so, it were a liverish and restless night.

CHAPTER EIGHT

♏ ☿ ♀

November 1641

The Corner House, The Strand

Saturn: He is profound in Imagination, in his Acts severe,
in words reserved, in speaking and giving very spare, in
labour patient, in arguing or disputing grave, in obtaining
the goods of this life studious and solicitous . . .

Winter was setting in early and Jane my wife was preparing to
visit her brother and their family in Nottingham to bring them
some cloth and spices for they were constantly short of money
and the luxuries we were accustomed to. As I have explained,
relations were not good between myself and my spouse; her
piety as well as constant bickering hath worn my patience to
the thinnest sliver. So when she entered my study without
knocking, interrupting a particularly complicated calculation,
I was greatly displeased.

'William, I would have words.'

'Patently, and patently I have no option but to listen.'

At which Jane did flounce and pout, placing herself
between myself and my books. 'Your behaviour of late hath
put this household in grave danger,' she announced in
solemn drama.

'Madam, you are audacious. It has been my behaviour of
late that hath provided and continues to provide this

household and yourself with a very good income. Faith, even provide you with coin for the very journey you are to take later this morning.' In truth I had no idea to which behaviour she might be referring.

'Do not play the ignorant wit with me, William. I refer to the nature of the peoples who come to this house seeking your horary advice. You cannot serve Parliamentarian and Royalist, housemaid and Lord without alienating one or the other. You play a dangerous courtship and one will find out about the other and then both will condemn you.'

'I am not a fool, Jane, I am careful to keep the politicks of my Querents from each other.'

'Perhaps, but I have heard from Estelle, the wife of the leather merchant who doth serve the Court that George Wharton, the King's Astrologer, means to destroy you, and I have also heard from Agatha, the wife of the Presbyterian minister I know from my hospice work, that he also means to discredit you and see you in the Tower before next summer. What say you, sir? I am your wife, you have a duty to protect me!'

At which I put down my quill and turned on her in wrath.

'Woman, do you think me such a small soul that I would cower under the petty politicks of our times? I know these enemies, I watch them closer than you could possibly imagine, but if you think William Lilly intends to stunt his vision to that of the partisan you are much mistaken. I may have the mind of a Puritan but I have the heart of the Royalist — and above and beyond this I am an Englishman with no desire to see my country divided!' My shouting sent the dog under the desk, and with my spittle hitting Jane's cowl, she did cower. I confess my anger had forced me to abandon control and of this I am not proud, but in that moment she embodied all that I loathed: the small-minded fear and cowardice both of the populace and of those I actively campaigned to fight. 'More so, I have a duty to my vocation, madam, a God-anointed gift to illuminate all men to their Fate, regardless. There is a bigger vision here than to sit out a possible war in silent anonymity. If you object so much perhaps you should remove yourself and live – at your own expense – under the pious roof of your Quaker brother!'

Now Copernicus, tail between his legs, bolted for the door, whilst Jane pale, drew herself up to her full height.

'I see I have angered you greatly, and yet all I wished for is to ensure both our safeties, husband.' Her thin reedy voice grated. 'But since the sight of me offends thee so much I take my leave and will depart immediately for Nottingham.' After which she turned on her heels and left the study. I did not stop her. Instead, I sat down, thinking how my longing for Magdalene, both as confidant and intellectual intimate, hath eclipsed all rationality.

And so it was I stayed in a paralysis of shame until I heard the horses depart beneath my window.

Later I went out into an evening all blue-white and frosted by the full moon and made for the White Hart Tavern and did drink with my friends, John Scott and Harry, where we were most entertained by the wit William Pool who kept us merry with obscene verse. At midnight, encouraged by the ale and fighting a growing hollowness within me, I found myself walking the streets alone, Pool having reeled off to the conquest of a lonely merchant's wife.

It was not long that I was beneath Magdalene's window, hoping she was not at Court. I was rewarded, for I saw her silhouette, her hair loosened to her shoulders. How long I remained there, turning my situation around and around like a prism, I cannot tell you, despite the cold and the snow that settled upon my shoulders and hood.

Although such union is a sin outside of matrimony, relations between my wife and I were of such desolation that I thought to fashion a logic by which I could act in good faith. For surely a marriage is not a marriage if nocturnal union is not acted upon and man and wife have become as strangers, therefore, how could union with my natural mate be sin? For God could scarcely regard my marriage a union as it was, never mind a holy one (most unholy is how I had begun to regard it lately). Surely Magdalene was my natural mate, in spirit, intellect and soul? And so I argued with myself, the snow falling in mute judgement about me until I was betrayed by a twig snapping underfoot.

'You are far too old for such wistfulness! Besides, you must be freezing!' Magdalene called out from the window.

'So cold I think me a statue!' I retorted.

In moments I was inside, the rest of the household sleeping, Magdalene's bedchamber as airy and spacious as her study was not, the four-poster bed, sparse in hangings except for the bed itself, luxurious in fur and quilt.

She studied me with a bemusement that irked me somehow, and so, struggling for my dignity I stared into the fire, warming myself before her hearth.

'I fought with my wife,' I told her without looking at her. 'She would have me be an ordinary man who desires nothing but a grey survival. She would have me be someone who questions nothing, a whipping boy to be kicked about by History.'

She moved nearer, and I could smell her body under the loose robe she wore. Oh, torturous proximity!

'That will not be, William, not in a thousand years.'

I could not turn to her nor step closer. 'She is frightened; she thinks I will be arrested if I continue to court both Parliament and the King.'

'What think thee?' Magdalene said softly.

Now I turned, 'I think I have no choice, not any longer.'

And we both knew this was a bigger truth than those simple words and she did place her hands upon me.

Faith, it was a perversity to stand there without lifting a finger, desire telling me to take her and damn the consequences, whilst Intuition pounded against my conscience like a mad drummer boy marching before his army.

'William, we have already transgressed; there is no great sin in ploughing the seed you have already sown.'

'It is no longer the sin I struggle with, but the consequences – not for my wife, but for myself. I cannot see how this would end.'

'But as seer you must know you cannot fight Fate.' She lifted her skirts, showing two plump thighs. 'Am I not woman enough for you?' I did not move.

'You want me to step closer?' She lifted her robe higher and now I could see the pink lips and button of her sex, then the full curve of her buttocks as she turned for me. 'For William, if I was to be any closer I would be upon you.'

'Then be upon me, lady,' I told her. 'Absolve me of the sin of taking you – for, help me God, I will.'

At which she moved close enough for me to reach out and pull her thighs across my face and, burying myself under the tent of her robe, I played her sex with my tongue and fingers, the sweetness of her lemony musk falling about me, filling all my senses like light and colour, the sounds of her pleasure feeding my own, and yet my body still lay untouched upon the bed. When I felt the moment to be ripe, I pulled her down upon my hips and finally I entered her and we were one.

Such a tight plum was she, I thought I would disappoint both her and myself, and so I paused then threw her upon her back and, hoisting her legs over each shoulder, rode her hard.

She reached her pleasure before me, with a scream I did think would wake the dead (at the very least the maid) and send the town crier running. But, in her ecstasy I did my own meet, and a great shuddering release it was too, the likes of which I'd not experienced for many a year.

Afterwards, lying back in each other's arms, the day now creeping across the wooden floor, she did call for Rosie, who, to my embarrassment, arrived in the chamber bearing a plate of fruit and claret. At the maid's appearance I made to pull the bed sheet up over my head, but laughing, my lady tugged them back down again, and in full post-coital disarray I was forced to confront the maid.

'Mr Daisy is ever so shy,' the maid commented as she left the refreshments by the bed.

'You know it's Master Lilly!' I called after her.

'Aye, and a wilting one at that,' the wanton servant retorted as she shut the door. I turned to Magdalene.

'Are you not worried about the servants' tattle? Are they not loyal to your husband?'

'My servants are loyal to both of us, but they know my husband and they know me. My husband only has eyes for other men. Indeed, it was the King's father's own favourite, Buckingham, who did approach my father with the match and I married with full of knowledge of my husband's inclinations. I am fortunate that he allows me my own passions, with the proviso I am discreet and keep such matters within these four walls.'

I pondered this arrangement, but then, thinking upon my own unhappy marriage, and upon the peccadillos and extraordinary circumstances in which both love and fortune places people, and the grievances experienced by my Querants through these very same emotions, I concluded such practicality might have its attractions.

'Where is your husband now?'

'He is with the King's nephew, Prince Rupert, fighting in Holland.' She curled up to me.

'He is a Chevalier?'

'He is a soldier, close to the Prince and the King; I fear one day he will fall out of favour. Prince Rupert is a charming but violent man.'

'Indulged and violent so the rumours say.' The rumours I knew to be true, but again I feigned diplomacy.

'His behaviour in Holland at the siege of Breda was questionable – he should never have charged the Spanish. I fear Prince Rupert's hot-headedness prevents his excellence at soldiering.'

'You are a woman of much education, military as well as the politick?'

'Three years imprisoned in Austria has left Prince Rupert chafing at the bit. The King knew this when he ransomed him – but the King is also blind when it comes to family.'

'This I saw in his stars. What make you of the Earl of Stafford's execution? They say the King sacrificed him knowingly . . .' I pressed now, eager for her perspective.

'Wentworth played a dangerous game, ambition was his folly – his rule in Ireland has done the King no favours and so later he was made to pay for the fiasco of the Scottish revolt. But you could argue his only fault was following orders. A fault he paid for with his life. The King bears his execution badly and doth feel both guilt and anger.' She was bipartisan in tone, and I loved her for it.

'I fear more heads will fall, following such unwise orders.'

'And now Ireland. Methinks England is besieged from all fronts . . .'

'And from inside as well – a sick man in a mad world, in danger of flaying his arms out to punch blindly into the shadows.' I spoke my fears hoping that to utter them would be to lessen them; instead, it had the opposite effect. Magdalene leaned over and embraced me.

'Yet here we are, a Royalist bedded by a Puritan.'

'Well-bedded?' (Oh vanity, stay thy tongue!)

'Very well-bedded.' She miaowed. 'Despite our differences you and I will be of help to each other.'

I rolled away and studied her. I could not see any guile; a spy is a spy but all information is useful. It's a matter of interpreting it well, I reminded myself thinking, *If I lose my heart I still cannot afford to lose my head*. Besides, this liaison promised to be the most pleasurable of chess games and faith, I liked to play.

Later that morning I returned to the Corner House, where Mrs Featherwaite had the good sense not to ask where I had spent the night. I confess, dear Reader, this state of affairs continued on through the next few weeks – little did I realise it would be years.

CHAPTER NINE

♂☾♌

The fourth day of the month of January, 1642

The House of Commons, of which I happen upon that day to be residing within

Aries is a Masculine, Diurnall sign, moveable, Cardinall,
Equinoctall; in nature fiery, hot and dry, cholerick,
bestial, luxurious, intemperate and violent: the diurnall
house of Mars of the fiery Triplicity and of the East.

If November and December had been cold, January did show us
her harshest face with many lakes and streams frozen over.
London turned into itself; all this Christmas there was nothing
but private whisperings at Court, and secret councils held by
the Queen and her party, with whom the King sat in council
very late many nights. It was a tense atmosphere, febrile and
most unhealthy for governance, my only joy a letter I had
received from Cullum Monroe informing me of his safe arrival
in Rotterdam. Now in Amsterdam, he was to sail on to Seville
in the Spring. The youth wrote of both his relief and of his
excitement at the treasures he had discovered in both the
Hebrew and Christian libraries of that same city. I confess, once
I had placed the letter back down upon the table I did wonder
whether this intimacy was to be the nearest to a son I would
experience – certainly my Natal figure would indicate a great
lack of natural progeny. I have not one planet placed in the

fourth house at the time of my real birth, the fourth house signifying family. Perhaps this is the reason behind my great ambition?

There is something else in my Nativity that compels me to make my mark upon the world, an aspect that secretly fills me with terror — my ascendant by direction will be a very hard square to my Mars and the Moon in five years' time — this could signify my death in 1647. I would not be the first Astrologer to have predicted his own demise, but I am of the belief that a man can overcome his destiny if he hath knowledge of his proclivities and when he is vulnerable. I have told no one of this, for no one knows the true date of my birth — like many Astrologers I have made a rumour of an alternative date to confuse my enemies.

Meanwhile, outside the palace discontent and the divide between royalty, merchant and apprentice was becoming pronounced indeed. Several petitions had been organised, with thousands signing — the only voice for a poor labouring man.

My own community — the pious members of the Church of England — were divided, some sympathising with the old order the King represented, and others desiring for a more rigorously unembellished church. I, like many of my community, vacillated. This was not uncommon.

We had seen riot after riot, people demonstrating in their thousands over the Root and Branch petition — a bill that demanded the end of bishops, deans and chapters. The apprentices, as usual, were the most vocal. Young employed men with a bleaker and bleaker future afeard for their professions, with no wives to blunt the knife of their frustrations (except for the whore and strumpet), these youths increasingly held London to ransom with their protesting.

My baker and my butcher had their windows smashed,

and the daughter of the man I bought my pickled fish from was sorely abused by an errant gang. Politick became an excuse for the most abhorrent behaviours — thirty thousand this Christmas alone running amuck through the streets demonstrating for change. Even the King grew afraid.

Meanwhile the auspices for the new year of 1642 did not look good. I had sent several messages through Magdalene to warn the Queen of the planetary reversals and obstacles our good King faced. A man armed with foreknowledge is a man armed indeed, or so the proverb goes, but both hubris and arrogance was the Achilles' heel of Charles the first — I had seen it in the heavens that had stretched over his birth time, but, as you know, Dear Reader, my warning hath been ignored.

Jane arrived back from her brother's in Nottingham for the New Year Day celebrations, the conversation between us, as well as any affection, now past the pretence of etiquette. Did she know I had taken a mistress? I think not. I suspect she thought it beyond my imagination, nor did she see that another might desire me. But we were cloven together in the eyes of God and, despite Jane's cankerous nature and the misfortune of her Saturn squared with Scorpio, she kept house well enough (although frugality was not a virtue of hers) and her main cost to me was of her visits to her Quaker friends and to her needy family.

In those festive but hollow weeks, we talked of nothing but small matters of a practical nature. This kept us civil. But of the mind and spirit there was no exchange, the bedchamber as thankless as a grave. And so you can imagine my weekly delight upon returning to the conversation and intelligence of my mistress.

And so to the day leading up to that fateful occasion on

which the King did blunder and set this country upon the path of civil conflict.

I remember I had managed to steal an hour in the arms of Magdalene. It was barely light . . . I had told Jane I was to early morning prayer. Outside the world was hazy with the dawn, herself mere fingers of blue lustre that crept across the frosty roofs and ice-kissed branches. I did so love the anonymity she doth provide. St Clements had just pealed five of the hour, the beadle on his rounds setting the neighbourhood dogs barking, yet within this cacophony my mistress's bedchamber were an oasis. I lay beside her sleeping form, my body and spirit aglow with the life force such congress ignites, speculating upon a discourse we'd indulged earlier upon of John Dee and his alchemy, when Magdalene woke.

'William, have you horaries later today?'

'There will be the unexpected visitors, but my only actual appointment is a new mother whose child was born on a full moon during a Mercury retrograde seeking to address these planetary afflictions upon the child.'

Magdalene sat up and curled her fingers into my chest hair in play.

'It would worth your while to spend the day in Parliament. I know there will be much commotion there and I, as a known courtier, cannot be there but you . . .'

'To what purpose?' I caressed her naked back, again marvelling at how such intelligence ended up being contained in such a comely vessel.

'Let's just say that the Queen was heard to issue an order to her husband . . .'

'The Queen ordered the King? That is an unnatural state of things.'

'He loves her much, and cannot refuse her.'

'I could refuse you,' I teased, pushing her hands away in jest.

'A man can always refuse his mistress. His wife is another case entirely. The Queen has her man's *colei* cupped in her hand. *Go, you coward, and pull those rogues out by the ears, or never see my face again* were her exact words, although naturally I cannot swear by this.'

At which I sat up. 'And who are these so-called rogues?'

'I would venture that Pym is named amongst them.'

'The King would not dare! Such an action would only enrage the people further!'

'Go be my eyes, my love, this is the great turning of history.'

'Yes – and if the King continues in his actions we will all be on the roasting spit of it. Who else knows of this?'

'The Lady Lucy Hay – as she is said to be Pym's lover, the King might find he has more of a hunt than is expected.' Magdalene was right; since Earl Strafford's execution and the Irish rebellion, England had been reduced to a jittery rumour mill running amok like a headless pheasant in the fowler's yard.

Every week brought fake reports of a French invasion from the east and an Irish invasion from the west, not to mention the cunning Scots who continued to eat into the northern border. And with these reports and Fear and his helper Imagination, at times it felt as if the Papists were coming at us from all sides, with the King and his Catholic Queen a rotting heart in a diseased body. Now the counties, dreading an army on their borders, had applied for arms and men from Parliament; North Wales, Cheshire and Lancashire were particularly uneasy. How much was truth and how much was terror fanned by Pym's leaflets and the Protestant reports of new violence upon ordinary English folk was hard to ascertain. But one thing was certain: as I predicted, the King did not look beyond his own Court and was increasingly ignoring the needs of his people whilst reports of Republicanism from Germania and the promotion of such revolution only fuelled the discontent.

Leaving the bed, I pulled on my breeches, my mind calculating all possibilities. If I were to warn my Parliament friends I would place both Magdalene and myself in danger. We both knew the Court was a sieve when it came to hiding information – there were as many spies inside Whitehall as there were inside Parliament so I had little choice.

'I will go and be your eyes and ears,' I promised her.

It was a bracing walk back to the Strand, the wind blowing flurries of snowflakes across my path. It seemed that civil war was inevitable, but would it come in a year, months or days? It would be bloody and terrible, but how bloody we had no idea, for war is only ever an abstract, an imagined nightmare until one is actually in the midst of it. Even then there is disbelief as all one's higher senses are eclipsed by the grinding and most immediate need to survive.

I wondered on my own Fate and that of the people I loved: my vocation, a few good friends, the custom and peoples of this country and lastly of my frailty – Magdalene de Morisset.

Since the sighting of the Royalist spy, Vindecot, in the company of her husband, I had been careful in only sharing useless tattle about various Parliamentarian friends and clients with her. There were a few occasions I had deliberately led her astray with a harmless piece of information that I knew she would report back to the Queen and her courtiers. Sometimes, I confess with some chagrin, with the knowledge that such false information might serve both my purpose and that of my client. I was sure Magdalene had gleaned my ploys, and in turn had toyed with me in a similar manner. After all, I knew her to be an excellent strategist. Could this visit to the House of Commons be another ruse? Either way, I would find out.

By the time I arrived home, the morning sun had begun to catch at the icicles hanging from the eaves of the Tudor houses with their high red-tile roofs, white daub walls and dark criss-cross beams, some with the upper storey so over-hung they almost touched their neighbours opposite, and I warrant they would be able to hear each other's whisperings, secrets, nay, even their merry-making. Such proximity only served divided London and I did worry for the loyalty of mine own neighbours – there was much coin to be gained as turn-coat. Nevertheless, despite all the turmoil within, without Mother Winter had made an angel-lace of the frosty twigs and branches of the trees. Dirty London had turned all silver, falling mute like a shy virgin holding his breath before a beautiful woman. What did this day hold – revolution or tyranny? There was an air to it that murmured of the dangers of a voided Moon, a restless Mars and the obsessive shadow of Saturn.

As I stepped into the lane, the cathedral bell tolling six o'clock splintered my tranquillity.

At midday, after analysing the urine of a man afflicted by the wasting disease, then, casting a horary for a head servant enquir-ing about some lost silver within the great household he worked for, and finally treating a distressed mother with an afflicted child, Jane left the house to travel beyond the city walls on an act of charity and I ate mutton and leeks in the kitchen, with Mrs Featherwaite fluttering about me like a hen upset by a fox. After promising I would return later with some ribbon and silk the housekeeper had wanted for a furnishing, I donned my best cloak and set out for the House of Commons.

Looking down from the public gallery, I could see the lines of the politicians seated below, some now standing and shouting to make their point, others openly dozing in the aisles. Suddenly the man sitting beside me (who wore the badge of the guild of saddlers) nudged me as a muscular man with the broad head of a patriarch rose to his feet to speak – the member for Cambridge whom I recognised immediately.

''Tis Oliver Cromwell, a real firebrand; they say he be the fiercest man of the party,' my neighbour murmured reverently. Indeed, Cromwell made a powerful figure, some five feet ten inches in height, crudely dressed with his features large and roughly hewn, but he was upright and defiant in stance; already infamous, and a man to put your money on. I knew his Sun to be in Taurus, and bull he was proved to be from head to toe.

Addressing the Parliamentarians in a booming voice he spoke of a loyal Irishman – a certain Owen O'Connell who had warned Dublin of the uprising, and for his services had been promised by the very same Parliament a place in command of a company of Dragoons. Yet the Lord Lieutenant (a servant to the King and a Royalist) had failed to action this appointment.

'Is this the respect the King shows to Parliament?' Cromwell thundered. 'Are all our directives to be ignored! And our heroes disrespected!'

When he sat back down a great applause rippled through the House; truly, I thought, this is a leader. After which the House descended into its usual tedium. A stick-thin and laconic member from the north, his see-saw accent soporific, began arguing against disafforestation, describing the hardships this practice had afflicted upon the peasants and poor folk of his villages now they no longer had the right to gather free firewood from the forests. His wheeling, flat voice drilled on and I began to fall asleep, thinking Magdalene's information must have been false when I was woken by another sharp jab from my neighbour.

'Something's afoot,' he whispered, pointing down. Below, in the pews, MPs were turning their heads and glancing about nervously.

'Why this commotion?' I asked.

'This is a subject that the great Pym himself likes to address, and yet he does not appear to be in the House. This is most peculiar and disturbing. Pym was here only an hour ago. He is expected to stand and respond.'

We were interrupted by the sound of a commotion from the front of the hall. A moment later the King entered, accompanied by about two hundred men, some in the uniform of his pensioners, others in the florid clothing of the mercenary, but all armed with swords and clubs.

Faith, seeing him like that, surrounded by his men, one realised how short of statue he really was – yet dressed so royally and immaculately, his presence veritably glistening with dignity and Stuart grace, which, for a Puritan like myself, made one waver in one's opinion. The whole House was now in outrage; Speaker Lenthall, a tall, singular figure, stepping back in fear from his chair, whilst the entire place exploded into shouting as the King's men wove their way down the aisles.

'Order! Order!' Lenthall slammed down his hammer to no avail. Finally, the room quietened as the King moved forward, his lame leg evident in his faltering steps, and I could see the rumour the Monarch had the rickets as a child was true.

'By your leave, Mr Speaker, I must bor . . . row your chair,' he addressed Lenthall, in polite but stuttering tone, and Lenthall (who towered over the Monarch) stepped reluctantly aside. I, with the other men in the hall, watched aghast, astounded at the audacity and sheer insolence. It was unheard of for the King himself to enter the place for the commoners – reserved solely for the mercantile and guild class, the people's hall – without announcement and most threateningly with a whole platoon.

Was the King here to dismantle Parliament as he had in the past? Did he mean to finally quell the voice of the populace and the workingman? Had the Queen's galling finally driven him to some ill-advised gesture of extremity?

Calmly the King sat in the Speaker's chair as if it were his own throne. At his side, his twenty-three-year-old nephew, Prince Rupert, in full Chevalier regalia, his sword poised by his hip, alluring in beauty and arrogance, gazed imperiously about as if all before him were inferior, whilst beside him stood two tall guards with pikes in hand.

The Monarch slowly glanced about the hall as if to study the faces of the politicians standing before him – some enemies, some friends, but all wearing expressions of utter disbelief at his action.

'I must declare that no King that ever was in England shall be more careful of your privileges . . .' His voice rang out in the muted silence. 'Yet you must know that in cases of treason . . .' And here, a muttering and an anger swept through the incredulous onlookers. Ignoring it, the King continued, ' . . . in cases of treason,' he repeated for emphasis, 'no person has a privilege . . .' His declaration was underscored by the loud thud of his guards locking the doors of the hall. Faith, I confess I then began to fear for my life and the lives of all those others now trapped within those walls.

The King turned to the speaker. 'Speaker Lenthall, I wish for members John Pym, John Hampden, Denzil Holles, Arthur Haselrig and William Strode to step forward. The rest of you have nothing to fear . . .'

(And here, dear Reader, surrounded by so many armed soldiers and in such disregard for the law of the land it felt that all in that hall had everything to dread – from arrest to execution.)

At this point Lenthall stepped forward, and truly he was a

brave man then, to be confronted with the King's wrath and the fury of Parliament hot upon both shoulders.

'May it pleasure Your Majesty, I have neither eyes to see nor tongue to speak in this place but as the House is pleased to direct me, whose servant I am here . . .' he argued most courageously, at which the King stared, amazed at Lenthall's impudence to question his authority, until he lifted his hand to signal for his soldiers to begin searching the House.

Immediately the guards started to look for the named men amongst the Parliamentarians, who, in bravery, closed ranks, and began to mock them on their search.

My companion looked wildly around. 'None of the men he seeks are here – someone has betrayed the King!'

'More pertinently, the King has betrayed democracy and besmirched the privilege of the House,' I retorted, outraged by what I was witnessing – a King acting without the permission of both his people and his political advisors, an inflated nobleman thinking he is on a hunt – for that is what he resembled, that day, God save my soul for thinking it.

The soldiers, riled by the jeering and now desperate, began searching under tables and benches to the growing ridicule of the Parliamentarians. Meanwhile I reflected upon the face of the King; his expression upon entering the building triumphant that he had finally snared his prey, the blank look of incredulity that the five men he hunted were not to be found, his brow and eyes clouding over with frustration and vexation.

In truth, for all his good breeding and politeness, I thought this to be a man who neither understood compromise nor had the diplomacy to conduct himself to any advantage. He was a gasping fish out of water, standing there, displaying a complete inability to relate to his fellow man, the assumption of his superiority obscuring any humanity as profoundly as an eclipse. It frightened me to see him thus.

Finally, after an eternity, realising that indeed his birds had flown, the King ordered the doors to be unlocked, amid the murmuring of discontent: an admission of defeat. As his men left, his chief-in-command most liverish, actually knocked the walking stick from under the corpulent member for Berkshire before leaving the hall.

Once the Royal entourage was out the door the whole House broke into lampooning cries of 'Privilege! Privilege!'

I cannot remember when I was so proud to be called a common Englishman.

Outside Westminster a crowd had gathered in the square, entertained by an entrepreneurial bard, a songster who had already composed his ditty of the events, with the King a subject of much ridicule, whilst an acrobat dressed as a skeleton juggled three plaster heads of the Monarch in a dangerous gamble. My spirit all a jangle with what I had witnessed, I made my way to the nearby tavern – so appropriately named Hell – to calm myself and glean the extent of the outrage. Already the occupants had spilt out onto the street, the air abuzz with chatter and politicking. The tavern was heaving with Parliamentarians, lawyers and all manner of workingmen – fishmongers, tinkers, aldermen, beadles and pamphleteers – all crowded in to hear the latest news. I have noticed that both disaster and revolution are great levellers and, in huge uncertainty, all and one is equal in his secret fears. In one corner a lone fiddler played a patriotic ballad until someone threw a pewter tankard at him, whilst at every crowded table a Parliamentarian held court, describing humiliation and outrage at the King's actions. The younger men – merchants, scribes, apprentices – occasionally breaking into cries of 'Down with the King's men!' were quickly stifled by their wiser and more cautious companions, but all of them taking note.

One young blade (as Puritan as they come with his cropped hair, and austere clothes) leapt to his feet to address the whole tavern:

'And if the King has arrested the goodly Pym and the rest, would we have stood by to watch them lose their heads!'

As one the rest shouted back, 'Nay!'

After which a thin preacher, his skin gaunt and serious across his face, climbed upon a chair and with arms outstretched began to recite Psalm 68 (a favourite with the good Cromwell I was told by an old drunk breathing cider in my face). 'May God arise, may His enemies be scattered!' The baritone of his voice cutting through the pipe smoke and clamour. 'Let them also that hate him flee before Him . . .' Now the tavern was hushed, all staring up at him their faces hungry for leadership, 'As smoke is driven away by the wind, may you blow them away!' His audience now in his hands, 'As wax melts before the fire, may the wicked perish before God!' Was this revolution at its conception? The moment ordinary men threw off the dictats of society pushed beyond rationale? Was this to be anarchy?

Then there was that silence, the deep void in which human emotion can swing either way, and I did suspect a riot, but an older patriarch, silver hair to his shoulders, climbed up beside the preacher and calmed the men by telling them now was the time to plan, not to protest, for it was becoming clear that the King meant to stifle and destroy Parliament and with it the voice of Protestant England.

The seeds of republicanism were sprouting before me and I was powerless to stop them. Instead I kept my silence and stared into my jug of ale. What if the King's men had found Pym and the others? He would have surely executed all five and stuck their heads on the Tower Bridge to the fury of all of London and the Protestant world beyond. These were just men, men who had argued for the defence of England against the Irish, who had questioned the King's insistent taxing for both the ornamentation of his palaces and for an army that might at any minute be used against the very same citizen.

Behind me a man murmured, saying he had heard that Pym and his men were hiding out in St Stephen's, a Puritan church on Coleman Street, and that he was sure the King would lack the courage to follow him there.

Then I overheard a young clerk from the Old Bailey, still in his robes, tell a fishmonger that it were Lady Lucy Hay who saved the five men by informing her lover Pym himself earlier that morning, to which the fishmonger raised his jug in a toast to the lady, followed by several others, and I wondered whether the said lady could ever guess she was being celebrated in a tavern called Hell or that a preacher would a recite a psalm in such a place that very day.

So . . . Magdalene's information was solid and true. This pleased me, as did the power of Lady Hay's influence to change such actions as the arrest and execution of men. If I could cultivate the right clients – both Royalist and Parliamentarian – I too, perhaps, could save the realm and appease the people. The whole madcap day had set me strategising.

When I arrived back at the Corner House, Jane was waiting in most ill temper. Screeching like a banshee, she accused me of neglecting my duties as the household provider because Mrs Featherwaite had sent away Querents that very afternoon. No amount of pleading or placating convinced my wife otherwise, not even the argument that I had a duty both as an Astrologer and advisor to the politick of this land to witness history. Jane is the most shrewish of women, and to rub salt into the wound of my humiliation she baled me out in front of my own servants. For this alone I cannot forgive her.

After, she locked herself in her own chamber at the top of the house and banished me from her bed. No hardship there; besides she is a woman most afflicted with the flatulence, a condition I attribute to her fervent praying, fasting, and Quakerish ways.

That night it was a blue moon. The lunar Goddess herself seemed to bear down on me through the high window of my study, her frigid light criss-crossing over my wooden floor and the figures I had spread upon it and upon my desk, the coal fire in the grate battling the chill wind that crept under the door and came whistling through the rafters and the crack in the window. Now, feeling an ague coming upon me as well as melancholia, I abandoned all pretence of sleep. As the great and wise Astronomer–Astrologer Kepler said, the whole business of acute illness depends upon the return of the Moon and its configurations with the planets and it is vain to seek explanation for it anywhere else. I am sure you have felt the affliction, dear Reader, but the power of a full moon (particularly when it is in Gemini) stirs up the brain and makes a dangerous nonsense of our meditations. Even so, the momentous events in Parliament had set my nerves alight yet I was determined to stay wise and calm.

I have taught my students Life is short, Art long, Experience not easily obtained, Judgement difficult and therefore it is necessary that a student not only exercise himself in considering several figures, but also that he diligently read the writing of others who have treated rationally of this Science. Therefore, that evening I sought out the astrological calculations by the illustrious astronomers I admired.

In search of calculating the chain of events to come I spent several hours poring through the horary predictions and the astral readings for the profound events in the history of England.

I had decided upon three junctions: the battle of Hastings in 1066 and the piercing of King Harold's eye by the Norman king which completed the invasion of the Norman French into this fair land; the signing of the Great Charter by King John in 1215, limiting feudal payments to the Crown, allowing swift justice and the protection of church rights and which I feared King Charles sought to undermine, and finally, the defeat of the Spanish Armada by the navy of Queen Elizabeth in 1588, a double intrigue, knowing how much influence her Magi and Astrologer John Dee had upon her and her realm.

I was looking for similar aspects and interpretations — some parallel observations to illuminate potential trouble to the kingdom. We all knew that Mars conjunct to Saturn indicates civil strife and that Venus conjunct Mars brings turbulence, but I was searching for more specific indicators. And so I went to the writings of Valentine Naibod — his commentary upon Alcabitius the eminent astronomer, Herr Kepler in his book *On The More Certain Fundamentals of Astrology* and finally to the writings of John Dee himself, and then compared them to the figure for the event that day in Parliament. To my considerable relief, after much study I finally concluded war would not be upon us quite yet.

I was just ascending to my bedchamber when there was a rattle of gravel against my window. I opened the pane and glanced down. A figure hooded in a plain cape stared up. For an instant I feared it were a Querent wanting news on a missing child or murder, such are the manner of folk that arrive after midnight, but then a cloud moved from the face of the moon and I could see the face more clearly. Magdalene's eyes were visible under the hood.

'William, 'tis I!'

'You take a huge risk, Madam, one that endangers both of us!' I told her, hoping my voice be taken by the wind and not heard by the household or my neighbours, although, thank the Good Lord, my wife was fond of a sleeping draught – one of my own concoctions, heavily laced with both mead and poppy, popular with ladies of a certain age.

'We are in the eye of the storm, an insurgency. Who knows where we will land tomorrow? Besides, I have been sent by the Council.' She indicated a waiting hackney standing in the shadows.

'A summoning I cannot ignore,' I replied with a wry smile and, turning back to my room, did take my jerkin from its hook. Out in the corridor, I slipped past Mrs Featherwaite's bedroom and was relieved to hear her heavy snoring, knowing she hath consumed a large quality of plum brandy in celebration of Pym's escape and was therefore dead to the world and any other disturbances.

Once in the privacy of Magdalene's panelled bedchamber I saw she still wore the plush clothing of her Court dress under her drab cloak; lace and silk under hessian. It was, indeed, as if she had fled some grand feast.

'I was told to give this to you, William.' She handed me a letter.

To the Philomath William Lilly, as a newly elected member of the Council you are called to the Grand Council of Theurgy on the 25th of February – St Walpurgis Eve, the messenger of this letter will take you to the meeting place at midnight.

'I am honoured and I will be there.'

'I know, William,' and here she did kiss me, 'I have come straight from the Palace of Whitehall. There are already young apprentices on the prowl for Royalists and Papists, and the courtiers are near hysterical with fear. So, you witnessed the events in the Commons today?'

'It was an affront to Parliament and liberty. It also augurs badly for the King.'

'This is what I dread. Oh William, how could such a Monarch be so blind to all that is London?'

'The Queen?'

'He is furious with her. Upon his return, empty-handed, she ridiculed him in front of the courtiers, calling him coward, scornfully saying that he would not be able to stop Pym himself from impeaching her, for surely that will be Pym's next move. The King hid his face in shame, whilst Lord Goring paced about in useless anger, offering to seek out and execute with his bare hands the traitor Pym and his four friends if necessary, whilst the Court is full of stories, fresh from the country, of Catholic aristocrats being driven from their lands by the Protestant rabble. William, I'm frightened!'

'And yet you came to me again, a risk indeed. Are you sure you weren't followed?'

'My coachman is to be trusted.'

'I am glad of it.' I pulled her toward me, the heavy incense of the Court still twisted in her hair.

'Pym has church and the people, the King has what?' she whispered into my chest.

'So far, the Tower and the army, but the army is made of men, and the men are of the people and primarily of England. They too feel the threat of the Papists, they too fear the Queen will make our King, the *English* King, kneel to France and Spain and ultimately to the Pope.'

'Will there be a war?'

'Not tomorrow and not the day after, but yes, unless God intervenes and changes the will of truculent men. What will the King do now?' I asked.

'He will appeal to the City, to the aldermen and the guilds, to give Pym up.'

'That will never happen. London is Puritan. If the King meant to court the merchants and tradesmen he should never have enforced the ship money tax.'

'Then I fear he will ride to the Tower tomorrow and appeal to the military. It is as if Whitehall Palace is encircled with apprentices, furious with rage and all manner of Puritan, each with his own grievance and each intent on thwarting the King and his command.'

'There is truth in this.'

'And if the Court should fall, would you protect me, William, despite our differences?'

'I shall endeavour to do so to the best of my abilities — may God forgive me my sins,' I added, almost involuntarily, but hearing this she did step back.

'To love how we love cannot be a sin — nothing that is born of Natural Order is.' Her voice was without doubt and I confess I did envy the clarity of her emotion then.

'You speak like a Cunning Folk, who let the spirit speak before the intellect.'

'We are all part of Anima Mundi.' She touched her heart then mine. 'This was ordained.'

And with that I did unlace her silk bodice and with the touch of a hesitant youth did peel layer upon layer from her body until she were clad in nought but a thick strand of pearls that did hang to her belly.

I stood her before me and slowly traced the path of those sea jewels, one by one, across her skin, pausing at the nipple until I reached the place where they hung shimmering before her sex. Then, kneeling, I did part her with my fingers, playing the pearls against the hardened button of her pleasure, pushing them in and out, to replace them with my tongue, until, shuddering, she clenched my hair with her hands.

*   *   *

Later, when she was sleeping, I crept from the bed to use the pisspot and noticed something had fallen from the pocket of her cloak. I bent down. Lying in the silver of a moonbeam, staring blindly up at me, were the dull eyes of a poppet stuck with pins.

It had the long black hair of Lady Lucy Hay and was stitched with the colours of that same lady's house. Shocked, I glanced back at Magdalene. Was she Witch? And if so, why attack Lady Hay unless she meant her to falter in her protection of John Pym? Or was it something more personal? And if she cast such wickedness upon one who has declared herself Presbyterian, what did my mistress think of mine own Protestant faith? One day will she make a poppet out of me, with pins stuck in its eyes and throat? Or will our entwined Fates as Occultists play second fiddle to our political allegiances?

Whilst she still slept, I carefully pulled the pins from the poppet then threw it in the hearth (in which it burnt up in a green flame) and in the pocket where it had lain I placed a plain wooden cross I had been given by my mother in the hope I would at least save one soul that day.

At five in the morning, with that noisy moon now fading into the sunrise, I did leave my mistress's bed to walk through the waking streets, the atmosphere of violation still hanging like a foul air over the narrow lanes, the debris of rioting peppering in an array of broken glass, torn flags and the smashed wood of both the shop stalls and taverns. Drunken apprentices did sleep in doorways and I did even see spilt blood upon the cobbles. I was agog, the rights of men and the duty of a king pressing upon my mind most heavily, until I came upon my own house. Then, with the skill of an silent thief, I returned to my own bed, to arise an innocent later with the household – thus nothing was amiss.

*   *   *

That day King Charles did indeed ride to the Tower to look for Pym.

Amid many protesters, to his intense humiliation, the Monarch was both shouted at and cheered, and with London splintering like worm-infested wood it was no surprise that he found no support amongst the guards of the Tower. Instead the soldiers denied him access, announcing they had no idea where Pym could be.

At the same time, on the other side of the city, John Pym and his four companions were entering the Guildhall to cheers from the aldermen and the guilds, whilst outside Whitehall Palace a rabble now gathered to shout that jeeering catchphrase 'Privilege! Privilege!' coined by the ministers of Parliament during the King's invasion of the House – a dark echo of the Monarch's own impertinence upon Parliament and the People.

London was declaring itself before my very eyes and all I could do was bear witness.

Later that same day I was returning from Pudding Lane after meeting with my printer friend, Harry Pickles, and my partner in magick, John Scott, where we did have much discussion on whether the King might declare open war and how the merchants and guilds of London might respond for we are firstly a mercantile city, a nation-city – London's needs are not that of the North or even of the West and East.

The narrow lanes were, as usual, a clatter of vendors, urchins darting from one side to the other, overhead washing strung from windows across the lane to the opposite windows, flapping in the stagnant breeze like bedraggled pirate flags while feral dogs and wooden carts careered madly from side to side as their drivers hurried to commerce or home – in short, the usual mayhem that is my city – when I came upon a crowd aflame with mockery. Before me was a bedraggled parade of open coaches with a paltry number of servants walking by foot abreast the vehicles. In the main coach sat Queen Henrietta's mother, the Queen-mother of France, her chin held high, much reduced and aged since last I set eyes upon her, departing from London in company with Thomas, Earl of Arundel. A sad spectacle of mortality it was, and brought tears from mine eyes, and many others, to see a poor Queen, ready for her grave, necessitated to depart hence, having no place of residence in this world left her, but where the courtesy of her hard fortune assigned it; she had been a stately and magnificent woman of Europe and to see her so reduced was the cause of much sorrow. It seemed to me to be an illustration of the growing irreverence for both the King and all his family. Another crack in the constitution of what we knew to be England.

The next day, the sixth of January, I woke to the town crier just outside my bedroom window.

'Hear ye! Hear ye! All march upon the city to protest the King's outrage! 'Prentices and clubs!! 'Prentices and clubs!' His shouting was followed by the rolling roar of a huge throng, with its feet and chatter. Still in my nightshirt I went to the window. King Mob was flowing down the Strand like a great river; all manner of people – country folk, working men, whole families, even a farmer herding before him a dozen terrified sheep, streaming down toward the city.

'Where are you going?' I yelled down to a young ferryman.

'To the Abbey! They say the King is there!' he answered before he was swallowed by that huge snake of humanity. I shut the window fast and thought about the position of both the house and my standing if there was to be a revolution.

After ordering Mrs Featherwaite to make sure no one was to be let in that day, I instructed Simon, her nephew, to follow with the crowd and report back on any incident he did witness.

In truth, there was such violent turmoil, infectious and dangerous to one's spirit, that I thought it wise to stay within the safety of my own four walls. Indeed, I contemplated a return to Surrey. But then the thought of abandoning both my Querents and Magdalene seemed impossible.

In the evening Simon returned, his jerkin torn and with one black eye. I found him in the kitchen where Mrs Featherwaite fussed over him, administering all kinds of herbs and sweet-meats to please the lad.

I had assumed he was, like his aunt (he did grow up in the Tower Hamlets) to be staunch Puritan, but now I queried what manner of fisticuffs he had indulged in.

'Faith, good master, it were the King's supporters, outside Westminster Abbey itself. When a group of them courtiers came out from prayer, Sir Richard Wiseman amongst them, we – that be me and the 'Prentices I was running with – started yelling for liberty and justice and an end to the taxation and the Papist Queen Henrietta then a group of Royalist supporters, young blades, city boys and some right ringletted and feathered Cavaliers, set upon us with fists and sword. Our Roundheads fought back, but when the soldiers finally parted us it was clear Sir Wiseman had come a cropper – dead he were – upon the cobbles. And this hush ran through the rabble like it were church. People were shocked, Master Lilly, to see a King's man killed like that, so we scarpered. I don't know who killed him, whether it were one or many, but I ain't ending up in the Tower.'

At which his adoring aunt wiped the grime and blood from his forehead whilst he did wolf down the bread and dripping she'd given him. 'And you won't,' she told him. 'Master Lilly has very powerful friends, he has. You was just doing your Christian duty. Fighting for godly men and for England.' She looked to me for support.

'You did well, lad.' I slipped the youth a farthing. 'Learn you anything else?'

After pocketing the coin, he wiped the grease from his chin. 'Yes, master sir, they were saying that down at the Guildhall the Parliamentarians won the day. Many were shouting for Parliament and Privilege, whilst some still shouted for the King, but there weren't enough on his side and now the rumour is he's running scared, most likely for Hampton Court.' His aunt hung on his every word as if he were John Pym himself. 'I'm telling yer, us Roundheads will soon be running London, you'll see. It'll be death to all Papists and all them poxy French and Spaniards,' the youth boasted, puffing his chest out like an undersized cockerel.

'If Sir Wiseman *is* murdered, that will be grim news indeed. We will board the windows for the next few days – but I warrant once the King leaves the city it should get quieter,' I ventured.

'You don't think John Pym will rise up against the palace?'

'I think Pym a politician, not a war general; there are others who are even more ravenous for such a position,' I answered carefully. One could trust no one, including one's servants, such was the fragmentation of the English people, and I did not want any uninvited visitors from the Tower Hamlets nor a summons by the Royalist guard. But the boy still looked at me slyly.

'Like that minister from Cambridge – Oliver Cromwell? They say he is fierce and godly, and that he could be the great rescuer of godly England.'

Again, I regretted bringing Simon into my employment; he was sharper than I had imagined. 'What do you know of Cromwell?'

'I have seen him speak, master sir, he gives a convincing sermon, and they say he fought well in both the Scottish and

Irish wars. I would march under his banner if it meant saving Protestant souls,' he answered boldly.

His aunt clapped her hands in joy. 'My sister had bought you up well, Simon; you will make a great soldier for the army of God.'

'Mrs Featherwaite, do not encourage him so. There is no war yet and there is no such army.'

'You wait, sir Master Lilly, we are training in the Tower Hamlets and proper professional with proper soldiers and generals teaching us. We'll be a force to reckon with before the year's end,' Simon crowed.

'I'm sure you will,' I replied dryly; outside the air was still peppered with the distant thud of cannon fire and the breeze smelt of war.

On the tenth of January the King and the whole of the Court left for Hampton Court and with them a great source of revenue for the city was lost. The silk merchants, the weavers, the actors, fishmongers, whores and all trade that supplied that great, sumptuous machine of the Palace suffered. As for myself, I lost Magdalene, as, in fear of her life, she did depart with the Court, sending word she was still mine in thought and spirit.

Two days later the King moved his entourage out to Windsor Castle, such was the terror of the uprising in London.

In this time of my life I felt a great loneliness despite the presence of Jane and the bustling panic of my own household – it was as if the invisible cord between myself and my mistress was pulled as tight as it could be, a cord of a profound and mysterious sensibility I felt keenly. But above and beyond these supernatural ramblings I simply missed our conversation; it was a scholarly journey that circled the globe and travelled centuries effortlessly. There was no other I had such discourse with and the ambience in the city was now incendiary. Half the guilds were furious with the loss of revenue they feared would continue as long as the King and his courtiers stayed out of London, whilst the other half argued for Parliament and gloried in the possibility of curtailing the King's high taxation in blatant disregard for the traditions of trade that had run successfully from the time of the Magna Carta until now.

Meanwhile rebellion grew fat on fear, hate and nationalism. Eighteen days later, on the twenty-eighth of January a certain Captain Skippon marched in great secrecy to the Tower (I know, for Simon Featherwaite, awash in sudden manhood, ran alongside his soldiers in great excitement). The good Skippon apparently attempted to get the Sergeant commander of the Tower and his men to join forces with the Tower Hamlet militia and Parliament. Skippon's gamble did not work and for a while the Tower guards held out.

But by February the Tower had fallen to the city and was now guarded by the trained Roundheads and the East End — disillusioned apprentices and the elder brothers of the likes of young Simon, and even I knew such was the discontent that one could summon whole battalions overnight if needed. Londoners were poised to fight each other, the whole city a bone-dry tinderbox awaiting an inevitable spark.

On the twenty-third of February, just after the Sun moved into Pisces, Queen Henrietta departed for the Netherlands with her eldest daughter to raise funds, it was rumoured, for a Royalist army.

Here in the Corner House Mrs Featherwaite was convinced 'the Papist Witch' had pilfered the crown jewels to sell for arms, a view unfortunately shared both by Jane and many of my neighbours. Out on the street corners pamphleteers sold caricatures of the Queen and all manner of propaganda. It had become dangerous for a man to wear a feathered hat or any dress seen as 'Cavalier'. What was once deemed traitorous was now fashionable, the order of authority turned on its head like a pauper drunk on anarchy.

I feared for Magdalene, an anxiety interlaced with a powerful longing, which, if I let it, could quite take my mind away from a task in hand – whether it be a horary figure for a sick child, or a herbal remedy for an affliction of gout. To my deep chagrin the woman haunted me and my desire for her grew like a periwinkle flower through rocks, no matter how I tried to repress it. I could tell no one, which only increased my melancholia and the sense that I was but an island surrounded by a rising tide of dread and ignorance.

Finally, the twenty-fifth of February arrived and in the late afternoon of that day Venus was in good aspect to Scorpio (the protector of secrets and other sinful activities) and in the ninth house – a house of the Philosopher and the Occultist.

At six of the hour I dismissed my last Querent and told my wife I had a meeting with some fellow Astrologers. As it were the night Jane attended her Quaker praying circle she seemed relieved we were not to embark on our usual quarrel over money, household duties and suchlike – not to mention the differences in our politick. Dear Reader, I confess it took all my skills to contain anticipation of the coming liaison and I marvelled at how Magdalene contrived to travel from Windsor castle through hostile territory back to her house.

The last of the winter still lingering in a frosty mist through which the sun swam in a pale gold, I was washed and my linen clean. Prudence abandoned for visions of satiated desire, I did set out for Chancery Lane. And I confess, for a man of middling years, my heart thudded most uncomfortably as I wound my way through the back lanes to her house. A street away I discovered a young urchin of some six years, near naked and blue with the cold, washing her clothes in a filthy horse's trough. And may I be blessed, I did give her three farthings to purchase some new shawl; there are so many of these new-found orphans running amuck – the offspring of poverty.

By the time I arrived at the doorstep I felt most unholy and was about to turn tail when her maid opened the door with a twinkle in her eye.

'Why, 'tis Master Rose – you are expected.'

'Master *Lilly*,' I corrected her as I stepped in.

'Flowers or men? What does it matter? They all fade and die in the end,' she murmured and again I wondered at the nature of her relationship to my lady; it were more than maidservant, I suspected, and with her accent of the country there was something of the Cunning Folk about her. Was she just assistant to my mistress in her practice as medic or something more portentous?

Magdalene was waiting in the front chamber; she was thinner than I remembered and the strain of the last few weeks was etched on her face. I waited until I heard the maid close the door behind her then I embraced her.

'I only feel safe here,' she whispered, 'and yet we are now in opposite camps.'

I stroked her hair, the cup of her skull fragile under my palm and so painfully precious to me that I knew I was, in that moment, a conduit to a future – one in which I knew I would lose her and yet I couldn't tell or warn her. Instead, I let my lover slip from me and compose herself, for that is how it is those with second sight, when past, present and future fold over each other and one is given a window to see through the panes of all three.

'You were sorely missed . . .' I told her as she reached to pick up a pearl inlaid comb that had fallen to the floor.

'You are lucky I'm here; I was anxious the Queen might insist I went with her to the Netherlands. It is possible that she might still send for me, but I persuaded her I might be more useful to her in England.' Her smile was wry.

'You are her eyes and ears?'

'The Queen has many spies.' Again, that tension between us, but even if we were of differences politickal, our souls were fused in a manner I had no words nor any rational logic for. 'I hear that the Queen's Chapel on St James hath been made into barracks for Parliament.'

'I'm sorry, Magdalene.'

'I worshipped at that chapel with the Queen; it had good Catholic worship.' Her voice was guarded as she walked to the desk, and now my eye was drawn to two ornate gilded masks, the kind one wears at carnival; one was in the shape of the head of a Fox, the other a Raven.

'Trust is earned, not given – even between lovers.' I spoke carefully.

'Is that what we are? Not sparring partners, nor peers in the mystic arts?' she asked softly.

'All that and more.' But our differences hung between us: she could never be mine, and I hers – unless in death.

Instead of answering she picked up the two masks and pressed the golden Raven's head upon me.

'The Grand Council means to survive, not just this war, but the colleges and the new ways of thinking that are tearing the mechanical from the natural sciences. The great threat of nova scientia, Descartes, Hobbes, Francis Bacon . . . they will see the magick of the senses and psyche buried. We need to fight back and you are now one of us.'

And when I looked back up at her she had donned the half-mask of the Fox, her hair cascading behind the gilded ears.

We were standing at the entrance of a small banqueting hall where two rows of black candles set in ornate candlesticks, depicting all manner of gargoyles, ran down either side. The flames danced against mine eyes and I blinked to fasten my sight through the half-mask I had been made to don upon arrival.

We had driven there by coach. Magdalene had insisted that I travel blindfolded, and again I entrusted her with both my life and my reputation. I sensed we were near the river for, as I had stepped out of the coach, a damp and salty breeze whistled about my face, placing me near water – and by the stench, the tide was out. There had also been the faint cries of seagulls, the lapping of water against rock, the surface beneath my feet spongy. But now, facing the open door, the dampness in the air suggested we were below ground – a cellar or crypt, yet as my eyes focused I found myself staring at something far more disconcerting.

Before us, in the centre of the hall decorated with hangings and celestial statues some of which were adorned with wreathes and other bizarre flora, sat a circular table topped with marble, inlaid with a large pentacle. Seventeen individuals sat around this table, each person wearing a half-mask similar to the ones upon our faces.

Each gilded mask was of an animal, amongst which I counted a peacock, the bulbous, startled eyes of a frog, the proud brow of the bull, a horse, and the crest of a cockerel. It seemed a confederacy of animal familiars, and in any other circumstances a festive atmosphere might have prevailed. But, dear Reader, I confess a sombre and most intimidating air hung over the gathering, as if it were more wake than symposium.

Gleaning my apprehension, Magdalene took me by the hand and drew me on, placing me between the Bull and the Peacock whilst she sat opposite between the shimmering scales of a Dragon's head and the white feathers of a Dove. Now at greater liberty to examine my fellow companions, I was intrigued to see that their dress (other than the masks) indicated all manner of man – from Cavalier to Puritan, from wealthy aristocrat to the humble yeoman – and that of the nineteen of us five appeared to be women.

It were no accident there were nineteen present, and dear Reader, the mathematicians amongst us understand the magnificent character of the number: it is a prime number, a number of great occult significance, and most powerful in its assembly in the doing of ceremonial magick.

Once seated I could see the full design of the table top, that at the pinnacle of each arm of the inlaid pentacle there was a jug of herbs – Cunning Folk magick to ward off evil spirits, each herb linked to an astrological sign: for Aries I recognised a sprig of wormwood (I myself have used this in the treatment of headaches, a common malady of the Ram), Taurus: Yarrow (good for a tea for the throat), Gemini: Harehound (excellent in an infusion for the lungs), Cancer: Myrtle (I have used this in a tea for digestion), Leo: Eyebright (an excellent remedy for heart murmurs), Virgo: Marjoram, (a herb that calms the Virgin's nerves), Libra: Bergamot (to be rubbed against the kidneys), Scorpio: Catmint (good for impotency), Sagittarius: Chervil (for the liverish), Capricorn: Tarragon (an excellent balm for the arthritis), Aquarius: Comfrey (which will correct a poor circulation) and, lastly, a bunch of fine Sage for Pisces (to be placed in a bath for aching feet). My observation was interrupted by the individual beside me who rose to speak.

'Fear not, Master Lilly, we are most grateful for the shelter and assistance you gave to the talented Cullum Monroe, who is now safely in Cordova and studying under the great cabbalist Abraham Azulai.' It was the Bull, his voice familiar to me, and yet in this outlandish garb my memory struggled to place him. 'And for this effort you have been elected a member and brother to us all.'

'I am honoured and am humbled to have been finally called to the table.' My voice rang out in the echoey chamber.

'As you can see we, as Occultists, students of astrology, men of the natural sciences and Magi, are gathered from all wakes of life and consider our vocation above petty terrestrial politick.'

'Indeed.'

'And yet it is this very politick that has prompted this meeting. We are under attack. More than ever there is a need to become as invisible as mist. Individuals such as Nathaniel Bacon, that most dreadful and Puritanical head of the Council of the Eastern Counties, a fanatic who knows no difference between white and black magick, nor the beneficial nature of horary astrology, he has made it his campaign to destroy all the old knowledge.'

'And not just the old knowledge, but the wisdom of the Cunning Folk.' A man wearing a mask in the shape of a Drake spoke, in a broad western country accent. 'Many have become fearful. They are frightened to heal for terror of being branded Witches.'

'There is a greater need to ensure recognition from Oxford and Cambridge universities, to legitimise our arts.' This time it was the Dove, a genteel woman's voice sounded out from behind a mask and I fancied I recognised the Lady Eleanor Davies, a psychic and visionary I had met just once when she approached me on the making of a Sigil to ward off the image of her dead child who did haunt her dreams.

'A greater need? I would say it was essential, or all will be lost to the obscurity of Time and the censorship of history,' spake the Dragon, and I instantly knew the voice and distinctive gestures of the elderly Henry Gellibrand, a secret almanack maker, the astronomy professor at Gresham college; I had met him on several occasions. 'There is no greater way to ensure the passing of our knowledge to future generations, otherwise the

nova scientia from the Netherlands and Germania will undermine all that we stand for.'

'I agreed, the omens are bad,' I intervened.

At which all at the table turned toward me.

'Neptune, the house of the secret arts is in the fourth house
– the House of Death – for most of this year, and is a very bad
conjunction to Mars; we are all, whether Parliamentarian or
Royalist, under attack and in threat of extinction. And yet, in
this time of war, I feel there is even greater craving for knowledge and certainty of the Future. This is where the Astrologer
can assist – foresight gives strategy and strategy is how one
survives.'

'But they will call it sorcery, Master Lilly! And I, for one, do
not mean to burn!' It was the Frog who cried out, in a voice that
sounded suspiciously like a Royalist client of mine, Jonas
Moore. Ever the diplomat, I feigned ignorance.

'Walk the middle way. Keep your head down and be careful
of finite prediction, would be my advice. This war will be upon
England for many more years, I fear,' I advised.

'I have seen this also,' Lady Eleanor Davies confirmed.

'Even more reason to unify and protect each other with information. I propose we develop a method of communication, one
that cannot be brought down by arrows or swords,' I elaborated, sensing the sway of opinion to my side. 'In this way, if we
hear of a possible raid or persecution of a fellow member of the
Council we can send warning . . .'

'But what nature of messenger?' the Bull insisted.

I studied the Dove, an idea forming. 'Perhaps homing
pigeons, but instead of carrying messages, the pigeons themselves could be the message. We could concoct a code around
the actual appearance of the bird. That way, if the bird was
caught, it would be meaningless to our enemy.'

The Dragon looked at the Bull who glanced meaningfully at

the Peacock and Magdalene murmured across the table, 'I told you, he is a natural leader . . .'

'A code?' the Bull queried.

'A pigeon with a black tail to tell of a possible raid, a pigeon with a white tail to speak of passing danger and that now all is safe, whilst a pigeon with brown wings would be a call to a sudden meeting. Such messengers are above arrow and sword, and if captured, silent and innocent,' I elaborated.

'But do we all keep pigeons?' the Peacock interjected somewhat nervously.

'We will now,' the Bull announced, and after a show of hands the motion was passed, after which I felt most vindicated. Just then the man wearing the mask of a Cockerel thumped his pewter goblet upon the table.

'I have another proposition to make to the Council,' he announced.

'Proceed . . .'

'I, being of pacifist persuasion and not wanting a war between my countrymen, propose that we do gather our powers and magickal knowledge and call upon Demons – or as some amongst us like to call them, Angels – one to visit the King, another to visit a powerful Parliamentarian like Pym, for example.'

'Faith, he would die in his sleep of shock!' someone jested, but no one dared laugh for the Bull looked on, most disapproving.

The Cockerel continued, 'Or perhaps Oliver Cromwell, since I wager he will play a powerful soldier role in any upcoming conflict.'

'And what would be the point of this conference of Angels?' the Bull inquired.

'To convince the King to compromise and meet Parliament's demands and for Cromwell to have a vision of the bloodshed true war will entail. I know there are some in this room that have already summoned such spirits to great effect and are capable of doing so again.'

And I did feel the heat of his gaze upon me. I was careful not to react but waited, though it was a fact that I have both attended and witnessed the summoning of Demons and Angels in ceremonial magick.

'As there are both Catholics and Protestants, nay even Lutherans, around this table, I foresee a philosophical schism,' I countered, deliberately not committing myself to any action.

At which the Peacock did cry out, 'Indeed! This brings to the fore the nebulous subject of predestination. As a Catholic I believe that God has both appointed and ordained from eternity all events occurring in time, particularly those influenced by Man's "free" will. To manipulate great events that are already set could be a mortal sin.' This voice I recognised both from Court and tavern, the Royal Astrologer George Wharton, my nemesis and rival.

'You are suggesting this war is a God-sent inevitability?' the Cockerel countered, irate. 'If so, this is not the God I recognise. As a humanist I believe the murder of a man to be a sin — no war is just.'

'Then perhaps you should be a Quaker,' I blurted out, thinking upon my wife Jane and her beliefs.

'Do you not think it possible, that us Philomaths and men of magick cannot influence political events and perhaps prevent this war? Master Lilly, your reputation precedes you in this arena of the manipulation of Anima Mundi.' Now it was the Horse who spoke out in a thick Scottish brogue.

'If it is achievable it would be a worthy application of such craft. I, myself, a high-church Protestant, have no clear allegiance, but I do not want civil war though I cannot speak for the others around this table,' I replied, 'however, I can say that free will and determinism do not exclude each other; rather that, as the Ancients believed, there is the Fate one cannot escape – Ananke – and there is the Fate that can be negotiated, Heimarmene. This war is Heimarmene.'

'You do realise that if such an magical intervention would become public it would condemn all of us to death?' The Peacock's wavering voice silvered the air.

'I, for one, would be prepared to die pursuing such a cause.' Thumping down her goblet, the Dove nailed her fear to the table.

At which the Bull brought down his hammer. 'Those in favour of the invocation of angels in an attempt to prevent a war?'

Slowly, from behind the masks and high-necked cloaks, there was a show of hands.

'Note there are nine Ayes,' the Bull announced grimly. 'Therefore, as that would leave ten Noes, the case is decided. We, as a united Council will not conduct any such ceremony. Is that clear?'

We sat in the coach in silence; outside there was just the sound of the clattering wheels over cobbles and gravel, the coach lurching from side to side as the driver attempted to avoid the channels that ran down the centre of the streets filled with stinking water and the offal of the day. Magdalene had taken off her mask and was resting her head against the cushioned seat. It was still light, being at that time of dusk in which both pick-pockets and children flourish. The fading sun painted the profile of her tired face in golden stripes and I loved her then in all her vulnerability. As the coach travelled on, I watched her with a new respect, my mind agog with a thousand questions, but before I could even begin the coach came to an abrupt halt.

Magdalene sat up, now wide awake. 'About time!' she declared, and reached over to open the coach door.

Just then two men, the hoods of their cloaks pulled low over their faces, climbed in and sat opposite us, and I found myself staring at the masks of the Cockerel and the Horse.

'William, meet Harry Goldsworthy and Hamish McDuff.'

The Cockerel and the Horse both slipped their masks off. Harry Goldsworthy was a young man of not more than thirty years of age, of aristocratic bearing, noble in brow and nose, his eyes burning with an intensity that betrayed fierce intellect and perhaps a mania. Hamish McDuff was far older – fifty years or more, his hair a fading red streaked with white, his face craggy, reminding me of an ancient cliff moulded by both sea and wind.

'Master Lilly, 'tis an honour, sir.' Hamish held out a huge hand, of which two fingers were stumps, and I took him instantly to be an old warrior, perhaps of the Highlands. 'It were me who brought young Cullum to the Council, therefore I am doubly indebted to thee, sir, and am acquainted with thy craft and consider thee to be a great Magi.'

''Tis not a title I would adopt publicly even amongst friends,' I said, for I have a suspicion of flattery.

'But you're not amongst friends now, sir, thou art amongst fellow students of the occult and can call thyself by thy true title.'

'What means this encounter?' I demanded, still unsure of these new companions.

'We intend to stop this war, for war it will be, by the end of this very summer.' Harry now spoke, his tone full of youth and the fire of belief.

'You will summon Angels and go against the will of the Council?' I asked.

'The safety of a few souls against the loss of many is not a great argument,' Hamish answered in his deep gravel voice.

'I agree,' I concurred.

'So, you will help us in our ceremonies?' the younger man

pressed most anxiously. I glanced over at Magdalene, who nodded. It were true; war would serve neither party, but, in my opinion the King had to agree to compromise, but knowing his Natal figure, I believed this was near impossible.

I leant forward, a strategy manifesting in my mind. 'Charles is less ready to dismiss such a visitation as a symptom of madness or stress, and yet it will be he who will take the greater persuasion.'

'We could ask that he be told it is against the will of God and that such obstinacy is a sin?' Magdalene suggested.

'But what Angel?'

'The King is dominant of Mercury, the Sun and Jupiter. The ruler of Mercury be the angel Raphael: this is who we shall invoke for his visitation.' Magdalene argued further, 'And if of Parliament, we think there are three choices, the Earl of Manchester, the Earl of Warwick and the Earl of Essex.'

'Nay, your man must be the member for Cambridgeshire – Oliver Cromwell. I warrant he is the greater force and the men are drawn to him,' I countered.

'Not Essex?' the younger man volunteered.

I could not tell him how I had seen Cromwell's destiny shimmering about him as clearly as sunlight that day in Parliament. ''Tis Cromwell. He be the right man and it would be the Angel Zachariel for that summoning, for he rules Jupiter, one of the planets Cromwell is dominant of.'

The others exchanged glances then seemed to accept my greater wisdom.

'But when?' Harry asked.

'Within weeks. We are in the eye of the storm but soon it will break and with it bring war. I have in my library some great works of the invocation of Demons, drawing upon the teachings of Trithemius and Ficino as well as other ancients. I have conducted several invocations before, some successful, some less so.'

'But we will need five men,' McDuff pointed out, 'and we are only four?'

'I have a partner in these matters, a man to be trusted, and a close friend John Scott. He will stand at the fifth pinnacle of the pentacle,' I reassured him, knowing John had partaken in similar ceremonies.

'I have a property, a country mansion south of the city – it is removed from eye and ears and will be safe,' Harry ventured. 'I am without parents and wife, and I keep but three servants there.'

'You must let me decide the time, and I will inform both of you, through Lady de Morisset,' I instructed. The others nodded, then, after shaking hands again, they did slip out of the carriage and into the night.

Later we returned to Magdalene's fashionable house off Chancery Lane. And there, in the privacy of her bedchamber, before the fire, she did describe how she, herself, was recruited by the Council some five years earlier when word of her skills as both alchemist and medic became known.

'The survival of such knowledge is more important to me than the Monarchy,' she told me, at which I did draw her down to the bed, for now our lives were in each other's hands, and I did caress her well and most thoroughly, her pleasure as much of, if not more, import than my own. I swear to you, dear Reader, I did love her more than life. Afterwards I lay in her arms, all intellect and torment surrendered, watching the shadow play made by the candlelight upon the drapes.

'I will send you my best pigeon in the morning – an innocent delivery to a loyal Querent – and you will return my messenger with your best bird. I will do a horary on the most favourable time for these two invocations then send you my decision and you will inform the others,' I told her, mediating upon my plans.

'You see how powerful we are together, William?'

I dared not answer. The strands of all possible futures twisted like smoke above me, but I was yet to find a thread that gave Magdalene and I . . . hope.

By seven that evening I returned to the Strand. Jane was at Newgate market and upon her return she found me in deep and fervent prayer at the foot of our bed. An action of mine she (for once) thoroughly approved of – although I could not tell her of what I prayed for – and that night we did share a bed, more as sister and penitential brother than man and wife, but it was a truce and of some comfort.

The Reader might think me callous or indifferent. It was as if I only knew my true emotion when Magdalene de Morisset was actually standing before me; the rest of the time I fought the longing to be with her as valiantly as George slayed the Dragon, yet I believe (and still do today) that my affection for my second wife – little as it was – was never altered by my love for my mistress.

The next morning I sent my best pigeon in a single wicker cage by messenger boy. Two hours later he returned with Magdalene's own homing bird. Later that day I cast a horary for the invocations, and after consulting my grimoires and other like texts found the most auspicious dates. In the evening haze of my garden I held Magdalene's bird close (her thumping heart against my palm a secret thrill) and did wrap the time and dates written on tiny scroll about its leg, then threw the bird against the sky – all love and prayer to fly with it.

CHAPTER TEN

The fourteenth day of the month of March 1642

The Corner House, The Strand

Taurus is an Earthly, Cold, Dry, Melancholy, Feminine, Nocturnal, Fixed, Domestical or Bestial Sign, of the Earthly Triplicity, and South, the Night-house of Venus.

It was on a day when you could smell Spring under the frosty air, I had just finished a horary for the wife of a silversmith who had imagined her husband had taken a mistress and had given the same woman several pieces of jewellery belonging to her. The wronged wife's question had been answered most clearly (and a little harshly) by the stars and it had been difficult, for she did love her husband, to tell her the entire truth – there was indication of a babe in the reading, and not hers by the looks of it – but truth enough I told her. She had just asked where she might confront this young woman when we were interrupted by a commotion from my front chamber.

Mrs Featherwaite's indignant voice roared above that of a yeoman's (judging by his broad accent) and, objecting to both the smell and dress of the visitor, she demanded that he leave the house immediately, whilst the country gentleman insisted that he see me straight away. Both were as loud and tenacious as each other, so I ushered my Querent out the back door and went to meet this irate peasant.

He was an individual of a most uncommon appearance, dressed in hessian, simple leather wrapped around his naked feet, and carrying a walking stick fashioned from willow with a carved head of a ram as the handle. He appeared to be of more than three score and ten, with grey hair and a beard he wore, unkempt, and to his chest. There was a strong smell of pig manure, hay, and something I can only describe as sweet – the musk of elderflower, perhaps – emanating from his person. A bunch of charms, bells and Sigils made from a variety of magical metals hung from a leather belt tied about his waist.

Upon seeing me he ceased his argument with Mrs Featherwaite and stopped stock-still.

'Master Lilly – or should I say Magus Lilly? My name be Hector Able of Canewdon, sir, a humble yeoman of the Essex county, both a good Christian and a Cunning Folk. It is a great honour . . .' At which this ancient person (at least two score older than myself) lowered himself to the floor and genuflected. I immediately indicated to Mrs Featherwaite to close the shutters and the doors – for to host such people was a danger – then helped him to his feet.

After settling him with a good jug of mead and cornbread (he had walked all the way from Essex) we retired to my study.

'Master Lilly, I have travelled far to you, good sir, and the last journey it will be, for I have seen my own death and know it be upon me within the year. I was hoping for a natural death, but I know it will not be. I have seen violence in my water.'

At which I noted the time he spoke, thinking he sought a horary answer. The old Wizard caught my eye.

'Nay, Master Lilly, I am not here to ask thee of thy wisdom; I have quite a different task. I wish to convey to thee my own knowledge. My seed has proven barren. I am without heir or child, yet I carry the teachings of natural magick of my father and mother, and before that my great dame, then all the way up the Ables until my Saxon ancestor, himself a priest of that people, stood on the proud hill of Canewdon.' He glanced around the room, at my books and tomes – many of them the teachings of great Occultists from the time of the great Egyptian Magus Hermes Trismegistus to the learned John Dee. 'I am talking, Master Lilly, not of bookish craft, but the ways of the field and forest, of the eyes in the hills, and the calling of water spirits to save a harvest. You might call it low magick, but it is the treasure of my family, the only treasure, and I wish to pass it on before I am murdered.'

'Murdered? Is this what you see?'

'As clear as I see thee now . . .' At which he leant closer (and faith, I had to hold my demeanour for he did stink!). 'It is the Roundheads; they have taken over our church and put fright into our pastor. Good folk and the "wise" have had slander daubed upon their cottages, "Witch" whispered behind their backs for nought but curing a neighbour of a rash and other simple magick like the taming of pigs and dividing water. Don't mistake me, I have no fear of the Reaper, I am more than ready to fly with the wind and go back up into the sky as light. It is merely the violence of my death I have not calculated upon.'

'When did you see this vision?'

'Upon the sunrise, the three sunrises ago,' he answered after counting upon his fingers – the middle one being missing. 'The whole world is about to change, Master Lilly – I suspect you too have seen this in your calculations, and it will be fast and bloody. Happenstance I might be lucky not to live to see it.'

'Could be, could be, Mr Able, but tell me, do you have spells, instructions for talismen and Sigils I might otherwise lack?'

'I do.' Here the old man's face broke into the wildest excitement, like sunshine after rain and a small wonder to see. He placed a worn leather sachet upon my desk. As he opened it, a curious scent of both meadow and brook, of sea at high tide and of hot summer's grass floated out.

'I have carried this strapped to my breast for three days for fear of theft or betrayal.' He slipped his wrinkled hands into the sachet and pulled out a handmade book, the stitches of rabbit gut crude and large along the spine, the leaves of the book a coarse parchment. 'I had the good widow Smithers write it up for me, as I have no letters nor numbers. I keep them all in my head, this knowledge, taught to me as it was in practice but not in words,' he explained, handing me the slim volume.

I opened it with hesitation; it has been my experience that such items are lovingly put together, but such natural materials have a tendency to dissemble upon touch. I have seen spells writ in blood upon scraped goat's skin, burnt into tree bark, or pressed into clay tablets, and I fear for the preservation of such fragility.

But I was to be pleasantly surprised, for here the magical calculations were written in ink in plain English and in a good hand (good enough for me to 'see' the studious widow Smithers who had writ them; a broad-faced silver-haired woman bent over a quill, her lips twitching in concentration as she wrote down the old man's whispered magick).

Hector Able's rumbly voice interrupted my reading. 'I have divided them up into four sections, Master Lilly, to make it easier: *For the Medic, For the Harvest, For finding of Love* and the last section — one which would see thy true self hanged — *For revenge upon thy enemy and other undesirables*. I wish thee to learn this, and all the rest I plan to teach thee while I still have a working tongue in my mouth,' he concluded, planting himself firmly upon my good morning chair, and I could see that, despite his humble attire, in his sphere he were considered royalty.

'But why me?' I ventured, smiling at his audacity.

'Thou art too modest. Thy fame has reached the county of Essex, and it will be greater; this too I have seen in my cups. Now tell me, Master Lilly, art thou humble enough to take instruction from an old Cunning Folk Wizard, or have thy city ways made thee too high and mighty?'

I glanced down at the book; already I could see a spell for the breaking of scarlet fever that would be much useful in my practice as medic.

'We shall strike a deal, Mr Able: I shall give you my evenings for a month and you shall teach me all that thou knows. Will that be time enough?'

Again, he calculated, counting his fingers. 'My death comes the full moon after next.' A statement of fact given without a smidgeon of emotion. 'So, Master Lilly, we have a deal.'

And so it came about that the cunning man of Canewdon lived with me for a month and every night we sat and he taught me all he knew, and it were a great privilege.

That night I sent my bird to Magdalene. In a scroll tied about the bird's ankle I told her of Hector Able, of his great gift, and of how I wished her to have been beside me, as fellow student and practitioner. I also enclosed several spells for health, a good harvest, a cure for boils and a herbal tincture he had instructed was good for the lessening of rheumy fever.

I was well pleased and content enough in both my learning and practice when a week later the Astrologer and publisher John Booker published his almanack on the Vernal Equinox for this year of 1642. I did know the Astrologer, for he did publish several of my leaflets, and the last time I had been struck how his voice resembled the booming baritone of the head of the Grand Council of Theurgy – the Bull. But if he wanted me to know he was of the Council, he gave no indication, and therefore I was not encouraged to expose both him and myself.

I shall frame this revelation for thee, dear Reader; in the years 1632 and 1639 John Booker made his fame though a prediction upon a Solar eclipse in the 19th degree of Aries 1633, a most ill aspect for heads of states, both the King of Bohemia and Gustavus of Sweden dying during the effects of that eclipse – bad fortune for them but good for John Booker. And I confess there was a time when I called him the greatest and most complete Astrologer in the world (he was but a mere year younger than myself, but much advantaged by beginning his studies earlier and being a great Latin scholar) and his correct prediction of the deaths of both Gustavus Adolphus and the Elector Palatine had impressed me. Sadly, this latest almanack did not. It were a poorly worded, shoddy piece of so-called craftsmanship, thinly skewered in favour of the Royalists. However, it were more the lack of rigorous calculation behind his predictions that infuriated me.

To my amazement and chagrin, despite its obvious failings, the almanack was received with great seriousness in Parliament, the Tower Hamlets, Church, Court, even in the taverns and whorehouses as my visits with William Pool to the White Hart have testified.

Booker hath prophesised that cruel and bloody counsels shall be put in execution the latter end of this month of March. Everyone, Royalists or Puritan, is in terror of this prediction. This is more a cold reading of the times then a true calculation, I warrant, but the almanack still had great sway.

Again, I find myself thinking upon the importance of creating an almanack in good plain English like the Lutheran prayer book, a tome based on hard calculation and one that would not patronise the ordinary man with hocus-pocus vagueness. Instead a book of daily predictions grounded in proper astrological observation – an almanack of intelligence for the people, not the twaddling flotsam of the snake charmer's nonsense like Erra Pater's, a fantastical citing of lucky and unlucky days. Pity the farmer and the poor serving maid who live their lives by such a nonsensical guide! Or the erroneous prophecies of *The Sphere of Pythagoras* (my laundry woman swears by this one!). So many fake pedlars of fortune and misery, and so many of them capitalising on these troubling times, 'tis no wonder I have until now been loath to add my name to many of these ill-wrought and base almanack-makers.

I am determined I will create my own standard. I will write for the learned man, the reader, a man of letters and of the politick – the Querent who lives the broad and Christian life. I pledge this now to myself and to Magdalene, for she alone is my mirror-soul in Theurgy.

Meanwhile my life begins to fall into two opposites: the domesticity of my married life – laced as it were with disagreement and profound difference – then the other, the secret world Magdalene and I create within the four walls of her bedchamber and her study chamber. It is a wondrous thing, this wielding of knowledge. In truth, we spend as many hours debating the writings of Abbot Trithemius and the magick ceremonies described in *Le Livre des Esprits* as we do spooning.

April, May, June passed, and yet, like a man wading toward his own drowning, I could not stop myself from seeing her. I was the Yellow Hound howling in the Moon card. I was the balancing Acrobat walking the rope over a rushing river. I was the Fool about to step off the cliff whistling. Every occasion I left my mistress's house and turned into Chancery Lane to creep like a thief back to the Strand I swore it would be the last time I visit her bed. It never was.

As the days moved toward the date of the invocations, the arms of clock spun faster. Two weeks before the ceremonial magick I had promised Harry Goldsworthy and Hamish McDuff, I did begin to prepare myself, through abstinence and fasting and daily prayers, to both the angels Raphael and Zachariel (as I learnt in my youth from my teachers such as Mr Evans). My wife, thinking my faith invigorated, was most pleased. Foolish woman.

Finally, the date I had chosen at the zenith of the summer in July arrived, and the conference of spirits was upon us.

CHAPTER ELEVEN

The twenty-first day of the month of July 1642

The Hunting Lodge of the Goldsworthy Family, Richmond Forest

Gemini, it's an ariel, hot, moyst, sanguine, Diurnall, common or double-bodied human Sign; the diurnall house of Mercury of the airy triplicity, Western, Masculine.

The family mansion of Harry Goldsworthy was situated to the south of the city, near the palace of Richmond. The estate sat in a small forest and was, at this time, empty.

We stood, the five of us, having drunk a magical potion I hath prepared, in a circle in the banquet hall of the hunting lodge (some acres from the main building), dressed in ceremonial robes Magdalene had sewn herself, embellished with various magick hieroglyphs as instructed in the grimoire by Apollonius himself. Chalked upon the floor was a pentacle with a circle, the five arms of which were marked with Cabbalistic symbols invoking the Angels and protecting us from wrongful invocation of Demons. A crystal glass was placed in the centre of this symbol, as I meant to trap some of the power of these summoned angels.

As master of the ceremony I resided at the head of the pentacle, holding the grimoire ready to call forth the Angel Raphael, for we had reasoned that the first visitation should be to the King in his bedchamber at Windsor Castle, to persuade him to arrive at a compromise of power between himself and Parliament.

In a low song, I did begin the first prayer, the others joining in, swaying in a kind of trance so as to allow the Anima Mundi, the Natural Soul of this Earth, to flow through them, her power fastening us to the floor in a growing heat.

As the chanting grew louder, a spark of yellow and violet light did appear in the centre of the circle. Encouraged, I became more fervent in my prayers, invoking the Angel to service us in the pursuit of Peace and in protection of both England and its citizens. The spark, dancing like a fairy, now split into two points, then five, then six, until the all of the points joined to reveal an outline of the Angel himself – a figure of some eight feet, the tips of his wings stretched high above his head. To my relief, the angel appeared in the form of a beardless youth – a most benign manifestation.

The light Raphael cast was most supernatural and blinding, a bluish aura that illuminated the faces of those gathered in a harsh starkness; Magdalene was beautiful in her ecstasy, whilst McDuff was white with fright and I did fear he might fall to the ground and break the circle.

Beside him, Harry Goldsworthy remained unnaturally calm whilst John Scott, my partner in magick in these matters, looked on, his face rigid in its impassiveness. Gathering strength from his stoicism I began my instruction, remembering that the grimoire had warned of the peril of appearing in any way in awe or subservient to the summoned Angels, as this could lead to great danger.

'Raphael, we, gathered here, do salute thee and empower thy great power, and we command thee to make thyself known to King Charles and to tell him of the great danger he will face if he doth plunge England into War. Thou must instruct him otherwise and make him see a compromise with both Parliament and the Peoples of this land.' My voice rang out, true and undaunted, and when I finished, the sound of a trumpet – not of this World – filled the hall and seemed to darken my crystal with its music.

At the end of this singular note, the Angel did disappear, leaving the five of us staring across at each other, drained and exhausted, until Hamish McDuff slipped to the floor in a dead faint.

Once plied with hot mulled wine he recovered and we proceeded to the second invocation. Here I did incite the prayers to invoke the Archangel Zachariel – the angel of surrender. This time it took far longer and I did fear Zachariel might not appear at all. I had almost abandoned hope when a small funnel of wind arrived at the far side of the hall. A spiral of whitish fury, it spun toward the centre of the pentacle, throwing a chair and a table wildly along the way. I knew then he would appear in a far fiercer manifestation.

We stood firm and not once did our circle break. But the terror rose in the back of my throat, and Faith, dear Reader, was the only thing that kept me then from faltering. In a burning cloud, the Archangel Zachariel manifested as a man with the head of a lion, fire was his mane and his eyes were aflame. As my hair and robes flew back I commanded the Archangel to go to Cambridgeshire and show itself to Cromwell, to tell him to expect the King to compromise his power, but that Parliament must be prepared to make peace with the King and stand down some of its own demands, as all men worship the one God and England cannot lose its crown.

At which the wind grew so fierce around the Archangel I did fear for my life, then just as suddenly it was gone, and a sweet tranquillity entered the hall in its wake.

Afterwards I collected my crystal from the centre of the pentacle and was most pleased, for now the glass were cloudy with a golden light in the centre of which a bright spark fluttered.

As I began to walk toward the door methinks I saw a movement outside at the window. I looked again; there was nothing but the forest beyond, and thinking I was imagining the movement I did not tell the others.

That evening the five of us, sober and in a dumb wonder at all we had witnessed, decided upon our next step of action.

An hour later Magdalene went back to Windsor Castle, anxious to observe if there had been any change in the King's attitude, whilst McDuff rode out to Cambridgeshire to see if he could catch rumour on the state of Cromwell's mind. Only Harry Goldsworthy did stay back in the house as I mounted my horse with John Scott by my side, to ride back to London, my crystal packed carefully in a side saddle, my spirit now electric with hope.

Two, three days passed and I heard nothing, and the time turned dully in my usual routines.

As for the Politick, it continued to deteriorate, the city was now emptying of all Royalists and Catholics, except for the few merchants and aldermen who had the good sense to become invisible. Hatred festered in hearts and in fields, on barges and in taverns, the pulpits, and the reading chambers. War was now a carbuncle ready to burst. And with the theatres closed and emptied of actors London was becoming a grey shell of a city, a sinking boat that were leaking laughter by the day, and it saddened me to see it so. Many holy statues considered decorous were pulled down or condemned for being idolatrous. The preachers had fled or changed their altars and services to placate the Puritans in a mincing dread. The East End had its cropped-haired soldiers ready to fight for the godly kingdom as the King continued recruiting his own forces from the army and supporting aristocracy, whilst the Queen was still in France raising finance for her husband. In short I saw no evidence that our strategy had worked and I feared the worse.

Finally, on the third day, a messenger pigeon came from Magdalene.

William, my love, I have watched the King most closely and have befriended a valet of his, a member of his bedchamber who did report to me that several days past the King had a most unpleasant 'nightmare' in which he claimed an Angel most mighty fierce did visit him in his bedchamber with a great light (as bright as the brightest day), and this Angel did tell him he must make peace with Parliament else face the most uncertain future both here on Earth and the hereafter. The King, who took great fright, did call upon his spiritual advisors that very night (rousing them from their beds). Cantankerous in their irritation they all stood before him, but alas the interpretation he did choose to believe was from a French Catholic Priest (of the Queen's staff) who did convince him the Angel was in fact a Demon sent by evil Protestant forces to sway him from his true path. And thus the King decided to ignore the warning. We have failed.

The days grow shorter in dread here at Windsor; many of the officers and arrogant youth are bursting with false valour, and confidence to begin this war. I am appalled . . .

Overwhelmed by disappointment I lowered the looking glass I had used to read the tiny lettering. My despair was interrupted by a youth bearing a message from Hamish McDuff. Fearing bad news, I reluctantly broke the seal.

I have now been at the inn of the Toad and Nettle in Cambridge for over three nights. I told you I had a spy in the house of Cromwell and

verily he did prove his worth. Two nights ago he reported that the
master did have the most obnoxious visitation from a terrible Demon
after church one night. Lucifer himself (so the master claimed)
appeared before the fireplace whilst Cromwell was reading one of the
psalms, and in a great roaring did command that the politician cease
his militaristic ways and look for a truce with the crown, else find his
head staring from a bridge for many a decade. This apparition was
so terrifying and wrathful in his manner that Cromwell himself did
consider calling a priest to exorcise the house after the creature had
disappeared. Apparently, it were only his good wife Elizabeth who
convinced him it were merely a fear of failure that had manifested
and now, (God help us) the leader is more convinced than ever to call
the King's bluff and if necessary enter into battle. I cannot tell you
how dismayed and shackled I feel after all our efforts . . .

A wave of fatalism swept through me; it seemed no matter
what we did, the cogs of this war would turn regardless.

☼ ⚲ ♌

CHAPTER TWELVE

The eighth day of the month of August 1642

The Corner House, The Strand

Cancer: Cancer is the onely house of the Moon, and is the
first sign of the Watry or Northern Triplicity, is Watry, Cold,
Moyst, Flegmatick, Feminine, Nocturnal, Moveable, a
Solstice Sign mute and slow of Voyce, Fruitful, Northern.

Now the summer was baking in flies and thirsty dogs. Mrs
Featherwaite hung herbs about the doors to ward off plague and
other pestilence that comes with the relentless heat and I did
chastise the nightsoil man for throwing his filthy cargo about
my step one morn.

Every dawn of the second week of August I scanned the
skies, praying for a break in the stars, a sign that would give me
hope that my beloved country would avoid civil war. It did not
come, and God, in his wisdom, allowed Mars to clash with
Saturn most brutally.

Finally, on the twenty-third of August, I took a walk along
the Strand and came upon a pamphleteer I knew. Jonka Hessel,
as he was known, was a local character loved by the street and
town folk alike, a Dutchman of some sixty years and an importer
from that same country of the most scandalous and treasonable
literature; an aged refugee of the religious war that raged in
Europe these twenty years and more, whose bald head was

reminiscent of a turnip and whose toothless grin was always of cheer. You must know, dear Reader, I am a great consumer of daily events; a necessity both for the informed gentleman but also for the learned Philomath, as nothing is unconnected. There are many weekly news books to choose from, for they, as well as the printing presses, have sprung up like mushrooms in these years: *Mercurius Britanicus*, *Mercurius Veridicus*, and *The Kingdom's Weekly* are just a few I subscribe to. In service of my craft I seek as broad a spectrum of events as is possible, and Jonka's information was to the moment and most accurate.

'War!' he cried in that guttural accent of the Lowlands, waving the pages at me. 'The King hath raised his standard in Nottingham! England is at war with itself! 'Tis King and Parliament at each other's throats! Prepare young men and 'prentices! Arm and shield thy women! 'Tis War! Good Master Lilly, we will need men like you — uncertainty is a fortune teller's bonanza!' he announced to a gaggle of indifferent children, all nit-picky, shifting black toes in dirt, at which I bought a pamphlet and hurried home.

At the Corner House there was yet another piece of grim news — Harry Goldsworthy, betrayed by a servant, had been arrested on charges of sorcery and was now awaiting trial in the Tower. Shocked, I collapsed upon a chair and, casting my mind back, did try to remember whether that shadow at the window of the hunting lodge I saw fleetingly could have seen who else attended the invocation. Was it possible I too might be arrested?

The very next day, the twenty-fourth of August, the Battle of Edgehill was fought. Despite Parliament's forces being of greater number, the better trained Royalist troops held them off and neither were the winner. Now all of England slaughters itself, and I, William Lilly, jump at every knock upon my door.

Later that evening I received a message from McDuff that I should meet him in secrecy at an eating house next to a tanner's yard by the dockland.

I left the house at nine o'clock. An evening fog full of putrid vapours brought on by the heat hung about both store and dwelling. Methinks it were as if the spirits of the dead to come in the bloody conflict were gathering above our very heads. Even Jane was convinced I would be murdered, such was the panicked nature of each Londoner that night. But I had to go: my life, Hamish McDuff's, and that of Magdalene herself were now in great danger. If Harry confessed under torture we would all be hanged, and I knew the Grand Council would not save us.

The eating house was one of those establishments in which the malodorous stench of the hung meats and pickled cabbage attacked one's nostrils and destroyed one's appetite upon entering. A poor man's tavern, it was not a place either McDuff or myself would naturally frequent, and it was therefore the perfect clandestine meeting place.

The huge, craggy Scotsman sat at the back, his hat pulled low upon his brow. When I joined him at the grimy table, slithery with old pig fat and bacon rind, he barely acknowledged me.

''Tis dire, Lilly; Harry is already on the rack once, but I heard he did not break, brave lad. However, I fear his tongue will not survive more torture.'

'Was he the only one seen at the ceremony?'

'I believe so. It were an itinerant looking for favour with the local sheriff, a man who hath no love for the Goldsworthys.'

'What do you want me to do?'

'You could visit him, William, at the Tower, in your guise as medic. If he had a way of ending the torture, a painless way . . .'

'They have not executed him yet.'

'But they will, a date is set. But they mean to torment him until he has given up every name of those he was involved with, and any other Occultist in the city. The whole Council could be betrayed.'

'He is still a young man.' I looked over at a dog gnawing at some offal under a table, thinking how this dog's life were so much simpler than my own, and I was envious then: to know nothing but hunger then the fulfilling of it; of immediate animal pleasures that kept us all innocent. Thinking I was after his meal, the dog looked up and growled at me.

'This would be a sin indeed,' I finally answered Hamish.

'It is not a sin to release a man from absolute terror. I know that the Parliamentarians who now own the city wish to make poor Harry an example of their power and of their desire to cleanse the city of any Popish witchcraft they regard as being of Royalist persuasion.'

'But Harry's family are Protestants.'

'His mother was not. Will you help?'

'I will visit him prepared, but I will only act if it is his own desire.'

'If I could swap places with him I would . . .' McDuff gave a great hollow sigh and I did feel sorry for him, knowing that Harry Goldsworthy was his great friend.

When I returned home I locked myself in my study and concocted a tincture that would guarantee a quick and painless death.

The next morning I dressed myself in the long cloak and mask of the Physic and, escorted by the young Simon Featherwaite (for, as fledging Roundhead, I knew he had some influence) we did ride to the Tower.

As I predicted, the guard at the gate recognised Simon from the Tower Hamlets and the makeshift battalion he was a member of. The two young men, all bluster and shiny self-righteous violence did push each other about in good humour and it were not difficult to persuade the guard that I had come to mend the body of Harry Goldsworthy to ready him for more of the rack. Which, the guard cheerfully announced, was to be later that day, and was to be supervised by a young and most learned expert on such unholy matters as sorcery, Matthew Hopkins, a rising star in the witch-finding profession, a young man I once knew. I hurried to the cell.

I found Harry collapsed upon a bed in the corner of the stone room, his wrists, neck and ankles bearing the purple band of the rack, both eyes circled with bruises. Aware of the guard who had escorted me standing at the door, I sat down beside poor Harry and took out several poultices I had prepared for such bruises. Groaning, he opened his eyes.

''Tis you,' he murmured, although I did wonder if he was not in a delirium.

'Pray, stay still, dear sir, and let the ministrations of a good doctor mend your flesh.' I spoke loudly, pressing the poultices upon his wounds, again so not to raise the suspicion of the guard. Harry clutched at my wrist; I saw then three of his fingers protruding at strange angles – the bones shattered, and a great sorrow rose up in my throat I fought to contain.

'They tried to break me, William. They did not succeed, but they will try again and I fear my willpower will not survive the pain.' His voice was little more than a harsh rasp, the steel collar they must have used to fasten his head to the rack having destroyed his throat. 'I swore an oath and I will not die a Judas.' He collapsed back upon the bed. After glancing over to the guard who was turned away, I bent down low so only Harry could hear me.

'You don't have to.' I pressed the small vial of the poison I had prepared into the hand that was still intact. 'Two drops and you will be in Heaven by the next clock tick.' His fingers closed upon it, the skin smooth, and I was reminded that he was not yet a man of thirty.

'Will they kill me anyway?'

I confess, dear Reader, I knew the Reaper lay in Harry's cards whatever path he chose, but to take hope away from a condemned man is one of the hardest things to do. I could not look into his eyes, but let my gaze wander to his battered body. It was as if his spirit had already begun to hover above him.

'They will, Harry. 'Tis best if thee join thy family in the hereafter, I know they are waiting for thee,' I told him, thinking to give him some comfort. Again, with great effort, he whispered to me.

'We saw them, William, we saw those angels. Perhaps they will carry me to Heaven. Help me.'

Carefully covering my actions, I then did take the poison and slip a couple of drops into his mouth. 'Sleep, my friend, and forget your troubles.'

As I left I told the guard that Harry was sleeping, then on the way out, in my haste, I did bump into a young clerk hurrying with his servant down the dark, cold corridor.

'Why! 'Tis my old friend William Lilly! Do thy not knowest me?' The clerk was young, but carried himself with the arrogance and authority of an older man. I stared at him for a moment, wishing only to be out of the building, then recognised the once shipping clerk, Matthew Hopkins, now only twenty years in age, curly blondish hair to his shoulders, with a beard and moustache to match.

'Of course, Matthew Hopkins; what brings you to this sorry place?'

'I am here to observe and perhaps assist; thou know I have a growing authority on witchcraft and sorcery. There are occasions when the guard calls for such knowledge. And thyself?'

'I am here as a medic. And now that I have administered my services I must leave. But, Master Hopkins, my door is open for thee at any time.'

'I thank you. And safe travels, Master Lilly.'

After which I hurried back down the corridor, knowing the ambitious shipping clerk's interest was now alerted. For him to pursue with such zeal a Devil he sees in the shadow of so many innocent souls, Master Hopkins strikes me as a personage haunted with terrors of childhood.

Later I was too distressed to return to the Corner House but instead found myself at St Antholin's where I did kneel upon the cold stone floor, praying for my soul until well past midnight.

On the evening of the next day Hamish McDuff called at the Corner House and did thank me for my service to the Council. I had no words for the heaviness of Harry's death weighed upon my conscience, and yet I could not go to Magdalene to take solace in her wisdom and bed.

Windsor Castle had never felt so far away.

CHAPTER THIRTEEN

The month of September 1642

The Corner House

*Leo is the onely house of the Sun, by Nature Fiery,
Hot, Dry, Cholerick, Diurnall, Commanding, Bestial,
Barren, of the East and Fiery Triplicity. Masculine.*

On the seventh of September, that fair town and strong-hold Portsmouth was conquered by the Parliamentarian forces, a defeat most humiliating and strategically disastrous for the King as much supply and arms came through this port.

Later this same month the King moved the Court away from Windsor Castle to Oxford, taking with him Magdalene.

I was disconsolate, and to hide this I trebled my labours. As my Dutch pamphleteer had predicted, it was fortuitous for the Philomath that such fear ruled the day. The query, 'adhere to King or country?', was most common as men and women tried to ascertain the future and their own fortunes.

Wives worried for their husbands and sons: whether the men had left to join forces with King Charles and Prince Rupert, or march with the Roundheads, their anguish was the same, as was the dread of losing property and livelihood as both armies tore through villages and boroughs, stealing plate and ransacking field and mansion for supplies and shelter. This, and the usual ailments I was consulted for, helped distract me from my lover's absence.

My frantic labours bore fruit and soon I had cause to hire another chambermaid, for which Jane was grateful and did dissuade her from her shrewish ways — for a week or two.

And thus my long, noisy days and empty nights did pass. Many were the letters I began to Magdalene and then abandoned in the privacy of my study. Such was my longing to share a tippet of knowledge that had come upon me that day, or another of the good Master Able's Cunning Folk magick, a thread of a connection to an ancient spell I might have come upon in one of my own grimoires, or a herb Magdalene could educate me on.

I missed her like a cripple misses a limb, and there was a growing intelligence within me that I must have been wedded to her in another life or perhaps even in a future one, which was not consoling.

It had been a rainy day: one of those mornings when the Sun himself is reduced to a pale orange spectre striving to caress the grey Earth. I am not fond of such weather, the nefarious climate of nostalgia and infirmity.

At ten of the hour there was a great knocking at the door. Afeard it might be some politick bullyboys, I sent Mrs Featherwaite in case I had to make a quick escape. To my surprise it were a countrywoman, one I recognised having seen her in great clarity in the vision of my second sight. Mrs Smithers, the good widow who transcribed Master Able's knowledge with such loving detail.

Despite the neatness of her bonnet, there was a bruise over one eye, and her cloak was torn, her short boots stained with mud. She clutched a hessian bag that twitched and shook of itself, which I ignored, figuring it to be a ferret, perhaps, or the like. To the gentlewoman's surprise I called her name before she had a chance to introduce herself, after which she fell into my arms in great agitation.

'Master Lilly, they have murdered him! Ransacked his cottage and violated his body! My poor dear Mr Able! He hath been murdered, I tell thee, as he did predict!'

At which I sent Mrs Featherwaite to brew Valeriana and Skullcap, such was the condition of the poor woman's nerves. After an infusion, she was finally coherent.

''Twas Nathaniel Bacon's mob — the most pernicious of thugs, yet some of these lads I did nurse upon my own knee and school. Why, some of their own mothers have been delivered of these lads with the help of the very same cunning women those boys are murdering now. It is the most insidious of evils, to turn country folk against their elders and their own legacy of knowledge. Their minds have been poisoned, Master Lilly. No longer is there respect for the old and the *wise*.'

'Master Able?'

At which her face distorted with the horror of the memory. 'I found him in his own back field, his limbs splayed out in a cross, a stake driven through his heart pinning him to a tree. His dog and cat hanged with him.'

'A death most horrible.'

'Aye, but they did not get Solomon.' At which she opened the hessian bag. The long beak and head of a raven poked out to survey me with an eye most intelligent. At my feet, my spaniel Copernicus growled.

'Solomon was Hector's companion, they were not to be parted 'cept for the time he were with you, Master Lilly. He'd had him since he were an egg, and the bird has an old soul. But he will not stay with a woman. He is a man's bird, and a wise man at that, which is why I have brought him for you. It's what Hector would have wanted. I just pray his heart gave out to fright before they tortured him.'

The bird hopped out of the bag and on to my desk, where it stood looking at me most quizzically, then with one flap of its great black wings perched upon my shoulder.

'I told you. Solomon belongs to a "wise" man, and now he hath chosen you for himself.'

The raven gently rubbed his beak against my ear, as if to answer. I confess I was pleased with his company. 'And the cottage?' I asked.

'Ravaged, Master Able did not have much, but what there was is now smashed up or lying half-burnt outside – his mother's spinning wheel, a bench and table, his mortar and pestle, the straw pallet upon which he did lie. But one thing I did find was a page from a pamphlet of yours, torn out and pinned above the door – your name encircled. It is a warning, Master Lilly; I know they have a list and now you are upon it.'

A shiver ran though my body. To be suspected is tolerable, but to *know* one is being watched terrifying.

'You must take precautions. I fear they know Master Able visited you: one slip and they will put you in the Tower.'

At the word Tower, Solomon did screech. Copernicus barked and I was forced to move the bird to the edge of a chair.

'I am a cautious man, Widow Smithers, and I have friends as powerful as the noxious Master Bacon, for all his posturing. But this is tragic news indeed; Hector Able was a rare man, there'll not be another like him. Did he get a Christian burial?'

At which the good widow laughed bitterly. 'A good Christian burial? Did you not hear what I just told you? They would not allow it – for they have branded him Wizard. Forty years serving our parish church as curate, and they brand him Wizard! Nay, I buried him myself in unconsecrated land down by the river, a place I knew he loved. Canewdon is not a village I now recognise; fear hath settled upon it, neighbour betrays neighbour, and I'll not be able to live long in it. Take care, Master Lilly; look to your wife and household for there are eyes everywhere. Is there nought you can do for the Cunning Folk of this country, Master Lilly, a man like you with friends both in Parliament and in Court?'

It were a plea from the heart, and one I heard loudly. I thought of Hector Able, of his peculiar mannerisms that were, after a week, both endearing and familiar, of his courage and of the great gift of knowledge he hath bequeathed then decided one act of bravery merits another.

'There might be,' I answered, careful in my promise, but as I looked up she were gone, a breeze tumbling a few strands of silver hair across the carpet. Solomon, staring up at my amazement, cackled gleefully.

It was only that same afternoon that I had another extraordinary visitor brought in by Mrs Featherwaite, an old woman, genteel in her dress, with several gold bracelets visible, thin, tall and bent over, her head and face covered with a shawl. She moved with such convincing decrepitude that I was forced to keep my distance, worried she might be a leper. To my great surprise, once Mrs Featherwaite had left the room the old woman flung her shawl back and I recognised the features of Tobias Young, albeit much thinner and gaunter.

'One of the witches from *Macbeth* – played her in 1632 – but I apologise if I startled you. I did not wish to be recognised by the Roundhead thugs,' the actor explained, standing upright in his true form.

'Understandable, Mr Young, nevertheless it is a sorry state when some of the finest texts in the English language are regarded as sinful. It is not an opinion I share with my Protestant colleagues,' I reassured him.

At which the actor grasped my hand most pitifully, and I could see how harrowingly recent events had etched themselves upon his person.

'I know, William, I know, and that is why I had to see you.'

'I thought you must have been with the other actors, at Court in Oxford? Did not the King take his theatre folk with him?'

'He did, but I found I had to come back – I have left people I cannot live without in this city. I have not been in London since Christmas and find it much changed.'

'It is dour, with the theatres closed and all secular joy banished. I myself have lost a close colleague, a learned Occultist and Philomath, to the rack. The Puritans protest too much and I am suspicious of any man who makes too much of a show of piety. It makes me wonder what sins he wishes to hide,' I replied, after going to the door and ordering Mrs Featherwaite to bring ale, cheese, and apples, for the actor did look starved.

'Indeed, and Master Lilly, I am keeping a list – for some of these pumped-up ruffled-collared joy-kills I remember as the most debauched and lusty of my audience. It is as if they have gone and blanched their souls overnight like soggy almonds and banished their vices as well as their lovers, bed boys and the rest, the hypocrites! To call themselves the greater Christians! But the journey here, and the hardships I had to endure! At one point, this snivelling bed-louse of a coachman tried to defile me, all for the cost of a measly passage from Hedington Hill. Why, William, it were almost rape! Faith, I did not know whether to be flattered or appalled. He did, however receive a boot to the balls. Ah, the trials of being a woman. All the world might be a stage and all the men and women merely players, but let me assure you it is men who have the better parts!'

At which Tobias collapsed into a chair and began fanning himself with a much-valued volume of Tycho Brahe's astrological observations. I carefully removed the volume and replaced it with an Nativity of a minor client of no consequence.

'Please, best to keep your voice down; my housekeeper might think it beyond a miracle that my dowager visitor has suddenly grown testicles.'

'That, I fear, have quite shrunk in the face of War. It is one thing to find yourself playing King Henry upon the battlefield of Shrewsbury, it is quite another to be *on* an actual battlefield. Tobias Young does not have the constitution,' the actor lamented. 'I am a natural coward and, in truth, acting is a manner of hiding.'

We were interrupted by Mrs Featherwaite. Gazing most sympathetically at the actor she held out the tray of food. At her gesture, Solomon flew across the room and, perching on the tray, began pecking at the bread.

'Stop it, you damn bird!' Mrs Featherwaite said. 'Let others eat first! You'll not be keeping this vermin in the house, surely, Master Lilly?'

'This "vermin" was a last gift from a beloved friend; besides, I think he be an excellent judge of character,' I answered firmly, taking the tray to ensure the ever-spying housekeeper didn't get a closer glance at the good widow, who had struck the most tragic of poses as soon as she'd sensed an audience. A performance most effective.

Mrs Featherwaite grasped my elbow in concern. 'Oh, Master Lilly, do be kind on the poor old soul — she's lost all her sons in Ulster, and her own husband slaughtered on her doorstep by them Papists; do give her some hope with them predictions of yours. She's a godly soul,' the housekeeper begged me, whilst peering over at the intrepid widow, who smiled weakly back as if he were the dying mother of Christ himself.

'I will, I will,' I promised, pushing her out of the door then swinging back to the actor. 'Tobias, a less embellished performance would have sufficed. Now I'll have to invent a whole second act after you've gone.'

'Couldn't resist, I *so* miss the stage. Oh dear Zeus! Is that Cheddar?' Miraculously revived, the starving widow sprang up and began devouring the bread and cheese. 'I can't remember the last time I ate Cheddar cheese — the whole county is with Parliament, a pox on all politics! Even the King's kitchen has run out of oranges. And as for soap!'

'Perhaps now the Monarch will learn what it means to alienate both the merchants *and* the navy,' I retorted with a certain smugness.

'Not that the King cares, he is now at Edgecote. They say he will be again in battle by next month. Oh, it is never ending!'

'Interesting . . .' I took note of the information. 'Why are you here, Tobias?'

'"*Love is a smoke raised with the fume of sighs,*"' he quoted, at which I countered, '"*These violent delights have violent ends.*"'

'Indeed, but I am a foolish man of middle years.' And the actor had the grace to blush. 'It's the matter of Mistress Quake, my beloved.'

'Your widow?'

'The very one you helped secure with your horaries. Before the King's declaration we were so very happy. Although she were Presbyterian and had reservations about my profession, every night she was there up in the balcony, like a planetary goddess gazing down on me. Her very presence fed my performance. We were Romeo and Juliet, Abelard and Eloise, Tristan and Isolde — and now . . .'

'Odysseus and Penelope?' I added helpfully. A comment that made him whimper most painfully, thinking I was inferring a great separation.

'She hath fallen under the influence of a terrible man,' he explained, 'the Puritan preacher, Reverend William Bridge, who professes a great hatred of Queen Henrietta and all that she supports. So now the good Mistress Quake really does think I am the Devil incarnate and will have nothing of me. You must help me, for she respects you and thinks of you as a godly man. You must be my ambassador. Go argue my case to her, reinstate our love.'

'You cannot go yourself? Surely she will not recognise you as Old Woman Hatchet?'

At which he took offence.

'Oh, callous disbeliever, I am one of the Weird Sisters from *Macbeth* – but then, why would I expect you to know the difference?' He buried his face in his hands, and the wig slipped several inches over his forehead. 'In truth, I have already visited her and it was a disaster.'

'How so, Tobias? I know the woman loves thee. It cannot be that bad.'

At which he groaned further. 'It is, and worse. You see, knowing her serving maid is most pious and most disapproving of my influence, I was compelled to keep up the pretence until Mistress Quake and I were alone and out of earshot. And so, with my best Ulster accent I did spin the most terrible tale of a widow newly arrived from the Irish troubles, her sons and husband murdered, now seeking alms from godly fellow widows. I was most effective—'

'As my housekeeper can testify,' I added wryly.

'But the more I spun my woeful tale, and the closer I crept toward my mistress, who thought she were patting the hand of a bereaved old woman, the longer the serving maid stayed to listen, and now, revelling in my captive audience, the more extreme the horrors got the more my hands sought comfort, and the more my mistress, kind soul that she is, fell into grieving with my old lady until we were both weeping.'

'A sorry state of affairs indeed.' I was having trouble containing my laughter. 'But how did it end?'

'Badly. Eventually, in a croaky voice, I pleaded for water, thinking this would be the way to rid us of the maid, and finally the servant did depart, at which point, unable to control my longing, and forgetting I was still Mrs McGrady, I did kiss her passionately . . .'

'And?'

'She took fright, as she still did not recognise me, and thinking me some unnatural creature she fainted dead away. Oh, to have been a lesser actor! And to my shame, knowing the maid was to return and in terror I would be reported to the Puritan authorities, I ran. William, dear, dear friend, your house was the first sanctuary I could think of.'

'I thank thee for the compliment. But this strikes me more farce than tragedy.'

'It will be tragedy if Reverend Bridge's bully boys get hold of me. You must help me: you must send a boy to Mistress Quake's house and tell her to meet me here; she'll listen to you. You must persuade her my profession does not damn my soul. Please, Master Astrologer, I fear that with this war I might not be able to see her for months, perhaps even years. How cruel this Age is!'

I sat down. He was right, of course; the world felt as if it had begun to divide and there were many families, couples and enterprises that were beginning to splinter through distrust, hatred, and suspicion, but how to use Tobias? I thought upon Magdalene and how I could shield her from afar. I then thought of the crystal I had taken from the ceremony at Richmond, and of the power trapped within it.

'I'll do this on condition that once you return to Oxford you take a parcel to my good friend, Lady de Morisset.'

'Such good friends are dangerous for married men.'

'Even more dangerous for unhappily married men.'

'Indeed, I had the mixed pleasure of meeting your wife on the way to your chamber.'

'Jane is a – distinctive woman.'

'She is indeed, and of course I will carry your parcel to your dear friend. Eros knows no wars – he shoots his own arrows with no regard for borders or any other petty human machinations. Marriage? Pah! "*Hanging and wiving goes by destiny,*"' he quoted.

Frightened he was about to launch into another well-rehearsed soliloquy, I interrupted. 'And know, Tobias, that I intend to use you sorely in the future, a man who can transform into a woman, or whatever he wishes is useful in these times, and can go anywhere as a messenger.'

'Anywhere he is happy to risk his neck.'

'Have courage, dear friend, if you can fool your lover you can fool anyone.'

And so it was. I sent a message to Widow Quake who was at my house within the hour and I did persuade her that, as theatre is an aping of life and, as life with all its peccadillos was given to us by God himself, then surely an actor was merely the conduit of God's will and as such was as holy as a cleric.

Truly, dear Reader, my argument was so good I myself was persuaded, and after Tobias had removed his wig, the good widow did fall on him with such joy and hunger I was compelled to leave the chamber.

And later, in a shard of moonlight, I wrapped the crystal with its trapped power most tenderly as if I were caressing Magdalene herself, and the next morning Tobias did take my parcel back to Oxford. Once I knew the actor was safely on his journey I went to the back of our walled garden (in which I have planted many magical and medical herbs) to the dovecote

I had placed there since the meeting with my fellow mystics. Thinking of poor Harry Goldsworthy and Master Able and of others of his kind, I reached in and collected a bird with two grey wings — the markings that would call a meeting of the Grand Council of Theurgy. Standing upon an old anvil I released it and watched it fly away, a pale curl against the dark blue.

I swear you could smell the unease that swept across the city that day, a truly Scorpio messenger carrying the reek of secrets, of betrayal, of the angered face of thy neighbour. It cut through hope and the very sunlight.

CHAPTER FOURTEEN

Autumn 1642

The Corner House, The Strand

*Virgo it's an earthly, cold, melancholly, barren,
feminine, nocturnail, Southern Sign; the house and
exaltation of Mercury, of the Earthly Triplicity.*

Several days later a tapping on my glass pane drew my attention.

I opened the window and carried Magdalene's faithful pigeon inside. As docile as a kitten, she let me unwind the scroll wrapped around her puny bird-leg.

My most beloved of Philomaths, Tobias did bring the crystal and it now sits before me, the wonder of its celestial light doth illuminate my bedroom most magically, and I do feel its protection, even though its discovery would see me hanged. Here in Court there is the most fractious of atmosphere; Sir Samuel Luke has a circle of intelligence through which he asserts who is a spy for Parliament or not – his investigation knows no limit and many of the good citizens of Oxford have also fallen under suspicion. Monsieur Vindecot is newly arrived, and although he is a friend of my husband's, he doth not regard me so well. I fear he will soon set against me, and the Frenchman hath the ear of both the King and Queen.

Weekly they hang people in the square, both food and clean water is scare, as is lodgings. I, myself, am forced to share rooms.

Nevertheless, the Court itself remains confident of a victory — many cannot believe the ill-trained 'rabble' of the Parliamentarian army could possibly defend the well-trained and well-armed Royalists — particularly popular are the heroics of Prince Rupert and his cavalry. They proclaim him the epitome of the heroic horseman. In truth he is a Cavalier, a dandy with a penchant for killing as I well know, having met him through my husband and good officer of his own cavalry. The Prince, who tasted war as a boy and trained on the battlefields of Germania and Holland, lives and breathes for nothing but war and blood.

I have heard word that the Council will sit again in a few weeks. This cheers me greatly, and I might surprise both the Council and yourself with my presence, for without you in my bed and heart I am nothing . . .

My reading was interrupted by the cry of Jonka the pamphleteer in the street outside, for he did know I liked my news swift.

'Essex defeats the great Prince Rupert at Edgehill! The Royal standard torn from the hands of the Royalists! A great victory for Parliament, but many dead!' came his distinct shout with his guttural accent. In moments, I was before my house, as neighbours and other pedestrians gathered about the crippled Dutchman.

'Ho! Jonka, what news? The King's troops beaten?' If this be fact this was news indeed, as until now the professional soldiers of the Royalists were stronger upon the field, for Parliament was a motley army, stitched-up from Roundheads, farmers, 'prentices and working men, few trained soldiers amongst them.

''Tis true, the Earl of Essex held the centre of the skirmish whilst Prince Rupert broke Parliament's left flank.'

'Yet he was defeated, you say?'

'Hubris and a grave miscalculation. The Prince did underestimate the People's infantry – they say the Royal standard went down but was then repossessed.'

'Prince Rupert's Achilles' heel is his arrogance,' I retorted, knowing full well Jonka, as a Dutchman, was partial to the Prince, who was many years living in the lowlands.

'And Essex his naivety!' At which we both laughed, for poor Essex was much ridiculed as the cuckold of London, having been divorced by his wife for failing to commit his nuptial duties. This humiliation hath not prevented him from becoming a fine leader and I think him a better man for it.

Back in the house I studied the pamphlet. Essex had countered Prince Rupert's advance through a surge of reinforcements and it was said that the lives of the King's sons, Charles and James, were for some time in great danger. Oh, foolish Prince Rupert – he is a man very ill-starred, perhaps more so than his uncle. But it was clear to me that there had been no conclusive outcome amidst the bloodshed for one side or the other.

However here in London there were celebrations amid the Puritans and Mrs Featherwaite's nephew Simon, now a fully trained Roundhead with a shaven top to prove it, was of much cheer.

Speaking of Simon Featherwaite, I confess I have my own suspicions of the zealous lad. I fear he has some inkling of both my liaison and my secret visits to the Grand Council of Theurgy, as once, coming back from Chancery Lane, he saw me creeping into my own house like a shamefaced villain. My distrust could be an unreasonable anxiety of the imagination – there be many a Londoner now overly careful of who they praise or where they worship; nay, even of the poppy they might place in a buttonhole for fear it might be seen as Popish decoration. I am convinced some even try to censure their dreams in case they may speak out in their sleep, for fear the cat might hear them and report them to the good Roundhead sergeant who patrols their parish.

And so I court the youth to make him indebted. I have also been most careful to praise the actions of Essex to Simon's great approval, and upon seeing the lad crestfallen one morn, I extracted the cause of his bruised demeanour. Nancy, the neighbour's maidservant scorned him, and so I fashioned him a Sigil based on one of Hector Able's spells to secure her love. The Sigil did work (although I believe the courting advice I gave him and the farthing to buy Nancy a kerchief was of some assistance) and they are now courting.

Even so at the corners of the neighbourhood whispering and suspicion gather like snails on lettuce. One man's terrorist is another's revolutionary. But to be safe I made sure that Jane and I were seen at St Antholin's, where, along with my other most zealous neighbours, we listened most attentively to the anti-Papist ranting of the preacher and sang the loudest so our Puritan fervour be renowned and *unquestioning*. I hate myself for this artifice.

I have also been warned by my printer to have care of a fat woman, aged about fifty, known in these parts as Parliament Joan. They say she is ever watchful for Royalist sympathisers in all manner of society, including my own.

There are double agents both in London and in the now Royalist capital of Oxford, and I worry that Magdalene's capricious nature might lead both of us to err.

That night I returned her bird, with a love sonnet and one of Master Able's remedies for *grand mal* she had asked for; as she has had much success with his other remedies. Despite the dangers, I cannot bear the separation much longer, and I had begun to contemplate a journey in which I will risk much, and not just reputation. Meanwhile, the night I have called the meeting of the Grand Council draws nearer.

The next full moon I found myself sitting at that grand oval table, herbs smouldering in the corners of the cavernous crypt, masked and in attendance with my fellow Occultists. As I expected, there was only seventeen assembled. I was not expecting Magdalene and I could not help but notice the absence of poor Harry Goldsworthy.

'It were your bird that called us together, Master Lilly . . .' The Bull's thunderous voice rang out. 'Pray, what is to be such urgent cause?'

'The deaths of two noble Magi – firstly the death in the Tower for sorcery of one of our very own members, Harry Goldsworthy.'

At which Hamish McDuff, wearing his Horse mask, shifted most uncomfortably in his chair.

'The accusation was that he partook in an invocation of a Demon. Yet we ourselves voted against such an invocation only weeks before his arrest?' The Bull looked accusingly upon my person. 'I believe there are several amongst us who executed the invocation of these "Demons" against the wishes of the Council.' Outrage ran around the table catching like an errant wildfire before the Bull turned slowly toward me. 'What say you, Master Lilly?'

At which I stood. 'It was I.'

After which Hamish reluctantly rose to his feet. 'And myself.'

'But I was the leader,' I declared. 'We could not resign ourselves to the inevitability of war, and felt it to be our duty to do whatever was needed to prevent such an outcome.'

'But you failed – and a man is dead as a consequence.'

'Harry was betrayed! You have to understand there is a new threat coming – which brings me to the second death I must speak of, the persecution and most torturous murder of the good cunning man, Hector Able of Canewdon.' My companions glanced at each other: the man was obviously known.

'Hector Able is dead?' The Dove, Lady Eleanor Davies, seemed particularly distressed. 'He was a most accomplished Magician. He would have seen his own death.'

'He did,' I answered most carefully, knowing the implications, and beside me Lady Davies did sigh. Everyone there knew of the horror and bravery second sight entailed.

'Then why did he not run?' the Bull asked.

'Because I think he meant to martyr himself. He spoke of a new dark age, one in which much knowledge and magick will be both hunted down, destroyed, and ridiculed.'

'Hector Able was more than a simple Cunning Folk: he was a Magus.'

'If they can kill him they can kill us all!'

'Nathaniel Bacon goes too far. He means to evoke the Witchcraft Act upon us all. I have had dealings with him and he has a personal grudge against such things; it is said his young wife died in childbirth after a local Cunning woman failed to save her.' Now it were the Dragon who spoke, and again, my mind went back to that first meeting – it were the good Henry Gellibrand, the professor from Gresham College; he would have known Master Bacon through academic circles.

'And so now we all pay the price?' the Dove queried.

'Indeed we shall, for he has a new ambassador.' This was my opportunity for persuasion. 'There is a new nemesis on the horizon, a shipping clerk with political aspirations, and he wishes to build his career upon the blood of all who sit in this room. I have seen him stalking the corridors of the Tower. His name is Matthew Hopkins – Nathaniel Bacon is his patron, but it is said he is well set with the Puritans. I know this man. He hath visited me on a number of occasions, for horary readings on the fate of his employer's vessels. He hath an eager mind and questioned me greatly on the making of Sigils, the difference between white and black magick, and how Christian I felt it to tell of the future – as if reading the mind of God himself.'

'So, this Matthew Hopkins is young and ambitious, with some knowledge – he is a dangerous foe, indeed.' This time it was the Peacock who contributed to the discussion, his distinctive accent and undertone of superciliousness unmistakable. 'I blame Parliament, Pym, and his rabble rousers; they are branding all manner of activity unholy.' George Wharton, Astrologer to the King and staunch Royalist – his rhetoric unmistakable, aimed this last comment at me – perhaps the only individual of some Puritan sympathy at the table – the Peacock's head turning and staring at me directly, as if looking down its beak. 'It is a means to unite the populace through hatred and suspicion.'

'There is some good to the politics of the common man, and, in this Parliament, serves the nation,' I retorted, aware that I was under attack.

'Perhaps, but I'm telling you John Pym will have our heads impaled upon the bridge given half a chance, and as for John Thurloe – I have no doubt he has every one of our names on a list and a spy in each of our households!' George Wharton was close to an hysteria that infected the rest of the Council.

I knew of Thurloe, a young man previously acquainted with Matthew Hopkins. A zealous, ill-mannered man who, like Hopkins, was most ambitious and had already begun to build his career on the ruined reputation and lives of others. He was the son of the rector of the Abbes Roding, and also heralded from Essex. It was said that in Parliamentarian England he had a great future. Banging his fist upon the table the Bull shouted, 'Order, Order,' and all fell silent again.

'May I make a suggestion?' I ventured, at which the Bull lowered his great wide head. 'In these times it is best to keep thy enemies close. I shall endear myself to Matthew Hopkins. This will enable me to have foreknowledge of both his plans and raids upon innocent villages and households. I am able to walk with my two feet upon two planks without falling into the river.'

'As most tricksters! Do I need remind my fellow practitioners that William Lilly is a sworn friend of Parliament? The rest of his sentiment is born through opportunity only,' George Wharton hiding behind the mask of the peacock retorted spitefully.

'I refute that!' I retorted. 'I love my King as much as the next man, but he is victim of his own ill-starred destiny as the next mortal. I did try to help him, and by Jove, I would do so again!' Half the table leapt to my defence whilst the other half (Royalists, I suspect) leapt to their feet, and I feared the turmoil outside the hall might mirror itself inside.

I was close to tearing off my own mask when the Bull again called for order.

'Please! Can we conduct ourselves like civilised men? I urge you to resume your seats! What means do you all hope to achieve by promoting panic! Can't you see we are one and the same, and as such will be condemned for it!'

And so it was, after much chastising, the others found their seats and the circle was closed again and the Bull continued, 'There are members of this Council from both sides; I urge you all to rise above the temporal nature and pettiness of the political divide that tears asunder our good England and let it not tear apart our own Council,' he pleaded, at which the Dove interrupted, 'We need to elect a leader who is advisor to both camps and is trusted by both sides.'

Now the Dragon spoke up, hands trembling. 'Master William Lilly, it is true you dress like a Puritan and yet you advise both Court and Parliament and have many friends in many places. I, for one, would like nominate you as leader of the Grand Council of Theurgy.'

'This is a grave mistake,' the Peacock muttered, but was ignored.

'And I will second the motion,' the Dove confirmed.

'Those in agreement raise their cups,' the Dragon announced.

Slowly, various members lifted their cups to indicate their support. There were fourteen in total.

'The Yeas have it. And so I confer the honour of becoming the leader of the Grand Council of Theurgy upon you, Master Lilly – will you accept?' the Bull concurred.

I glanced at the rest of the table. Along it, the three members whose cups had stayed firmly upon the wooden table – the Dragon, Peacock and Bull – formidable foes indeed. Could I afford enemies within as well as without? I thought of Harry Goldsworthy, of his courage, and of Hector Able and those long evenings we spent together, his great lion head with its mane of white hair bent over my bench as, carefully, he'd grind together a paste, or draw out the symbols for a Sigil he knew would go toward the saving of souls, hearts and minds. And I wondered at Hector Able's own horary magick. Had he somehow, in his powers, created this moment in a future he knew he would no longer be a part of? Was this the gift, the last part of his legacy he had told me would only become apparent after his death?

'Master Lilly, we await your answer?' The Dragon's stern voice brought me out of my reverie.

'I am honoured, and I will take up the position and can promise I will employ all my diplomacy to ensure the protection and preservation of both the profound art of astrology and the study of the occult. For God and the legacy of this great country.' And from beyond the flicking candlelight I saw Hector Able's ghost smile.

*   *   *

Outside, it was still dusk, and I could see I was on the edge of a thicket beyond which the silhouette of the city lay. The sound of children playing floated over the treetops, and somewhere an owl hooted. I marvelled at the prosaic nature of life so different from the mysterious world I had just emerged from, then, hoisting myself up, took saddle upon my horse.

CHAPTER FIFTEEN

⊗ ♃ ♄

Winter 1642

The Corner House, The Strand

Libra is a Sign aeriall, hot and moyst, Sanguine,
Masculine, Moveable, Equinocuiall, Cardinall,
Humane, Diurnall, of the Aerinall Triplicity,
and Western, the chief House of Venus.

The wheel of Time hath spun and a great frost is upon us, as it
hath been for many a winter these past years. Sometimes the
sky is so dark I wonder if London itself hath fallen out of favour
with Apollo and he hath turned his flaming chariot from us for
ever.

After the battle of Edgehill the king and his men took
Banbury, then arrived to great jubilation in Oxford. In this
I did not know where my loyalties did lie; I did wish the
King a long life yet I did fear his obstinacy. At this same
time Prince Rupert's Calvary rode toward my beloved
London, taking Abingdon, Aylesbury and Maidenhead.
However, the town of Windsor proved his undoing, as many
of the brave Parliamentarians were there. It was then I did
hear the rumour – from friends who did sit at Westminster
– that the Royalist officers demanded peace talks against
Prince Rupert's wishes whilst the King did agree with the
notion of a truce. Alas, it was not to be and the fear of Prince

Rupert and the violence of his men grew daily in the city as they advanced.

Then on the thirteenth of November (a most inauspicious date) after Parliament lead by the Earl of Essex had suffered a beating at Brentford the day before, a huge force of the King's men, some thirteen thousand trained Royalist soldiers, faced the People's army upon Turnham Green, the last place before an invasion of London would be possible. My own household was galvanised by the terror of invasion. Simon Featherwaite marched to the battle as did half my neighbours and both the butcher and his boy, with cries of 'God bless Earl Warwick!'.

It was a case of defending London, our homes and all that free commerce and speech did stand for. And I myself was sorely tempted to join this army of ordinary Londoners. In the end it were twenty-four thousand who faced the King's troops, and after small losses he did retreat. Methinks he did wisely know that to conquer London at that moment was not to conquer the hearts or will of the populace within.

But despite the furore and chaos of this war I find I am lonely. 'Tis a wonder a man, surrounded by the bustle and noise of one wife, two maids, a housekeeper and her errant nephew – not to mention the constant stream of Querents who flow through my house like an endless river – could be so solitary. But believe me, dear Reader, I am.

I have taken to talking alone to Solomon the raven of Magdalene; thank the Lord he is not a parrot and therefore has not the tongue to betray me. There is a chagrin to this transgression of the heart in a man of my age that is difficult to live with. I had thought a man nearing forty years in age immune to such folly, but Venus (and her grinning infant) reminds me most painfully that we cannot choose who we fall in love with.

Increasingly, I found my intelligence of interpretation rising above and beyond the mere placement of the planets. I have found I can read the persona of the Querent in colour and in light. This helps guide me. How I wish to share this discovery with Magdalene!

Meanwhile, huddling about the hearth in the White Hart I bored both the good John Scott and my friend and relative, the unconventional William Pool, with my cogitation. Oh, for one of those conversations in which my mistress's wit gilds the air with its gold. I long for this as much as I long for her body.

My one consolation is that I believe I am being guided in the bigger questions, by God and the Angels. I strive (despite my one failing) to be pure of thought and heart – for the more holy thou art, and more near to God, the purer judgement thou shalt give. Some days I confess it is as if a great light is shining through me and that I am a mere conduit to a higher illumination, yet the responsibility of such power weighs heavily.

As if in answer to my prayers (and perhaps my more secret doubts) I felt this most keenly when I was visited by a great well-wisher to the Parliament, a London merchant who hath given much coin to Cromwell's cause, a portly man who despite his most Puritan exterior wore an ermine vest beneath his conspicuously black and plain tunic, his valet mincing behind him. His question (after much small talk and bluff) was 'If Prince Rupert should get honour by our wars or worst the Earl of Essex, what should become of him?'

As required, I took note of the time this blustery merchant placed the question and he then departed, leaving behind the faint scent of cloves and the plucked petals of a rose he had pulled apart in his nervousness.

'Tis tradition, as you know, dear Reader, that the Querent should be signified by the ascendant and its ruler, but the truth is, I was many hours studying the resolution of this question, for it were clear that in the rest of this particular horary the ruler of the ascendant had lost his importance.

Perplexed, I spent the night drawing figures over and over – studying the positions of the planets and houses as this question fell not under the notion of ordinary rules, nor as I believe, must the Astrologer expect particular rules to govern his fancy in every question. It was well said in the Latin – *Per scientiam ad te*, 'By you and by the science' – for I do daily resolve such questions as come not into the ordinary rules of Guido or Albohazin Haly, two great mystics I do follow, but have some room to fashion these rules in my own intuition. I do not prostitute my art to please a Querent, but there is a magick that comes from the self in the reading of symbols. It were this God-given power that spake to me that night.

Finally, as dawn crept across Mother Thames, I concluded that Prince Rupert should gain no honour by this war, for all the talk of his superior soldiering, and that he hath no prospect of defeating the Earl of Essex.

I gave my answer later that very same day, and my Parliamentarian Querent was most pleased. As for myself? The horror of this war tears into my dreams, and I imagined myself as wayward and vulnerable as the aerialist walking upon a wire stretched over a tumultuous sea, the scales of justice hanging from each hand: one tip to the left and I fall to my death, one tip to the right and I will meet the same fate.

A week later, as I had promised the Grand Council of Theurgy, I did travel to meet with Matthew Hopkins at the tavern at Manningtree. We sat outside in a wintery sun and the shipping clerk, his fair hair greasy, his beard scarce hiding pox scars and an acne, did question me with a most unpleasant curiosity.

'You know why I wished to meet with you, Master Lilly? And the importance of such an meeting given the dark and troubled times this country and its governance is moving toward?'

'I believe you wish to exploit my expertise in manners of the occult?' I answered lightly. The cider was excellent and the sea air was balm to my lungs after the foul vapours of the city, but I intended to mislead the zealot into all number of misconceptions and false trails.

'Indeed, I think you one of the great experts in this field, and I am, as you know, most impressed with your predictive astrology.' He filled his jug again. 'However, I wish you to teach me the best ways of detecting a Witch, the signs both ordinary and extraordinary. I have studied the *Malleus Maleficarum*, and I am in the process of developing my own techniques of interrogation, but to have the opinion of a great scholar like yourself . . .'

Faith, this glorified shipping clerk knew the weakness of a man's heart; he did use flattery like a sword. And, as much as I detested him, I did soften.

'Firstly, I would not arrest any woman unless she hath horns,' I told him most seriously.

'Horns?' he repeated, incredulous. Seeing him falter, I quickly expanded my explanation.

'Yes, horns. And I mean two bony nodules symmetrically placed on either side of the skull, bestowed as they were by the very Devil himself. Such gifts, according to the seer Ficino are always given during a ceremony on All Saints' Day, where Lucifer himself doth lay hands upon his devotees' heads and thus the horns are sprung.' By Jove, this was good cider! I could see Hopkins' eyes grow wider and wider and, inspired, I continued, 'There are only three or four sacred sites where this ritual is rumoured to occur; perhaps I could take you there?' I elaborated with the most sincere of enthusiasms.

'You would do that, Master Lilly?' Faith, the credulous fool was actually grateful!

'To serve the purging of these most insidious and dangerous individuals who threaten the purity of England, I would. You know me to be the most devout Protestant.' And here I threw in a little gesture I had learnt from my actor friend Tobias Young to underpin my sincerity.

'I have heard of your religious piety and the frequency with which you attend the sermons of St Antholin's, a most admirable institution. But tell me, what were you doing in the Tower a few weeks back?' Hopkins asked.

'I was there in my capacity as a medic. I had been called there to attend the sorcerer Harry Goldsworthy. His interrogator feared he would not survive a second interrogation and thus confess the names of those who had made magick with him.'

'But he did die most suddenly.'

'His heart, weakened by the rack . . . It was most unfortunate, for there are far cleverer methods of extracting the truth, as you have no doubt read in the *Malleus Maleficarum*?' I told him with great conviction.

'Indeed, and I look forward to applying them to my own practice. So, William, you will join me with several other learned men in my pursuit of such creatures? I am depending on your knowledge of the many signs and symbols that betray the Witch.'

'It would be my civic duty,' I answered, reaching out to clasp his clammy hand.

I spent the rest of the afternoon teaching him nothing, instead leading him into false signifiers and astrological symbols. As Matthew Hopkins is half-educated in such matters he swallowed all I taught him like a huge, bloated fish about to be hauled to the shore. This was of boundless satisfaction to me, all the time thinking of both Hector Able and poor Harry Goldsworthy.

*   *   *

Christmas this year was a hollow affair, with many of my more Puritan neighbours claiming that such ceremony was Popish and unchristian. I would hear none of it, and at the Strand House we did hang holly and dried cloves and oranges over the door. Later, as in earlier years, the children of the neighbourhood knocked for mince and other sweetmeats; again I was reminded of my own lack of progeny so marked in my Nativity.

I laboured until the eve of Christmas day and then (to the great annoyance of my wife) I did see a Querent after Church in the morning – a Royalist gentleman who had a quantity of plate stolen from his house.

My working life now had a whirly-gig madness to it, one that was edged with danger. Mrs Featherwaite did usher in a Puritan merchant through the front door as I did hurriedly usher the Cavalier gentleman out the back. Let it be said that Master William Lilly refused no man on grounds of the colour or lace of his collar. However, I am tiring of the fractions this conflict has thrown up like so many toadstools after heavy dew. I have a particular dislike for the Ranters, amoral preachers who oft appear naked in their street sermons, ranting that God doth not belong in a church nor in any institution but is within each man and that private ownership of both land and goods is wrong and, most wickedly, that sin is mere product of Man's imagination. Monstrous in their amorality I perceive them as heretics. Methinks there will be many such folk who will appear in these coming years of anarchy.

Yesterday morn I saw three men and one Irishwoman hanged from the 'Tyburn Tree', at Tyburn village, where the most enterprising locals do charge a half-penny and have erected stands for the thousands who turn out for such events. Hangings have always been most popular with the Londoner, but it seems to me in these times of prejudice and fear King Mob takes an extra delight in such executions, as if to witness another contortion at the end of the rope delays or denies the possibility of their own deaths.

The four prisoners, dressed in their best and full of fake gaiety, waved from the open cart as it trundled down from Newgate prison. They did arrive at the gallows cheered on by a much appreciative crowd. Some had packed picnics and ale, bringing their whole families for both the education and entertainment, other watched in silent fascination. Hangings are particularly popular with the apprentices, a brave death being the most celebrated.

The prisoners then mounted the gallows in sullen defiance, the woman, (a young Auburn-haired woman and most fetching in a blue muslin) was a particular favourite and men threw flowers as she took her place beside the rope. Their crimes were claimed to be Papist spies for both the King and for the Pope. The rabble, in good spirits, shouted encouragement to the hangman as the four, one by one, were pushed from the block.

Only one prisoner, a tall stick-bone youth with a man's hands and the body of a boy did cry out for his mother. It were a pitiful sight. Upon witnessing his companions dying before him he did piss his pants – to the merriment and booing of the onlookers. Later I could not eat my supper for the memory of it.

I received another winged messenger from Magdalene, written in Latin. She told that the Queen was still in the Netherlands, having lost her patience with the King, and in missives most ungracious was urging him to secure the city of Hull, a most important port, and that Henrietta did now question the King's soldiering. Truly, this Queen is a meddlesome warmonger, determined that England and King should reach no compromise or treaty unless one defeat the other – that a woman should seek the blood of a nation upon her hands!

As I read Magdalene's letter I did try to find her in her minature handwriting, the arch of her neck in the swallow of a J, her open lips in an O, the swoop of her eyebrows and regal nose in a T. A man dying of thirst clutching at snowflakes. Is there a word, a sigh, a hidden term of endearment perhaps embedded in the astrological symbols? To my intense disappointment, I only find it in the cipher she has enclosed in the Venus. Is she tiring of me? Has she found another? I am rendered helpless through geography and desire.

Much of London is now surrounded by earthworks, great trenches and mountains of which every day (and even on a Sunday as it has been decreed Lord's own work from all the city's pulpits) whole families, women and even small children arrive with all manner of spades to help with the defending of London from the King's men.

It is most righteous and most godly propaganda to be seen standing over such siege work and the most prominent merchants of this city will have it. They say even the Lady Mayoress has spoiled her hands with the red clay of London. Inspired, my wife Jane (who cares not a jolt for this mercurial city), Mrs Featherwaite and my two young maidservants, have joined with this motley army of shovellers. Londoners have made London a citadel with their bare hands, and it is powerful watching to witness their digging.

The real truth, dear Reader, is that the stories of thievery, rape, and looting most dreadful, committed by Prince Rupert and his feathered-hatted comrades, have galvanised the city and terrified it into a fortress. Prince Rupert is the new ogre of children's bedtime tales and the King a heartless dictator who will sell children to Papist cannibals and make all of England French. Fear now clamps the tongue of many a sane man, and no one dare contradict preacher, Roundhead or vehement spinster.

CHAPTER SIXTEEN

The events of early 1643

The Corner House, The Strand

Scorpio is a cold, watry, nocturnal, flegmatic,
feminine sign, of the watry Triplicity, fixed and
North, the house and joy of Mars, feminine; usually
it doth represent subtill, deceitfull men.

In the New Year I did receive an intriguing Querent, Mrs Lisle,
who was known to me as a fervent Parliamentarian with a most
forceful nature one was careful not to slight. She bore with her
the water of 'a close friend and of a powerful man indeed' and
was insistent I give her a diagnosis of the urine and instruct her
as to how I might help her friend, whom she feared was dying.
As her husband was a vocal critic and enemy of the King, I was
diplomatic in my words for she did indicate that the patient
was a man of great influence and should my diagnosis be correct,
could be of much help to myself and all that I stood for.

I took note of the time that the fluid had left the body of the
patient and calculated a horary that told me the patient would
recover but that there would be a relapse in a month's time.
Relieved, Mrs Lisle hurried away but not before paying me a
whole guinea.

After she left I sent Simon away to shadow her carriage and
later he reported that she did disembark at the house of

Bulstrode Whitelocke, a man in Parliament I do admire for his reputation as one who walks the middle ground, and, like my good self, judges a man as a man and not for the politick he followeth. This could be an advantageous circumstance indeed.

I was dining at my favourite tavern, the White Hart, when I overheard a tall, young fellow, who rashly wore a feather in his wide-brimmed hat, speaking with the accent of a Lancaster man, boast how he had just ridden down from Prince Rupert's camp. Picking up my pewter jug I sat at his table.

'Know you the Prince's cavalry?' I asked.

'Aye, sir. I did ride with the Prince and his men until two days ago, and with them I saw such acts of indifference and cruelty that I deserted and made for London.'

'I can believe it.'

''Tis one thing to believe, another to witness. The Prince watched as his men stole the crops of a poor widow farmer, much abused and violated her daughter, then hanged the poor woman when she did protest. I am for Parliament now.'

'Then take your hat off, young fellow, or be mistook for Cavalier, which in these parts will lead to your own hanging,' I suggested. 'Tomorrow you will visit a barber and have him shorn you, and then wear the colours of Parliamentarian London upon your head. Know you the Cavalier de Morisset?' My heart was in my mouth just to say my lady's name, but I did conceal it well.

'I do. He is one of the favourites of Prince Rupert's and not a bad man. His wife is also favourite with the Queen, and I heard Henrietta was most displeased when de Morisset did not accompany her to the Netherlands.'

I cannot pretend it were pleasant to be reminded Magdalene was, in fact, someone else's wife. But I let the young soldier prattle on. 'Of course, now the Queen is back in England – and whatever you might think of her, she is a brave woman.'

'How so?'

'Her great determination to return at all – for when she first attempted to sail back from the Netherlands she was forced back after nine days at sea, and only twenty hours from Newcastle a most terrible tempest blew in and the ship almost upended. You think the Queen would give up, but no. Even when her Astrologers warned her to abandon the journey.'

'I hear she is master of her own Fate, and treats such guidance with dangerous contempt,' I answered dryly, and dear Reader, I confess a certain schadenfreude, for I now understood that the Queen hath a disregard for all my kind and no longer took her criticisms personally.

'In this she was correct, and did land a few weeks later at Bridlington, and this is the second part of her bravery. For the royal party did come under attack from the pursuing naval vessels – that good harbour coming under heavy cannon fire – and whilst most of the Queen's courtiers took shelter in nearby fields the Queen did retrieve her pet dog Mitte despite the cannons.'

'Brave indeed. Is it also true she had difficulty selling the larger pieces of the Royal jewels in Holland in her efforts to raise money for the King's army? I also hear that she is appealing to the Scots and wishes to settle the rebellion in Ireland so that she can bring back the Royalist troops to defeat Parliament? Faith! The woman has more balls than both her husband and her dog together!'

At which the soldier looked upon me with that mixture of curiosity and suspicion that is so particular to our times.

'You are very well informed. Perhaps you are a friend of de Morisset?'

'No, I have been in employment of the wife.'

'What is your profession, sir? A dressmaker?' he asked surprised.

'I am an Astrologer, a reader of horary.'

'Ha! I see how the Queen might rub thee. Would I know you, good sir?'

'I am Master William Lilly of the Strand.'

At which he spluttered his beer into a pretty froth. 'I do know thee! You are infamous for your predictions and for your doctoring. I believe my aunt might have used your services on more than one occasion. Former Lieutenant Meriwether Jenkins at your service. I suppose Lady de Morisset was also a Querent of yours? They say she has an interest in such matters and is no small practitioner of such crafts herself.'

'Who says?' I asked innocently.

'Why, many at Court. She is beautiful, too. I have seen this myself; however, it is also true her husband is almost as pretty.'

A remark I chose to ignore, for fear my emotions would expose me. Now he leant toward me, quite giddy with the drink. 'Rumour hath it that she is without bedfellow. 'Tis a crime to have left such fertile ground unploughed.'

His crude comment made me recoil. Faith, I could have punched the man.

'They say the Queen and the royal party will travel to York,' Meriwether Jenkins continued, oblivious to my disgust, 'and I heard but three days ago that the Queen hath asked for the Lady de Morisset to join her there, regardless of the great danger. There is many a Parliamentarian regiment between Oxford and York. She will have to travel with a good guard.'

'The King will provide her with such.'

'I could have volunteered myself – to protect such a lady would be no hardship – but I have made my mind up: Parliament is now my guiding light.' He peered at me closer. 'I don't suppose you are in need of a good soldier? A personal guard?'

'If such a need arose, I would think of thee, Master Jenkins.'

After I thanked him for his information I put him in the way of a good lodging house.

And so I learnt where my mistress was, and the great peril she would face travelling. And I did wonder if the crystal I had sent her would give her protection and ensure her safe passage, rendered helpless as I was, in the miles between us.

My spirits were only lifted when I received another visit from Mrs Lisle, begging me to come at a fashionable house; her friend, the honourable Mr Bulstrode Whitelocke, was attending a banquet there and had fallen ill.

'Dear God, Lilly, methinks I am dying!' The corpulent politician was reclining on a divan in the back parlour in a veritable fog of stench, his velvet doublet loosened to reveal the huge pale orb of his stomach, above which a sunken and rather puny chest was visible.

Several maids fluttered about the man who was at once vomiting into a bucket then shitting into a chamber pot. 'Save my life and I shall be eternally grateful,' he declared pompously despite his affliction. I did note he was sweating profusely and that his belly was extended and hard, but that his colour was good. After instructing that he should drink some salty water to further expel whatever poison that might be within, I insisted upon interviewing the cook.

A thin Frenchman in a paroxysm of fear, the poor man could hardly speak.

'There was no poison, I swear! Everybody else is not ill!'

'Be calm. Just tell me what Mr Whitelocke did eat?'

'Trout! And a good many portions, but the fish it was from the river this very morning!'

'Please! I am dying! Dying!' Bulstrode did yell out just then before emptying his stomach once again at a most dramatic volume. At which the cook paled and fell to his knees praying.

'Bring me a portion of the very same fish,' I ordered, pulling him to his feet, 'and quickly!'

Whilst the cook fetched a sample, I examined my patient further, checking his tongue and his neck for lumps and pustules; I found none and I could see with the purging the pain was lessening. However, Bulstrode groaned even louder.

'Sir, you did predict that I would live?'

'I did, sir, death was not in your water . . .' at which I glanced over at the chamber pot and did see that even now his piss was clear and healthy, 'and I predict you will not die now.'

'Oh dear God, pray you be right! And you are the best predictor in London, are you not, Lilly?'

'I am indeed,' I confirmed, observing he was remarkably loquacious for a dying man. We were interrupted by the cook entering with a portion of the accused trout. It was, as he had said, very fresh and most delicious in taste and smell.

'So how many portions of fish did you consume, sir?' I asked Bulstrode delicately.

'A good eight – decent trout is difficult to obtain in this damned siege,' he answered.

'I predict you will live; more so, by tomorrow morning you will be back in rude health,' I declared. 'Two teaspoons of syrup of fig and a further purging of the stomach and, my good man, happiness awaits. In the meanwhile, I suggest that you restrict yourself to a mere two portions at table, to rest your stomach.'

I confirmed this later with a horary asking the question: would Bulstrode make a full recovery? The outcome was most positive. And so it was to be proven, for within a week Bulstrode Whitelocke was cured and I received a visit from the gentleman. So grateful was he that we did become good friends.

'Tis a wonderfully advantageous thing to be able to cure a man, predict his future and reassure him of his luck all in the one consultation, thus my influence amidst the Parliamentarian politicians grew mightily at this time.

The Queen was now in York, in the care of the Earl of Newcastle, intent on travelling to Scotland to raise forces with supporters of the King. I had word that Magdalene was to join her and daily I prayed she would arrive in safety.

To my surprise Bulstrode confided in me that John Pym and Hampden had sent secret messages to the Queen herself, appealing to her sense of duty both to husband and country and begging her to persuade the King to consider a peace treaty. In great arrogance, Henrietta did dismiss all their entreaties, no doubt this will prove fatal to the Monarch — who is weak but not, I believe, an evil man.

After this information I did send a message to Magdalene, pleading with her to influence the Queen to both compromise and peace whence she should be with her husband. There was no reply. Had I lost her? This was a silence full of dread.

In March I was walking past Denmark House when I saw a crowd gathered at the gate, jostling and pushing against a barrier of soldiers.

'What happens here?' I asked a nervous knife grinder who had stepped back from his cart.

''Tis Parliament's soldiers. Since the Queen's chapel adornments have been decreed as idolatrous they mean to destroy them,' he told me, crossing himself as he spoke, 'but the priests who guard them have barred the door.'

I knew of the Capuchin friars who were the custodians of the Queen's chapel and I knew of its beauty having seen with mine own eyes. There was a particular altarpiece, by the Dutch painter Rubens, a rendering of Christ himself on the cross that was so wondrously realistic you could see the human flesh of the saviour in all its mortal frailty. It was truly a terror to the spirit to stand before this painting and see Christ so recognisably a man. And although the Puritan in me did not agree with such art, something in its aching beauty pinned it to – dare I say it? – the erotic (for our Saviour here was the most beautiful of men) and away from the transcendental but it is great art nevertheless. Rubens hath been the Court artist, brought to England by King Charles, as hath the venerable van Dyck, another Antwerp artist also much loved by the aristocracy. Van Dyck hath been persuaded to the Kingdom by Master of the King's music Nicholas Lanier, my 'patron' Artemisia Gentileschi's once lover and imagining these so-called civilised men ripping through those canvases with pikes and spears made me think of Artemisia's own powerful but beautiful visions. This was evil indeed.

'This is a sin! The Monarch's possessions belong to the Nation also!' I cried.

'Then go fight the soldiers yourself, for the priests have nothing but God on their side. Me, I cannot afford to be arrested.' The knife-grinder, not more than fifteen I warrant, shrugged and went back to his trade, whilst I pushed my way through the crowd.

I arrived at the entrance of the chapel just as the soldiers managed to break through the door, pushing asunder the friars. There were two officers at the front, busy issuing orders as soldiers wrestled with several of the priests.

One silver-haired friar, his face etched with the wisdom of Moses, stood before Rubens' altarpiece, his arms stretched out mirroring the cross depicted in the painting behind him. Two soldiers wielding sledgehammers lurched toward him.

'Out of the way, old man!' one yelled at him.

'I will not allow you to desecrate our Lord!' The priest did not move.

'This is not a holy depiction of Christ, but an idolatrous misrepresentation.' One of the leaders now faced the friar. 'Step aside else I will have thee killed!'

'And who are thee? And who ordered these acts of vandalism?' The friar held firm, and I was full of admiration.

'I am Henry Marten!' the leader proclaimed pompously. 'I am here on the order of Parliament itself! And for all decent Puritans who have tolerated the Queen's fake and Popish idolatry for long enough.' After which he smashed a marble stature of John the Baptist as an infant to demonstrate his authority.

'This is a sin! You will all go to Hell!' the friar retorted before a soldier knocked him cold against the marble floor, then cast the first rip through the painting with an iron bar. It was like watching the face of the Christ being torn in half before me. I could not bear to witness.

I shook all the way home, and upon my return did lock myself in my study to wonder on the banality of such destruction. Later I did hear they also smashed the vestry statue of the Virgin and Child and did destroy another of Saint Francis (one of my favourite saints) in the chapel garden. May the good Lord forgive them!

The day after May Day the Puritans also tore down the Cheapside Cross. The monument hath stood there since before Queen Elizabeth, an island of statuary in a sea of carts and wagons. It were our Lady and the Christ Child in white stone (dimmed by soot) with a large golden cross and atop a dove. It were a favourite with the Jesuits and it had power and some unspoken magick; a touchstone of faith for the working folk who passed it day in, day out. I myself, as a country youth much in awe of the bustle of London, did love it, and there were occasion in which I did touch it myself for good luck.

Even so the Roundheads toppled it, another piece of London, to the ground. The lead was made into bullets – and so the dove transformeth to vulture, the bird of death.

So much beauty destroyed in the name of Puritanism! How can these be holy acts?

Today I heard from a good Parliamentarian that the Queen was impeached for high treason in absentia. There is now a high price on her head, and if she is ever taken captive I fear for Magdalene's life. Her silence is a paradox; it both terrifies and liberates – I cannot stop thinking about her and I spend my time shoehorning both my apprehension and desire into the mundane tasks of my craft. It is a fickle distraction.

CHAPTER SEVENTEEN

Summer 1643

The Corner House, The Strand

Sagittarius is of the fiery triplicity, East, in
nature fiery, hot, dry, Masculine, Cholericke,
Diurnall, Common, by-corporall or double-
bodied, the House and Joy of Jupiter.

Praise the Lord, I finally have had word from my mistress.
Magdalene is with the Queen and they are met with the King
and his Court at Kineton, near Edgehill, where that terrible
battle took place. She writes of how joyous the reunion of the
royal couple hath been. Methinks this ironic, for if Henrietta
truly loved her husband she would advise him other than she
has, for she hath set him upon a fatal path.

Magdalene also tells me how much the distance between us
hurts her, soul and heart, and I am bereft. Despite the peril, I am
determined to see her. It is becoming more and more dangerous
to take the road to Oxford even by day. Famously treacherous,
there is a patchwork quilt of divided loyalties with allegiances
switching from village to village, farm to farm. A traveller is
shot for a trifle: sometimes for their provisions, even for the
leather of their shoes, sometimes for a wrong word.

In August I dined with Bulstrode Whitelocke. Originally a
deputy lieutenant of Oxfordshire, his family's seat is in Fawley,

Oxford (his good wife being the niece of the Earl of Rutland). But the Royalist troops plundered it, desecrating Bulstrode's most precious possessions, even using his manuscripts to light their pipes, and so now his family is in Henley. Such stories are commonplace, with raiding parties acting with impunity on both sides.

But when Bulstrode is in the city he is in dwellings in Whitechapel and it is in this relatively humble dwelling the banquet took place. The food was excellent: venison, a good sweet red cabbage, and a most delicious suet pudding to follow. However, I found the gentleman much down in mouth, but there were several others there – Sir Philip Stapleton, Robert Reynolds, Sir Robert Pye the younger, and Sir Christopher Wray – all powerful men I intended to turn in my favour.

As Bulstrode was familiar with Oxford and all the routes there, I hoped to draw him aside and plumb him for a way in which I could embark upon the journey. But to talk in confidence was impossible. Bulstrode himself was bursting with news: having just been appointed governor of Henley garrison and, as a peace commissioner, he had just returned from the Royalist Capital, Oxford, albeit empty-handed.

'Faith, although I was one of the first to warn the Speaker of the King's ambition for an army.'

'Very prescient of you, Bulstrode, but truly this king has been spoiling for a war since he tried to arrest Pym and his good colleagues,' I remarked.

'Methinks he himself is not a warring man; when we visited Oxford he was prepared to listen to Parliament's proposals – 'tis the company he keeps about him.'

'The woman on top of him, you mean,' Sir Philip Stapleton jested, and the others laughed.

'Perhaps, but you are wrong if you think him a feckless man. I saw for myself, that there in the garrison they have made of fair Oxford, he showed ability and judgement,' Bulstrode responded. 'But the King's weakness is to trust others' judgements over his own. This is not the trait of a true leader.'

'The key is the Queen,' I said. 'She will not have the King or his army surrender to Parliament. I heard that she has even tried to convert Prince Rupert to Catholicism.'

'And he's a Calvinist to the tip of his sword,' Stapleton added.

'And a rapist to the tip of his cock,' Robert Reynolds retorted.

Ignoring the comment, Stapleton turned to me. 'But tell me, Master Lilly, you appear to have a very good source in Oxford, a client, perhaps a female one, close to the Queen?'

Suffice to say I kept my gaze steady. 'I am already in the pay of Parliament, and contribute what I can to the cause,' I volunteered, wanting only to draw the conversation away from who might be my informant in Court. Thankfully Bulstrode, reading my dilemma, distracted Stapleton by filling our jugs with wine.

'But will the Queen allow the King to agree to meet us halfway?' he pondered aloud.

'She will not stop until England is on its knees to the Pope,' Robert Reynolds retorted darkly. 'There will be royal blood spilt.'

'I still believe there is a sane and middle way through all this madness. We are not a peoples given to division,' Bulstrode voiced my sentiments exactly.

'You are right. I cannot imagine an England with a King. But tell me, Bulstrode, who is your butcher? I have not tasted pig as good as this for some eighteen months.' Again, I tried to lead the conversation into safer waters, but it was not to be.

'I found my butcher's son a position in the garrison, and so his father's gratitude is measured in good cuts. But back to the point: I can only express abhorrence at the notion of good England without a crowned head of state.'

'But the days of blind servitude are numbered! Land tenants deserve the right to be protected by their lord, just as the merchants of this good city should not be expected to be taxed to the point of absurdity merely to humour the King's taste for gold and expensive Italian painters,' Reynolds blurted out.

'You sound like one of those – what are they called again, Sir Christopher, those radical serfs?'

'Levellers, Bulstrode, and I think Reynolds is no Leveller. He merely gives voice to what our own eyes have observed. The people have spoken and, in the main part, they have chosen Parliament,' Sir Christopher replied.

'Which is why the King must allow talks; he must find a way that isn't humiliating to either parties,' I voiced.

'This is not a King, this is a petulant child who is only concerned for his lavish Papist ways and to ornament his palaces,' said Sir Robert Pye, a sombre man, the member for Woodstock and the heir of Sir Robert Pye the Elder, a Royalist and member of the King's Court.

I looked over. A grim, angular man in his middling years, there was nothing of the jolly about this Roundhead. Much given to religious posturing, he adopted such zeal to compensate for his aristocratic and Royalist parents by my reckoning. There were many like Sir Robert Pye, who, until a few years ago had no concern for their fellow men, least of all the labourer or street merchant struggling to make an honest wage.

At his comment the most meaningful of glances happened between Wray and Stapleton whilst Bulstrode remained oblivious.

'I was treated with much disrespect and derision at the

Court in Oxford both in January and in March,' Bulstrode confessed. 'At one point I feared for both my life and for the papers in my protection that were to be delivered to the King, and yet I have been industriously labouring to promote all overtures for peace.'

'Indeed, Bulstrode, you are a martyr to this cause, and hopefully not literally so,' Sir Robert Pye interjected, 'for I fear Parliament will send you out again, bearing another olive branch to that ingrate. I hate that this war is nothing but skirmishes, like rats fighting across a chessboard. There is no real frontline.'

'Except in the bed, dining table, and tavern,' I countered, thinking of my clients.

'I suppose you could argue most of the West of England is Royalist, and the East for Parliament — but then you have our men at the west of Plymouth, the loyal Gloucester, Exeter and brave Bristol — who all stand with London and are fortresses against the King, but for how much longer? Master Lilly, you are the prophesier at the table, what do you see for King and Country in your crystal ball?' Robert Pye continued, with a certain curl to his tone I cared not for.

I smiled wryly. Sir Robert Pye was a friend of the fanatic Nathaniel Bacon and a close friend of Cromwell, who was the member of Cambridge. Cambridge was now the home of the central committee; the organisation that ruled the seven counties included Essex — the murdered Hector Able's county. Nathaniel Bacon was the same villain the Grand Council of Theurgy warned me of: the fox lays his trap, and I must watch how my chickens run.

'I am no teller of future or if it be so, only with the scholarly and Christian craft of astral mathematics of which I am a humble student,' I replied in a cloying voice, fearful as I was of ridicule.

'Humble indeed! Master Lilly hath cured me twice and predicted the outlook successfully. I believe him to be the greatest Philomath in the country and one to be of great assistance to Parliament,' Bulstrode interjected.

'That might be the case, but if Master Lilly were to employ any unchristian methodology or by ways of the occult to secure his results . . .' Robert Pye fixed me with his gaze and I wavered not.

'I am an Astrologer, sir, my studies stretch back as far as Plato and Socrates, and further to the Ancient Egyptians, but Theurgy it is not.' In this I did not tell the whole truth.

There have been cases in which I ensured an outcome by calculating the most favourable time to persuade an unwilling suitor, or compel a wayward philander to visit a certain place at a certain time in order he confront the woman he had wronged. Was this magick? Was this witchcraft? I certainly had learnt the art of summoning spirits, scrying as well as divination. But was I to tell this Roundhead I had a crystal ball? I wished not to burn.

'So, tell us, Philomath, do you see a future for the King or for Parliament?' Pye insisted, and now with all eyes upon me I had to answer.

'I believe the stars tells us there is still hope for appeasement,' I finally concluded.

At which Bulstrode slammed down his pewter mug in triumph. 'I told you so! We must still persist in our negotiations, for England and its people.'

'If only the rest of us shared your optimism. I fear this war has only just begun, and it will bankrupt the best of us, both morally and financially, by the end of it.' Wray lit a clay pipe from the candle flame, and the sweetness of his tobacco floated down the table. 'I have heard rumour the King is to send Prince Rupert and his men to escort the Queen from Stratford-upon-Avon, to take her through our counties and troops. He is anxious she will be taken captive.'

'We can but live in hope,' Robert Reynolds muttered into his port. Ignoring the comment, Wray continued to address me.

'Perhaps, Master Lilly, you have heard the same? From your little bird with the bright plumage?'

What did his sharp words insinuate? What hath the good knight gleaned? Did he know of Magdalene de Morisset and her congress with me? I studied his visage; the wide, pock-marked face had a benevolence about it, a Jupiter countenance without a trace of suspicion, and he knew nothing yet he hath assumed my informant was a woman.

'Surely you must have many a nervous wife or mother come to you as Querents, wanting to know this of their son, their husband?' he elaborated.

'Or their father,' Sir Robert Pye added bitterly, reflecting no doubt on his own estrangement with his Royalist father who hath a reputation as a tyrant.

I breathed easier; Wray's assumption was general not specific.

'I do, and I would never betray neither their private anguish nor their political allegiances. I have, however, heard that the Prince is already with the Queen and that the Royal party is due to arrive in Oxford in early August, assuming their progress goes unencumbered.' My answer was careful.

'I have heard this also, and that the Queen, at every lakeside or pretty copse, insists upon a picnic and Rupert and his men dine al fresco as if on a jolly hunting jaunt. It is an insult to those who have already died for their country, and more so to those who will. The woman has the stubbornness of a mule and the arrogance of Papist minister who regards his "flock" as ignorant. It is a dangerous combination,' Stapleton added ruefully.

'If we had the exact road and location they are travelling upon we could ambush the party. King Charles would negotiate if we held his Queen.' Reynolds peeled a pear thoughtfully.

How would Magdalene fare in such an attack? If the Parliament forces were successful it would mean her arrest and execution. I was about to argue against such action when Bulstrode spoke for me.

'This is not the way to peace. The Queen is so disliked by the populace I fear she would be torn to pieces before we'd have a chance to lay down the terms of ransom. And we know that would be disastrous for all in this room, for who knows in whose hands England will lie in a few years' time.' Bulstrode sighed, then gestured to his servants to clear the table, somewhere in the huge fireplace a coal exploded.

'Master Lilly knows,' Pye quipped.

'But does he?' Robert Reynolds concluded, at which all turned to me.

It had passed twelve of the clock when I left the house, and as it were a warm summer's night, I took the air in, perchance to think along the river in my strolling. It were a half-moon, a crescent of most beauteous yellow, a smile on its side, a sliver of gold suspended so far from these streets, cities, fields, castles and trenches, away from the warfare, the killings, the suspicion and hatred now festering between men who were friends, brothers or neighbours only a year before. And I did long to be up there with the moon, away from the perils of this age.

It was September when I heard another great cry of Jonka the pamphleteer outside my window.

'Battle at Newbury! Great victory for Lord Essex and Parliament, the King's men slaughtered in the thousands! Read the letters of a soldier who fought there himself!'

As Bulstrode was amongst those who fought with Parliament,

and Magdalene's husband was serving under Lord Digby for the Royalists, I did sent out my maidservant to purchase the advertised newletters. But as I am shrewd, I also procured an illegal copy of the Royalist pamphlet *Mercurius Aulicus* to read of the same battle.

When I had the two accounts I spread them out upon my table and did look for the naming of any dead. To my great sadness, I saw the names of friends slaughtered on both sides – the Secretary of State Lord Falkland, who I shared a table with once at Bulstrode Whitlocke's house; Colonel Tucker, a man the young Simon Featherwaite was enamoured of, now shot down by cannon fire, and there, in the lists of the Royalist dead, stripped naked and lying like felled wheat in a field, most probably, I found the name of Magdalene's husband staring up at me like a retribution.

I sat there, until beyond my window the Sun had passed the top of the pear tree, and only then I did begin a letter but found I had no words . . .

Seven days later Fate provided me with an opportunity to ease my conscience and perhaps to see Magdalene. A woman in her middle years, of comely appearance, well dressed in damask and velvet, but her demeanour wizened by grief, visited me. As is the way with my art, I took note of the moment the Querent presented me with her question – was her son still alive? An officer with the Parliament troops who was taken prisoner at Marlborough and then imprisoned in Oxford castle in January. It were a twisted tale, like many of its time, with family fighting family. For the officer's own father was a Royalist, but so disgusted at his son's alliances he hath refused to pay ransom to the King for his only child, despite his mother's pleas.

Finally, in despair, she had sold some jewels and was now in a position to pay the ransom. But she had heard that these prisoners incarcerated in the castle of Oxford were deprived of water and food, and were existing in their own filth, and that the commander of the prison, a William Smith, was ruthless and many had been tortured to convert to Catholicism and therefore the Royalist cause. Again, she asked in a fearful whisper as if frightened of the truth, 'Does my son live or not?'

I did take note of the aspect of the Querent herself, the planet that embodied her son (Saturn the planet of restriction in the twelfth house – house of imprisonment at a hard angle to Mars – the ruler of all soldiers) and the horary indicated that he did still live. However, I could also see that the trajectory for the subject was potentially disastrous and that he would not live much longer unless there was some intervention.

When I told the woman, she did weep and her suffering moved me.

'Madam, I am to Oxford myself; I hope to enter the Royalist city incognito and could seek out your son and deliver a message of comfort, even see if a ransom could not be organised?'

'In that case let me help you! I have an ally at Court, a good friend to my husband who did know her father well – Jane Whorwood.'

'I have heard of her.' Indeed I had. It was rumoured Jane Whorwood was a paramour of the King himself – Magdalene had made mention of the lady having been described as having russet locks and being most loyal to his majesty.

'Use my name and I promise Jane will help you in any way you need. I believe her to have a Christian soul and good heart, despite her politick. And I know she hath much respect for the Philomath. '

'In that case I will leave for Oxford by the end of this week.' My intention was now clarified.

After she left, the magnitude of my promise descended and left me shaking, with only Solomon the raven to witness my sudden apprehension. How was I, a man of middling years, not a soldier nor even a brave man, to survive such a journey? Yet to stay meant I was half a man; to leave meant I risked being no man at all; and to succeed in my quest would make me far more than a man. Sighing, I reached for my maps and the next day I began to prepare.

I sent Mrs Featherwaite out for provisions and decided it would be most prudent to hire the young deserter, Meriwether Jenkins, I had met in the White Hart Tavern.

And so, with this in mind, I did visit his lodgings, only to find the good landlady of the property most distressed, her hands a-flutter in her anguish. When I did inquire as to whether the good gentleman was to be found within, she broke out into a low wail.

'Ye be Master Lilly? The kind gentlemen that did help young Master Jenkins?'

'I am that man. And I now wish to employ him in good service.' I spoke slowly and carefully for fear she might misunderstand me in her grief.

'That be impossible. Oh, he were such a good kind lad, his only crime was not knowing whether he be feathered or plucked!' she exclaimed followed by more such nonsense I did wonder at the state of her wits.

'But is he within?' I insisted.

'Within! He is without! Without anything that maketh a man. You will find him at Tyburn tree. They hanged him for a spy! A spy, Master Lilly, and his only crime indecision! Those Roundheads, they'd hang a cat for being idolatrous because it has long, pretty fur!' She spat into the gutter in way of protest, and I thought her brave for being so plain speaking.

There was a nasty chilly wind encircling Tyburn Hill. The hanging had been that morn: three lads – all for supplying information to the King's men. The old crone whose job was to watch the corpses were not robbed, sat at the foot of the gallows, a bitter knot of a woman, much pinched with misery and cold. Above her the bodies – youths not yet twenty and five years of age – spun slowly at the end of their ropes, their mottled, swollen faces a testimony to terror, each crumpled labour turned into itself at death.

My brief friend was the last, and it grieved me greatly to see so a young life taken in such calculated exhibition.

At my appearance, the crone's hand shot out of the pile of rags she wore for clothing, her blackened fingers twisting with the wind and my own fearful sadness.

'Farthing for a prayer for their damned souls,' she croaked, more crow than woman.

Instead, I paid her a shilling to take the body down and to ensure that Meriwether Jenkins had a decent burial, and the next day I contracted a member of the militia, the Red Brigade from the Tower Hamlets – Daniel Jenkins, a burly man of some thirty years – as guard and escort. A lad from Cheapside, who, because of an injury had not soldiered these past few months, he was a good man of few words and much solid advice and I did trust him on sight. More importantly, he had travelled as far as the town of Cumnor in recent times and knew the roads and all their dangers to Oxford. I was resolved, and intended to put my life into the hands of my Maker.

CHAPTER EIGHTEEN

The first day of October 1643

On the road to Oxford two miles outside Uxbridge

Capricorn is the House of Saturn, and is Nocturnal,
Cold, Dry, Melancholly, Earthly, Feminine,
Solsticall, Cardinall, Moveable, Domesticall,
Four-footed, Southern; the exaltation of Mars.

We set forth on our journey, myself on my reliable and much loved nag, Pegasus, and Daniel, my escort, on a far more impressive mount, a towering stallion who, like his master, had seen battle. Soldier and horse rode before me ever wary of what might lay around the next curve of the lane. Although most of the land east of Oxford was Parliament's territory, the lands west of Oxford were occupied by the Royalist troops led by the notorious Prince Rupert, infamous for unexpectedly heading east from the city and attacking Parliamentarian troops in sudden raids. To be caught in such an attack is what I feared most, as well as the marauders who roamed the countryside.

A gentle rain drizzled down upon us, scattering droplets over the animals' ears and making damp the cloth of my hat. I think we had been riding for several hours, having spent the night in a tavern in Uxbridge, and there was already a growing excitement gathering about the pit of my stomach (the seat of emotion for many ancients) to think I would be able to hold Magdalene two days hence.

With this, and the sighting of a comet, the night passed and what that might portend rang through my mind in rhythm with the swaying flanks of the horses as well as the meditation the sharp country air bestows. In truth, dear Reader, it were the nearest I had experienced to tranquillity for many a month when suddenly Daniel's horse reared up and the air about us was filled with shouting.

'Stand down or die!' A man of some thirty years, thin and brown from a regime of earth and sun, a hood made from badger's skin stitched roughly over his head, sprang from behind a hedge, a musket pointing straight at Daniel. He was followed by three others: a boy of fourteen or so, stunted in poverty, one arm a stump, whilst in the other hand a pike, and two brothers, twins by the look of them, not more than twenty years, one still wearing a jerkin sewn with Parliament's colours whilst the other's battered hat with a pheasant's feather poked through the brim declared him a Royalist. The brothers pulled Daniel from his horse.

'I pray you, we are ordinary men! Simple travellers on the road to our friends and family!' I cried, quickly dismounting to avoid the pike thrust in my direction.

'There is no simple and there is no ordinary in these days. Hand over your gold and coin!' The leader peered at me from under his badger skin.

'We have no gold, and the coin we have is to prevent us from starving on our journey!' I pleaded, thankful that my money was safe hidden, sewn to the underside of my old saddle slung across Pegasus.

'Think we care that you starve, or that your friend here lives?' There was now a knife held at Daniel's throat.

'You would kill a fellow soldier?' my companion managed to croak.

'We are not soldiers! And you are a fool to give your life up for a cause that loves you not.' The boy now spoke, his voice not broken, and yet he had the anger and pain of a full-grown man, 'England is run by money and it maketh no difference whether it be a King on the Throne or that there donkey!' At which he pointed to Pegasus, who neighed; not so much in terror as being mistook for a donkey methinks.

'You were soldiers, I warrant, and perhaps from both sides?' I was playing for time, knowing the longer we spoke the less we were faceless unfortunates in the way of a good meal. The leader spat into the grass.

'We are our own army now, with our own laws.' He lowered the musket and nodded to the brother with the knife, who then deftly cut Daniel's gold cross from his neck and pocketed it.

'Deserters!' Daniel spat upon the ground.

'*Deciders* – deciders of our own Fate. Essex or Charles – they will both have the peasant's head on a spike. Go back to London and see how many of your good soldier friends have been given a roof or a job for their labours!'

'You have a point, Brother,' Daniel replied, 'but for my liking it is the King who hath bled us all dry.'

'Enough of this lovemaking!' The leader thrust his face so close I could smell his breath, pickled by the stench of hunger. 'Give us something, else I shall be forced to kill you for the leather on your back and those fine shoes.'

I reached into my pocket and pulled out the amulet I always carry on such journey, three medallions inscribed with magical markings, in gold, silver and copper. 'Take this, it will bring you luck.'

He peered it, swinging it by the cord before his eyes then bit into one of the coins. 'It's gold,' he informed the others before turning to me. 'What strange amulet is this? Art thou a Wizard?'

'He is a Philomath, an Astrologer who can tell you whether you will live or die, prosper or fail. And a much respected one too,' Daniel informed, still struggling to free himself. At which the boy did push the end of his blade against my doublet.

'*This* decides whether a man lives or dies.'

'If he is so good, how come he did not see my ambush?' the leader, ignoring the youth, questioned Daniel further.

'Because I was not looking for it,' I replied calmly.

'Let me kill him anyway; no prediction or good omen has ever saved me, nor my arm.' The space behind the boy's eyes was cold and closed; he had witnessed too much death and was beyond redemption. I now held my tongue. I was not afraid; I was convinced we were not to die that day.

Somewhere in the forest a cuckoo sounded her strange call whilst Time turned a mocking somersault.

'Nay, 'tis bad luck to kill a Wizard. Search them for gold and we'll take the stallion and their shoes,' the leader said and I exhaled.

The deserters had stolen everything except Pegasus, the old saddle still tied over the horse's back. Daniel was much humiliated and angered, having lost both his horse and several bottles of claret he had intended to sell at great profit in Oxford (claret being the rarest of commodities in that siege town). The rain had worsened and we looked like two sewer rats, or the most miserable tinkers imaginable. Even so, a great joy filled me at having escaped with our lives and so we plodded on through the mud and gravel. We walked five miles in our bare feet before spying a farmer hoeing in a nearby field.

'Good day, Brother!' I yelled across the glistening heads of the cabbages.

At which the farmer turned warily, then seeing the state of our dress raised his hoe like a weapon.

'Ye not come nearer – I have neither bread nor meat to offer thee!'

'Kind farmer, we are good folk who have been robbed this very day!' At which I showed my bare, bloody foot for him to see. 'We seek just shelter and water!'

'How do I know that? Do you know how many times we've been raided these past few months! And now my own wife is sick and ailing and I cannot take her to town for fear of these roads!'

'But then you are in luck, sir, for I am a physic!' I pointed to Daniel. 'And this is my godly assistant!'

Daniel, pulling his jerkin down, tried to look studious.

'You don't look like no physick!' The farmer still did not lower his hoe.

'What ails your wife!'

'A rash that has crept over her hands and elbows and leaves her skin cracked and bleeding to the point she cannot cook nor work the land.'

'Dost thou have a herb garden and perhaps a sheep or two?'

'Aye.'

'Then I can cure her, sir, by my oath.'

Now he lowered the hoe. 'I suppose you'd better come by the house, then.'

I applied the poultice I had made from the grease from the sheep's wool and the flower of Chamomile and Juniper berries, carefully smearing it upon the bleeding hands of the farmer's wife – a comely woman in her middle years who had humbly laid her cracked and reddened hands upon the simple wooden table as if they were plates of meat that no longer belonged to her body.

'I am most grateful, sir, 'tis a miracle indeed for a physic to arrive in these parts. Anyone who hath such skills hath been pressed into service by the Parliament army. Every mansion and estate from here to Oxford hath been made into a hospice for the wounded soldiers and the dying.'

'We would have our property if we had not been set upon,' Daniel growled from a chair before the hearth, his own bare feet now wrapped in a goat's pelt, a bowl of stewed turnips upon his lap.

'I know these men, a motley bunch of anarchists and deserters who answer to no god nor law and have no allegiance except to their stomachs and pockets. You are lucky they did not kill you for the pleasure of it alone.' The farmer, having taken a liking to the truculent Daniel, threw another log on the fire.

'Is there no physic nearby?' I asked, carefully wrapping cloth about the hands to bind the medicine to the skin.

'Oh, there was sir, before this war,' the farmer's wife answered. 'Elsa, a local wise woman, lived two fields yonder. She did all the healing for the village and the farms. The childbirthing, fever-rousing, and had remedies for all manner of pox. She were good, too. They said she'd never had a death at her hand.'

'What happened to her?'

'A mob. They came for her in the middle of the night. Some neighbours, some from High Wycombe. I believe they thought her a sorceress, but methinks it were Old Malcolm after her land. 'Tis a crime to take an old woman like that.'

''Tis a crime to have neither physic nor Cunning Folk for the curing,' said the man. 'I hate this war. It means nought but trouble for us farmers. Twice I have been raided, by both King and Parliament, and as far as I can tell they all steal, eat, and rape the same.' The farmer held out a bone for his skinny dog.

'Hush, Alfred, else they will come to take you too,' said his wife.

'Let them! We'll be dead of starvation by next summer at this rate.'

I tied the bandages and stepped back from the table. 'How does that feel?'

'The itch hath stopped – am I cured?'

'You will be by tomorrow morning, but you must reapply the ointment until the redness is gone.'

'But how is she to wash and clean and tend the sheep?' the farmer asked.

'That I cannot answer, but she must wear the bandages for a good few days.'

'This is the fancy of a rich woman,' he grumbled.

'Better to have no hands for four days than no hands for a month, Alfred.'

'That's true, woman. And you gentlemen will need shoes on the morrow, to help thee to disappear.' At which he unfolded his gaunt bone-rack of a figure and left for the other room.

'Please excuse, my husband, he's a man of few words and much unhappiness.'

The farmer appeared with two pairs of crude boots in either hand.

'They ain't much, but the soles will hold until Oxford though they won't protect thee from the treachery of the Royalists once you're there. And if I were you I'd avoid Thame; many hundreds have died of gaol fever this summer there. 'Tis Essex's men, they have crowded out the town and lean too much on its generosity.'

I took the shoes, the ghost of someone's feet still moulding the leather, the shape of so many journeys walked. 'Can I pay you?'

'No, I have no further need of them.'

'Then perhaps I can pay you in kind, for I am also an Astrologer, sir, and can tell thee of thy future?'

At which the farmer's wife sighed wistfully. 'Oh, Alfred.' He glanced over at her, and I did see an emotion pass over him like a cloud, not anger nor sadness but a terrible resignation.

'Nay, I don't want to know my future nor hers neither. Not in these times. 'Tis enough to know we are still alive.'

But later, when Daniel and I was settling in the soft hay of the barn for the night, we did hear the door creak open, and the pale yellow hair of the farmer's wife moved below.

'Master Lilly?' she cried, and Daniel, thinking this be an illicit visit, tactfully turned his back to me as she climbed up the ladder.

'Are you in pain?' I asked her.

'Nay, but before when you said you could tell us our fortune . . .'

'You wish for a horary? Do you have a specific question?' I did sit up and she settled at my feet like an excited little girl.

'I do.'

At which I glanced out of the barn window at the sky, looking for the formation that could at least give me a reading for the hour and day.

'I wish to know if we could have another child,' she asked, entirely without guile, and I looked into her face, surprised; as she was a woman of at least forty and five years. 'You see, the shoes my husband has given you belonged to our son. He was killed by Prince Rupert's troops at Chalgrove this past June, trying to protect John Hampden. He was our only child, was he, so tell me, is it possible God might favour me again?'

Her desperation was evident in her eyes. I glanced again at the sky. Venus was the first star glistening in this early night; behind her, trailing like an unwanted child was Sirius. The vision gave me an idea.

'God will bless you again, but it will be a foundling, a child you will take in as your own,' I told her, thinking this war has made many orphans and to encourage a home can only be a Christian act, after which she kissed my hands in thanks.

At High Wycombe we managed to buy a cheap horse for Daniel, as well as a dagger and a musket that had seen better days but was fearsome to behold. As we had arrived by midday we decided to ride on to try and reach Thame before sunset and then Oxford the next day.

The sun, although dim, promised another three hours of light by my calculations as I watched it flicker through the tree branches passing above me, the rhythm of the hooves clopping against the gravel of the path filling the air. We had just crossed a small bridge over a stream and the forest was thick on either side when the path opened up into higher clear ground.

Since our attack, I had become wary of both woodland and field — the forest meant we were concealed, but it also meant a potential attacker could be hiding; open land left us vulnerable but allowed us to see for miles. I rode with my gut strung tight around my heart, whilst the taste of fear made my mouth bitter. I could only trust in God to protect us.

For the last half hour I had felt we were being watched, but every time I turned to search between the tree trunks and through thick brambles there was nothing but shadows, and, no doubt, tree spirits who mocked our desolate mortality. Riding in front of me Daniel also looked around with unease and, just as we were about to emerge out of the green twilight, he held his hand up and we halted, horse flanks trembling, nought but birdsong and the lace-patterned afternoon falling about us.

My companion slipped out of his saddle and, careful not to break a twig underfoot, walked to the edge of the forest, his body as tense as any hunter. He peered out at the grassy rise before us. I said nothing. Suddenly all birdsong stopped and the horses, pinning back their ears, widened their eyes at an unseen sight.

A moment later the air was full of cannon fire and shouting and before us we watched in astonishment as a cavalry of mounted Royalist soldiers launching a surprise assault rode across the open path to attack a small camp of Parliamentarian men still sitting beside their tents and horses. The screams of the injured men, the sunlight glinting off the raised swords, the sudden thunder of the horses' hooves frightened our own mounts as we struggled to control them.

I watched in grim fascination as the Parliamentarian men ran frantically for arms, some still in their undergarments, others clambering on horses, some simply picking up whatever served as weapon at hand. The Royalists, better dressed and better armed, bore down upon them, the scarlet plumes of violent injury sickening to behold.

'What now!' I shouted to Daniel over the gunfire and noise. We both knew the road was on the other side of the skirmish and we could not reach it through turning around and riding back through the forest.

'Follow me and do not falter!' Daniel replied, as he launched out into the sunlight. The smell of gunpowder now hung in the air and the sky, only moments before tranquil, was now peppered by small puffs of grey smoke. Pegasus, smaller than Daniel's mount, in sheer fear I believe, shot forward and galloped like he'd never galloped before, following the frantic but determined pace of Daniel's steed as we rode toward the road ahead.

I am not a young man, dear Reader, and as I held on I did think whether this would be considered a noble death, and if I were younger, would I risk my life in defence of my fellow Puritans? My own terror pushed time and my experience of that momentous ride into a staccato of images: a cavalry officer slicing through the neck of a foot soldier who was trying to dismount him, the pike he held welding around his head. A horse tumbling upon the ground, its rider thrown, then two of Essex's infantry leaping upon him, one man running from out of a burning tent, his hair and clothes alight. We were there and not there, invisible witnesses caught in the glare of sunlight bouncing off a steel helmet. No one appeared to see us, and if they did they were too busy in battle to care. Finally, we reached the road and kept on galloping for a good couple of miles. We did not talk until nightfall.

CHAPTER NINETEEN

The third day of the month of October 1643

Outside the battlements of Oxford

Aquarius is an aierial, hot and moyst Sign, of the
aiery Triplicty, diurnal, Sanguine, fixed, rational,
humane, masculine, the principall house of Saturn
and house wherein he most rejoyceth; Western.

Standing at a crossroads marked with an iron cross much
vandalised by the fluctuating politics of the day, we stared
across a great expanse of water and earth, the autumn sun catching at the water of the flooded fields like a silver tracing of
Mercury running through an embroidery of blue and brown. A
heifer and her calf, marooned on an island in the midst of this,
looked up at the echo of our voices, then, indifferent, returned
to their grazing.

These ditches were the Royalist enforcements, built by the
besieged townsfolk themselves, structures to discourage an
army from approaching. Daniel had dressed me as farmer, a
field hand armed with a cart of potatoes which we had purchased
at great expense in the town of Thame, now headquarters for
Essex's Parliament army, the last outpost before Royalist territory, for we knew that besieged Oxford was part starving and
such fare would incur little questioning at the gate. Daniel
instructed me to speak in a broad West County accent (the west

counties being of Royalist persuasion) and, knowing his own gait and attitude would reveal him to be once a Parliamentarian soldier, thought it wiser and less suspicious if I approached the new Royalist capital alone.

We agreed to meet at that very cross in two weeks' time when the sun was again at mid-point in the sky and I did say goodbye to him and my good nag Pegasus. After which I pulled the hood of my tunic over my brow and ascended upon the cart (drawn by the most cantankerous mule).

I set the cart upon a narrow road that ran between the fields, and as I drew nearer I saw the huge cannons placed upon the fortifications and did think me lucky not be with Essex's foot soldiers confronted with such weaponry.

At the entrance two Royalist soldiers came out to greet me before the gated stone arch that lead into the city itself.

'Farmer! State thy business!' The larger of the guards armed with a pike stood before the cart most menacingly.

''Tatas — a gift from Wiltshire, for the Queen herself.' At which I threw open the sackcloth cover. The two men stared down most ravenously at the potatoes and the smaller one had started forward as if to take them himself when he was blocked with a swing of the pike.

'Wait, it could well be a trap,' the larger one told the other, then stepped forward himself.

'From the West, art thee? And how could thee travel all the way here through hostile lands?'

'I knowest the small roads and lanes, and travelled by night for fear of capture.'

At which the soldier thrust his hand down through the pile of potatoes as if looking for something.

'Take care, good sir, for these are for the royal kitchen, and I warrant the Queen herself would not want them damaged,' I warned him as a good farmer would.

Ignoring me, he pushed the potatoes aside but found nothing but the wooden floor of the cart. After pocketing five of the potatoes himself, he waved me on my way. As I passed under the stone arches, and into the filthy crowded lanes of the garrisoned city, I looked back and did see the two soldiers fighting over those same five potatoes.

The streets were so piled up with litter and all manner of refuse it were difficult to navigate the cart across the pebbles. There were many folk about, all sorts mixing in a madness of desperate industry. Each dwelling had people lingering about the doors and windows and it seemed as if the city were packed to the rafters with refugees: Cavalier London in its entirety had decamped here, and I passed several taverns in front of which young men lolled in plumaged hats and finery, drunk on ale and the fearful inertia waiting for invasion brings. Servants of the Court, wealthy families, and young gentlewomen in soiled lace traipsed along with merchants and the poorest of the locals – it were society turned like an hourglass upon itself, the sands that define us trickling over every social convention. I confess that it did both mesmerise and revolt me – for what is Man finally but naked before his God?

I thought to seek out Magdalene immediately but then decided it would be wiser to stay my hand and think of a safer strategy to reach her. Besides, there was one who could help me in this endeavour and after asking the way from a cleric hurrying to a sermon, I did hear that the actors and artists of London were housed at Basing House, a military outpost before the city walls on the other side of the town. I drove through the centre and then out again beyond the fortifications.

*   *   *

'By Jove, I have not seen such fine potatoes since Christmas last! You could pay ten whores with these beauties. We are gut-foundered and living off pottages of rats and boiled grass. Occasionally I get to smuggle in the collops the Court servants get handed down by their masters – dollops of glorified pigs fat and old mince – but it is meagre, meagre fare. Oh, by Zeus, 'tis good to see you, Master Lilly; a Philomath is much needed in this metropolis of lost hope. We just have George Wharton and he is a charlatan at his craft.'

Tobias's room were at the back of the red-brick tutor building, a cell not more than a cupboard with a straw mattress and a single chair upon which he had hung many costumes and a wig. The actor himself, thin beyond recognition, collapsed upon his straw pallet, his demeanour crumpled in melancholia.

'I have not come to practise my craft, although I would be happy to oblige any Querent once my own tasks are completed,' I answered warily.

'I see . . . you are here for a lady?'

'And I intend to visit the said Lady, but I am also here to try to secure the release of an officer with Parliament imprisoned in the castle of Oxford for some nine months.'

At which Tobias shivered then crossed himself. 'In that case, it would be better to assume him dead. I have heard they are swimming in their own shit, and that the commissioner is most harsh there.'

'I will still campaign. I have made a pledge to his dear mother. And I have some leverage with Mistress Jane Whorwood.'

''Tis, true she has the ear of the King – and faith, if I were in the King's shoes I would give her more than my ear, as her beauty would deafen me to the goddess Fidelity, but then I am not an uxorious man, nor an uxorious husband or indeed even a husband,' he concluded, shrinking even lower in his misery.

'But the King is?'

'More's the pity. There is something inflexible and untrustworthy about such a publicly moral man, do you not think?' The actor's tone was wry, and I chose not to answer. 'War and hunger have seen many promises turn to dust. I myself have surrendered to despair. There is nought in Oxford but quarrelsome courtiers and rowdy soldiers; the city overflows like a sewer, and the Court is a dull, paltry mirror of its true counterpart. The Queen is anxious, and little takes her mind from the cannon fire. I heard she hath been deposed by Parliament and there is a good price on her head?'

'Ten thousand pounds.'

The actor slumped further into his shoulder blades. 'That means the gallows for this poor Tobias. If the King loses this war I fear there will be such a dark horizon – a country devoid of joy, entertainment, a hellish place with the most long-winded sermons whistling about, gathering nothing but sanctimony and hypocrites. Pity the clown! Shed tears for the Fool no longer able to transport us to those childish joys that maketh the very Sun smile!'

All delivered in a loud and dramatic turn of phrase and, at the word Fool, a swarthy little man with the most rotund physique I have seen upon a torso, dressed in chequered shirt and pantaloons, appeared at Tobias's door.

'Did you cry clown?' he enquired with an Italian lilt.

'Oh, begone, Gianni!' Tobias cried. 'Leave us actors to our *acting*!' at which the little man scuttled away. Tobias turned to me. 'You see who I am forced to share my lodgings with? Circus performers! Jugglers! Bear baiters! The lowest of performers.'

'It is indeed a tragedy,' I replied tactfully.

'If only! It is merely the most prosaic of deprivations. So, you've rode through the city?'

'I have, it has been struck most low.'

'Low? It has been reduced to squalor. the King is housed at Christ Church, the Queen is in Merton College, and all those closest to her are lodged there – including the ladies of the bedchamber,' he finished with a knowing grin. 'But then, love is the greatest balm for the Spirit, and Master Lilly, as usual your timing is impeccable – although I suppose it should be for a master of the horary prediction.'

'I fear possible arrest if I present myself baldly at Merton College. The Queen has reason to see me silenced.'

'And when are you to petition Jane Whorwood?'

'Once I have seen my own lady.'

'Who is far harder to reach, billeted as she is with the Queen herself,' the actor concluded thoughtfully, then stood and walked about me as if he were assessing the measure of me both breadth and width, a most disconcerting sensation. 'The Queen has commanded a masque to take place tomorrow night – the centrepiece will be a representation of Botticelli's Mars and Venus—'

'An appropriate theme! With the Queen as Venus?'

'A *pregnant* Venus, but Venus nevertheless. She chose the theme to embody the power Love has in War – in other words, her hold over the King. Her interpretation, and none of us dare contradict her – she is uncommonly foul-tempered these days; methinks 'tis fear of capture.'

'And who plays Mars? Not the King, surely? Perhaps Prince Rupert?' I suggested playfully – an absurd idea, perhaps treasonable.

'Prince Rupert! That Calvinist beard-splitter would not indulge in such foppish entertainments! Besides, he is in battle. No, the most beautiful man in Oxford will play Mars, the young Cavalier Edmund Cressy, who is most elegant in body and in dance. Whilst the Queen's favourite, Jeffrey Hudson, and three other dwarves will play the cherubs. We will open with the unveiling of the tableau, then the whole scenario magically transforms into two choruses – one of the handmaidens of Venus, performed by the most comely of the ladies of the Court – the other chorus the soldiers of Mars, which I myself will lead. How is your singing voice, William?'

'Passable.'

'And I suppose you are presentable in hose and bare skin?'

'Tobias, I am a man over forty years!'

'But you have height,' the actor observed thoughtfully, then suddenly clapped his hands. 'It is done! I shall return the favour you once extended me and play Cupid.'

'I am to be part of your soldier chorus?' I was not sure to be appalled or bemused.

'Fear not, I am a very good teacher.' His eyes softened in memory, and for a second I felt myself looking with him back at the past. 'You know I was one of actors who performed in that masque of masques – *The Triumph of Peace*?'

At the name, images of that grand parade began flashing through my mind like light off a blade. 'I remember it well, I saw it with mine own eyes, proceeding along Whitehall – it was a spectacle that seemed to have descended from the Heavens, to landed lightly upon the cobbles. I believe my current patron, Bulstrode Whitelocke, composed some of the music.'

'He did, but it was Inigo Jones who designed the production, and at such expense!'

'But remember, it was extravaganzas like these that have helped turn the people against the Queen,' I chided the actor.

'But worth every penny! Such cultural levitation transports the soul a hundred times better than the most fervent sermon! Unfortunately, Necessity is my new taskmaster and this masque is a mere production of thirty players and a measly question of some papier mâché and a little silk.'

'Nevertheless, 'tis sad to think a masque so named was performed for a king who is now so embroiled in war. What character did you play?'

'I was Jollity – though you would not credit it now. I wanted to play Justice, but I lost that to a pompous ass who once played Caesar to my Marc Antony – I was younger then.'

'Can you get me to my lady?'

'Your face will be concealed in a helmet and I will blacken your skin so that you resemble a Moorish warrior; not even your mother would know thee. Lady de Morisset, and I believe Jane Whorwood, will both be in attendance. But now, let's see if we cannot get these potatoes prepared. Tomorrow night is a lifetime away.'

After we had eaten, as the quarter moon shone down upon the cannon and tethered horses in the courtyard of Basing House, I went to sleep in Tobias's cramped chamber upon a straw pallet and was much bitten by fleas.

The Presence chamber in Merton Hall, although far smaller than the one in Court, was of an imposing size, and it was here I now stood, dear Reader, concealed behind a curtain already dressed for the soldiers' chorus, a heavy helmet pressing down upon my brow, waiting with five other players Tobias had recruited from Basing House.

As I turned my leaden head from side to side, I could see clearly through the slits of my helmet fifty guests sitting on chairs facing a makeshift stage, a pretty podium that was curtained. The audience was mainly the ladies of the Court, dressed in their best robes with one or two showing the most discreet darning and artful concealment of the current shortage of both silk and velvet. There were also a number of Cavaliers, and various courtiers – I recognised the poets Denbigh and Davenant, the Queen's favourites, standing at the front, as well as several young aristocrats, some of whom I was surprised by, as I had thought them of Puritan persuasion and still in London.

I confess I did find the silks and gilded cloths all aglow under the candlelight, and the array of fruit and fine wine most appalling and Popish in appearance. Poor London in its black and grey! A most Christian monochrome, as if colour itself was sinful, and perhaps it was, for here I found myself thinking upon the deprivations many were suffering both outside this castle's walls and in the capital itself – same war, different politick, same suffering, to what avail?

My grim reverie was interrupted by a gaggle of four ladies entering the hall, twittering amongst themselves. There was one, seemingly in mourning, who walked amongst them, the silent eye of the storm, her dark skirts brushing across the branches of rosemary and thyme spread upon the stone floor, her hair hidden by a veil. All stilled as she passed.

I leant forward to peer closer, the weight of my helmet heavy upon my shoulders, the coarse bear fur tickling my neck.

The beloved is always trapped in memory through movement – I wouldst know Magdalene at fifty yards, through the turn of her chin, the sway of her hips, the pale knot of her hand held against her dark skirts. The greatest magick lies in this crystallisation of time, oft the sole opportunity of catching an image of our affection and keeping it suspended for a lifetime like sunlight in a drop of dew. And so it was that I first saw Magdalene in Oxford, luminous in her widow's weeds, a swirling mirage of bruising sorrow, oblivious of my presence, in an ignorance that made me fall in love with her again, seeing her at last without guile or strategy.

I made to move forward, but Tobias did halt me.

'Faith, dear friend, you cannot afford to be recognised so openly. Not here, in the Queen's Court – it is a pit of snakes,' he whispered, pointing out a man I immediately recognised — Monsieur Vindecot. 'You will condemn yourself and your good lady by doing so. Wait until after the masque; at the banquet you will be able to get a message to her. But look yonder.' He indicated a tall, handsome woman with flaming red hair, her beauty only slightly marred by pockmarks, standing at the back of the hall, demure in her demeanour and with a quiet dignity that impressed me. 'There is the King's favourite, Jane Whorwood, the woman you need to coerce. Few realise how close she is to our Monarch, and certainly not the wife.' Just then a great cymbal sounded and all turned to the stage.

The blue silk curtains, emblazoned with the arms for the House of Stuart and with the Angel and Lion for the Queen's family, were being hoisted up slowly to reveal the re-enactment of Botticelli's painting of Mars and Venus.

The pregnant Queen, draped in white silk and gold brocade, a blonde wig artfully arranged about her face — and placed to conceal her crooked teeth — her small but voluptuous body mirroring the lounging Venus exactly, down to the naked foot which I noted was heavily rouged, kept her position with a professional poise learnt from her actor friends. The young knight playing the sleeping Mars was beautiful enough to turn the gaze of a man who loved women, such was the perfection of his physique and muscularity. The youth was, as in the painting, near naked, a white cloth covering his modesty, his eyes closed, his cheeks flushed as if just finished in the act of love, his red-gold hair tumbling to the shoulder. He was, however, young enough to be one of the Queen's sons, and if there was any fault to this scenario it lay in the age difference between these two.

The onlookers burst into applause whilst beside me Tobias snorted in ridicule. ''Tis a female January and a male May, more like, but still poetic,' he quipped, referring to Master Chaucer's famous tales. But I, thinking upon my first wife, who I was most fond of and of whom I was some thirty years younger, thought it of little importance, as Cupid always provides a blindfold and, where the others see age, the lover only sees beauty. All this returned to me as I gazed upon the very young Mars and the pregnant Venus, defiant in her vintage.

'But do they not look splendid? Do you not agree, Philomath, does not my artistry impress you?' Tobias pressed.

'Indeed, you have made a veritable pageantry out of royalty,' I retorted.

'All is pageantry,' he replied in a whisper. 'The Church, the Court, even the rhetoric of the Roundheads. The populace is made to believe by show. Us actors are just more honest in our artifice. This is the elixir of success. You of all people know this to be so.'

Before I could disagree with him we were interrupted by a wave of laughter from the front row of spectators. A small dog I assumed to be the Queen's Mitte, surprised to see his mistress in such attire, had broken free from the arms of one of the ladies-in-waiting and run up onto the stage where he now did whimper and paw at 'Venus's' feet.

The Queen retained her composure and moved not a muscle, but the three dwarves, all holding Mars' spear behind Venus, did, as one, march around the prostrate goddess and aimed the spear at the dog, chasing him off the stage. Delighted, the audience burst into another round of applause whilst the errant lady-in-waiting ran up and collected up the beast.

'You see, a true professional. I have trained Her Majesty well,' Tobias remarked as Venus stood to arouse Mars from his post-coital slumber. As she did, several handmaidens to the goddess, dressed in diaphanous silk, gold thread woven through their loose hair, their bosoms almost entirely uncovered, appeared from behind the painted wooden trees singing some dreadful refrain written by Denbigh (whose poetry always reminded me of a frothy French lace – portending to much, amounting to nothing). Just then, one of the gilded dwarves blew a goat's horn trumpet. The note cut through the scene and seemed to send the silks a flutter. Tobias jabbed me in the ribs with his elbow.

'Prepare thyself – this is our cue.'

The four of us entered, stepping forth with military swagger, to sing beside our tousle-headed celestial leader.

'*Oh Hark, Venus, your lover Mars must to war,*' I sang, with Tobias bellowing beside me,

'*Grieve not, good goddess, for he will return triumphant!*' (Cheers from the audience.)

'*And vanquish all thy foes so that you can reign supreme!*' This last line was a veritable challenge. I confess the words twisted about my tongue and near gagged my conscience, but it moved one audience member, for the drunken fellow, standing upon his chair and overcome by patriotism, began singing along only to fall back headfirst into the audience.

I used the commotion as an excuse to peer beyond the candles at the foot of the stage. Finally, I saw Magdalene staring back up at me, her face agog as if she could not quite trust all that was before her and I knew she had recognised me, despite my blackened face, helmet and bear skin.

At the banquet afterwards, my heart pounding an unnatural excitement, I engineered a seat near my lady, yet away from the Queen to avoid further recognition. The beautiful Mars (who somehow preserved his modesty despite his scant loincloth) sat at one end of the table surrounded by a gaggle of admiring young Cavaliers, shiny with drink, all raucous with a determination to shun Death who seemed to hover above the cannons clearly seen through the windows beyond.

The Queen, still dressed as Venus, crowned by white lilies, sat at the other end, surrounded by her ladies of the bedchamber, her poets and courtiers.

Servants flitted like gadflies about the table, refilling goblets and replenishing plates. I was careful to keep my face turned from the Queen, again disgusted with this pantomime of luxury for so the rest of England did suffer starvation.

'Lads, mark the suckling pig!' Tobias suddenly shouted as two servants struggled with a huge silver plate that was placed in the centre of the table. The ravenous actors lunged forward, and I noticed several lumps of meat being slipped into pockets and under the folds of costumes.

''Tis for later, at Basing House,' Tobias explained, pushing some toward me. 'We have not seen meat for many a day and we save what we can. But faith, drink, William! And please lose your serious demeanour else risk being spotted for a Puritan!'

I stole a glance at Magdalene. A man of about fifty years of age, short and unprepossessing, appeared to be trying to engage her at every turn; an unwanted suitor, I wagered. I watched as she filled this man's cup over and over until his head lolled in drunkenness. Finally she glanced back at me, indicating that she would leave. A moment later she made her way towards an archway, I waited, then followed unnoticed by the others.

As soon as I stepped out of the hall and into the Queen's privy chamber, Magdalene pulled me into the folds of a tapestry and we embraced.

'You risked all to be here, William!'

'It was too long a deprivation.'

''Tis a powerful alchemy between us, and now it is even more dangerous, as I have been widowed.'

'I heard, and I am sorry for it.'

'He was a good man, and a good protector. My estate is much reduced by this war; now I have nothing but my wit. You saw Lord Pennington?'

'The young swain who hangs by your side?' I couldn't help jesting, for he was no youth.

'Do not be deceived by his fawning manner; he is a powerful man, close to the King, and campaigns to have me by Christmas. I must escape to London – I must, William.'

I buried my head in her hair; I wanted nothing more than to have her back with me, but the image of four spies I had seen at Tyburn gallows rotating slowly on their ropes hovered before me. 'Now is too dangerous; they are hanging spies daily and there is still talk of the magical invocation we carried out. Whoever spied upon us did not see our faces except for poor Harry, and Matthew Hopkins visited him in the Tower before his death and spoke of it in Manningtree when I did visit him.'

'Does Hopkins suspect?'

'Nay, not yet. I did fill his head with fake rumours of whom it might have been – which did surprise him greatly as some I named were Presbyterians and Puritans, most demonstratively zealous. I know Hopkins would not risk his own career by spreading such rumours. But he mentioned you. You have some grudge with him?'

'My husband once cut him in a business transaction – Hopkins hath not forgotten.'

'And now you are in his sights.'

'I don't care, I'm coming with you.' After which she held me most closely, and my heart did sink for I knew I could not protect her in her own city.

'Nay, you must be patient; there is still no tolerance in London for one so close to the most hated woman in England.'

'I have no patience nor time left, William! The Queen carries another child, and she hath night terrors and prays for both her life and that of the King. If she dies in childbirth I will be one of many who will be blamed. I fear God might not be Catholic.'

'He might also be deaf,' I answered. Somebody passed nearby and we froze until the footsteps faded. 'Can I be with you tonight?' I finally whispered.

'My chamber is at the back of Merton Hall, out of earshot of the Queen's bedchamber.' At which she touched my face. 'I cannot quite believe it is you, Othello, or some Moorish prince?'

'Not Othello, but simple William Lilly and you have him by more than just his ear.' I pressed her hand upon me to prove it.

'So . . . I think now is not the time for talking.'

Love is made sweeter through obstacle and conflict. I had always regarded this an irony, the way in which one's travails sharpens desire. I had walked through fire for this woman, navigated fields of fighting men, narrowly avoiding arrest, trial and torture. She was my Nemesis and my Mecca yet there has not been a more rapturous crucifixion, although it would be blasphemy for me to say so. God alone was my witness as to how hard I fought to resist such a transgression, but then he was also a witness to the ecstasy of my surrender. Dear Reader, you must decide yourself if I were sinner . . .

Magdalene's chamber was small, as cramped as a monk's cell. The bed was a simple cot set into the wall, a curtain drawn across, and barely slept one person, never mind two. A large wicker basket of clothes and linen filled the wall opposite, atop which was a straw pallet upon which the maid slept. The room lacked the luxuries an aristocrat required, and brought to mind the plainness of my own bedchamber when I was a mere clerk; because of it there was nostalgia and a tenderness.

She lit a candle, and this reunion, which I had spent so many months imagining, flickered into such vivid colour that I wondered if it were not a dream, a mirage sent to make me crazed in my singular longing. But then she kissed me, her taste real, her flesh warm. We fell upon the bed, which promptly collapsed beneath our weight, this accident making much merriment amid our lovemaking.

Afterward, we held each other as if we were drowning, the noise of the musicians and the revelry below still echoing up those stone corridors, the hostile world closing in more dangerous than before.

'What now, William, will you stay in Oxford for a while? There is horary work here aplenty if you are careful. The Queen has still not forgiven you your dire predictions, but the King is more circumspect and there are admirers of yours within the courtiers.'

I traced a path along the sweep of her breast; all dissolved was I, my wit blunted by the love-making.

'I will not stay more than ten days.'

'Ten days? Barely time to know thee again. How do I know that, once you have gone, you are true to me, that I am your secret wife in Spirit and Wit as you have vowed?'

What could I give her that was of the greatest value to me that could prove my affection, yet be invisible to all others?

'I will tell thee something no other living being knowest, information that can unravel me. As a fellow Philomath you will understand the value of it, but you must promise not to divulge this information to a single living soul, not in my own lifetime.'

'I promise.'

'Then take my true birthdate as a pledge. For I have deliberately claimed it is otherwise, to confuse my enemies and to conceal my real nature.' After which I did lean across and place the truth into her ear and she did smile, then kiss me plenty in kind, for she understood the value of such a gift. And we did spoon again, after which I cradled her like a child, before speaking again.

'Sweet Megs, there is another reason I am in Oxford. I have promised to attempt to secure the freedom of a young officer of Parliament imprisoned in Oxford Castle.'

'This will not be easy – the commander of the gaol, William Smith, is most brutal.'

'I plan to solicit Jane Whorwood. I have been told she will give me a sympathetic audience.'

'She is a perplexing woman, one that defies her husband by standing with the King. However, she is also a follower of astrology and is most learned in these matters. She will hear thee. But I have another path of persuasion and perhaps together we will sway William Smith's hand.'

'How so?' I asked, distracted by the blush I had placed upon her cheek. But, all business, she pushed my hand away.

'The commander frequents the house of a friend of my maid. One of ill repute, but I have found such places most useful in the collection of information and have a girl there myself in such service. Men with their breeches down are much undone, and men who face death on the morrow moreso.'

'You mean to bribe him?' I sat up.

'It will be easier to secure ransom if we have leverage.'

'Such intelligence in the body of a woman,' I marvelled.

'And such prophecy within the mind of a man,' she countered. 'But you should know my wit alone will not save me from the wrath of the Queen. Prince Rupert's protection finished with my husband's death and the Queen's favour is waning. She still has not forgiven me for not accompanying her to the Lowlands and if I should fail her in her birthing . . . But there is yet a greater danger . . .'

'Tell me . . .'

'There was the wife of a merchant here, a young woman who I tried to help with a canker of the womb through herbs and the application of some sigils, but God took her regardless.'

'And now the husband blames thee?'

'He is powerful, but he is not an aristocrat. However, he has gone to Monsieur Vindecot who now spies on me and suspects me of all sorts of evil doing, including influencing the Queen to her detriment. I fear he will reach the ear of the King and His Majesty is most concerned that we Royalists do not provide fodder to the Puritans' accusations of idolatry and witchcraft in Court. William, of all the dangers this is the greatest and could be the unmaking of me. If Matthew Hopkins should hear of such talk . . . Tell me what I should do? Make a horary for me, William.'

Oh, the Philomath's worst fear, to have to cast for one so close. Yet I thought on the fatalistic prediction of my own Natal figure, how until then I had navigated the deleterious aspects – my Sun in the house of the Bull set against the fatal opposition of Saturn in Scorpio in the house of the magi, the eighth – who knows if I would be able, myself, to avoid my written fate. However I had another gift, the manipulation of events, and this I had not learnt from books, or any manuscripts, but from a secret astrological lodge. Could I apply the use of magick or invoke Spirits on Magdalene's behalf? I had the craft, yet instinct told me not to act.

'William?' Magdalene ventured.

'There is a timing,' I finally answered. 'I feel it like an ache in my bones and this is not it.'

'So you cannot save me?'

'You will save yourself.'

To this day, I wonder what perversity made me refuse her so.

CHAPTER TWENTY

The tenth day of the month of October 1643
Garrison Prison, Oxford

Pisces is of the Watry Triplicity, Northern, cold Sign,
moyst, Flegmatick, feminine; nocturnal; the house
of Jupiter and exaltation of Venus, a Bycorporeal,
common or double-bodied Sign, an idle, effeminate,
sickly Sign or representing a party of no action.

I had been in Oxford for a week now, travelling in disguise
from Basing House to the city itself. My time had been spent
visiting Magdalene, when she was freed from her courtly
duties, and casting horaries for those she had secretly
arranged: courtiers and the occasional merchants, but also for
Tobias and many of the exiles at Basing House – artists,
actors and writers. I am proud to say I was of comfort – able
to give news of London, its luminaries, and for a small
payment, (which I wavered in instances of extreme deprivation) of the fate of their possessions and loved ones still
marooned in the capital.

But George Wharton, my rival Astrologer, hath now heard
rumour of my presence in the city and I knew I had to leave as
soon as I was able.

Finally, I managed to see Jane Whorwood who graciously
promised to seek audience with the King to ask him to allow

the young officer — Lord Pendle — a visitor from his mother. And indeed she had succeeded, for now I was in the prison itself, standing in an outside chamber; a woesome place through which the prisoners must be marched before being placed in the dungeon. A wooden bucket sat in the corner, filled with putrid water, and I dared not go closer for fear of contamination.

The stench of the prison was most foul, the worst soup of human waste: the smell of rotting flesh and stone walls running with slime. I'd bribed the captain of the guard, and then the guard himself, and now I stood waiting for them to bring me the prisoner I promised to free.

'Here he is, sir, your good friend Lord Muck, a little worse for wear but still standing.' The guard pushed a creature I at first took for an old man, his beard and hair matted with filth, the clothes upon his back rags, the skinny flanks of his buttocks rubbed raw through holes in his breeches. After pressing a sovereign onto the guard, who obliged me by stepping outside the small chamber, I turned to the wretched man before me.

'Lord Pendle?' I ventured, stepping forth.

The man recoiled as if I meant to attack him, and methinks he were much abused. I pushed the parcel I carried into his hand. He tore it open and, like a starving beast, bit into the hunk of bread that was within. 'Who are you?' he finally asked, his mouth a mash of crumbles.

'I am friend, sir, and have come from your dear mother,' I told him gently, but by faith, it were hard to stand near him, such was the odour of unwashed flesh. Trying not to flinch, I reached into my pocket and handed him the letter I had kept by my breast. He opened it slowly, then did weep upon reading its contents.

'She tells me my father is unmoved.' His voice was broken and thin (I wager you can tell how long a man is to live from the timbre of his voice – both hope and despair lies in the disharmony of it). 'I will die here within the month, good sir. We are given five farthings a day and there are forty men living in a room barely bigger than this chamber. I stand in my own shit – already many have perished of gaol fever – we are tortured to force us to give up both our religion and our politick. I myself have been lashed. Ten men under my command have died the most ignoble deaths, and yet my father will still not solicit or pay ransom for my release.'

'The King has his heart.'

'And the Devil his soul. And who are you, sir, to perform this kind duty?'

'William Lilly, an Astrologer your mother did consult.'

'I know of you, what soldier doesn't. But you are in the enemy's camp now?'

'Pray stay silent on this. I abhor the injustices of man upon man, regardless of his politick and the treatment of your men here is a great injustice.'

'I wished for a noble death in battle – I never imagined myself dying at twenty, ankle-deep in my own shit.' He was most bitter.

'Have faith. I will have you released with the month.'

'In that case you must be a miracle worker as well as Philomath.'

'Perhaps, but for now I must ask thee to do nothing to offend and stay low amongst the others. You will know when I call for thee. Meanwhile, wear this close to your breast.' And I handed him a Sigil I had made especially, knowing the time of his birth from his mother. 'This will protect you.'

'A Wizard's trinket? How will this fill my belly and ease my thirst?'

'I will also try to persuade your jailer to provide more than the daily fare until I secure your release.'

I made to go, but a bony hand shot out and clutched my own wrist.

'Before you take your leave, Master Lilly, tell me, how fares London and all its citizens? We have had no news for months and I fear all hath fallen to the King?'

'Not so,' I whispered, for to give hope and tell such information would be a hanging offence in such a place. 'Parliament hath taken Lichfield, Reading, Wakefield and Gainsborough. Most importantly, the good Earl of Essex hath won a great victory at Newbury, on the twentieth of last month. I would say the King sleeps uneasily, if at all.'

'This will make us all want to live!' The hand that still clutched my wrist shook with excitement. Gently I prised it free.

'I myself, would like to see peace and compromise,' I told him. 'England needs both King and Parliament.'

Just then there was the rattling of keys as the guard let himself in and the young Lord Pendle pulled me nearer. I had to hold my breath for fear of breathing in his pestilence.

'You must move fast, sir, faster than the gaol fever moves through this prison if you wish to free this prisoner,' he told me.

Later that day I'd arranged to meet Magdalene outside the church of St Mary the Virgin, as I arrived there was a cry of 'Fresh bread!' and we were enveloped by a horde of people pushing toward the vendor. Magdalene stumbled, but I managed to pull her to her feet and into the darkened entrance of a beer cellar.

We crouched between the empty barrels, the stench of fermentation prickling our nostrils.

'I believe William Smith can be swayed for the right amount

of coin, I sent a message through his woman,' Magdalene whispered.

'Jane Whorwood has also been petitioning.'

'The captain has indicated that if there should be a break out at a certain time of a certain evening, he and the guards will be conveniently absent and will not pursue until some six hours thereafter.'

'And how much coin is the good captain expecting?'

'Twenty gold florins – and one for my girl.'

I studied Magdalene; she had risked her life by such negotiation.

'Do you trust the captain?' I ventured.

'I believe he is greedy and this makes him as good as the terms he suggested, no more and no less.'

'It would have to be tomorrow night; the young Lord Pendle will not see the end of this week if I do not get him out. Can you get word to the captain and pay him his bribe?'

'I can, but so soon, William?'

'You know George Wharton will betray me to the Queen if he can find me. And the Queen hath good reason to silence me,' I told her reluctantly.

'Look around you, William, even the rats have fled this city.'

'Not fled, eaten.'

'I tell thee, I will not survive without you.'

'You must, for a short time longer.'

'Then take this for your travels . . .' At which she reached into her pocket and presented me with an object wrapped in soft goatskin.

'It is the magical glass in which you caught the angel – it is your turn to be protected by it.'

At which we did hold each other. 'Are we to see each other again?' she whispered. 'If Oxford is taken and the King should lose . . .'

'We will, of this I am certain.' And I enveloped her with my cloak so that we were in a place without time, politick or creed.

The next night I waited in near total darkness outside the walls of the castle itself, Oxford castle looming up before me like a huge beast, tense in squat disapproval. The two horses I had tethered and ready were restless in a sweating apprehension, the only light the silver of a crescent moon glinting on the surface of the moat. We were standing beside a stone tunnel used for the disposal of rubbish and other matter that ran straight into the moat, sewerage trickling down the centre of the vent. The stench near turned my stomach, and I guessed it had been chosen as a final humiliation for the young officer.

I had made a horary for the most auspicious time and was sure it was from that moment and for one half hour further as Jupiter the planet of expansion was in a good aspect to the twelfth house – the house that represented goals, fortresses and other places of restraint. But now I was full of doubts: what if our prisoner would be delayed in some unpredicted manner, or that the guard on duty had not received his coin? This and a dozen other fears assayed me like a swarm of wasps. Sensing my anxiety, one of the horses whinnied and I reached across to run my hand over her warm flank. The touch of my hand reassured her and she quietened – farmer's son that I once was, I was thankful then I could still whisper to the souls of animals.

I glanced back at the castle. I had learnt the night watch was about to change its guard on the battlements above and it were at this precise moment the young Lord Pendle must arrive.

I waited, time a vice on my guts. Just when I had abandoned hope there was the echo of footsteps and from the entrance of the tunnel a gaunt figure appeared, clamouring across the slippery stone. As he stepped into the moonlight the young lord's haggard face was illuminated and I ushered him over.

'Were you followed?' I whispered as I handed him the reins of one of the horses.

'Only by two of my compatriots until the guard made a great pretence of catching them and losing me.'

'Are you able to ride?'

'Anything for liberation.'

'Then steel yourself; we have a hard and fast ride to the Reading Cross where my man waits.'

We were interrupted by the clatter of footsteps, and we did stop still, thinking we had been betrayed. To my astonishment, a figure, slight and female in a hooded cape, stepped out of the shadows.

'William!' Magdalene's pale face peered from under the hood.

'Magdalene?'

Without a care for protocol she rushed to my side. 'You must take me with you, William! Monsieur Vindecot has petitioned for my arrest tonight! The nobleman who blames me for his wife's death hath persuaded him I am guilty!'

'But there is as much peril on the road ahead as there would be for you to stay here.'

'If I am arrested, I am hanged by tomorrow night. Before Vindecot got to her ear the Queen listened to my advice. Now she believes I will murder her own unborn babe.'

On the castle turrets, I could see the moving lantern of the new guard.

'We go now.' I hoisted Magdalene on the saddle before me then climbed up behind her. Lord Pendle was already on his mount. In silence we walked the horses until we were out of arrow range and it was only then that I dared look back at the city, thinking of all within, then we galloped away as fast as we were able.

CHAPTER TWENTY-ONE

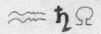

The thirtieth day of the month
of November, 1643

The Corner House, The Strand

**The First House: It hath signification of the life of man,
of the stature, colour, complexion, form and shape of
him that propounds the Question, or is born . . .**

Winter had frozen over all the horses' troughs and ponds of
London, the Sun had not fallen upon a blade of grass nor
windowpane, the low sky was a lead weight on mind and spirit,
the deprivations afflicted upon the populace to finance
Parliament and the New Model Army were grievous. I myself
was tired of rabbit and cheat bread and false wine made from
nettles. I found myself dreaming of Banbury cake, dripping
with raisins, and so did barter my services for a store I knew a
wealthy merchant's wife had set by. As a consequence, Mrs
Featherstone did bake a most glorious slice and did cheer my
spirits for a day.

Magdalene had been back in the city for several weeks and,
at my insistence, had not yet returned to her house on Chancery
Lane. Instead, she and her maid Rosie lodged with a good
Puritan family who thought they be abandoned, pious souls
requiring sanctuary and asked no questions. I told her to stay
under this guise until the Queen and Monsieur Vindecot, as

well as several powerful members of Parliament, lost interest and found better quarry. I knew not where she was so I was not tempted to visit for fear that I should accidently lead one of Hopkins' men to her. But knowing they were well and alive was solace enough for me

Of my Oxford trip, my wife Jane suspected nothing. She believed I did journey to replenish my stock of herbs for my medical practices. Upon my return, a flurry of Querents both highborn and low querents did await me, most anxious over my mysterious absence. And, for once, my wife seemed pleased to see me, a pleasure of only seven days or so until she began to find fault with me again (as, in truth, this were her greater amusement).

This last night I had a terrible vision that did wake me from my slumber in a crazed panic. It were Cullum Monroe, his body twisted and writhing in chains, his young, beardless face splattered in blood, and he did plead with me, saying over and over – *forgive me, forgive me*. When I woke, my cheeks were wet with tears. I did wonder upon the vision; was it premonition or fear? Should I send message to the Council or not?

Outside the garrison of London, the war raged; more ambushes, more deaths, more confusion – were the good Scots to save Parliament? Was Spain or France to come to the rescue of the King? Would London hold? I pushed my fears to the back of my mind and concentrated on my industry. Such dread was profitable business for me and I was able to hire an extra servant (a maid for my wife) and made sure my household was well stocked for the winter in salted meats and dried fruits.

One morning I had just given a diagnosis for the Pleurisy to an elderly gentleman when I was interrupted by Jane, suspicion painting her features most darkly.

'There is a Querent, William, who says you must see her immediately.'

'Tell her I will be with her shortly and ask her to wait in the outer chamber.'

'There are others before her, who have been waiting since noon.'

'It is a matter of life or death?'

'So she claims.'

At which I pressed the package of balsam and borage upon the elderly gentleman, then ushered him to the door.

'Send her in, Jane, and reassure the others I shall be as quick as I can be.'

At which my wife looked upon me with skewered gaze.

'She is comely and young. Are you are a godly man?' At which I lost my temper and dismissed her most angrily.

A few moments later a young woman her head and face covered by a veil (and, this being indoors, I assumed a gentle-woman fearing recognition) entered. Thinking I was to receive a query I glanced at the hourglass and toward the sky beyond the window to calculate the time.

To my surprise, my young visitor pulled the bolt across the door then the curtain so that we had nought but candlelight to see upon each other. I was suddenly aware that I was entirely alone. Remembering the recent attacks on the Cunning Folk and other Occultists my hand wandered to the knife I kept hidden at my belt. Could her urgent concern be the matter of my own life or death? Solomon, sensing my discomfort, squawked upon his perch, and puffing up his feathers lowered his head ready to defend me, bless his avian heart. The young woman stepped closer and my hand tightened – the city was full of untrustworthy creatures who had taken to whoring or spying, for both paid good coin. To my relief, the young woman threw back her hood and revealed herself to be Rosie, the maidservant of the Lady de Morisset.

I now assumed her to be the bearer of grim tidings and took fright.

'My lady, is—is she well?' I faltered.

'She hath had news, Master Lilly, and must see you most urgently.'

'Bad news?' I sat down heavily, knocking several manuscripts to the floor, where they lay as exposed as my emotions.

'I believe there is action to be taken to ensure both my mistress and perhaps your own life. You must come tomorrow.'

'What if I am followed?' My mind struggled to think quickly.

'You must make sure you are not. We lodge at my sister's in St Saviour's parish.' At which she smiled, a sad mien to her pretty mouth. 'You have a suspicious wife, sir, and I see that she is a Quaker.'

'Jane knows nothing, but I fear I cannot trust her.'

'Then come to us tomorrow night; it is the first house on Ploughman's Way. Bring no guard or witness, 'tis safer.'

At which the maid covered herself again and turned to leave, before which I grabbed her arm.

'Tell me, what is the spirit of my lady?'

'Lady Morisset is strong, sir, and will be more so for the sight of yourself. Bid me go, I have far to travel.'

I pressed a shilling into her hand, then after pulling the curtain back, watched her disappear into the twilight of the afternoon.

My next Querent was a young woman asking about the faithfulness of her suitor and I confess, dear Reader, I had to bind my tumbling emotion to concentrate.

The next morn I convinced my wife that I had an evening to play bowls with Harry Pickles, my printer friend in Lincoln's-Inn-Fields (one of the few entertainments a good Puritan man could morally afford) and that Jane should take the occasion to attend one of her Quaker meetings she knows I loathed to go to. Disapproving of Harry Pickles, but pleased I was uncharacteristically encouraging of her faith Jane complied, and I even gave her coin for a new bonnet for the occasion. So easily is marital strife solved!

And so it was that I found myself travelling toward Southwark in a hackney carriage I had hired for the purpose. I held my good self deep against the seat within, a hat drawn low upon my brow, for I had no wish to be recognised and I was popular with the street folk who thought it good luck to touch an esteemed Astrologer. I had also taken the precaution of giving the driver an extra shilling for his silence. It is normally a luxury to travel thus, but the covert nature of my journey had started to fray at my nerves.

I stared out of the window as we lurched and bumped across the potholes, the horses driving us through the narrow streets passing both hovel and mansion against the stench of the tanneries and open sewers, passing, too, small gatherings of men, many missing a leg or an arm, or whose faces had been blown into monstrous asymmetry. These returning soldiers, too maimed to fight or work, had become a silent force in the city, forgotten by Parliament, who squabbled amongst itself about the monetary compensation for these poor men.

And yet there was industry. We drove by a blacksmith, silhouetted in the doorway of his dwelling, the roaring hearth behind him, swinging his hammer with graceful rhythm down upon the anvil as he fashioned a blade – no doubt to be used by the young soldier slouching against a wall smoking a pipe, his makeshift uniform barely able to declare him of the New Model Army.

There were also the mingling pedlars, shouting their wares – jellied eels, chestnuts, pamphlets with the latest news, the vegetable stalls, and the fruit (much of which hath been grown in the small gardens of London herself, as most orchards have been raided by the armies both King's and People's) and the whores, one of which, when we were snared in traffic, pushed herself against the coach's window, offering herself to me. At Billingsgate I even saw an alehouse, obviously once of Royalist sympathy, renamed; a large black line had been struck through The Crown and Hart and the new name, God Encompasses Us, was scrawled beside it, indicating the faith of the new owner, likely a Freemason.

Those who had fled to fight the Royalist cause had had their property and businesses seized, power tipped up topsy-turvy. As the coach flew through the gathering night I wondered what protection I could offer Magdalene now – if any.

But Life turns, even at the End of Days. Mankind is an animal of habit, no matter what lies low on the horizon. In this thought I found comfort, and, regardless of my terrors, my excitement mounted with each travelled mile.

Finally, we turned into the parish of St Saviour. This was still the People's London, but twenty miles west was Royalist-held territory. There were open fields, now, some populated with the tents of the newly homeless, others with cows guarded closely, and you could see the wide sky, another great comfort to me, as I stared up through the carriage window, Venus in her red robes bouncing along the road with me as if to cast down her blessings.

The coach turned into Ploughman's Way, a broad street that, to my relief, did not, in the night, stink so much, with just a few pigs nonchalantly eating refuse alongside the dirt road. The house – a large brick mansion of quite recent construction – stood sandwiched between two others, an older cottage at the end of the lane. We pulled up, and I could see a figure at a top window peer out down at me behind a curtain. I stepped out of the coach, gave an extra farthing to the driver and told him to find a tavern and to return in two hours. I waited until he drove off before turning to knock upon the oak door.

*   *   *

'We are right happy to have our sister and her . . . friend . . . back within our midst, Master Lilly, and of course, your own honourable self. I know your work, sir. You are a cut above the rest, I told Mrs Jeffries, a cut above, none of yer when-to-plant-cabbages nonsense or how to beget sons or when the best time is to cross water, but good common sense and most accurate prediction of this King we 'ave all been suffering under.' Mr Jeffries, Rosie's brother-in-law, a cloth merchant virtually aglow in self-satisfaction, poured himself another glass of ale to the thin-lipped disapproval of his pinched wife. 'We ourselves are very good Puritans, but we also wish the Church reformed, and truly believe man is born equal in the eyes of the Lord and as such should be treated equally in both the right to own land and farm it. In fact, we have been reading the words of a Mr Richard Overton, a brave man not loved by Parliament.' I had indeed heard of the Leveller, Richard Overton, having had many an argument with my friend Harry Pickles about the renegade – as, most anxiously, I did not want my good friend to be imprisoned for the illegal publishing of the Leveller's philos-ophies, whose views seemed to me to advocate anarchy. And I would have argued the case now with Mr Jeffries if I had not been at his table, eating his stew, and my lady been at the mercy of his discretion; so instead I was forced to smile and nod.

We were sitting in a low room around a large table; the whole family were in attendance – Mr Jeffries at the head, as rotund as a glistening beached whale in his black robes, his pencil-stick wife beside him, and their four children, two daughters of six and eight, Hope and Charity, one as round as her father, the other as slim as her mother, and two boys – Honest and Labour – at ten and twelve years indifferent to their parents' argument, and busy scoffing the gruel before us.

I stole a glance at Magdalene. Clothed plainly in a black dress, every strand of her hair carefully covered by a cowl, she sat opposite me, Rosie beside her. We had not touched nor had a chance to exchange words, so keen were the Jeffries to make a formal impression upon this esteemed Philomath; all was jumping within me as I longed to touch her.

'Mr Jeffries . . .' Mrs Jeffries, her voice as thin as herself, interjected with a warning note, 'I'm sure the godly Master Lilly is not concerned with the humble views of a working man.'

'Not at all,' I interjected. 'Mistress Jeffries, I place the views of the working man highest of all. The Leveller Richard Overton is an interesting man, but I fear I tread a path betwixt the warring parties.'

''Tis a pity, Master Lilly, for I know Richard Overton hath a great respect for you, and that you are his most favourite Astrologer.'

'In that case, sir, he hath great judgement.' But I did not elaborate, for fear Mr Jeffries was trying me somehow; it was the habit in those days to ascertain where a man stood – in my opinion, usually on a thin plank over water – whatever he said or believed.

Mrs Jeffries, after glancing nervously at me, piped up, 'I think there is a lot to some of them more traditional almanacks. Why, my youngest sister got herself a very good match with an aged widower, most generous in form, no beard-splitter nor swill-belly, and that were following the instructions laid out in *Poor Robin's Almanack*.'

'The fornicator's handbook might be another title for it,' Mr Jeffries quipped and I liked him for it. At the comment, Rosie guffawed loudly as Mrs Jeffries feigned shock whilst Magdalene discreetly covered her laughter.

'Mr Jeffries, not in front of the children!' Mrs Jeffries scolded.

'The children know how whence they came to be. Besides, 'tis a gross insult to our guest to compare his great craft to such twaddle! Why, 'tis like comparing bear-baiting to Shakespeare!' he retorted, then turned to me. 'Forgive my wife. She is an ignorant but well-meaning woman. Mr Lilly here is quality, a pox on your *Poor Robin's!*'

'But Mr Jeffries, you should know I do not hate the King, I wish there to be peace,' I insisted.

'Aye, peace is all of our wishes, but what of those lads – our sons and brothers who have perished for an ideal? We must keep fighting, for the chance for all man in England to be able to stand tall and to be treated equally,' Mr Jeffries answered with the passion and conviction of a lay pastor, which, I warrant, he might have been.

'And what of Woman, is she not to stand equal too?' Magdalene now spoke out, her bearing and accent betraying her. I held my breath. It was then that I realised that family knew who she was – and they must also know how much they were risking by sheltering her.

Mr Jeffries glanced over at the young serving wench in the corner, who, not understanding, stared sullenly back. Suddenly there was nought in the room except the crackling of the fire-place and dogs barking somewhere on the meadow outside. Finally satisfied the serving wench knew nothing of the true identity of my lady, the master of the house swung back to the table.

'Well asked, Margaret, our-good-sister-in-faith,' Mr Jeffries said loudly and awkwardly in case the maidservant might not know who the suspiciously well-mannered guest was. 'Woman is equal in her humanity, but she is not equal in the powers of the mind nor body. She is a different creature in her entirety, not less but not equal,' he continued, avoiding the angry stare of his wife who clearly disagreed.

I reached under the table with my foot for Magdalene's, and thinking I had touched it I did caress it with my toes, but to my disconcertion Mrs Jeffries suddenly blushed and did give me a most coquettish glance. Shocked, I did withdraw my foot as if it were bitten. Meanwhile Magdalene's mettle was up.

'History, not God, will be the judge of that,' Magdalene snapped back and I did pray she would not argue with this man upon whose charity we now depended.

Ignoring the retort, Mr Jeffries addressed me. 'I have another son, Master Lilly, from my first wife. He is a soldier with Lieutenant Colonel Cromwell's regiment of cavalry. Perhaps I should visit you in your house upon the Strand and ask of his future? I fear for my boy. He is much loved.'

'Amen,' his wife whispered, as the other children shifted in their chairs uncomfortably.

'I will cast a horary for him tomorrow and at no charge, then I will send word.' At which, near tears, the good merchant grasped my hand across the table and Mrs Jeffries, to my further discomfort, did wink at me.

'Too kind sir, too kind,' Mr Jeffries sniffed.

'Not at all, I am glad to obliged.' I extracted my hand tactfully whilst Mrs Jeffries thrust a large, snot-smeared handkerchief toward her husband. 'And thank you for your hospitality and good fare,' I continued, 'but now I must have words with my good lady friend.'

I stood, with Magdalene by my side, leaving tearful Mr Jeffries a fluster and Mrs Jeffries blushing. Rosie turned to her sister.

'You 'eard what Master Lilly said: time to lend them your back parlour,' she told them plainly with a grin.

The parlour was darkened, the wooden shutters drawn, and the air musky with neglect. I suspected it were for the merchant's formal engagements before the war when there was cause for entertaining wealthy clients and impressing them with silk coverings and brass candelabra. I pushed the door shut behind us and drew the bolt, enclosing us in a dim light broken only by a sliver that crept under the door. I like this anonymity of darkness, I always have; it is as if in this eternal twilight man and woman becomes something far simpler, stripped of all that defines their standing.

I moved to touch her but she stayed my hand.

'I know you must be angry with me, William, to endanger us both this way.'

'You must have good reason.' My words stuck in my throat; I thought betrayal or a death at least to risk such exposure. So many people had been imprisoned or killed it had become an irreversible knowledge just to hear the words and I had become a coward in this way. 'Are we revealed?'

'Not yet, as far as I know.'

'So, who has died?'

'Two days ago I received news from Oxford, from a nun I knew there who heard it from Monsieur Vindecot who heard it from the Spanish Ambassador who is close to the Queen. Prepare yourself, William.'

At which I did sit.

'Cullum Monroe—'

'No.' I did not want to hear confirmed what I had seen in the youth's face so many months before.

'. . . was burnt at the stake in Cordova, after an auto-da-fé.'

'This cannot be!' The World tightened like a noose and I knew I had lost part of my future in that death. Covering my face, I caught my grief between my hands wherein it scratched and bit and tore. I had loved the youth.

'He was careless, and was betrayed. The Jesuit Inquisition had accused him of witchcraft.' Magdalene took my hand.

I looked across at her; she was without expression – she had lost too many people.

'This is dreadful news indeed.'

'There's more, William. He confessed under torture, telling of the Grand Council, naming names. The Inquisitor, a Jesuit with a good command of English – and also a ruthless politician – sensing barter with Protestant England, took notes. Most of the names were nonsense, the boy was delirious with pain by then, but our names were clear and he did repeat them. Vindecot will try and use the information as a tool to negotiate for Royalist prisoners.'

'If Hopkins should hear of this—'

'He must not! Or he must be made to think Vindecot has a hidden reason to want you and myself dead.'

'I must mislead him further.'

'And you must also endear yourself further in Parliament, make yourself their man entirely both in prediction and medical remedy. You are close to Bulstrode Whitelocke and he has influence . . .'

'I will try . . . What about the Grand Council?'

'They have already started their politicking: there is more power than you know behind those masks.'

Outside we heard the church bells ringing for the evening service.

'You will have to leave tonight, so we don't have long.' She moved toward me. 'This attire does not become me, William; it constrains more than a woman's natural inclination to express her femininity, it constrains the soul.' She slowly tugged the cowl from her head, the russet locks tumbling across her shoulders.

'You are beautiful anyway.' I pulled her to me, my hands running up under the coarse fabric of her heavy black skirt. To my delight, she was naked beneath.

'How do you like your chaste sister Margaret?' she asked softly.

'I like her a great deal . . .' After which I pulled her onto my knee and, loosing my hose, we did make love in that silence and sorrow, keeping our bliss mute for fear of being overheard, my hand over her mouth and her hand over mine, as, with most studied slowness, we did pleasure each other. There are many forms of Love as Venus herself could testify, the spiritual, the emotional and the physical; one is transported by all, and yet it is rare to be embraced by all three. So it was for Magdalene and I . . .

Afterwards we rearranged our clothes (as if wool and linen could conceal such transgressions). I lit a candle, the flame tinting Magdalene's face in gold and pinks reminding me of the portraits of saints by that good artist Rubens I had seen at Greenwich Palace.

'It is difficult to be apart from the Queen; there will always be an affection there despite our differences.' Magdalene's whispering brushed against cobwebs. 'This war and the hatred of her hath taken its toll, William – she plans to travel back to France.'

'She will abandon the King?'

'She means to drum up support from the Kings of France and Spain. She is not the woman you met three years ago.'

'But just as stubborn.'

'She has her beliefs and they lie in the hierarchy of monarchy. The King is anointed by God to rule, he is His representative. She cannot foresee another way of ruling. Just as in the matter of philosophy she abhors the notion of predestination and all that Calvin and Luther stood for; to brand the Pope as the anti-Christ is the greatest of insults and sins. She cannot see it in any other way.'

'And yourself?' I knew the answer, but perhaps I needed to hear the words, that she was a Catholic.

'I am tired of the running, the fighting, the debating. There is only one God. It now seems to me unimportant how we worship Him, only that we do. Belief should be enough. We are all Christians and, after that, Men.' She looked up at me, despite this sanguine stoicism there was a fear buried in those eyes; fear of discovery, fear of betrayal? I decided to ignore it.

'They say there are many thousands slaughtered and we are but two years at war.'

'The Royalists might win yet,' she ventured. 'The Queen loves her husband, but I fear he has disappointed her in this.'

I chose not to reply to this argument.

'I will take your advice; I will ingratiate myself with powerful allies in Parliament, and persuade Matthew Hopkins that Vindecot is merely intending to discredit good Puritans with his Popish and vile conspiracies. But you must trust me to advise you also.'

'Yet I am no man's wife now, and master of my own Fate.'

'Magdalene, neither Royalist nor Parliamentarian know whether you have fled the country or are in hiding. 'Tis better you stay here until I tell you it is safe to return to your house.'

'And how long will that be?'

'As long as it takes for me to throw our persecutors off the scent.' She smiled at me. 'But the heart has its own clock and will not run to self-imposed schedules.'

'Magdalene, there is no room for the slightest impropriety. Infidelity is now a hanging offence. This new London is a city ruled by both Saturn and Mars, full of men who police themselves as harshly as any zealous judge, who delight in destroying the reputation of their neighbour, justified or not, who compete to prove themselves the most pious, who will cut the head off a man for dancing on a Sunday. You embody everything the Puritan loathes – you are the child of French aristocrats, indulgent, decadent, of Popish descent. All this you must be seen to abandon if you are to survive, and sweet Megs, I wish us both to live.'

She pulled on her cowl and went to the window where, lifting back the curtain, she glanced out at the night beyond.

'The full moon was yesterday,' she told me without turning.

On the journey home I thought deeply about Magdalene's stratagem. It was true that my political influence was growing, thanks to my patron Bulstrode Whitelocke, whilst at the same time my secret efforts had not gone amiss amongst the Royalists in Oxford. I was gaining a reputation as a fair and levelheaded advisor who could be bipartisan in his judgements. But persuading the fanatic Matthew Hopkins of Magdalene's innocence was going to be far more challenging. As the coach bumped and swayed across the road I decided that Vindecot himself must be made the weak link. If I could only find a way of illustrating that the French diplomat and spy was himself involved in sorcery and had fabricated the story to discredit myself and Magdalene, and in doing so, Parliamentarian England. Only then might I be able save Magdalene's life and my own standing.

When I had returned to the Strand, my wife was at the door, her forehead ploughed with a particular anger, her lips shrivelled in that pursed manner I found most chastising. She held a letter in her hand which she waved at me as if it were a rail of rotten fish.

'What's this, William? A declaration of love in a feminine hand, found in your own desk!'

My heart jumped. Had I left some incriminating evidence out upon my desk? I peered at the envelope; it was not of Magdalene's hand and I knew who had brought it to me.

'I can explain—'

'Explain it to the court! I will have you branded as adulterer, and that is both a mortal sin and a great hypocrisy in one who doth give advice in matters both of matrimony and of the heart..'

'In which case, Madam, you would have no income or livelihood. For you might recall your dowry was far less than you and your relatives had me believe.'

'How dare you!'

'And how dare you accuse me! The letter was brought to me by a Querent, a young woman who suspected her betrothed – a William Stewart – of courting another, hence the written address *Dear William*. The letter she found in his waistcoat pocket and brought to me to assess the handwriting and the nature of her love rival. Nothing more, nothing less.' This was the actual truth, but Jane's accusation had shaken me greatly. She stared at me, eyes pinholes of fury no lighthouse could rival.

'You think me a fool?' She spat rather than spoke.

'I think you a most pious woman who exasperates her husband with suspicion and a grievous lack of faith both in his craft and in his professional demeanour. You are no asset in this marriage, but there it is, we are united at hip and heart, until death decides to free one of us.' As you can see, dear Reader, I spoke brutally, but marriage is a game of chess and, in this instance, I was forced to gain the superior position.

'I will believe you this time, but from now on you are barred from my bed,' she announced, then turned on her heel in the most imperious manner and was gone. I sighed – this was the third time this year she hath banned me and in truth I could see some convenience in this arrangement.

The very next day, the thirtieth of November, Fortune threw an opportunity in my path that was to prove my saving. It came in the manifestation on my doorstep of a wealthy merchant, advertising his devotion in Puritan black, whilst betraying his wealth in the quality of the fine white lace, the singular decoration about his appearance.

I saw straightway he was greatly troubled.

'Please, dismiss your housekeeper and other servants – this meeting is to have never happened,' the merchant instructed me and, uncharacteristically, I acquiesced as I could see he was on government business and not an official to argue with if one valued one's head and future commerce.

The gentleman placed himself squarely in the centre of my study and examined me for a good minute; I did not flinch.

'Master Lilly, you have a great admirer in Bulstrode Whitelocke,' (by my Lord, his voice was as booming and deep as a viola da gamba) 'a man much loved and respected by Parliament, and it is on his recommendation, and his alone, that I stand before you, a reluctant Querent, but a good Puritan, and it is on behalf of a great advocator of our cause that I am here.' Now his expression was exceedingly solemn and I did steel myself for the possibility he bore a most ominous query. I laid mine hand upon his arm, in both trust and truce.

'I understand; rest assured I am a Philomath of utmost discretion.'

Reassured, the Merchant began to stride about the room.

'I have come straight from the leader John Pym's house and on behalf of Westminster itself. We are greatly concerned for our friend and patron who has been taken grievously ill.' At which he produced from the depths of his cape a small flask filled with the dark amber of a man's urine – undoubtedly of the patient's.

In sober dignity, he handed it to me. And I did think upon that day I witnessed the King in Parliament attempting to hunt down this very leader.

'Tell me, good Master Lilly, is John Pym to live or to die? The fortunes of Parliament in war could depend on this. And, if he is to die, when?'

I immediately took note of the exact time and the position of the stars, for this be the ancient methodology of horary in health questions and in the diagnosis of urine. I care not when the fluid was passed, or when it was taken out of the house of the patient, but only when it and the question is presented to me.

'I am honoured to undertake such a commission; I am a great supporter of John Pym. Tell me, is he able to walk, eat or pass anything except his water?' I asked the gentleman, whose agitation had only grown stronger at the wait.

'No, he cannot. He is confined to his bed and is in much pain in his stomach. He does not know we have brought this to you.'

'And he will never know,' I promised, although by looking at the colour of the politician's urine it was apparent his health was grave. I began my calculations immediately. 'I understand the urgency of the query, and can have an answer for you in a very short time.'

'In that case I will wait; there is a coach and horse outside that can take me straight to Parliament with the verdict.'

After which the gentleman settled himself upon a chair outside my study whilst I began to draw up a figure. As Pym's ailment lay in the stomach I looked for the position of the ruler of the zodiac sign Cancer – the Moon, as Cancer ruled the stomach – searching for where the Moon had moved to in the last few days and where it was moving to in the near future.

To my horror, I saw that only twelve hours ago it had been conjoined by both Mars and the evil star Antares – whose very presence indicated great sickness and possible death. John Pym had been taken ill the day before so this was an undeniable logic. I then looked to where the Moon might be moving to calculate a possible time of death. Naturally, I examined the eighth house (which is considered the house of death) to see which sign was currently (at the time of the question) situated in the eighth house. It was Aquarius ruled by Saturn. I then drew out a trajectory – the Moon would take eight days to find itself next to Saturn and therefore I concluded John Pym would die in eight days, which, coincidentally, would be on the eighth of December 1643.

It was a grim and saddening judgement, and I paused, contemplating the implications. Such a death would change the course of this war; Pym was mightily active in the raising of funds for Parliament as well as providing a great figurehead but I had no choice but to be the messenger as the fatal judgement was written in the stars.

However, to the amateur Philomath I advise 'tis best to mention not great evil to happen to any prince, only some danger of it. This is sanguine advice, as there might be other circumstances to change a verdict – with foreknowledge a man can take some precaution to avoid travel, say if in his Nativity he hath a vulnerability in the house of travel (a placement of Antares in the eighth house).

Nevertheless, there have been many cases in history where men have tried to cheat an Astrologer's prediction on his time of death and failed. The most famous being the Italian Philosopher, Magician and Cabbalist Pico della Mirandola – whose *Disputations Against Divinatory Astrology* is much cited and feted. However, it must be noted Pico's own death was predicted by three Astrologers to be before his 33rd year, and sadly, the Philosopher did die in his thirty-second year of life regardless of the disputations he wrote in a desperate wrath, hoping by doing so he might live a full life.

Even the great master Nostradamus predicted his own death with great accuracy. I, myself, am most nervous for the year of 1647 as I have great vulnerability in my own Nativity.

So it was with these grim examples foremost in my mind I did deliver my verdict. This is the burden of the Philomath: to tell of what we see in a manner that is never entirely without hope; to live with such foresight is another matter and oft taints my working day – in this my Christian belief is my salvation.

And on the eighth of December, as my horary figure had forecast, John Pym did die and all of Parliamentarian England grieved to see a good soul taken so soon, none more than myself. And as a true and reliable Philomath, I am now greatly popular with the Politicians of this city. All this will prove most useful in my strategy to discredit Monsieur Vindecot's information and dissuade others of the truth of poor Cullum Monroe's forced confession, but I grieved for poor John Pym.

Frost has stripped the trees and citizens had taken to eating the geese, waterfowl and other beasts they could hunt in the grand forests like Richmond. There is little bread and all silver plate from households both Royalist and Parliament hath now been taken to pay for this endless war – we all eat off slate and wood.

The goodly John Pym was buried and I heard that Lady Lucy Hay, his mistress, was much distressed, and yet Parliament survived. Daily we heard of the triumphs and cool determination of Colonel Cromwell and his New Model Army. I took a cautious temper in this. It seemed to me that this time belonged to such men of uncompromising inhumanity – the Prince Ruperts and the Colonel Cromwells of our era – men who will slaughter for an ideal.

I was not this man.

CHAPTER TWENTY-TWO

⚥ ♂ ♂

The first months of that most war-like year 1644
The Corner House, The Strand

The Second House: From this house is required
judgement concerning the estate or fortune of him that
asks the question, of his wealth or poverty, of all movable
goods, money lent, of profit or gain, loss or damage; in
suits of law, it signifies a man's friends or assistants; in
private duels, the Querent's second; in an Eclipse or
Great Conjunction, the poverty or wealth of the people.

This year did begin in the most energetic of manners — a
frenzy of both the politick and of battle. Methinks Mars did
favour this year for his bloody struggles. On the twenty-
second of January the King did summon those members of
the Long parliament that did support him to Oxford to set up
a mirror parliament that would serve both him and his
Royalist strategies. I have heard that the eighty-two peers and
a good third of the commoners from the House did appear at
the Christ Church hall. I found this most disturbing and
disrespectful of the Parliament that sat in Westminster and
was of the People.

Only three days later there was a battle at Nantwich. The
Royalists lead by Lord Bryon were in the act of besieging that
fair town when the Parliamentarians, with Sir Thomas Fairfax

riding at their head, appeared to save those brave citizens within. As Fairfax and his men approached, the freezing weather did thaw most suddenly and the snow and ice did as water rush into the River Weaver causing it to rise – leaving Lord Bryon and his cavalry on one bank and his foot soldiers and guns upon the other. Naturally Sir Fairfax did exploit this situation and the Royalists were defeated. If ever there was an act of God I would hazard that this sudden thawing was such, and that (as I had predicted), both He and the Stars are with Cromwell. I believe this had prevented the King from forming an army in the North-West, and no amount of Catholic Irish he doth bring over the sea shall change this. This is a great weakness indeed.

I was to church now, at least twice a day, where I prayed for both King and Parliament and hope the two will be reunited. I talked to my God, for I could now see that I alone will have to show how, as a Philomath, my art serves Him, and is a Christian Astrology, not a demoniac evil nor a sorcery to malefic purpose.

Increasingly I thought upon this paradox. I did discuss it with my good friend and pastor, Hugh Peter, who was most political, and like me, no hater of the King, and even at the Grand Council of Theurgy, for increasingly the country ran rife with stories of witches, the summoning of Satan himself in the service of something or other, as more and more Englishmen found fault with Englishmen whether it was their politick, their religious beliefs, or county of birth. 'Tis easy to hate, methinks, and Man hath a great fear of that which he doth not see: the invisible, the spiritual and the mysterious. This was an ignorance ambitious men like Matthew Hopkins exploited; and despite the misinformation I fed him, his influence grew like a canker.

I found my sanctuary in church. There was an organist there through whose music my soul escaped the growing rattle of despair. Often, sitting there at the end of a sermon, my knees hard against the wooden pews, my mind soared up with the notes as they wheeled and swooped amid the gilded saints and coloured glass like a flock of swallows drunk with Spring. This meditation was the only respite from my labours, of which I was most vigorous, having now almost completed my first almanack for 1644.

I had been galvanised out of anger at the inadequacies of my fellow Astrologers – primarily George Wharton now publishing under the name of Na'worth, who fought for the King through his own almanacks and through the Royalist newspaper *Mercurius Elencticus* and also John Booker, Wharton's rival and my good friend. Despite the fact that they were both members of the Grand Council of Theurgy, they were children, tilting at each other with blunt wooden spears and did both the English public and the profession a great disservice with their bad craft. They went to war – in insults and on the page. George Wharton hath accused John Booker of being traitor and of taking the meaning of 'a man of three letters' – as Rex (King) – where in fact it were John Pym, whose demise he himself had predicted (or so he claims). Wharton twists all planetary aspects to serve the King, whilst John Booker was little better, and it had been his almanack of this year, which mentioned *Cave ab homine trium literarum* predicting the King's downfall and denouncing the Irish rebellion. John had given these predictions in Latin and from ancient and Arabic sources – thus removed the reading from the ordinary man. But I wanted to improve upon these paltry offerings; I wanted to give such future prophesying back to the ordinary man and write in plain English, but also with intelligence and not with the quackery or hysteria of the penny pamphlets popular on the street. Until then I had remained silent in this very public of arenas, but in the New Year I was determined to roar.

A few nights later I was hurrying back from an evening sermon at St Antholin's. Hugging the shadows I had a dagger for protection in my belt and was careful of my presence. After some time I became aware that there was a man trailing behind. Aware it might be one of Hopkins' henchmen or Thurloe's fingermen, possibly having now been told of Cullum's confession, I slipped my hand into my jerkin and my hand tightened on the knife. Peering into the half-light, I could see that the streets were empty, except for a beggar asleep against a barrel outside a bawdy house. If I were to be murdered there would be no witnesses.

I turned into a narrow lane near the house, but the footsteps behind me continued echoing across the cobbles. I ducked into a doorway, and waited. The footsteps slowed as the man, puzzled, seemed to look for me. As he took faltering steps past the doorway I grabbed him.

'Who art thou! And who is thy master?'

I pulled the hood off his face. To my amazement it were Tobias, aged and much begrimed, but the actor nevertheless.

'Master Lilly! Forgive me, I have just arrived back from Basing House and am in need of a roof and bed.'

'Toby! I mistook you for a villain! Come, of course I will give thee a roof – and bath I warrant, for you do stink!'

'The goodly honest stink of the exile, my friend, for I left Basing House four days and nights ago and have been sleeping in ditches since.'

'Why such a sudden departure?'

'I had a patron of whom I was most fond, endowed with a fortune and a comely young wife; he was to war, like many at court, his wife sad, a withering lily in her loneliness, so naturally . . .'

'You provided a much needed . . .'

'And appreciated service!'

The night-soil cart trundled past trailing a stench, the whistling night-soil man tipping his cap at us. Just then three drunken bargemen turned into the lane, two of them ill-humoured and evil-livered jostling each other whilst the other made water against the wall. I was suddenly thankful for Tobias's company and humour. The actor continued his prattle. 'Alas, when the husband came back to Oxford he was not so appreciative of my services. In fact he hath placed a modest sum upon mine head – in truth, a little too modest, I am certain my demise might be worth more. But these are hard times . . .'

'Indeed, a famed and celebrated performer such as thyself is surely worth at least fifty ducats. And so you fled?'

'I am safer in this Puritan city where the women, in this new-fangled plain garb, are as enticing as donkeys.'

As we walked on, it occurred to me that Tobias's reappearance might be fortuitous indeed. 'Tobias, I believe I might be in need of your services in a vital deception, but it will require courage.'

'Fear not friend, my valour as a man is pitiful but as an actor playing a role it is as great as Hercules, particularly after a bath, a hearty meal and a good sleep.'

'And so it will be, Tobias, so it will be.'

The next day I called a meeting of the Grand Council of Theurgy, homing pigeons having scattered the messages to the individuals North, South, East and West and not just within the confines of London. The place to which I called the members was unusual, secrecy now being of most utmost importance if we were to survive.

I confess, dear Reader, I had moral qualms about the false vignette I had devised to befuddle and mislead any pursuers, but in times of war and great persecution necessity hath no limitation – so I had called my fellow Philomaths and Occultists to a wake, to be held in a hall of a Puritan church I knew well. The advantages being, firstly, the hall hath a door that could be locked and few windows too high to be looked through, and secondly, I concluded the last place a hawk looks for prey is in its own nest. In this I had to be most precise in my instructions to my fellow Philomaths (written in tiny Latin bound about the passenger pigeon's leg) *dress as if attending the funeral of a close friend in the Puritan manner.*

As the rector of this church hall was a close friend I had no problem securing it and I did explain that the deceased was a recently impoverished gentleman and I was providing the means for his friends and family to grieve in dignity so I would require the utmost discretion. Naturally, after being given a godly sum of money, the rector was most happy to comply and had the sense to stay mute upon the subject.

The corpse was set in a coffin upon a table in the centre of the hall. I had left it open to appear more authentic if we were raided. The elderly man laid out in display (in rather fine clothes I had purchased at cost from a war widow) was the cadaver of a dead street pedlar I had borrowed from an anatomist with the proviso it was to be returned the next morning.

There were black curtains across the two high windows to signify a wake and to doubly ensure it was impossible to see in from outside. Four large wax candles flickered in each corner of the hall, making the dim light sombre and grand. A single lily (I could not resist the ironic symbolism) lay upon his chest between his hands – placed in the prayer position by myself.

I was on my knees praying (in truth for forgiveness for committing such a travesty) at the head of the coffin when I heard the first of the 'mourners' enter the hall and I did pull down my own mask of the Raven. I turned to see the Bull standing at the other end of the coffin.

"Tis a very grave and sad occasion,' he said without a trace of mirth. 'I presume our dear friend died of exasperation at the state of the nation. I know I could,' he concluded then took his seat. Within minutes, fifteen of the nineteen chairs I had placed about the coffin were filled. The Bull, the Dove, the Peacock, the Horse, the Dragon and several others I confess I did not know the identity of, but when Magdalene walked in wearing her Fox's mask I confess I struggled to keep my composure.

When all the places were finally filled I stood. 'You must forgive the extremes I have gone to, to conceal the true nature of this gathering.'

'I forgive you, but not the stiffness of this damned Puritan collar!' the Frog, my old client Jonas Moore and a confirmed Royalist, jested.

'Still, 'tis genius, methinks,' Hamish McDuff, in his Horse mask, retorted. 'The last place to look for an ant is in a wasp's nest.'

'We are all in great danger, graver than before, of this there is no doubt.' The Bull (John Booker) was solemn in tone.

'Cullum Monroe betrayed us! He should have died in silence!' Hamish insisted. 'Others, braver, have before.' And it was as if he'd conjured up poor Harry Goldsworthy, and that it was his tortured corpse lying before us, and not some anonymous tramp.

'Only two were named.' The Dove's trembling voice, Lady Eleanor Davies, sounded out, and all eyes fell upon Magdalene and myself.

'But the Council's existence was verified and that places all of us in danger.' Magdalene was defiant.

'The question is whether the French diplomat Vindecot will be believed?' Henry Gellibrand — ever rational — spoke as the Dragon.

'I can make sure that he isn't.' Now all turned to me. 'But it will require a great act of artifice, the manner of illusion that only we, as a collective, are capable of.'

'What exactly is your stratagem?' Henry asked.

'Instead of waiting like rabbits in traps for the city guards to smash down our doors, I will go to Nathaniel Bacon and John Thurloe, perhaps even Hopkins, and tell them a French Querent of mine hath visited me to warn me of a conspiracy by a secret Occultist and Royalist who plans to divide good Puritan, create distrust and chaos amongst the Parliamentarians by claiming there are certain Witches and Wizards amongst them where in truth it is the very same secret Occultist – a Monsieur Vindecot – who is the true Wizard.'

'But will they believe you?' Lady Davies was unconvinced.

'They will, after I have shown them the secret altar he hath dedicated to Satan in his house—'

'Which is boarded up and in Bloomsbury! Why, I have dined there myself before the war,' the Peacock, George Wharton, exclaimed excitedly.

'. . . filled with all manner of alchemy and Demon apparatus,' I concluded.

'It could work.' Hamish finally broke the silence that followed.

'And I can help,' the Frog, Jonas Moore offered. 'I inherited Vindecot's gardener after the diplomat fled to Oxford. The man has no love for his previous employer, but he is attractive to the ladies, and, if I remember correctly, was in much favour with Vindecot's housekeeper.' But again I found myself wondering, knowing his Royalist sympathies, if Moore was entirely trustworthy. Jonas, intuitive that he was, read my fears. He leant forward and placed his hand upon my arm.

'My friend and mentor, the safety of the Council is far beyond the matter of the politick. In me you must have trust,' he told me in a low voice, unheard by the others before we were interrupted by Magdalene.

'Excellent. This will allow us a manner of entry, perhaps.' A smile showed below her mask.

'I think perhaps the appearance of a Demon or two during the inspection could close the deal.' The Bull was wry.

'And I know the Demon personally, a very competent and trustworthy Thespian who is greatly indebted to me.' I offered.

'When do you intend to carry out this plan?' The Peacock was cold in voice — George Wharton, as the most powerful Royalist amidst us, had the most to lose. 'I am assuming you will also throw the scent off any idea Vindecot, or for that matter Hopkins, has that there might be members of the Grand Council within the Court at Oxford.'

'Naturally. As soon as the Council has given its permission and we have created this secret chamber that will be the undoing of the Frenchman, and the misdirection of Hopkins — trust me, I shall have him heading down the wrong road entirely.'

'Then I propose we vote on this immediately for we will need to act. I fear we have little time to save ourselves. All those who agree please raise their hands?'

I glanced about me and was most pleased to see that the Ayes had it.

'It is decided then, and now, Lilly, for the sake of this poor man's soul let's ensure he is buried quickly and with our gratitude,' the Bull concluded the meeting, after which the door was unlocked and the mourners of this fictitious gentleman left, most diminished in sorrow.

Meanwhile, in the Corner House there is a new levity. Tobias will be staying for a whole month and is paying me in service both as my assistant and in cheering my wife — faith, Jane has even begun to wear ribbons in her hair! The actor hath seduced her by playing the pious disciple and has even been persuaded to accompany her to her Quaker meetings, thus leaving my evenings to my own devices; I am much indebted.

*　　*　　*

It was only four days later that I found myself standing in the entrance hall of Vindecot's shuttered dwelling. We had broken the barred door and were standing in the entrance hall in near total darkness, our nostrils affronted by the musky smell of stale air and old perfumes.

I had, of course, already entered the house with Vindecot's own gardener who, for a bribe, had seduced his housekeeper into giving him a key, and with Tobias's assistance had dressed it for the occasion.

Matthew Hopkins appeared dressed for battle, although what battle I could not say, except there were penny amulets about his neck and a clove of garlic hanging from his hat. The shipping clerk stood beside me, inhaling sharply as if buttoning down his fear. I had primed him well for the appearances of Demons and witchery most insidious and evil – a well-planned attack upon the moral and spiritual soul of Puritanism itself. Accordingly, he had come with two soldiers of the government and his own assistant John Stearne, armed with pikes and daggers. To what end I did not know, as spirits cannot be defended with such weapons. After warning them, in the most dramatic of manners, not to move too fast for fear of disturbing any supernatural presence still hanging in the ether (at which the taller of the soldiers crossed himself) I did light a candle, the flare of the flame revealing the extravagance of our surrounds.

The walls were hung with ornate tapestries and the untouched décor suggested that the spy had left for Oxford in a hurry, for many of his possessions were still in place, this being the sinister ambience Tobias had striven for. Plates of both gold and silver sat upon a long table with crystal goblets set as if awaiting invisible diners, one still half-full of wine, another tipped onto its side as if a guest had fled without warning. In the centre sat a bowl full of rotting fruit: an apple, a quince and a fruit of the East, a pomegranate, the red seeds spilling out onto the marble top. I placed the candlestick upon the table and, after picking up the pomegranate, held it aloof.

'I am sure a learned man like yourself, Mr Hopkins, is aware of the symbolism of this devil fruit and its links to the Underground, the ancient Hades us Christians more commonly call Hell?'

At which Hopkins nodded most vigorously.

'Each seed the trapped Persephone ate kept her trapped in Hades a month longer – as you can see the fruit is half eaten.' I elaborated dramatically.

'I suppose one could describe besieged Oxford as a kind of Hell, but I hardly think the table setting suggests anything except that Monsieur Vindecot has a taste for exotic fruit and left hastily. In fact, the whole place reminds me of a plague house – are we certain there is no disease lurking here?' Hopkins' fear made him as snappy as a terrier.

'Only the disease of the soul and spirit,' I replied whilst removing a rod cut from hazel wood from my bag.

'What device is this now, Master Lilly? I have not seen such a thing in the *Malleus Maleficarum*, nor in any of the lowlands literature on witch-hunting?'

'Tis a dividing rod for the detection of treasure but, in this case, will lead us to places wherein evil vapours still linger as a result of communion with the Devil and other unholy acts.' (May all great Occultists forgive me for such nonsense and foppery!)

'Most unorthodox, but then you are the maestro, Master Lilly – lead on.'

And so we began exploring the house in a faltering line, myself at the head with hazel rod in one hand, twitching it most dramatically when I thought my companions lessen in their terror.

The spill of the candlelight travelled across the walls and ceilings like a cat's eye, illuminating the wooden panels of the corridor, the carved heads of gargoyles and other grimacing beasts staring down at us above each doorway as if to ward off a great passing evil that might have walked these hallways, the rug beneath my feet as thick and soft as spring grass.

The first chamber we arrived at was a place of study. The walls were lined with books and there was a map inked on a goatskin hanging from a frame in the corner – it appeared to be of France, the Spanish Netherlands and Germania. On the other side of the chamber a Moorish desk sat open, with a scroll curled out upon it. One end held by the weight of a cat's skull on one side and a horseshoe on the other. The scroll was one of mine own, planted earlier by Tobias and myself – a text in Latin by an ancient mystic describing a ceremony to summon a Demon to provoke revenge, it hath wonderful illustrations and I had left the page open at the eating of an upside-down monk by four-tailed sprites in great relish. In great solemnity I did twitch my rod faithfully toward the desk with the three other men in greater and greater anticipation tiptoeing behind me.

'Methinks this is of grave matter,' I whispered to Hopkins, who, like a fish swallowing bait, did take the candlestick from me to peer down at the ornate lettering and drawing.

'This is profanity indeed!' He pulled his henchman, John Stearne, toward the desk. 'Observe, John, the agony upon the martyr's face and the two toes upon the feet of these Demons. The tail is familiar to us, Master Lilly, we have seen evidence of such tails upon some of the women we have in custody.' At which I nodded vigorously in agreement before moving toward the desk. The chair was pushed away from it, but a velvet robe, edged with ermine (borrowed from Tobias's thespian wardrobe), was flung across it, as if the venerable author of the scroll had just stepped away – another device of Tobias and myself.

'Look, he must have rushed from this very desk to flee London with the King, taking with him the unholy and Popish conspiracies he no doubt means to inflict upon the Puritan!' I exclaimed, whilst Hopkins looked on most gravely.

In the corner, a domed looking glass of the Dutch kind reflected back a facsimile of this farce and I was secretly ashamed seeing the four of us, candlelight glinting off the soldiers' helmets, the elongation of our faces and beards, the wide, white-eyed fear of my companions ... we looked like flies trapped in a web which I was spinning to save Magdalene, myself, and all others of the Grand Council, a web that could either liberate or condemn.

'He must be a powerful Magus indeed, this Frenchman,' John Stearne murmured as if it was dangerous to speak too loudly.

'He is, and there is worse to see. Prepare yourselves,' I told them and moved into the bedchamber. There was a lute in the corner resting against the wall, giving the impression the player had just finished his recital then stepped away; this had been very strategically placed by Tobias, but I shall speak of that later. A tapestry of a dwarf wearing the emblem of some unknown Frankish Monarch leading a unicorn out of a forest was hung opposite the four-poster bed draped with embroidered silks, and covered with furs, a large chest painted with a multitude of symbols at the foot of it. I stood at the door and held the hazel rod up high in the air, shaking it and making all manner of sighing and dramatic exclamation.

'There is evil here, I sense it too!' Hopkins announced as the three others watched the end of my hazel rod with great fascination as it twitched and drew me closer and closer to the chest. Finally, the rod came to rest upon the carved top.

Just then several eerie notes sounded from the unmanned lute, a marvellous device Tobias had 'borrowed' made for a production of *A Midsummer Night's Dream* in which Titania is serenaded by invisible angels. The music made my companions jump out of their skins and both guards draw their weapons. It was most satisfying.

'What Demon was that!' Hopkins had shrunk back against the wall.

'Methinks spirits disturbed by our intrusion, but we are made of stronger stuff and will not be cowed.' I stood over the chest. 'Master Hopkins, would you do the honour? A pure soul such as thyself will not be harmed in the opening of the casket, regardless of the evils it might contain.' At which to my secret pleasure, this fearless witch-hunter did pale.

'Methinks John is better suited to the task – why, he was only in church some three hours ago,' Hopkins whimpered.

'Only to fetch my wife . . .' John Stearne looked just as frightened.

'John, open the casket!' Hopkins commanded.

Reluctantly John Stearne knelt and slowly opened the lid. Immediately a couple of bats that had been trapped within for a good day flew out zigzagging in dire confusion as the invincible John Stearne collapsed in horror.

'Easy lads! Such things must be approached with great caution else thy soul will be stolen! I myself am wearing a Sigil to protect myself and shall explain the objects within.' And with a great act of learned concern I began to point at the various ornaments that surrounded the makeshift altar within which I had decorated with objects of goetia – black magick.

The skull of a goat's head sat on a violated Bible, bound to it with a twine made from human hair. Painted in chicken blood upon the inside of the top of the chest was a spell I had composed in ancient Hebrew – total nonsense, but I had peppered it with key words in Latin I knew Hopkins would be able to read: *Diaboli, mortem, et Puritan* and the like. 'See here, the word of

God upside and reversed to take on evil meaning. 'Tis a great Sorcerer, most skilled to sacrifice a goat and drench the holy word in its blood,' I elaborated solemnly.

The informed zealot nodded vigorously. 'Indeed, I have read this in the *Malleus Maleficarum* and this incantation written upon the lid is an unholy declaration of spiritual and most wicked magick upon the good Puritan!' To emphasis his point he kissed his crucifix, the others following piously.

'This turncoat Popish Demon-worshipper means to set doubt and dispute amongst good Puritans such as ourselves, so that we destroy ourselves, do you not see, Master Hopkins?' Seizing the moment I clarified most precisely. 'There are some this Wizard Vindecot hath named falsely as evil worshippers as part of this most wicked of plans. I fear my own good name might be amongst them.'

'Not you, Master Lilly, surely not! You are a leader in the fight against this moral corruption, an exemplary example of the good Philomath!'

'I thank thee for thy kind words. You must never forget I am a *Christian* Astrologer and I serve the word of God, but I fear there are other good men and women this — Judas — has named. Beware, Mr Hopkins, you do not fall into his trap of divide and conquer.' Then I did pretend that I had seen from the corner of my eye something hidden within the pages of the Bible. Delicately, as if handling poison, or some truly foul object, I pulled it free. It were a pamphlet, an announcement from Nathaniel Bacon describing his intention to root out all unchristian conspirators and devil worshippers and that he was declaring Matthew Hopkins the Witchfinder-General. The names of the men were painted over in blood. Hopkins stared down in horror. 'I too have been named,' he declared, close to a faint, then pulled the pamphlet from my hand and tore it in half. 'I swear, William Lilly, if this French

Wizard dare stray from Oxford but once I shall see him burn!'

'I am much relieved, sir, much relieved.' Which indeed did I was.

That evening in the White Hart with my friends John Scott, Harry Pickles and William Pool, amid great merriment we did celebrate and congratulate Tobias Young on his astounding theatrical skill. Outside in the square there was a bear baiting and I did place a whole sovereign upon the mastiff who I thought would win the fray. He was called Fairfax and the bear Charlie Rex. In truth, the bear was old, his shanks skinny and his fur mangy. It were an ill-matched fight, but winning I did double my money and later spent it upon sack: the best lubrication for friendship between men. Later (intoxicated, I confess) I did send word to Magdalene telling her it was now safe to return to her own house.

Outside the cold intensifies; inside the heart becomes petrified with a clenching dread. Yesterday as I walked the dawn to church I saw a young mother and her three children in rags sleeping behind the rigging of an old ship along the River's bank. The whole family were curled up like bleached driftwood, starving in the bone-white corners of their flesh, the babe's reddish-gold wisps of hair against her mother's vein-knotted neck. The woman, not more than seventeen years of age, I wager, was undoubtedly a young war widow without income and shelter.

This could have been the Nativity without Joseph or the striking down of some innocent pastoral nymph and winged cupids, for no man or father was there. Struck by the harsh beauty I stopped and stared, thinking them dead. Both guilt and a secret thankfulness that I was not them had me fastened to the cobblestones and I did lean down to place two sovereigns in the pocket of the woman. 'Twas only when I saw the breath rise and fall in the young mother's bosom could I walk on, chastened by their hardship.

This was London, and at every corner it hath made us indifferent in our charity. This city, nay, this country, was now full of such shifting tragedies. Poor Mrs Featherwaite was forced to lodge one of her three sisters, a soldier's widow, and her four children, and has taken to saving the turnip peelings and other scraps. My housekeeper did not complain, instead grew more in her conviction that the King was not the representation of God and that there was a better society to be found through Parliament and the practice of a democracy that has all men equal with no crown. I did then wonder whether the cantankerous woman will turn Leveller on me, or worst Ranter – and, if so, I intended to hold Jane responsible for this. At this time, my wife had fallen under the influence of John Lilburne, leader of the Levellers, and hath taken to the avocation that a man hath free will under God and therefore can choose his own destiny, the same for King or peasant. We differed on this and our arguments could be heard throughout the house. I feared the Leveller would lead this country and its good people into anarchy; a man needs a head just as a country needs a leader. Jane (she has her Gemini in Mars and is most given to quarrelling) did believe that even the common man, given his freedom and land, is capable of self-governance. Methinks she gives voice to any blasphemy just to annoy me and challenge my vocation. Today we exchanged not a single word and I held all my wit and essence for my mistress alone.

Meanwhile, there was no firewood to be had, not in the fields, the markets, nor in the streets. Jane found a hawker who had sold us burning peat – it made heat, but filled the house with a nasty smoke. The winter is now the coldest I could remember, so cold that one of the bells of St Thomas the Apostle cracked and failed to peal evensong. And – as in a fit of zeal the very altar rails had been pulled from the building by the Puritans for being idolatrous only three years before – this was seen as an Omen sent from God for many parishioners had secretly tired of the destruction of Holy objects most beauteous. I confess I did nothing to dispel the rumour.

The weather worsens; every day the street sweeper finds another frozen corpse. Some are Catholics who have lost their homes in this most judgemental of cities, others injured soldiers who had no work except to beg. I sent some peat to Magdalene's house, fearing she would freeze to death once she had no jewels left to sell. No message came back, yet I dared not walk over there myself for Jane watches me like a hovering hawk.

This morning I was woken by Roundheads breaking down the door of a neighbour's house looking for a Catholic cook. The blue-gilled master and his mistress shivered in their nightshirts, bare feet in the mud, whilst cropped-haired youths broke windows in a sullen violence. It were a pitiful sight, but none of the street including myself dared stand up against pike and zealot. I was disgusted with myself and, determined to pay penance for my moral apathy, I was to church, only to discover Parliament hath banned the playing of the organ and hath ordered the instrument to be destroyed in all the churches of London. I was most aggrieved. I watched as my beloved box of song was taken out of the building and smashed up as if it were the golden calf itself. If this be the enemy of the true faith, God help us when the barbarians are really at the gate!! Oh, why have I not heard from Magdalene yet?

CHAPTER TWENTY-THREE

♈ ⚭ ♀

The month of March and the rest of Spring 1644

An old river warehouse, most secret, East of the City

The Third House: Hath signification òf Brethren, Sisters,
Cozens and Kindred, Neighbours, small Journeys,
or inland-Journeys, oft removing from one place to
another, Epistles, Letters, Rumours, Messengers: It
doth rule the Shoulders, Armes, Hands and Fingers.

'You might have persuaded Hopkins that the French spy
Vindecot's information was false, but he still continues his
campaign. He hath now accused six women of witchcraft and
declares they have tried to kill him in Manningtree – this
"Witchfinder-General" has the blessing of Parliament, Colonel
Cromwell, and the Council of the Eastern Counties. This is a
grave development that continues to threaten us all!' The Bull
stood at the head of the table in a warehouse east of Putney
village. I thought I'd been summoned to be congratulated for
my efforts, but news of Matthew Hopkins' developing campaign
had continued to spread alarm.

'This Hopkins fellow is a frail man, I wager, and easily frightened. I might unleash some real magick upon his tail and see
him run!' a tall man with a Northern accent wearing the mask
of a Lizard rose from the table in anger, making the goblets
shake.

Several of the others nodded in agreement. I glanced about. Where was Magdalene? I knew she had been notified: was she too arrested, or worse? Anxious, I struggled to calculate the timbre of the meeting. There were some amongst us who would begin a subterranean resistance using all manner of conjuring and magick, calling upon Angel and Demon, Spirit, friend or foe to defend ourselves and others like us, whilst there were others who would retreat further underground.

'That would not be wise; remember, Hopkins is fiercely ambitious but easily misled.' I drew myself up to full height.

'And tenacious. Don't forget he would see half at this table burn,' the Dove, Lady Eleanor Davies, reminded us. Just then wax fell from a candle to sizzle in a bowl of rosewater. A silvery fear fluttered down like a net and settled over us.

'We must act! Between us we span at least four counties and powerfully so,' the Dragon boomed out from behind his golden scales.

'But,' I countered, 'in these times I think it best we stay below the surface of society until the darkness of all this ignorance has drawn asunder and we can step back into the light.'

'Now is not the time for passivity – think on who we have lost already.' Hamish McDuff was fervent.

'Nova scientia tears away from the old mathematics; I fear by the end of this war we will be as relevant as the horse was when the wheel was invented,' the Dragon elaborated mournfully, at which all turned to me.

'I agree. I must go to Manningtree and volunteer myself as guide to deliberately thwart Hopkins.' I was interrupted by the Lizard, who leant across the table to grip my wrist iron-hard.

'You do that, Master Lilly. Meantime, I will make a spell that will have him dead within five year.'

Outside there were daffodils sprouting along the riverbank, and a drake circling his mate in the frenzy of courtship this season brings. It made me think upon illicit memories, and those to be. It were dusk and there was a trading vessel in from Holland upon the water, having sailed its way through the Royalist barricades. Many stood at the shore to meet it, women hoping for shipments of spice and fresh fruit, men for news of the continent. For a moment it felt as life was before, when such vessels crowded the foreshore of the Thames and London was a whore for trade. The breeze carried the scent of spring under the stench, cannon-fire from the ramparts built to protect the city. It carried hope, and the reminder that the war could not continue for ever. Distracted, and fearing for Magdalene, I hurried through the streets to find myself standing outside her narrow stone house.

The windows were darkened, which did only make me fear more – was she gone, or worse? I banged violently against the door. Rosie, head swathed in a turban, peered at me through as she half opened it, the disarray of the room beyond her apparent.

'Where is your mistress?' I demanded. 'She was due at a meeting.'

'Oh, Master Lilly, it is not sensible for you to see her,' she told me, struggling to shut the door in my face.

'What do you mean, not sensible?' I pushed my foot through the door. 'Has she got my messages? The peat fuel I sent?'

'We did and were most grateful. I was going to visit thee in a few days but for your own safety I don't think you should enter.'

At which I drew back. 'Not plague, Rosie?'

'Not plague, sir, but smallpox. However it has been two weeks without fever so she is almost cured.'

'Then I will see her.' And so I pushed past her and into the house.

The rooms were beginning to show signs of the poverty the war had inflicted upon us all; a painting (a fine family portrait) that had been above the fireplace was now gone, along with a mechanical clock that was most valuable. The silk and velvet coverings to the furniture had been stripped, leaving the wooden furniture paltry and bare.

Rosie rushed around me. 'At least let me announce you.'

'There is no need of that.' Magdalene's voice rang out. She stood in the half-shadow of another door, her head and her face veiled by fine muslin. 'I did not want you to see me like this; I was waiting until I was sure I was no longer infectious.'

'I am not afraid.' Yet I hesitated, and in that hesitation she stepped forward into the light, to slip off the muslin, revealing the small crater-like indentations that now marked the lower half of her face.

'This is who I am now, William, a marred beauty that Fortune has chosen to stain.'

'This matters not to me, that you live matters.' And I led her into the bedchamber.

Lying upon the bed in the flickering candlelight I held her, thinking about our mortality and how, as older lovers, we had little but the moment, for both our pasts belonged to others and the future was an eclipsed world of uncertainty. Sensing my swirling mind, Magdalene stroked my furrowed brow.

'I thank thee for thwarting Vindecot's intentions. But I still distrust Thurloe, Bacon and Hopkins – their ambition makes them dangerous.'

'I have told the Council I will go to Manningtree to further endear myself to Hopkins and send his bloodhounds on a false trail.'

'A good plan.' She sat up and again reached for the fine muslin to cover her face.

'I have a poultice that will rid thee of the marks.'

At which she smiled. 'I think I have a better remedy; I am waiting for the skin to heal fully before I apply it.'

Outside, church bells, and the town crier walking past yelled the time and the thought of the Corner House and Jane closed in on me like a trap. I began pulling on my clothes. 'I have a lot to share with you, and now that you are openly back in London, there is no reason I should not visit you. I have begun an almanack, my first. I will call it *Merlinus Anglicus Junior*, or in plain man's English, *England's Little Merlin*, a small bound pamphlet of some twenty-two pages and of a size that will fit into the pocket of gentleman, maid or farmer.'

'This is to rival Na'worth's offerings or even John Booker's prophesies. Have you joined their race, William?' she laughed.

'Their contest is their own ugly business; I write out of sheer frustration at the incompetency of both Astrologers. My calculation is far superior and within the year the Nation shall know it.'

'Then I shall be the mistress of a famous man.'

When I returned to the Corner House I was much berated for my late arrival, having told Jane I was at a game of bowls. She thought me drunk and that I had visited a bawdy house after the game.

Later I composed a letter to Matthew Hopkins, again offering my services for his cause and as a Philomath who hath written much on the detection of curses, witches and summoning of demons through astrological calculation. In the morning I sent young master Simon off with the letter, for there are men in London who can ensure it gets to Hopkins' county.

On the twenty-first of March Prince Rupert did, with his cavalry and some Irish regiments of musketeers, save the Royalist garrison at Newark from being besieged by the Parliamentarian army led by a Scotsman – Sir Meldrum. At the White Hart I met with a soldier who did march with Meldrum and was later traded as a prisoner of war. He spoke of Prince Rupert's stealth in planning an attack by moonlight upon the troops, who were then holed up in the ruins of a hospice on the east side of the Trent. This has been a most pivotal triumph for the ruthless Prince and Meldrum did surrender much weaponry to the Royalists. And so, the pendulum of power swings again.

♃ 👁 ♎

CHAPTER TWENTY-FOUR

Spring 1644

The Corner House, The Strand

The Fourth House: Giveth Judgement of Fathers in general
& ever of his Father that enquires, or that is born; of Lands,
Houses, Tenements, Inheritances, Tillage of the earth,
Treasures hidden, the determination or end of any thing . . .

It is now nearly April and the months of this violent year run
like sand through an hourglass. I have spent them serving my
Querents and composing my almanack *Merlinus Anglicus Junior*.
I hath, prefacing it with words and wisdom most sensible. It is
now complete and is writ with true skill and comprehension. I
have also published my own Nativity within this volume, but
naturally I have misled my public, for an Astrologer's true
Nativity is his ace card he covers close to his chest. I have written that I have Venus in Taurus, in cazimi with the Sun and
Jupiter in Libra near Spica Virginis and Saturn in Scorpio, the
Moon in Pisces. You, dear Reader, decide which part of the
above be true, but I will tell thee my Jupiter is adjacent to the
fixed star of Spica Virginis – a most fortunate placement, as this
star Spica arrives with riches, success, renown, and when
conjoined with Jupiter the subject is to be most popular with
every advantage of social success and wealth. In this I am
blessed.

As for the publication itself, I have not spent on the spine; faith, it will be enough if it should last the year for the reader, for it is the predictions for 1644 both in seasons and in politics. I share with you some of writing within.

It's far from my thoughts that there's any bindings or inevitable necessity in what I predict by the radiation of heavenly bodies; the stars have no such unlimited laws, they are bounded, and give light to us or some small glimpses of the great affaires God intends upon the earth, but if we rely on our judgement, without relation to the immediate rule and direction of his eternal providence, alas how soon of wise men we become errant fools and idiots . . .

I have great pride in this document; it is a guide for the common man and aristocrat both, and is intelligent in its delivery. And I did reveal one truth of my Nativity that the year 1647 is one that will afflict me and that I shall be in great danger of my life. Surmising this as my ascendant by direction will be in a hard aspect with maleficent Mars and his sister the Moon. No doubt my enemies will be much heartened, but I mean to prove a man can overcome his own inclinations.

On the twentieth of April the King did send his nephew Maurice with some five thousand troops to the Dorset port of Lyme Regis to destroy the Parliamentarian garrison there. But despite a most ferocious bombardment of the garrison (as I did read) and after capturing the nearby Haye House, the governor of that good port Thomas Ceeley did overcome the battery and the next day relief came in the form of two ships bearing both food and ammunition. Another victory for the Puritans!

Meanwhile I have had my *Merlinus Anglicus Junior* circulated in Parliament and my good friend Bulstrode did make sure he was seen by the Speaker reading a copy. The Speaker, intrigued, insisted upon having one himself and so, impressed with the sensibility of the document, did speak of it highly to other members of the Parliament, all of whom then wanted a copy for their own illumination. After all, I have written about Parliament, the future of the war and the negotiation with the King amongst other issues, describing myself as *a friend to monarchy: to the Parliament of England. I am an enemy of Independency. I wish the Church reformed, and all sectaries at Amsterdam.* And have described a troubled and divided Court, and an afflicted kingdom at great length.

When I heard of the popularity of the almanack I sought licence from John Booker as he was the licencer of all mathematical books. This was to prove a mistake, as John Booker, taking offence (and I believe with some envy) at some of my predictions, altered the text to suit his political fancy and only then did he issue permission and it were this altered copy I delivered to the printer. Even then the printer, being of Presbyterian most impassioned, insisted five members of the ministry inspect my now much maligned and put upon text. Then finally, despite this meddling and censorship (that is England now) I had an edition in less than a week, of which I presented to some members of Parliament whilst complaining most bitterly of John Booker's alterations.

To my relief, the members ordered me to reprint it as I would see it, which I did, and that second edition was then met with greater accolade.

I tell thee this so that you can understand the sensibility of the times and how each printed word, song or performed display was subject to such penetrating scrutiny and how easy it was for an honest man to lose his head with heartfelt opinion and how so many of us became more and more afraid to speak for fear of insulting some such fraction or religious group. Na'worth (George Wharton hath most to lose as the 'Royal Astrologer') in particular did ridicule me, as well as other pranksters who did compose ditties and parodies, such is the jealous nature of the disbeliever.

Thank the Lord, my predictions, level-headed and bipartisan, were popular, and my craft solid. Importantly, unlike my rivals, the intelligence behind my calculations spoke for itself and it was heard.

Soon the pamphleteers had sold out the second edition. The title *Merlinus Anglicus Junior* was spoken and promoted in taverns, church halls and in the balconies of Westminster itself. My true destiny, as a conduit to God's will, began to take both shape and speed.

In the almanack, I warned of the Queen's malevolent effect upon the King. Of the danger of the rascal Irish who have joined with the Royal army to vent their Catholic anger upon the Puritan man, of how future taxation will make beggars of us all, of the evil of these new rulers of us in Westminster as well as the county Committee-men – who have nothing but their own interests at heart – and how in both armies, of King and of Parliament, there are some who intend to extend the war for their own monetary gains.

Finally, I told of a Peace that will come through compromise and not through total victory, as I could not see either relinquishing their positions. Understandably, I am popular with the sensible man, whilst there are others who would like me to predict an outright victory for the King – for George Wharton hath accused me in the most cowardly way, under his guise of Na'worth in another pamphlet, of being an impudent, senseless fellow and by name William Lilly.

None of which halts the march of my success.

It was in these weeks I received a reply from Matthew Hopkins, who is most pleased I wish to assist him again and hath invited me to one of his meetings at the Thorn Inn in the village of Mistley, his headquarters. There are to be other important men of influence there (or so he tells me) but as he is busy with his investigations this conference of minds shall not be for many months hence and I fear he will inflict great suffering until then. 'Tis best to keep thy enemies close.

It were in this month of April when Tobias did rush into my study most distraught.

'I cannot believe it! William, such disrespect! Such sacrilege! Such hatred for the Bard!' As he was all atremble I sat him down and plied him with some sweet wine.

'What is it, Toby? Thou art shaking?' He gulped down the wine, then reach for more before answering.

'They have demolished the great Globe Theatre to make room for further dwellings for the populace! I watched in horror as they pulled those great wooden beams that have embraced the most profound of experiences. Why, they might have torn down St Paul's itself. This is the final desecration, William. I cannot sustain any further insult. I return to Oxford tomorrow — better to be locked up in a garrison where at least I can still perform, than continue living amongst these sour-spirited, desiccated, so-called Puritans who think it is more Christian to live without joy or celebration!'

He ranted the rest of the afternoon then fell into a sullen sorrow and by the morning he was gone.

Methinks it is the first symptom of a dying empire to whittle at the joys and transcendent pleasures of the citizen.

The next month, on the twenty-fifth of May, Prince Rupert advancing into Lancashire did attack the Parliamentarian outpost at Stockport — outside that great city of Manchester. I was ashamed to read that Cromwell's men did flee and the garrison was well plundered before the Prince continued towards Bolton. I fear for the good puritans in the path of this blood-lusty prince.

316 || TOBSHA LEARNER

His attack upon that city was most grim; I have heard that his men, many who were recruited from the ranks of the Lancashire Catholics, were inflamed by a public hanging of one of their soldiers, after he were taken prisoner in an early attack. And they did storm the walls and sack the Puritan city most brutally. They say over a thousand Bolton townsfolk and soldiers were massacred. London is awash with news of this slaughter.

But back to more celestial matters. Four days later there was a spectacle in the sky of great interest to the Astrologer. Three Suns – King Apollo shadowed on either side by his astral twins – seemed to appear at midday and I did hurry with my apprentice to the highest point of the common and observe the apparition, dictating most copious notes to my scribe, of the exact time and placement of the planets. This is most interesting, for it were the birthday of the eldest son and heir of King Charles, Prince Charles. I think this will be most auspicious and ominous; either way, it is greatly significant and I will use such information for future prophecy.

Standing there, shading my eyes from the blinding sunlight. I found myself wishing I had my beloved Megs beside me, if only for her opinion and intellectual observation. Who thought a woman could be such a sparring partner for the mind?

Sleep eludes me and my labours are difficult for my mind spins like a child's wooden top. Magdalene hath bewitched me and I must see her to quieten my spirit.

On the twentieth day of June, capitalising on my newfound notoriety (for in truth, dear Reader, more and more people in these times, from peasant to bargeman, were more likely to consult an almanack before the Bible and I had become the most read author in England) I did publish a pamphlet entitled *Supernatural Sights and Apparitions Seen in London* and within it did include several of my own experiences included the appearance of Spirit Demons that fateful night in the Westminster Abbey when John Scott and I, along with others, were foolish enough to seek treasure and were chased by a huge invisible Demon and I did swear I would never again on hallowed ground or church conduct such a ceremony.

It was a time of great contrasts, for despite the war and daily horrors, my career flourished. I was invited to the table of all the great politicks and merchants and many of the powerful now sought my advice on shipping, on war, on the matters of commerce and heart.

On Tuesday past the Puritans pulled down the Strand Maypole – the coachmen's icon – the one place you could hire a hackney carriage, or flag down a sedan chair to any part of London. The drivers are much incensed; this has been their idol, their flagpole of a motley tribe whose power and source of gossip and information is not to be underestimated. I fear Parliament will pay for this and that they have miscalculated our city folk. The Strand now lies bare, like a beautiful woman stripped. Meanwhile the Common Council hath built barricades for the 'safety of the citizen', St James had a wall of bricks across it as did Holborn and various other thoroughfares. The city has become a quilt of warring tribes. How changed will us Londoners be after this war?

CHAPTER TWENTY-FIVE

Summer 1644

The Corner House, The Strand

The Fifth House: By this house we judge of Children,
of Embassadours, of the state of a Woman with
child, of Banquets, of Ale-houses, Tavernes, Playse,
Messengers or Agents for Republick: of the wealth of
the Father, the Ammunition of a Town besieged . . .

This last week I have purchased several advertisements to tell of
my recent accuracy in the insurance of ships. My old friend
Caleb Masson has done much to promote me, and now I wager
that amongst the serving maids and the aristocracy, up to a
sixth of my clients were of the seafaring community and these
did range from the query as to which is the most fortuitous date
to set sail, to insurers wishing to know either the fate of a missing ship or what was its odds of making the voyage before it
departed whilst other querents were the owners of the ships or
relatives of the crews.

The ship in question – *The Blue Star* – had gone missing
from a voyage to Spain; all were convinced she had been dashed
on the rocks and was most probably at the bottom of the sea
and so the insurers had been asked to pay out sixty per cent of
the ship's value. They had come to me to ask if she was indeed
sunk or whether she would finally reach port. I cast the horary

and was most happy to report that she would, indeed, reach port – if weeks late. And so it was: *The Blue Star* sailed into Portsmouth six weeks later and the insurers were most grateful as well as delighted with my services. The advertisement will look most impressive and handsome and I have taken several paragraphs in several of the papers.

Oh, blissful summer in all its joyous fecundity. The fruit blossom is almost blown and even Solomon the raven has taken to song. It is now August and new green rushes have sprung up along the foreshore of the Thames. The sun brings hope to London, as has Parliament's victory at Marston Moor, the most significant so far with some forty-five thousand souls at stake and one that has warranted the retreat of the King's men and is a great success for the leader of the Parliamentarian cavalry, Lieutenant General Oliver Cromwell. And thank the Lord, for the King did plan a three-pronged attack upon the capital itself, which would have finished London.

I read this in the paper the *Mercurius Aulicus*, which hath been smuggled into this city by way of Oxford. I observed in my stay in the Royalist capital that there were several Puritan well-wishers within the Royalist Parliament at Oxford who left information in the hole of a glass-window as they made water in the street – and what was put in that window was the very same day conveyed two miles off by some in the habit of town-gardeners, to the side of a ditch, where one or two were ever ready to give intelligence to the next Parliamentarian garrison. Such is the spread of information in a war – by secret allies and ordinary folk.

On the sixteenth of June Magdalene did inform me that the Queen had given birth to a baby daughter, the Princess Henrietta, and, as predicted, it was a most difficult birth. The King was forced to send for the royal physic, de Mayerne, who risked all, travelling from London. I did ask Magdalene if the

Queen ever received a book of my cures I had sent Magdalene whilst she were at Oxford, for as a physic I had good experience of such matters. To my joy she began to recite, 'For easy delivery take the whites of eggs and cattle soap and make it up into pills, adding to every pill the oil of Sabin and in time of need give her five pills of it.' Then she explained the Queen had much greater complications, least of all the threat from the Earl of Essex who was advancing upon Exeter where she had given birth.

I, myself, feel vindicated, for I had told in my almanack that the first week in July may prove bloody – I had taken the first house and the planet Mars in the figure to signify Parliament and the tenth house to represent the King – and although I predicted a better year for the Parliament I warned that there was no prospect of a peace settlement as the placement of Mars was quarrelsome and hard. My predictions have thus proven correct and this has made me famous.

The battle at Marston Moor was on the second of July, but I also cautioned that both June and July should expect to hear of war, slaughter of men, division, towns besieged, some taken, some plundered and I singled out the days around the fourth day of June (the King and his men were forced to withdraw from Oxford on the third of June).

This defeat has been laid at the feet of Prince Rupert, his hubris and arrogance his Achilles' heel. But the battle had also secured the reputation of Cromwell who, through cunning strategy, directed his cavalry most effectively. They say four thousand Royalist soldiers perished and as many as fifteen hundred captured. However Prince Rupert himself suffered a loss; his famous mascot and companion, the white hunting poodle Boye was also killed in battle. The same canine is well known to gossip-spinners and scandalmongers, as there are some godly folk who claim he was the familiar of the Prince in hopes to discredit His Highness as a Witch or Wizard (I know better, for there is nothing of the Craft about this haughty youth). Such reportage has been much ridiculed and parodied in the Royalist press — who, in the spirit of jest, claimed the dog was a better soothsayer than Mother Shipton herself, and that he could catch a bullet aimed at the good Prince with his mouth. If so, the beast was a great loss indeed!

The Parliamentarian victory has changed the climate of this war, and there is the faint scent of new purpose in many about the country and city.

I myself had the sad business of informing Mr Jeffries, Rosie's brother-in-law, the Puritan merchant who had sheltered Magdalene, of the horary I cast for his son in this battle and, most tragically, the portents bore out as I predicted: he was killed at Marston Moor.

Twelve days later, on the fourteenth of July the Queen — threatened by the advancing troops led by the victorious Essex — fled England for France as Magdalene had foretold.

The good city of York did now surrender to Parliament whilst the King hath lost the North. The balance swings both ways, but more so to Parliament, methinks. I have also heard that Matthew Hopkins hath increased his persecution of old women and Cunning Folk. And so, dear Reader, this deadly dance continues.

As for myself, life is both exhilarating and expensive; my wife Jane has begun to send monies to her family as they are in the North and are suffering and I have secretly sent coin to Magdalene. I take precautions and only visit my sweet Megs when there is a void moon in the sky, scuttling to her townhouse like some night beetle, hating myself for the compulsion.

I write this at my study window, the busy events of the past months completing my reverie, as doth the pleasure of knowing my latest pamphlet *The Prophecy of the White King* was published on the eighth of this month of August, and I believe successfully so, after talking with Jonka, the pamphleteer, who tells me it hath sold like sugarcake in a famine these past two days. This is a quiet joy, akin to the composer knowing his hymn is being played in churches around the land and I find myself in a state of happiness quite removed from the grimness that surrounds me.

As my quill scratched across the parchment, I was interrupted by a tapping: Solomon was perched awkwardly upon the windowsill and was knocking most insistently with his beak against the glass. Outside another raven stood upon my sundial, wings glistening in the light, her head cocked to one side as she stared back at my avian companion.

Solomon was in love. There was a tragedy in that, for I believed it was only now that Solomon had fully comprehended that he was genus Corvus and not an abhorrent son of the human species. He had suddenly become aware of both his captivity and limitations. I wagered there was a hidden philosophy in his action, and that I should release him. But the bird's querulous yet devoted presence calmed my whirring mind and I had grown too fond of him. Even so, I wished he would stop hiding the sardines I fed him between the pages of my manuscripts (soon the stench of Pisces will start to dominate my figures). Was I selfish? Show me a successful man who is not.

But I return to the matter at hand, my pamphlet called *The Prophecy of the White King*. Already, it hath caused fervour in Parliament and was lauded by the Parliamentarians and hated by the Royalists. The accusing paragraph ran as follows: *You see what storms, what miseries, what cruel wars our nation is once like to suffer by the means and procurement of a King called the White King, who brings over strangers to destroy us, and God gives us command to provide sepulchres and graves for him and them . . .*

The reason being I chose to describe my 'King' as the White King and 'tis well-known King Charles wore white at his coronation rather than the traditional purple.

As such the Puritans fastened upon the prophecy, seeing a Parliament victory in it. I supposed it a veiled prophecy, but I took it from an earlier ancient prophecy made in the Welsh tongue of the year of 667 AD.

I also prophesied that after a great battle upon an ancient seat near a running river the King will die. This alone caused great consolation in the Court at Oxford and great encouragement at Parliament.

My prophecy, most tragic, was then borne out as I hath mentioned earlier, at the terrible and decisive battle of Marston Moor. As my pamphlet was at that very time still wet with ink upon the roller, the accuracy of my prediction hath made me, by my own humble reckoning, the most famed Astrologer in the land. I was in the middle of writing a letter to an old benefactor when Mrs Featherwaite ushered in Harry Pickles, my printer.

'Faith, William, we have done it!' he proclaimed, the jowls and cheeks of his trout face uncharacteristically flushed by a scarlet joy.

'We have?'

'The first printing – all one thousand and eight copies – sold out and in three days! This, my esteemed Philomath, is astonishing. You are now Astrologer to the Nation, and a pox on John Booker and that Royalist Na'worth!'

'Oh, George Wharton has his place,' I answered mildly – humility being one of the conduits to success, a truth one should never forget particularly at the apex of one's career – 'but now shall we proceed to second printing?'

'We shall indeed, and averaging three pence a copy you might do better than just covering the cost and make a profit,

William, but just think of the advertising you shall gain from such distribution!'

'I wish only to serve God and humanity through my talent.'

'Then you will be happy to serve a great man in his purpose,' Harry retorted with a mysterious smile. 'I have a request from a most prestigious individual, one I hold in much esteem and admire greatly—'

'Richard Overton, the Leveller?' It were an intuitive guess, I knew Harry was a great follower of the Leveller and held few men in any reverence, but Harry, assuming I were practising my craft, was most awestruck.

'You see, there you are, a true seer! You knew what I was to ask! Mr Overton wishes to writ but needs to know it will be in the utmost privacy. He cannot be seen to have any doubt as to his own future and that of the movement.'

'I will be most discreet. And in turn I ask you to be most private about my service to him. As you know, I align myself with no group, Harry, but am in service to all.'

Just at that moment Solomon, at the window, did set forth the most piercing whistle and then resume his tapping. Amazed, the printer, thinking it be some untimely alarm, did startle.

'But faith, William, this creature of yours: is he bird or Demon?'

'At this moment he is a creature driven mad by love, which illustrates that the greatest fool is an old fool, for the bird is not young and yet he finds himself struck, as the French say, *coup de foudre* for the first time in his avian life. Alas, he is well tortured.' At which Harry's pale visage (for I wager the printer scarce saw daylight in his labours) was split by a smile for he did sense I was talking for myself as well as for Solomon.

Later that day I took a visit from Bulstrode Whitelocke himself, who was most pleased with the predictions within *The*

White King's Prophecy. He told me that Lieutenant General Cromwell wishes to have me and John Booker upon the battlefield before an engagement, as our predictions should boost the morale of the good plain men of England fighting for Parliament and for God. There was some trepidation in this, but in confidence, dear Reader, I was flattered.

On the Sunday evening I went to the Stepney Church to hear a sermon by preacher William Greenhill whom my wife doth worship as much as any God. It was a most frightening sermon of brimstone and fire, and the approaching apocalypse, Greenhill proclaiming that, if we do not change our ways and oust all indulgences and rid society of those who value wealth over humanity and of the urgency for all governance to be the word of God, we would be condemned to an afterlife of Hell. We were all left chaste and trembling, myself secretly afeared at the preacher's enthusiastic condemnations of all indulgences (including the joys of the flesh, a love of sweetmeats and dance).

Our little party, that is to say Jane, Mrs Featherwaite, her nephew Simon, our new maidservant Maisie (an impressionable girl now convinced she were to be kidnapped by Catholic Demons who were to swoop in from the sky) wound our way back through the narrow muddy lanes in a fearful medley.

Upon arriving at the Corner House we discovered a countrywoman of middle years sheltering beneath her cloak and with her a girl of no more than fifteen, a shivering silent creature, the marks of scratches upon her cheeks, her hair shorn like that of a leper.

The woman stepped forward, the rain dripping over the ermine collar of her cloak.

'Master Lilly?'

''Tis I.'

'Author of the veritable booklet *Supernatural Sights and Apparitions seen in London*, published just two months now?'

At which Jane startled and did push in front of me like a terrier guarding its dinner.

'Mine husband is no Wizard, Madam! If you seek such services you must go to a priest.'

'I cannot go to a priest for I fear they will mark her as Witch.' The woman spread her hands. 'Please, my name is Judith Dutton and I am desperate. My daughter . . .' She pulled the girl whose eyes were dark caverns, devoid of emotion and light, towards us. 'I believe her to be possessed, Master Lilly.'

I glanced about me fearing spies. To my relief, it being Sunday night and wet, there were nought except a lone rat catcher with his cage and terrier at the end of the lane, a sleeping knot of urchins at the foot of a stone archway, and a beggar shifting through a stinking pile of rags. Even so, caution had me quickly ushered the woman and the daughter into the house.

Mrs Dutton sat before me, Mary upon the floor, having thrown herself down like a dog before the hearth. 'We were staying at my sister's house in a small village near Newbury when Prince Rupert's men rode through. They saw my daughter as she were coming back from the well – four of them, who circled her with their horses, frightening her against a tree whence they dismounted and took her into a barn . . . Her screams were heard across two fields, but by the time my husband rode to her it were too late. She hath not spoken since – and if she doth it is in a man's voice.' She leant forward so that her daughter could not hear her words. 'Their violation of her body hath let a Demon in, a Demon who is full of anger and murderous intent. When he is within her she scratches and cuts herself, and I am afraid he will find means to kill her. Please, I want my daughter back!' At which she rolled back the sleeves of her daughter's long gown and revealed the most grievous and brutal cuts and welts upon the girl's pale flesh.

'What is the child's name?' I asked.

'Mary, sir, was what she were christened.'

Gently, I reached to lift Mary to her feet, but she flinched and whimpered, hiding her face in her mother's skirts.

'Oh good sir, she doth not suffer the touch of a man since that fateful day, not even of her brother,' her mother cried, but I took the child regardless and, holding her by the shoulder, pulled her to her feet. I looked into her eyes – and was ashamed for my gender to see such terror.

'Mary? Is it you I address?' I was hoping to hoax the Spirit of the child out from under the Demon who held her body like a fortress. To my horror, her eyes rolled back into her head and a convulsion like a rolling wave travelled through her slight figure.

'I am Trent, servant of Bael!' The voice that cometh out from this babe's mouth was monstrous, deep and with the growl of a large man; it seemed to shake the foundations of the house and echoed about my bookcases. Jane, in her fright, grabbed Mrs Featherwaite, who in turn picked up a poker as if to defend us all. I stayed strong, although in truth I feared for my own eyes, for I could see this Demon could scratch.

'Welcome, Trent, to my house,' I answered, my friendly greeting surprising the Demon, immediately the ferocity that had puffed the child into menace deflated. Seizing the respite, I turned quickly to Mrs Featherwaite.

'For goodness' sake, put down the poker and fetch me a large quality of salt as quick as you can,' I hissed and she hurried out, and I was able to go back to the child.

'Trent, you have possessed Mary Dutton for a good six months, is that not so?'

'It is,' the Spirit growled, but methinks in a higher register and behind it were the girl. 'I'll not leave my Mary, for I doth love her and protect her!' After which the girl did fall back to the ground and convulsed once more, froth upon her lips, a fit that had Solomon in the beating his wings in alarm.

We were interrupted by Mrs Featherwaite returning with the salt, quickly I poured a circle of it around the girl to keep her and the Demon contained. She quietened again, and, to the relief of those gathered, stayed within the circle.

'Did you see the attackers?' I asked Mrs Dutton quietly so as not to be heard by either girl or Demon.

'No, but the young stable hand did see them leave the barn afterward, laughing and joking amongst themselves, the stain of my daughter's hymen still upon them. They did put a torch to the barn, but after they rode away the same stable hand put the flame out and rescued Mary – what was left of her. Can you help?'

'I think I might. I have had success in the past in these matters, but you have to understand that this is not magick, nor anything of the Devil, but simply good Cunning Folk logic.'

'I understand.'

Behind us, Mary broke into the most violent thrashing whilst chanting in that unnatural and hair-rising voice.

'Scar, tattoo and Peacock's crest,

I cannot feel my breasts!

Peacock's crest, tattoo, scar,

My screams will not reach that far!

Scar, peacock's crest, tattoo,

I will revenge myself upon all of you!!'

'Peacock's crest?' I queried of the mother once the girl had finished the horrible rhyme and slipped back into a trance.

'One of the men, he wore a peacock's feather in his cap, I was told.'

'And I suppose another had a scar and the third a tattoo. She has not left that moment, this has driven her mad,' I ascertained.

'Can you make her well?'

'I can take the memory from the girl and put it in a box and with it the Demon will leave, and your daughter, God willing, will find peace.'

'But no husband.' Mrs Dutton replied sadly; both of us knew the girl was now ruined.

'There is other happiness and, some might answer, greater to be found. Where are you living?'

'By the Haymarket, in my brother's dwelling. He is the Beadle for the Parish.'

'I will come tomorrow and exorcise her, but your family cannot tell of this, not to a soul – and most importantly, not to your priest.'

Mrs Dutton nodded solemnly. 'Thank you, thank you, Master Lilly, but tell me, what is your fee?'

'No fee, it is a holy service, to free the child.'

But after they had left, Jane did turn on me, furious that I had charged nothing, accusing me most shrewishly of great naivety and stupidity, claiming that I would endanger her and the whole household through these demonic practices and that I had no manner of telling whether Mrs Dutton and her possessed daughter were not simply a trap laid by mine enemies to prove I was an Occultist, a devil worshipper, and worthy of the attentions of the Witch Finder-General, despite our 'friendship', his reputed Witch trials now the subject of pamphlets across the land. I retreated into my study, uneasy. Could she be right?

That evening I did consult Johann Weyer's *De Praestigiis Daemonum* on the nature of Demons and Spirits. Upon reading the grimoire again I was gripped by a great excitement, a sense that now, at the pinnacle of my powers, I was at last able to use such spells without personal affliction or the fear of the darkness that might have come upon me in the past with such application and by the time I stood before the low arch of the cottage in the Haymarket the next day I was prepared.

I had the kitchen cleared of all furniture and upon the floor I with great care drew out a chalk Heptagram – a symbol that is also known as a devil's trap. Within this I made all the markings and magical symbols for the Demons of the North, South, East, and West.

I had the mother lead the daughter into the centre and sit her down so that she were enclosed entirely. I then placed an open box of Rowan wood beside the Heptagram (having being taught that Rowan wood were the best for containing magick and Spirits).

'Trent! Do you have Mary in your arms?' I commanded the Demon.

The girl's head nodded most vigorously, as if the very Demon himself were shaking it.

'Excellent. I wish you to allow Mary to recall the day of her violation and tell of each outrage in exact description so might we revenge her upon her attackers. Do you agree, Trent?'

'I cannot let her go back there!' the Demon snarled.

'But she has never left there; you have not allowed her.'

'I have protected her,' he screamed, 'when no one else was able!'

'Let her go back. She is safe now.'

'You promise?'

'I promise. She is safe within this design.'

At which the girl, lying there like a babe, began whispering all that had happened on that fateful day. The way she was trapped, her terror, the tearing and rending of her clothes, her broken face and cut breasts, the attack and the faces of the men who raped her, her voice growing stronger and stronger, until her mother had to leave the room, and then my helper, until it was just myself, Mary, and, somewhere on the pulsing, febrile air, the Demon Trent lying just under the visible light, his twisted body turning in the recited horror like a worm torn from its hole. The attack was brutal, the men taking great pleasure in their torture, and I did wonder how the girl had survived at all. It were no mystery her mind had split in two to maintain a kind of sanity.

But finally she stopped and there was a silence. It was then that I did recite the Lord's prayer for exorcism.

'In the Name of the Father,
and of the Son,
and of the Holy Ghost.
Amen.
Most glorious Prince of the Heavenly Armies,
Saint Michael the Archangel,
    defend us in our battle against principalities and powers,
    against the rulers of this world of darkness,
    against the spirits of wickedness in the high places.
Come to the assistance of men whom God has created to
    His likeness
and whom He has redeemed at a great price from the
    tyranny of the devil.
The Holy Church venerates you as her guardian and
    protector;
to you, the Lord has entrusted the souls of the redeemed
to be led into heaven.
Pray therefore the God of Peace to crush Satan beneath our
    feet,

that he may no longer retain men captive and do injury to
    the Church.
Offer our prayers to the Most High,
that without delay they may draw His mercy down upon us;
take hold of the dragon, the old serpent, which is the devil
    and Satan,
bind him and cast him into the bottomless pit
that he may no longer seduce the nations.'

At my words, Mary began to retch most violently, bringing
up a dark, malformed matter, black with blood. And it was this
that I placed within the Rowan box, shutting the lid down on
the Demon for ever.

When her mother returned, the girl was sleeping, her face
flushed with colour, and upon seeing that her child was restored
in all her girlish health and innocence, Mrs Dutton did break
into relieved sobbing. I made up a tincture to calm her, then
had the child carried up to bed.

Before I left, with the Rowan box under my arm, I gave Mrs
Dutton instruction for the cleansing of the cottage and of the
body of the bewitched, telling her to take two new horseshoes,
heated red hot, and nail one above the threshold of the door,
but quench the other in a pot of the urine of the bewitched,
after which she was to put the pot over the fire, add some salt
and three horse nails until the urine was almost boiled away,
then keep the horseshoe and nails in a clean cloth to use again
in the same manner for three times. I did suggest she do this
the very next night as it were the full moon, a most effective
time. Take heed, dear Reader, this is a most powerful spell
against the invasion of Witches, both in the house and in the
soul, and, when it comes to Witches, even the most Christian
amongst us are susceptible.

CHAPTER TWENTY-SIX

Autumn bleeds into Winter, 1644

Chancery Lane, City of London

The Sixth House: It concerneth Men and Mid-servants, Gallislaves, Hogges, Sheep, Goats, Hares, Connies, all manner of lesser Cattle, and profit and losse got thereby; Sicknesse, its quality and cause, principall humour offending, curable or not curable, whether the disease be short or long . . .

It was now Tuesday of the empty moon. I had closed the evening to my Querents and told both Jane and Mrs Featherwaite that I will first to church and then to bowls with a game with both Harry Pickles and a shipping clerk, the name I did not bother to give. Since our argument, Jane had stopped asking for the explanations of my movements, and with the larder full (in these hard times!) and a new shawl (procured with some difficulty) upon her dresser she was almost sweet in nature.

As I made my way to the house off Chancery Lane, I was dressed in an unseasonably heavy and long cloak, beneath which I did conceal a bunch of turnips, a grouse and one head of cabbage, for I knew Magdalene's fortunes were much changed.

When I arrived, I saw that there was a mark on the apparently unused gate, a symbol daubed in red paint. I knew it well:

it marked the household as Popish, and was an invite for the bully-boy Roundheads to come smashing. I reminded myself to tell Rosie to make sure it is painted out.

I did not bother with the front door, knowing it too appeared unused – a deliberate deception. Instead, I walked around to the servants' entrance, checking the neighbours were not over-looking me and that I was unseen. Rosie let me in, promising to have a supper ready by ten after I handed her the brace of grouse and the vegetables. Her gratitude was pitiful, and I guessed they had not eaten meat for days. As I entered, I noticed a chill in the air and I was most anxious, for this is an invitation to both thieves and Witches and other such-like spirits, so before I continued I asked the maid for a scrap of parchment and a quill and did write the following upon it. *Omnis, Spiritus, Laudet, Dominum, Mosem, Habent, Prophetas, Exurgat, Deus Dissipenter, Ininice.*

'Rosie,' I told her, most emphatic, as I handed her the scrap, 'you must place this spell in the corners of the house in order to catch thieves and drive away spirits that haunt a house.'

'Yes, Master Lilly, it will be hung before midnight, but unless you can magick up some hope and a good leg of hung pork I doubt it will work.' The maid led me through the dark-ness of the parlour, now unused and unlived in, and it is strange to see these rooms I have known lively in colour and luxury, stripped of their silver and tapestries, the mirrors all covered, chambers reduced to echoing, hollowed spaces, the few pieces of furniture now pushed against the wall. As if to taunt, a mouse scuttled across the floor before me, fearless, its twitching nose engrossed in brazen trajectory.

Magdalene was in the larger of two back rooms in which she and the two servants now lived. She stood before a small fire that I warrant was lit only in my honour. She had covered her pockmarks with powder and sat on an ornate chair strangely out of tune with the stained and neglected wall hangings. An island of light and colour in a dusty cave, she was wearing a scarlet velvet robe that rippled with an opulence this city hath not seen for years, but on closer inspection was patched in repair. As I drew near she touched her gold and pearl earrings.

'I wear these in defiance. They are the only pieces I have left, the rest I have been forced to sell. The dress, too, in defiance of the drab mausoleum they have made of my dwelling.'

'You still have me.' I knelt before her to weave my fingers through her loosened hair. This was a pleasure I had never known with my wife.

'Do I, William?' Magdalene cast a disparaging look upon me, and I could see I had offended. 'Your booklet, this latest offering to the populace, how could you betray me thus?'

Offended myself, I moved away. 'I have stayed true and honest to my craft. I serve my profession and God above all else. You know I do.'

'The Queen gave you his birth dates. You have drawn up a birth figure! You know the King's vulnerabilities, as you know his strengths!'

'*The Prophesy of the White King* is based on a far earlier publication – on ancient prophecy, in fact.'

'Poppycock, William! *The Prophesy of the White King* is political; you knew it would endear you to Parliament and make you their invaluable mouth piece.' Furious, she tugged at my sleeve.

'You know I love the King despite his failings . . .' I took her hands, fingers icy at the tip, 'and as a fair and honest Philomath I'm obliged to speak my truth. There is more to this and you know it. The Stuarts began their reign when Saturn and Jupiter were conjunct with Sagittarius, in fire and strength, with King James in 1603 – but since a year ago this powerful fire cycle has been disrupted; Jupiter and Saturn now meet in Pisces and there shall be a sensible disturbance, if not final subversion, to those commonwealths and monarchies—'

'I have read your almanack. I do not say that it is ill crafted, merely that you were advantaged. They are saying you predicted the victory at Marston Moor.'

'I did. Magdalene, please do not put an arrow through the messenger, especially when he is your only protector.'

'I would like to, but I find I cannot. Do you really see no hope for a Royalist England?'

'Marston Moor was a great victory, Cromwell has proven to be a great strategist.'

'As you yourself are.'

'Enough of this argument. Tell me, how is it with you these past weeks?' At which she softened.

'I have found some employment, through an old friend of my husband. I am teaching French to a merchant's daughter which pays enough to feed my small household, whilst your own generosity allows me a few luxuries. And, thanks to you, I have seen Sir Bulstrode Whitelocke and told him I had information that could be most useful to Parliament and would be willing to sell it.'

'The information is sound, Magdalene? My reputation is at stake here.' I risked my life by asking, but I had no choice. Magdalene took umbrage.

'It is sound. Don't forget, I once had the ear of the Queen.'

'In that case, I have a favour to ask of you. Prince Rupert's men, you must have known some of them through your husband?'

'I did.'

'Know you of these three young cavalry officers: one hath a tattoo, another a scar upon his cheek, whilst the third wears a peacock's feather in his cap.'

At the description of the last youth wariness came upon her. 'And if I did?'

'Magdalene, this last week I did perform an exorcism upon a young girl violated by these youths. I have been successful in ridding her of the Demon who did enter her body when she was left for dead in a burning barn, but now I wish for justice.'

Magdalene walked to the hearth, the trail of her dress sweeping the floor, a great resignation in her movement. 'These are actions committed under war; no doubt the youth was urged on by his companions.'

'A life is a life, whether it be aristocrat or farmer's daughter; she is ruined, Megs.'

She sighed heavily. 'The youth with the tattoo is Sir Justin Smithers, the third son of the Earl of Frome; the young man with the scar is undoubtedly Sir Clements Gilsbury, son of Lord Gilsbury, for they are always seen together and the last youth is Sir Benjamin Tillingham and the peacock is in his family's crest. I know this for I am his godmother.'

'His actions are not that of a true Christian, Catholic or otherwise.'

'His father and brother were both slaughtered by the Scots, thus he hates all Puritans, Covenanters and the like.'

'To wantonly violate an innocent maiden is inexcusable.'

'He is sixteen year of age!'

'You have given me their names; one day their actions will be accounted for.'

'You think that day will come?'

'It will, and it will be a day when men are not judged by the colour of their gowns nor the cut of their beards, nor the manner in which they worship God. For on that day we will all stand under one sky, Magdalene. I have seen this.'

'Enough! I want to forget these differences between us, I want to forget the moral poverty of our times.' And she did place her arms about me. But in our lovemaking there was now something amiss – a kernel of mistrust had taken root – and no amount of caresses could rip it free. I knew it then and I know it now.

Afterwards, lying upon the rug, staring up I thought I saw the ceiling dissolve and there, beyond the stars, beyond other universes, and beyond that, perhaps, the face of the Almighty himself. If this were sin I would lose my soul, and yet, dear Reader, I cared not.

Some days later I did inform Mrs Dutton of the names of the young officers, carefully writing them upon parchment so that there would be no later mistake in identity. I also promised that I would do my utmost to find the youths and let her know where the men might be discovered, but I finished with the caveat that patience is the greater part of revenge. Her husband was a farmer, pressed into the service of the Parliamentarian army, but his wife, Mrs Dutton, did swear she'd give the names unto him, and though they were not rich people they would revenge their daughter's honour and her lost future for she were surely unmarriageable now.

Naturally, Mrs Dutton was most grateful and again did promise the utmost secrecy upon both the exorcism and my involvement. She also informed me that Mary had begun to speak in her own voice, although she still would not suffer to be alone.

However, the whole exercise made me anxious about my reputation. The hunger to find Witches and Wizards in the most unlikely places hath become the latest sport of the uneducated and the unhappy. Even Janko, my Dutch pamphleteer, had fallen under suspicion, for he was seen talking to his pet ferret and some jester hath claimed him Wizard – in truth, I feared this was really a revenge for the selling of Royalist papers which he hath done in secrecy since the war began.

When I arrived back at the Strand House I wrote a message to Tobias Young, who is now my eyes and ears at Court in Oxford and at the Basing House garrison, asking to search out the three guilty Chevaliers and let me know when they could be found at their most vulnerable.

Although it was only October, already snow buried the fields and there was much complaining from farmers across the land. Many had taken to forming their own militia beyond the politick of both King or Parliament, saying that they were raided just the same by both armies and have been left without livestock and farms — many of which had been annexed by both warring parties, sometimes several times over. These unhappy farmers were called clubmen, for they were often armed with cudgels, scythes and the like, attached to long poles. I did not blame these countrymen whose livelihoods and lands were constantly raided by both the King's troops and the New Model Army. Theirs was a natural disgust, born out of disillusionment and there is a danger they will rise up as a fifth column, bringing true anarchy.

The papers were full of stories of hardship and indeed, it hath grown both colder and hungrier for the Londoner. We were a city under attack; however, both the merchants and Parliament did have military gains and last week the city of Newcastle fell finally into Scottish Convenant's hands, Parliament's allies. It hath been a long bloody siege for Newcastle, with stories of many Royalists killed. Jane was much troubled, for her cousin's family lives there and she was afeard the men of the household had been slaughtered.

Here in the Strand I saw up to twenty or thirty Querents most days, and yet managed to compose new treatises and publications at night. This last week I cured a child of fever; the next day I was asked about the winner of a horse race, whether it would be the chestnut, the dapple grey, or the iron-grey? The Lord of the Second House is an indication of sudden fortune, and if the Lord of the Second be placed in the ascendant, the querent shall unexpectedly come into a Fortune or without. The chestnut horse was thus favoured. I did choose this stallion and was proved right, a most profitable prediction for both the Querent and myself. Life is both ordinary in its habit yet extraordinary in its events.

I do not sleep well.

This morning the serving maid ran in to tell me a messenger pigeon had arrived at the dovecote, flapping and preening itself amid my own birds. I went down and, catching the plume of my frosty breath betwixt my hands, took hold of the glistening creature.

The message told of yet another arrest for sorcery, this time of my friend Hamish McDuff and that he did throw himself from a window to be dashed onto the cobblestones below before they were to torture him for further details. I was much saddened; my first thought to go to Magdalene who I knew counted him as an intimate.

As I placed the message back upon my desk I noticed that my fingers were trembling. How long will it be before my own arrest?

After that day I did deliberately endear myself to Nathaniel Bacon, now the Recorder of Ipswich this past year. This most pious of men is the great supporter of Matthew Hopkins and he doth engender permission for Hopkins' exploits both within Parliament and within the Puritan brethren, therefore I was most pleased when he approached me to cast a horary in order that he retrieve some stolen goods that were taken from his house. My prediction helped greatly and the thief was caught and the goods retrieved. However, the man is frightening, a Puritan of strong conviction and head of the central committee; he took great delight in describing the gruesome minutiae of the wonderful works the Witch Finder-General was executing in Essex.

I confess, upon listening to Nathaniel Bacon's most colourful descriptions, the spittle upon his lip in his enthusiasm, I did smile and nod my head like a dumb china doll, for fear my true sentiments about such persecution might show. In God's true name I shall play this card for Hector and those other Cunning folk I have loved. In this spirit I have also supped with John Thurloe (he is the secret eyes and ears of Colonel Cromwell who wars for all Puritan England and is most zealous of all) having offered my services and study of such peoples (Sorcerers and known Occultists) for his advantage.

The winter has now pulled on its bleakest coat and many of the lakes have frozen over. Yesterday I took Jane and Mrs Featherwaite to a market upon the Spittel Fields east of the city where it is still possible to bargain for fowl and pig at a high price. The fields were white with snow and black with mud where many had trod. But there were caravans with ribbons and bright flags as, far from a church and any zealot, there was some entertainment there. To see such mercantile inventiveness was hope indeed, but then, these were Londoners, and understood how a frozen cabbage could be made to turn a profit. There were stalls selling roasted chestnuts, a spit of roasted pig turning over a fire made upon the ice itself, an organ grinder with a monkey, and a circus performer, all manner of stalls — even a barber cutting hair under a striped canopy. It were like a miniature city sat upon a great plain of white and very pleasing to behold, set against the grey horizon.

As we picked our way across the snow, Jane noticed a caravan set up next to a rib-thin pony mournfully chewing at a bale of icy hay. FORTUNE TELLER: ONE PENNY THE PALM, A FARTHING FOR LOVE SPELLS read the banner strung over the open door.

'William, you must go in; it would amuse me to see what a fortune teller has to say about another fortune teller's life!' As I have mentioned before, dear Reader, my second wife had a sharp, prickly wit with which she loved to wound.

'Nay, Jane, I am an important fellow now; a man like me should not be seen entering such premises.' And so it went on, Jane with some unspoken grievance or humiliation she wished to afflict, and myself too aware of the gathering spectators. Since the success of *Merlinus Angelicus* and *The Prophecy of the White King* my reputation belonged to the common man and I had been recognised.

Meanwhile our bickering had drawn the fortune teller herself to her door — a thin, raisin-eyed woman, dark in complexion, her skin as wrinkled as the bark of an olive tree. The gipsy wore the attire of the orient, although when she spoke it was in an Irish brogue.

'I know thee for who thou art and it would be my honour to service such a Philomath and Master as thyself, a free fortune telling . . .' after which she curtsied as if I were a King or gentry, a strange quirk of a gesture but respectful nevertheless.

'Go on, William, what harm is in it? Now you will know what it is like, to have the wings of thy Will clipped by predicted Fate.' Jane's irksome voice, dulled by the weight of the snow, nevertheless boomed in my ear.

'I have never clipped anyone's wings, Jane, but I will go in to humour thee.'

Inside it were dark except for a black candle upon a small table covered in the cards of the Tarot.

'Sit to my left, Master Lilly. This is privilege indeed, for you are the maestro, the Philomath of our times. I know it from the air you carry about thee.' Her flattery made me uncomfortable, in that it was pleasing, and I did settle where she instructed.

'It might be wiser, Mistress, to pitch your "tent" on Royalist ground: they are more tolerant of prognosticators than the Puritan,' I advised.

'Yet you yourself run a pretty business,' she countered in a broken mouth of yellow and black, 'methinks you run the gauntlet more than I. I can disappear, whereas thou — thou shine as bright as light, and light is hard to hide both in war and peacetime, but I see you too suffer with the curse of second sight; this is no small burden.'

Then, with a grim air, she did hand me the cards. I shuffled then gave them back after cutting them with my left hand.

The first card she turned over was the Tower; turning the next card it was crossed by the Lovers.

'There is great change, upheaval, and a great passion.' She then turned up the card above the Cross to reveal the High Priestess. 'A tryst of great secrecy with a woman as powerful as yourself.' At which she looked up and grinned most wickedly. 'I wager 'tis not the shrewish wife I have met outside!'

'And you would win your wager,' I snapped back. Chastised, the fortune teller turned over the next card below: the Skeleton wielding the Scythe — the Death card.

'This affair will not end well.'

Startled, I stood up, thinking of the great susceptibility in my Nativity predicted in the year of 1647. And it seemed to me, this woman had given both wings and voice to that terror. Stumbling back, I knocked the table over, the cards slipping down to the floor, a broken map of ill fortune.

Outside, Jane and Mrs Featherwaite were making merry, watching a juggler throwing three burning torches, his striped tunic and the red flame reflecting prettily against the blue-white of the glassy sky. In my eye he resembled the Fool, the Tarot card that had been staring up amidst the tumble of cards. The Jester, the idiot with the bells ringing at the end of his three-pronged cap, tinkling uselessly against the inevitability of one's own Fate, as he steps blindly off a cliff.

'You were short. Was she a charlatan? Tell me, William, do we have greatness in our future or should I sell the chickens?' my wife joked, the pleasure she took in her cruel wit a measure of how ill-matched we were and always had been. For the thousandth time I cursed I had not cast a horary on such a union before I married her!

'Neither charlatan nor Witch but a shrewd observer,' I muttered as a sickening panic rose up from my stomach.

In my haste to leave I hurried the two women over to the edge of the faire and would have left then, except they both begged for a jug of spiced wine, the scent of which was floating across from a stall, intermingled with the fragrance of roasting chestnuts and hazelnuts beside a turning spit of suckling pig but I did think dog. Thinking there was no harm in losing ourselves in the jostling crowd, and with a hunger born from the needle-sharp cold, we stopped and feasted.

When I stepped away to give alms to a young mother with babe in arms, I heard my name being called. Magdalene stood at some distance, wearing a cape and hat, Rosie bearing several parcels by her side.

'William!' Magdalene hurried toward me before I had a chance to show that I was with my wife. I glanced over my shoulder; Jane and Mrs Featherwaite were now watching a dancing bear, dressed in bells and ribbons and goaded by its German trainer with a short pike – black furry arms flailed in hopeless fall and there was a poignant grace to the clumsy beast as he slipped and spun upon the snow. It seemed safe to exchange a few words.

'Take heed, I am not alone.' I indicated Jane and Magdalene did glance at the woman most imperiously, then ordered Rosie to fetch her a wrapped coal with which to warm her hands.

After the maid left she turned to me. 'There is nothing to fear – you forget I met your wife the first time I visited you in Surrey.'

'And so she knows you as the Queen's emissary; isn't that cause enough?'

'She knows me as an eminent client who seeks your expertise. But we waste time, William, I have much foreboding.' She moved closer so that our conversation could not be overheard. 'When they arrested poor Hamish they found my name and address in his journal and written beside it were a hexagram, a pentacle, and the alchemist's symbol for sulphur. I fear all the good work you did misleading the Witch-Finder General is undone . . .'

'Why did they arrest Hamish?'

'On a political charge; they thought he was conspiring with the Scottish against Parliament.'

'What irony!'

'I am followed, and both Rosie and my valet have seen the same young man loitering outside my house. William, they will arrest me for Witch, I am convinced of it.'

I glanced about us: Jane and Mrs Featherwaite were several yards away, their backs to us; a group of youths – apprentices no doubt – drunk with hot cider were laughing and parodying the jester who, ignoring them valiantly, continued juggling; there were several beggar families crouching for warmth and for scraps given by the more kind-hearted stall owners whilst some well-dressed women with their merchant husbands were walking betwixt the pedlars and barrel-sellers. I saw no spy amongst all this, but then it would have been impossible to have known as so many were fingermen, happy to betray family, neighbour or friend for coin or a privilege from Parliament that placed a meal on the table.

'Were you followed here?'

'Nay, we left by the back door and lane.' She stepped closer. 'It has been a month, I miss thee . . .'

I didn't move; I could not afford to touch her or embrace. 'Endear yourself to Pastor Thomas Edwards,' I told her stiffly. 'He is the most powerful. Make loud your penance on your past allegiances, be seen often at prayer at his parish, Christ Church in Newgate Street. A zealous convert is the biggest prize of all to these preacher-leaders. Meanwhile, I shall make some inquiries.'

'Your wife, she approaches!' Magdalene's countenance was suddenly formal.

'And make humble your countenance, you are Puritan now!' I managed to hiss, before Jane was upon us, and I was forced to reacquaint my wife with my mistress.

'Jane, you remember Lady de Morisset, a client of mine who first visited us at Hersham?'

'Mrs Lilly, I am pleased you look well in these challenging times.' With great grace Magdalene took Jane's hand.

Jane, flustered by Magdalene's grand manner and flattered by her affection, smiled back, and to my amazement looked almost comely.

'I am, though these are difficult times for us all. But I see from your dress you have had a change of allegiance?' she answered with a slight curtsy.

'Indeed, I am known now as plain Maggie, and have severed all my Royalist ties, and know that I am closer to my Maker for doing so.'

Jane, thrilling with my mistress's newfound piety, nodded wisely. 'All men are equal at Heaven's gate, and humility is the shortest path to Heaven. I will pray for you,' she told Magdalene with an earnest severity that did secretly amuse me.

We were interrupted by a commotion across the fields. 'Parliament is lost at Newbury – the King has victory!' a youth scrambling to keep his balance yelled as he waved a pamphlet in his hand. Immediately dismay ran through the crowd like an ill wind bending reeds.

'Could it be true!' Magdalene exclaimed, revealing her true alliance as Jane turned to me.

'Oh William! All those men!' Jane reached for my arm, for we knew youths who had fought with Parliament in that battle.

'The King was outnumbered by a great many, so if this be true it is a great victory for him and a blow for Cromwell.' I snatched a pamphlet from the youth, pressing a farthing upon him and read. 'They are saying each side lost some five hundred men, but after nightfall the Duke of Manchester did argue restraint to Cromwell and he did hesitate and so the King and his men did depart victorious the next morn.' I looked up. Jane was crestfallen whilst Magdalene barely hid her triumph. 'They will to Donnington Castle next, I wager,' I concluded.

''Tis how you first predicted in your almanack, before that John Booker got hold of it and did his alterations, William: "*I can promise absolute victory to neither side this year*" . . .' Jane quoted, and for once I loved her.

'The almanack is for the next year, Jane, and although there are more months of battles before 1645 is over, I have predicted victory for Parliament in the June – a most auspicious time for battle as the King's ascendant Leo will be quarrelling with Mars at that point and he will be weak. I have spoken with Bulstrode Whitelocke . . .'

'What doth he say?' Magdalene asked anxiously.

'Parliament hath listened to me; they will wait for the most auspicious time to battle, which will be June. Take heed, ladies, you are looking at a man who has influenced the path of history. But even after that confrontation I fear there will be instability until January 1647, and then by January 1649 I believe the matter of power will be resolved.'

'But will we live to see it?' Jane sounded doubtful.

'You will, but my Nativity tells me I might not,' I answered.

At which both women looked alarmed.

A few moments later, Magdalene and her maid had made their polite departure and I found myself watching my love hurry away from me across the snow like a complete stranger whilst Jane stayed by my side. I did reflect upon the heart and the terrible paradoxes of its afflictions. And yet I was to juggle both women and my own sensibilities of both the politick and my morality for many more months to come.

CHAPTER TWENTY-SEVEN

May, 1645

Thorn Inn, the village of Mistley, Essex

The Seventh House: It giveth judgement of Marriage, and describes the person inquired after, whether it be Man or Woman; all manner of Love questions, our publique enemies; the Defendant in a Law-suit, in Warre the opposing party; all quarrels, Duels, Law-suits.

I was writing from a small and chilly room I was sharing with a most unsavoury man whose belches and farts would shame Falstaff himself; this, and his tremendous snoring having stolen all possibility of sleep.

Much had happened since Christmas; the King was in retreat in many parts of the country – Cromwell's power, assisted by Essex, grows greater by the day. I had now, unwillingly, found myself in the petty battle of words between myself, the Royalist Na'worth, and my associate John Booker, with whom I have had several altercations over the censoring of mine own works. The fact that we were secret members of the Council bore no sway to this battle of opinion: we were the most influential Astrologers in the country and much stood by our judgements. Until last year I'd stayed out of the fray, but Na'worth dragged me in, and John Booker, who, I feared, was jealous of the success of *Merlinus Angelicus*, hath also irked me to the point of public response. In truth, when I looked into the future I did not see England as a Republic and would not lie to please others, patrons or otherwise.

I also knew from fingermen I had placed both in the House and in the alehouses of Westminster, Magdalene was watched and in danger. It was for her and for the sake of the Grand Council of Theurgy that I was to the village of Mistley in Essex, a miserable, unenviable place, damp, dank and devoid of all intelligent discourse.

I was in the attic chamber of the Thorn Inn, an establishment now owned by that meddlesome and wicked fingerman, Hopkins himself. Since March his persecution of innocent women and men had increased in the most foul way, and yet I was not able to voice my true disgust but was forced to play lackey to his pseudo-mastery. To conclude, I was there to attend a meeting called by the 'Witch Finder-General' the next day with several other honorary and learned gentlemen.

One was John Thurloe. Cromwell had now made him Number One Argus, a poor choice, for I feared this man was capable of both betrayal and deceit, but I conceded that he had the best constitution to run a company of spies and intelligence gatherers. He was of the constitution of Scorpio, and insidious in his sly observation of all gesture and psychology of men.

Another was John Stearne. If you remember, dear Reader, I had met this oaf before and he now boasted he was the best Witch-pricker in these Isles, although I wagered there'll be better in France, where the enthusiasm of Witch hunts is even greater than in England. A thick-necked bulldog of a man, I could barely bring myself to look at him.

There were others called to this meeting – the purpose of which was to discuss the hunting down of all Witches, Wizards, Sorcerers and individuals that might be a threat to Parliament and to the souls of all Puritans.

This self-declared Witch Finder-General hath already tried an Elizabeth Clarke, whose own mother hath been burnt for witch-craft (Cunning Folk, I wager, perhaps squatting on land that a neighbour craved to own) an innocent widow John Stearne stripped naked and searched for Witches' teats — the means by which the Devil sucks from a Witch. I knew this, for John Stearne did recount the woman's ordeal with great relish over a jug of ale earlier that evening. He claimed to have found three such nipples; they then kept this woman without rest or sleep for three days and three nights until she did confess her sorcery and her keeping of familiars — cat, rabbit, polecat and grey-hound. In truth, at this point of the unsavoury account, I had thought of my raven Solomon with alarm; would he be consid-ered a familiar? So tortured, Elizabeth Clarke did then give names of others — and this list grew (as it does with villagers and their grievances), with Hopkins and his gruesome band of men interrogating some hundred people, revealing all manner of horrors, familiars, imps and devil-worshipping (all in Essex? Is this such an unholy, ill-fated place?) In total, some thirty-two were accused and will go to the Chelmsford court in July.

To my shame, I sat through this most explicit rendition mute, occasionally nodding sagely whilst within I seethed. Once John Stearne had finished, the spittle barely dry upon his chin, I made my excuses and escaped to my room.

Ah, my fellow traveller finally ceased his window-rattling snore. I then to sleep.

''Tis a great honour to sit with the most learned experts of the age and with them discuss the greatest scourge that threatens our godly and Puritan nation — the Witch.' Matthew Hopkins stood before the hearth of the Thorn Inn, a place he hath anointed as his unofficial headquarters, then pointed at me with one gloved finger. 'In particular Master William Lilly, for not only is he the greatest Philomath and most goodly in his service to Parliament, but he is also the author of *Supernatural Sights of London*, and is most observant in the locations of such evil, as well as the effects of the stars on the deaths of monarchs, the presence of ghosts and the like. I personally have witnessed his great skill at the detection of Wizards, and practitioners of the black arts.'

I was uneasy. I was the only man around the table who had any real knowledge of both the Occult – both Magi and Theurgy – and I had to surrender this in a manner that did not betray either Cunning Folk or the wise men of astrology, astronomy, alchemy and all these sciences that marry the magical, and still protect myself. This was not a pretty dance. And so I forced a smile at this charlatan, and ask you, dear Reader, not to judge me, for it is better to know what poison feeds thine enemy's soul than not.

Encouraged, Hopkins continued, 'As you all know, I have already thirty-two Witches and Wizards awaiting trial. However, this is just the very tip of the fork-tongued monster who lurks beneath the very conscience of our great country. Satan dwelleth in the most ordinary and innocent of places – in the hearths and homes of our villages, behind the face of the hag who poisons livestock with a simple muttered word, in the hidden glades of our forests, the depths of our caves. But the Devil also is in our cities and squats upon the left shoulder of some of our most powerful and revered so-called scholars . . .' Hopkins turned his steely eye upon me, and so I did look back innocently in mock horror.

'Perchance you mean the sects in my good London who worship Jupiter and Saturn as their only gods?' I asked as sincerely as I could muster. Such communities were known in the city and tolerated, as much madness was in those times.

'These Junonians and Saturnians worry me not; they are merely a motley bunch of elderly drunkards who dance and fawn in the worship of these planets. No, I speak of far graver and more powerful evildoers,' Hopkins answered. –

I looked down upon the table before me to avoid his gaze.

'A list hath come into my possession,' Hopkins announced, causing several present to look up in surprise, including, I noted, John Stearne. Obviously this had been the jewel in Hopkins' crown he'd been saving until now and nervously I did wonder how he came upon this list, whether if it was from one of his own enemies or whether poor Hamish had left more condemning evidence.

'I call it The Devil's List – coded, it contains all the names of all the Witches in England – and I believe I have broken the cipher. These names are not just the humble servants of the Devil but also the names of some very eminent men – most of which are of the Court and Papists!'

At which John Stearne nudged me, his noxious breath repellent. 'No surprise there,' he muttered.

'In fact, I believe there might exist a secret coven in London of these Wizards and Sorcerers, and that they meet and share information to avoid the holy Law of the Puritan falling upon their heads.' Hopkins' finger stabbed the air as if he were already to work with the foul bodkin he designed himself for Witch-pricking.

There was a clamour of approval about the table, John Thurloe, in his enthusiasm, slammed his jug of ale upon the table and several others applauded whilst looking nervously over their shoulders as if these demonic overlords were already at the door.

I leant back upon my chair. 'This is Catholic propaganda designed to divide the Puritan society – this is a battle plan to demoralise and give fright to our troops and we should resist it. After all, my fellow Londoners are zealous in their pursuit of Papists, secret Catholics and other such abominations. The business of saving souls is taken most seriously. And if anyone should know of such a coven, it would surely be myself. And I know of none that fits your description, unless you suspect the Freemasons of unholy activity?' I meant to confuse them with my piety.

'Truly, Master Lilly, there is not rumour of such a society amid your colleagues? For some are well versed in the occult. Did you yourself not carry a library of such-like books once?' John Thurloe stared across the table and I did not care for his tone or the threat that lay beneath his pebble-smooth words.

'These colleagues are men of science, and have studied the occult to arm themselves with the knowledge to counter the dangers of the black arts, as I have done,' I answered firmly. 'To remain ignorant is to remain vulnerable. I have already revealed a devil worshipper, a French Papist Royalist known to the King's Court. This was for the benefit of Mr Hopkins who can testify that it were my expertise that enabled us to root out the condemning evidence.' I spoke with a false calmness whilst holding the gaze of Thurloe, a man capable of betraying his own mother.

'Indeed, this is true,' Hopkins confirmed, but Thurloe's expression remained sceptical.

'But if you were to hear of such an organisation, I can rely upon you to report back to Master Hopkins and myself?'

'I can promise more than that. I know most of the haunted and evil places within the city, places that draw such creatures and their hideous covens to them. I can provide thee also with a list, and perhaps, Mr Thurloe, you might post some of your loyal men to watch?' To my hidden relief Thurloe leapt most enthusiastically upon my bait.

'This does sound most intriguing. To trap one of these demonic overlords in the middle of a rite would be validation indeed of the impure and unholy spiritual decadence of the Papist. I have good brave men who would not quake in the face of such evil.'

'They were brave indeed,' I couldn't resist quibbling, catching John Stearne's eye; the coward he was in the face of the quackery I created at Vindecot's townhouse. He glanced away.

'And the Protector would approve?' I asked as if I cared.

'To catch such individuals could only improve Parliament's cause and prove to the common man the extent of the moral rot that eats at the heart of the Royalist,' Thurloe elaborated.

And so the evening progressed, Matthew Hopkins' descriptions of the 'science' of both his Witch-hunting and of his 'interrogation' techniques increasingly sickening, but I listened, feigning great zeal. At the end of the meeting I wrote the list I had promised, determined to send Thurloe's men on a merry dance across London, from a small cemetery downwind from Billingsgate fish market, to a crypt in a church in the village of Wandsworth – none of which were frequented by anyone except perhaps ghosts. I couldn't resist adding to the list a particularly pungent dunghill I knew of beside the barricade at the Bishops Gate.

Suffice to say the Number One Argus was most grateful and told me he would send his young wife to visit for a horary on when next best to conceive, as he was, like most rich men, most disappointed with his existing children.

Eager to get back to London that very evening, I stood to leave, but to my dismay Matthew Hopkins pulled me aside.

'Old friend, I am thankful such an eminent man joins me on my mission. You know, William, more than most, how I respect your word.'

Oh Lord, how he fawned, and when he moved to clasp my hand I did repress a shudder! 'But master,' he continued, the embodiment of obsequiousness, 'know you of a Lady de Morisset?'

'I met her once or twice before the troubles.' Faith, how I kept my countenance plain and closed I do not know. 'Perchance you have an interest in her?'

'She is on my list – her name is disguised in code, but the description, I am convinced, is of her. She was also mentioned in the information given by Vindecot.'

My mind spun in frantic strategy. 'Does that not suggest a Royalist plot against her? For she hath abandoned both King and the Queen of whom she was a favourite?'

He lowered his voice. 'Could she be Witch? Answer me honestly, maestro?'

'Nay. I know she hath a reputation for eccentric and strange prayer when she were a Papist and was most fond of idolatry, but since her return to the city and conversion she is wholly Puritan and is seen most often at that godly preacher Thomas Edwards' sermons. Papist once, but never Witch – I stake my life upon it.' At that the Witch Finder-General studied me long and hard.

'Yes, I believe you would,' he finally replied.

It was too late to leave the Thorn Inn until early morning. I set off in a fog but by midday the sun was high upon my back. I arrived at the town of Chelmsford and did pass fields where they were drilling recruits for the New Model Army and noticed some appeared as young as ten year, others as old as sixty. Truly, this was a desperate war. I rode hard and fast, terror a ghost companion breathing into my left ear propelling me forward. I suspected I was followed, and I felt the curse of Hopkins' suspicion. Several times at the sound of approaching hooves I did hide poor Pegasus and myself in ditches. And as the road was peopled by highwaymen and marauding soldiers starved of food and gold, I was taking no chances.

By the time I did arrive at the village of Stratford it was past the tenth hour and the stars were high in the night sky. Pegasus was spent, and only when I hitched him to a post at the inn did I know I was out of the Witch-Finder's reach — for now. Later I did spread several Sigils around my bed and pillow for protection and I prayed — both for Magdalene and for myself.

CHAPTER TWENTY-EIGHT

♍ ☉ ☉

June 1645

The Suffering City of London

The Eighth House: The Estate of Men deceased, Death, its quality and nature; the wills, Legacies and Testaments of Men deceased; Dowry of the Wife, Portion of the Maid, whether much or little, easie to be obtained or with difficulty. In Duels it represents the Adversaries Second; in Lawsuits the Defendants friends.

The next morn was the first of the new month; I rode up the Strand and, upon seeing white walls of the Corner House, felt a renewed sense of purpose. The time of the Philomath and of the mystic sciences may be passing, but I was determined to ensure a legacy that wilt not dwindle with time. This and other portentous musings filled my mind as I entered my home, which appeared strangely empty. I found Mrs Featherwaite in the kitchen, scolding the kitchen maid.

'Where is Mrs Lilly?'

'In church, praying for your soul! She's been there since four this morning. She heard Thurloe's men have arrested several Philomaths last night, and fears for you.'

'They dare not touch me; Parliament is in pocket to me.'

'You have no argument here, master, and I told her as much. But she will not be comforted. She fears your almanacks contain truths uncomfortable for both Parliament and King and that you make enemies of both.'

The kitchen maid, a pale scrubby wisp of a creature, whimpered. Angry that Mrs Featherwaite had upset her so, I pressed a farthing into her hand.

'Polly, go fetch a bun and a loaf from the baker,' I ordered.

'There is no bread in the bakers, sir, just cheat bread made from millet – there is no real bread to be found in the whole city.'

'Then buy what thee can find!' I shouted, my temper fraying and, to my shame, the maid ran. I swung back to my housekeeper.

'Mrs Featherwaite, have I not been a good employer to thee?'

'The best, master, the very best.'

'And do you not wish to remain in my employment?'

'I do indeed, sir.'

'In that case, be doubly cautious of idle talk and dangerous chatter. I am as astute a politician as I am Philomath, but I will not be cowered, either by suspicion or the agendas of Kings and Ministers. Know that I merely am the messenger of the stars. I broadcast what they tell of man and of kingdom.'

'I understand, sir.'

'So, go fetch Mrs Lilly from church and tell her that for better or worse I am not in the Tower but back home. Meanwhile I shall attend my business. Where are my Querents?'

'I sent many away this morning, thinking you were not to arrive back in time.'

'Then send Simon out to the inn and to the Common to proclaim that I am back–. Quickly, woman! Enough time has been wasted!'

And so I went to my study, but not before I visited the dovecote and sent a message to Magdalene that she was to meet me that evening at a tavern in Blackfriars I knew would be free of fingermen.

By late afternoon I had seen two widows, a young girl enquiring about the faithfulness of her swain (he was not, and indeed, appeared to be courting several women) and an armour-maker who was concerned about the tardiness of payment from a client. After which Jane came back from church, full of relief at my return. I waited until she retired early then after wrapping myself in a cloak and hat, to make my way swiftly to the Blackfriars' tavern, a place frequented by nought but street folk – swill-bellies, rag-pickers, sellers of cockles, and town criers. My street friend Janko hath taken me there on occasion and, despite the dank and grime-laden benches, it boasted a good ale and oxtail pie. Best of all, it were empty of politicians, spies, and whores and I have used it over the years for many a clandestine meeting.

After I pressed coin upon the innkeeper he did lead me to a small chamber at the back where a woman was seated, her face and head entirely covered by a veil. I said nothing until I had shut the door on the curious innkeeper.

'Did you see anyone suspicious?' Magdalene spoke through the fine silk, like an ancient obelisk that had suddenly developed a mouth.

'We are alone.'

'Are we?' She still did not remove her veil. I walked slowly around the walls; there were no windows, no suspicious hangings or curtains, and outside on the street an organ grinder played his tune. I was sure we would not be overheard.

'To get here safely I first went to Church, where I knelt on the cold flagstones for hours, watching the man who had followed me in the reflection of the brass plaque upon the pew. It was only when evening prayers began that he finally left and

I could hurry here.' She lifted her veil and I could see the fear in the white edges of her pinched face.

'Hopkins has your name on a list,' I told her bluntly.

She flinched. 'They say he tortures the women with needles and hot irons, until they are mad with exhaustion and pain and will confess anything. Is this to be me?'

I slipped my hand under her sleeve; her fingers were burning. 'Never! I will not allow it.'

She pulled her hand away. 'You will be lucky if they do not take you too.'

'Magdalene, I told him he was mistaken, that you were pious and most goodly. Besides, he would not dare arrest an aristocrat.'

'Not yet, but after this next trial . . . Cromwell uses this fear to control the people and Hopkins garners support for him. He is evil, as is Thurloe.'

'Pack up your household, go to the countryside somewhere far from Essex, take on the guise of an invisible woman.'

'Then he will have won! I will not let Matthew Hopkins run me out of London. Not now when, finally, I have some livelihood, some hope of a life. And what of us?'

'Jane already suspects, and would betray me to the religious council if she had evidence of infidelity. My reputation would be ruined. Is that what you want?'

'My mind understands but my heart and soul tell me otherwise. This affection is ordained by Anima Mundi, the soul of the world, if not God.'

Surprised at this turn of conversion, I wondered at her meaning; did she suddenly want the convention of marriage? But I found I could not ask her. I was a coward, and in that moment more concerned with keeping my head and my life.

'If you cannot save me I have friends who will,' Magdalene, appalled by my silence, exclaimed. 'New friends in Parliament, powerful men who would place their neck on the block for me, William.'

'In this age, a man's trust is as fickle as the weather. I trust no one now, not even members of the Council. I can help you get a cottage, a place you can hide until this war and the era of men like Hopkins has passed.'

'No more running! If they come to arrest me so be it, but I am staying in London.'

'This is foolishness!' I tried to take her into my arms but she fought me.

'Perhaps we have little time left, but not because of Hopkins. If so I will spend every moment with you!'

'I understand you not!'

'You forget, you are fated to die in 1647. It is in your true Nativity.'

'Keep your voice down!'

Frightened she would alert the innkeeper, I put my hand across her mouth. 'All the stars show us are the favourable circumstances in which to act! But the action is taken in free will. Magdalene, all I wish is to save you!'

At which she bit my hand, more animal than woman. Bleeding, I snatched it back, anger bolting me to the floor.

Shocked at herself, she tore a shred from her petticoats and, pulling my reluctant arm to her side, did bind the hand.

'Forgive my anger. I do love thee, but as thou say, it is my destiny and I will choose to stay – I'll not spend another year in a different city, William. I want thee by my side – even in the stolen moments. We are married in Spirit, William, I know it now, and that is more than thou hast with Jane. I'll not surrender that.' After which she lifted her skirts, pressed my bandaged hand to her damp sex, the fighting having stirred her to passion, and to my shame I hardened.

I let her free me from my hose, her breasts now loosened, and she mounted me as I leant against the bench, her nipples brushing my lips as she rode out all her fury.

It was only afterwards, in the lancing sweat and tumble, I saw the amulet between her breasts. I recognised the symbols etched upon it, for I myself had made many such amulets for hopeful young wives, and in that I knew her mind, yet I said nothing.

CHAPTER TWENTY-NINE

Summer 1645

The edge of Epping Forest

**The Ninth House: By this House we give judgement of
Voyages or long journies beyond Seas of Religiousmen,
or Clergy of any kinde, whether Bishops or inferiour
Ministers; Dreams, Visions, forraign Countries; of
Books, Learning, Church Livings, or Benefices . . .**

A week later I called a meeting of the Grand Council of Theurgy.
Had Matthew Hopkins known he would be most aggrieved.
There was daily news of Thurloe's raids — the storming of the
most absurd places in search of Sorcerers, Devil worshippers and
even Papists involved in the sacrifice of children. Yesterday it
were the back end of Billingsgate fish market, famous for its
outdoor spooning I did know the place as a younger man. The
day before it were an empty well, located in the stinking yard of
a tanner's (I claimed a Witch did lower herself down there every
full moon to be nearer the Devil), the day before that an old
vintner's cellar near the docks. So far, both Thurloe and Hopkins
were convinced they were on a grand hunt that would make
them famous, or at the very least infamous. But I knew I would
have to contrive more false leads to keep them befuddled.

In the meanwhile, I chose an abandoned cottage at the edge
of Epping Forest for the Council's meeting. The war continues;

as I predicted, the Long Parliament's commissioners could not reach a peace agreement with the King's men and again the Treaty of Uxbridge failed. We were steeling ourselves for more battles and more dead men, but I still saw victory for Parliament. None of which I shared with Magdalene. We had not seen each other since our meeting in Blackfriars. I felt her calling out to me every night and I struggled to stop myself replying. I heard through my fingermen that she endangered herself by working as an apothecary, selling her own devised cures. This was dangerous news.

At the same time there was information from Oxford. Tobias hath collected places and times where the three young officers who raped Mary Dutton might be found alone and unarmed. With great haste I did send the information to Mrs Dutton and her soldier husband, and in gratitude they did send me back good coin and a fattened goose. I did not doubt I will hear of the officers' demise within the year. This, and more, meandered about my mind as I dismounted and tethered my horse one half mile from the cottage, deciding to walk the rest of the way through the forest in case of discovery.

It was pleasant; evening light flooded the sky as if there were no war and Armageddon was not upon England and her neighbours. Mayflies and dragonflies danced at the water's edge, somewhere a lark sang, trees were green with leaf, and I did marvel at such ill-founded tranquillity.

The abandoned cottage was at the edge of an estate belonging to Duke of Cumberland who had been killed at Marston Moor where some four thousand Royalists are said to have died and a mere three hundred Parliament men. I knew his son was sympathetic to our cause and the estate itself was boarded up as the family had fled to Royalist land.

Inside, it was dim with the last of the light struggling through the gaps in the wooden slats that covered the windows.

Most of the furniture had been taken for firewood and the room was empty, except for the traditional circle of thirteen chairs placed around one large candle, burning and dripping. Four chairs were empty – three were of members who had been arrested, the fourth would be Magdalene's place.

Nine of us sat, all masked, and I noted that many wore different masks from whence we last met, a precaution to being recognised, although I knew individuals from their voices. To my relief, Magdalene had stayed away. John Booker, with his customary Bull mask, was holding court.

'We have now lost three members, including Hamish McDuff, who like brave Harry, took his own life before interrogation. But I fear Hopkins' popularity, and any of us in this circle could be sacrificed to gain further support of the people – no matter how powerful our friends or how noble a family we might herald from.'

'Maybe we should disband until the fervour has passed?' Lady Eleanor Davies spoke up.

'There is safety in shared information. Perhaps we play at the same game and place trusted fingermen within both Thurloe's band and Matthew Hopkins' men to report back to us,' I suggested.

Another spoke out. 'I already have one such fellow, trusted, with eyes that can see in the dark. He is one of Thurloe's most zealous officers.'

'The Number One Argus already believes he has a list of all known covens in London. So far, he hath found nought but a homeless tramp asleep upon a dung heap, a scroll buried in a bottle I did compose myself, and an upside-down drawing of the Virgin drenched in goat's piss. The ease with which he swallows such nonsense is an embarrassment. However, as a strategy it is working – for the time being,' I responded, the others nodding in approval.

'Nevertheless, if any of us be arrested we should claim immunity as professional scholars, and that any powers we might have are for the good and are white magick.' Henry Gellibrand's frail voice sounded out, chipping at the rose-tipped air. 'If the importance of our work can be understood, I am convinced we will reinstate astrology, alchemy and the study of the occult back to its true eminence, as it was in the days of the ancients.' At which he swung around to his neighbour. 'Have you seen the drawing the Dutchman Christiaan Huggers has made of the planets — landscapes he hath seen through his new telescope? Venus has been stripped of her skirts! He parades her nudity like a cheap peepshow!'

'People like Matthew Hopkins cares not for the truth, old man.' The young man sitting opposite me who I had not seen before spoke out. 'He cares not for who is truly Witch or Sorcerer, or whether it be white magick or black. He cares only for the fat coin he is charging parishes for the pleasure he takes in torturing defenceless Cunning Men and Women, and how much favour such actions curry with government. As for scientific discovery, methinks it is inevitable — one day men will be able to fly as Angels, and we will know the peoples of the world as well as our own neighbour. Even so, we are custodians of older knowledge, of the Babylon and beyond. If they destroy us, they destroy our libraries, make mute our tongues. This cannot happen.'

At these stirring words the others began drumming their heels upon the wooden floor in approval. Verily, I too was impressed yet, as I looked upon this sprig of a man, I saw an early death. I wasn't the only one.

'A wise head upon a young neck, may it stay there.' Was this a compliment or a threat? To this day I do not know, but I do know that it were John Booker that spake.

'These sentiments are noble indeed but surely there is greater strength in numbers.' A man in an owl mask spoke — Nicolas

Culpeper, an alchemist and great medic I did respect. He gestured toward the table. 'I, like several others at the table, am also a member of what we call the Invisible College, a group of learned scientists and alchemists who meet both here and in Oxford to acquire greater knowledge of the world and all its wonder through experimentation and intellectual investigation. We are few, but powerful, I think, and have much, but not all, in common with the voices I hear at this table. What say you to the two secret societies meeting?'

'I would know more of your philosophies,' I asked.

'We follow the works of Paracelsus; we believe the macrocosm and microcosm are one. There are great minds amongst us, including Robert Boyle. We are Godly people, whose works are dedicated to the betterment of all men,' Culpeper replied.

'And what say the Invisible College of transmutation – the alchemist's quest to turn plain metal to gold? There are some amongst us who regard this as unholy – a sin.' Again, it were Henry Gellibrand who spoke.

'I confess this is an argument amongst ourselves; it is a great gift of God, but as it is a purely physical process I myself would call it ungodly and accursed gold-making.' Culpeper's religious dedication was well known.

'I think it prudent to draw attention away from the Grand Council and not toward it,' I interjected, thinking upon the suspicion cast upon all intellectual pursuits at this time. 'The Invisible College will have its own detractors, so let us deal with ours firstly and then, perhaps when both the times and men are more tolerant, God willing, review the possibility again. To this may I see the yeas?' And as there was a show of six hands I did not bother counting the nays. 'It is decided, then, the Grand Council of Theurgy and the Invisible College will not meet in the foreseeable future.'

Across the table I could see Nicholas Culpeper's shoulders sink in disappointment.

After we had left the circle the stranger who had spoken earlier drew me apart from the others.

'I recognise thee despite thy mask,' he told me.

''Tis the penalty of famed reputation,' I replied graciously.

'And justly earned, maestro. I too, am a Philomath, though a mere student against thy greater knowledge. But I believe we have a mutual friend.'

'Indeed?'

He leant toward me, lowering his voice, 'Magdalene de Morisset.'

Faith, I was glad I was masked; even so, I kept my voice indifferent. 'I have been of service to the gentlewoman a few years back, a matter of some stolen cloth . . .'

He did not flinch or show he knew otherwise. 'She hath mentioned you once or twice. I barely know her, but I sent her a goodly servant, one Susan Bodenham, sister of my own housekeeper, Anne. Both women are skilful Cunning Folk, and know old knowledge, most useful in ways of astrology, healing and fortune telling. She will be of great assistance for Lady de Morisset, who I believe has an interest in such matters.'

'A godly woman now repentant for her previous ways,' I added piously, wishing to make clear that Magdalene was above suspicion. 'She hath been most kind to my wife,' I added to clarify relations, 'and I trust this Susan Bodenham will not lead the good lady astray nor place her in any danger?'

'To the contrary, sir, such a creature can only give advantage to events, present and future.' At which he bowed and offered me his hand. 'John Lambe of Salisbury, at your service.'

'Your service, my good man, would be to keep your anonymity even amongst friends,' I replied, 'we all play a game here.' But I liked him nevertheless.

It was at this time Wharton, in guise of his nom de plume Na'worth, did again, from the Royalist capital of Oxford (for he was seen no longer at the table of the Grand Council of Theurgy) embark on a vicious attack of both John Booker and myself, angry at the Royalist defeats.

His almanack of this year 1645 published on the seventh of May did name me. It were an open attack upon myself and John Booker, accusing us of encouraging rebels and conspirators against His Majesty through our disloyal and ambiguous use of language, and suggested we were unprofessional and biased as Philomaths. Faith, this man has much blood upon his hands. Would those troops have marched so naively into battle if they had been advised the battle was doomed? Na'worth's *An Astrological Judgement upon his Majesties Present March: Begun from Oxford, May 7th 1645* was a guide to certain suicide!

I would not have taken such offence except in Na'worth's blank denial of the Heavens and the ominous signs that hung over the King as visibly as the highlands of Scotland. When his false and self-seeking pamphlet reached me, I did respond quickly with *The Starry Messenger*, describing why the King and his men courted disaster if to battle before mid-June. As soon as the pamphlet were finished I went straight to the press. For whilst writing it had felt as if every day was one month so pressing was the morality of correct prediction until it was public; I had made good use of the King's Nativity and found that his ascendant was approaching the quadrature of Mars, about June, 1645. This was a most unlucky formation. In *The Starry Messenger* I told it in plain English. If the King were to fight before the eleventh of June, victory would be stolen from him, and so it proved on the fourteenth of June at the great battle of Naseby, the worst defeat for Charles in all the War.

But my influence was more than just the publication of that pamphlet upon the outcome of Naseby. And I will tell thee, dear Reader, for I am sure you are impartial politically to this matter. In truth, the New Model Army itself did take my advice upon the timing of this engagement. For on the ninth of June I did by accident (or Divine Providence) come upon my dear friend and politician Bulstrode in the streets of Westminster and asked him news of both the King's men and the New Model Army. Were they upon each other yet? And he doth confirm that yes, they were very likely to engage, and, having the calculation of the King's vulnerability, so I did insist again (knowing Bulstrode hath the ear of both Parliament and of Fairfax) that the New Model Army should not engage until after the eleventh day of this month of June (two days hence), for it was only after this date that the Parliament would have the greatest victory they ever yet had.

Following my advice, the New Model Army did engage in battle at Naseby on the fourteenth of June. In the morning of that very same day I did publish *The Starry Messenger* with this same prediction within, that Parliament would win, and win mightily, in battle and so it was. Naseby was the most decisive battle of these years and if Parliament had not heeded my advice the outcome of the civil war might have been very different. This was the greatest confirmation of my skills as a Philomath and impressed all in Parliament, a useful ploy for my own promotion and survival.

But Naseby was a most brutal defeat for the Royalists: one hundred and fifty officers killed, and, more shamefully, the pamphlets did also report on the slaughter of the Royalist women by the Parliamentarians — over one hundred campfollowers, whose only crime was to have followed their husbands and lovers into the battle camps. The King himself and his nephew Prince Rupert did flee to avoid capture – to Ashby-de-la-Zouch, I believe.

Again, my reputation soared like Icarus, for the people read my prediction declaring a victory on the very day the victory itself was being won! This was doubly sweet, for *The Starry Messenger* was a counter foil to the false astrology of George Wharton.

But to prove to you I am more Philomath than instrument to Parliament *The Starry Messenger* did also contain a warning for Parliament itself. I wrote of the great unhappiness amongst the New Model Army officers, and that Parliament needed to pay its army to promptly divert disaffection and mutiny.

Naturally, there were some in Westminster who took great offence at my authority. One in particular, a Mr Miles Corbet, a pickled peppershaker and a pickthank who had run the poor Archbishop Laud to his demise. A man equal to Matthew Hopkins in his self-serving prosecution, arrest and questioning of innocent bystanders. Corbet was, unfortunately, the chairman of the Committee of Examinations – an institute to be feared.

And so it was that one morning there was a great knocking at the front door and Mrs Featherwaite ran into my study. Behind her were two armed guards and the Sergeant-at-arms of the Committee of Examinations.

'Master Lilly! Master Lilly! They mean to arrest thee!'

The tall, stern-faced gentleman, a sword in his belt, stepped up. 'Master Lilly, I am here to escort you to Westminster, where you will be examined by Mr Corbet, the chairman.'

'You are arresting me on what grounds?'

'It is the Committee's duty to search out falsehoods that might serve to inflame discontent against Parliament . . . and, in truth, you're not the first Philomath I have arrested, although personally I do believe you to be the best in the land, Master Lilly, but then I don't decide these matters. So, if you would kindly come with me . . .?' He was so uncomfortable in his duty that I did take pity upon him.

I donned my cloak and left my weeping wife and house-keeper and we made our way through the streets toward Westminster, three abreast — myself flanked by two guards — and as such were greatly noticed by the passers-by, some of who recognised my good self. Several ragamuffins and street children began following us, taunting the guards with rhymes and ditties at which they did respond in good cheer. As I walked, fear wound me tighter and tighter and I pondered on how I had fallen in such bad grace in so short a time. Had Thurloe fathomed my deceit? Had Hopkins fallen out of affection with his most favoured Astrologer? Was it even possible Magdalene had betrayed me? Miles Corbet was a man unpredictable and fickle, known to be cruel in his interrogation techniques.

My fear hardened into terror, but then, to my great luck (and the auspicious stars of the day) as we turned into Turnpike Lane we stumbled upon four of my friends — Robert Reynolds, Sir Christopher Wray, Sir Philip Stapleton and Denzil Holles — all members of Parliament, who stopped in surprise at the sight of the eminent Philomath Mr William Lilly being marched through the streets. I could barely believe my good fortune.

'Faith, William, 'tis lucky we come upon thee at this minute. Why look, I have the very pages of *The Starry Messenger* upon my person, and a heartening read it is!' Sir Stapleton exclaimed, pulling my pamphlet from his pocket.

I indicated the guards. 'I fear too popular. This gentleman is a messenger from the sergeant-at-arms. I am being hauled before the Committee of Examinations, to be questioned by Miles Corbet himself — no lover of mine.'

'Indeed not – Miles Corbet is a dour taskmaster whose fervour will lead him to an unhappy end; he will punish thee soundly, William,' Robert Reynolds added, smiling as he did. However, my terror must have shown upon my face, for Sir Christopher Wray interjected, 'Fear nothing; we four will dine, then make haste to be at the committee in time enough to do thy business – and trust me, we are far more favourably inclined to thee, Philomath, than the sour Corbet and chirping-mercy.'

At which they all did laugh, being somewhat intoxicated with both the evening and their own company but I did take comfort in their promise and indeed my friends made good their word, for when I appeared before the committee (after being confined in a dank, dark cell during which I had much time to reflect upon my mercurial fortune) the four esteemed gentlemen and supporters were firmly sat upon the committee benches with Robert Reynolds himself in the Chair.

I was called in, and when the miserly prosecutor finally appeared he did produce a copy of my almanack of 1645, which he waved wildly as if to emphasise a point, claiming that I had written that taxation would reduce all to beggary and that I had accused all Committee men of being the new lords of corruption.

In truth, dear Reader, this was not totally inaccurate, but I had also shown that the stars favoured Parliament and not the King, and, as a mere mortal, I cannot be held responsible for what the planets might indicate.

Yet there I was, facing the Tower and possibly execution for treason, my legs atremble, aware that Corbet hath condemned men on far flimsier charges. The prosecutor also claimed I had made much criticism of the commissioners of Excise, at which the other members grew quiet. Just then a Presbyterian Excise officer entered the court, a man I knew who had personal griev-ances against me and I swear I did feel the full weight of my

Fate totter – like two plump boys upon a seesaw – as unease filled the room. Corbet, feasting off my agitation, turned to a passage in my almanack.

'Why, here, in this very pamphlet, in plain print for any ordinary man to read, is just one of the inciting passages . . .' And here he pulled himself up grandly like some amateur actor and began to read from the almanack. 'In the name of the Father, Son and Holy Ghost, will not the Eclipse pay the Soldiers!' at which the Chamber fell about laughing whilst Corbet, not realising his gaff, looked up, bewildered. For instead of reading *will not the Excise pay the Soldiers*, he hath read *will not the Eclipse pay the Soldiers*, and thus undermined both his case and sensible authority.

'Have you any more against Master Lilly?' Reynolds cried, and then, to my dismay, the same Presbyterian Excise Officer I had seen earlier, stepped up.

'Yes, since Master Lilly's *Starry Messenger* was published I have had my house burnt down, and many of the commissioners have been assaulted and pulled by their clothes in the Exchange. The Philomath hath great authority with the common man and he hath turned them against the sensible and the sane,' the officer claimed over the laughter.

The elderly Sir Robert Pym (a supporter I knew) spoke out. 'Pray sir, when was this that your house was burnt and the aldermen abused?'

'Sir, the second of June.'

Pym then turned to me. 'And when did your book come forth?'

Before I had a chance to response, Robert Reynolds replied, 'The very day of the Naseby fight, nor need he be ashamed of writing it: I had it daily as it came forth of the press.' He spoke proudly in response and my supporters drummed their feet in approval.

'Then your house was burnt twelve days before *The Starry Messenger* were published — what a lying fellow thou art,' Sir Pym chastised, and I did take heart until another man sprang to his feet.

'My name is Robert Bassell and I am an honest merchant and a Presbyterian and I would have Master Lilly's books burnt. They are dangerous and incite men to acts against Parliament!'

Just then Mr Francis Drake leapt up and yelled, 'You, sir, smell more like a citizen than a scholar!' Again, the chamber erupted into chaos.

I was dismissed, then called back, at which the committee told me (to my great relief) I was discharged and when I pointed out I was under a messenger the committee ordered him, nor the sergeant-at-arms, to take any fees.

'Indeed, literate men never pay any fees,' Reynolds proclaimed as a final conclusion on the case and I was greatly relieved.

But many other astrologers of England were much startled and confounded by my predictions, especially one William Hodges, who I did respect, an older master who lived near Wolverhampton and who was a staunch Royalist. Hodges swore I achieved more through astrology than he could through Crystal gazing, of which he was a master, and although he was a great Royalist he could never predict anything positive for that party, despite desiring such predictions greatly. He would never meddle with Nativities and in things of other nature he always turned back to the Crystal. His Angels were Raphael, Gabriel and Uriel; however his life did not conform to the degree of holiness and sanctity required in dealing with these holy Angels. My partner in magick, John Scott, was a prodigy of his.

John once asked Will to show him the person and features of the woman he should marry, and in a field Will Hodges did pull out his Crystal and bid John to look upon it. Within John did see a ruddy complexioned wench in a red waistcoat drawing a can of beer. 'She will be your wife,' Will Hodges told him, at which John did take offence, telling him he was mistaken, for he was to marry a tall gentlewoman in the Old Bailey upon his return to London later that week. But Will Hodges insisted: you must marry the red waistcoat, he tells him. I tell thee this story because it is an illustration of the strength of Will Hodges's Crystal gazing, for when John did return to London he found his tall gentlewoman had married another in his absence. Then, two years after, John did refresh himself at an inn on the way to Dover, and as he came in he mistook the door and by chance found himself in the buttery where he saw a maid of the very same description drawing a can of beer. They were later married. 'Tis the truth! Such clarity can be achieved with a good Crystal Gazer, Magdalene did study with one of the best in England — Sarah Skelhorn. This made me disquieted.

There were several attempts later the same year to discredit me, but as they were of a personal and vindictive nature and the committee did not consider them charges worth pursuing. I now realised that popularity did not make one immune to arrest and demise: if anything it raises a man to new vulnerability. But what choice did I have? God hath placed me on the planet to speak for the stars and to direct Man to a greater fortune if he so wished to listen. It were the Presbyterian who truly hated all my prophecy and, if they ever came to govern, my books would be burnt and my head would surely roll.

♃ ☉ ♀

CHAPTER THIRTY

The month of September 1645

The Corner House, The Strand

The Tenth House: Commonly it personateth Kings,
Princes, Dukes, Earls, Judges, prime Officers,
Commanders in chief, whether in Armies or Towns;
all sorts of Magistracy and Officers in Authority,
Mothers, Honour, Preferment, Dignity, Office,
Lawyers; the profession or Trade anyone useth . . .

I was just grinding up some jet (the amount that will lie upon a groat) to keep it in a glass of Sack, then have my patient drink it for the treatment of Rickets – an excellent remedy, dear Reader – when my wife returned from her morning visit to the market.

'William, you will never guess what I have just learnt!' Her colour was high and she was most excitable.

'That cabbages are blue this season?' I replied, irritated I had been disturbed. Jane ignored my quip.

'Thy client's maid hath been arrested for witchcraft! I learnt it from Maisy, the fishmonger's wife, who learnt it from Honor Collins, the hatter's assistant, who learnt it from our butcher. And her an aristocrat! What was she doing communing with Witches?'

'What client, Jane? And do sit down – all your scuttling and flapping is ruining my craft.'

'Why, Lady de Morisset, that aristocrat we did come upon at Spittel Fields. And there I was, thinking she were most pious,' Jane answered with all the relish of the Gossip (which she was). I tell thee, the world did invert itself then. 'William, art thou ill? Thou look most pale suddenly.'

I turned to Solomon, to hide my face, and did take him upon my hand.

'This is grave news.'

'They say the maid's name is Susan Bodenham, and that her and her Lady were travelling to see a friend in Essex when Matthew Hopkins' men did come upon them and arrest the maid.'

'And Lady de Morisset?'

'I believe she hath returned to London. I pray your friendship with her will not bode ill for us, for you cannot afford another arrest, William. There are many, not just Miles Corbet, who seek your demise.'

Staring at her, I wondered if she had guessed at our affair, but her face was open and clear.

'Matthew Hopkins is not a foe. Why, he doth use me as advisor,' I reassured her, whilst dread rose within me like nausea.

'Nevertheless, it would be foolish to be seen associating with the woman. I fear they will arrest her too.'

'There is no good reason to think the mistress would be infected by the sins of a servant,' I answered, with a certainty I did not feel and an hour later I sent Tobias with a message for Magdalene to meet me in the crypt of St Antholin's, for I knew the pastor there and had keys to the church.

It were damp and the cold air of the dead seemed to seep from under the brass plaques and marble tombs. I stared over at a winged statue of the Archangel Gabriel and methinks I saw those marble feathers ruffle.

'William . . .' My name, whispered, hung like the sheen on a cockerel's crescent it were so lightly spoken. And I did wonder whether I heard it, or that I had wished it into being. Magdalene came out from behind a tomb, her hair hidden beneath a cowl. She moved toward me in a swelter of both fear and elation and we did embrace.

'We rested at an inn at Danbury,' she said. 'I think they must have been following us for some time. You warned me, William, and you were right. Poor Susan's arrest is just the first twist of the noose.' Magdalene shook in my arms, her shoulders stripped of their courage.

'Is your maid Witch?' I asked outright.

'She is clever with the Knowledge – her mother and grand-mother and sister are all Cunning Folk. She hath been of great help with my alchemy and cures.' Magdalene would not look me in the eye.

'Is she Witch?' I insisted.

'The only Devil she worships is one born of Nature, not evil! Oh William, I am much afeard! They have kept poor Susan from sleep now for three nights, and I hear that the Witch finder's bodkin hath been used upon her body, and that she has confessed that the Devil did come to her in the form of her dead brother.'

'Brother?'

'He was a Royalist soldier killed at Newbury and she was much grieved by this loss. Perhaps it did drive her out of her right mind.'

'What else has she confessed?'

'That she hath made spells upon her enemies and at my instruction . . .'

'Has she told them you are a Witch?'

'It is only a matter of time.'

'Could it be a trap? The master of your maid's sister is a

member of the Grand Council of Theurgy, John Lambe. He introduced himself to me; is it possible he is also a spy?'

'If so, we are all lost. But I think not. Susan hath spoken often of her sister Anne Bodenham who is reputed as a great healer in Salisbury and I believe John Lambe to be trustworthy.'

'Even so, we must take no risks. Magdalene, you are to return to your house and pack immediately, and destroy anything incriminating. I will send you Daniel Jenkins, the same private guard I used to take us back from Oxford, to escort you, but you must flee back to the King's Court or to the nearest Royalist garrison before dawn.'

'I cannot.'

'You must — it is your only chance of survival. Hopkins *will* find you and arrest you.'

'That pox-ridden fingerman will not dare arrest a noble. Even if he be Puritan.'

'Oh, he will, precisely for those reasons. I know he has you in his sights. Susan's arrest is just an alibi. You have a fast horse?'

'Not now.'

'Then I will send one with Daniel.' I pulled her toward me. 'You will leave as soon as he arrives. Take this . . .' I took off the chain I wore about my neck upon which hung one of my own Sigils for protection — Angel's Gold with the symbol for Jupiter, for luck and good fortune.

She placed it next to her bosom and I did hold her, the scent of her hair sweeping me back to all our lovemaking. Outside, an early cockerel crowed and I knew she had but few hours to leave.

'Go now, and don't tarry.' I pushed her away.

'Know I shall never betray thee, William Lilly!'

*   *   *

After, I went straight to Daniel's dwelling, and he did leave by dawn. Later, back at my window, I watched a flock of starlings twist against the sky like one joyous creature, unencumbered by the machinations of us land-bound mortals. In my mind's eye I was turning around my encounters with Magdalene, in the manner I calculate a horary, tracking the meaning of each moment, each decision. I was obsessed, even so intellectual dissection was no cure. I might as well have cut a man open to find his soul.

If we were fated, was it possible for me to walk away? Magdalene now held my happiness between her hands as if it were a fragile paper kite. To imagine a future without her was to imagine a world without music or hope – and my world was dark enough.

And when the first sunlight fell upon the rug I confess I did pray, my supplications broken only by the sound of Solomon rustling his feathers, impatient to be out in that morning light.

Over the next three days I did conceal my fears in a deluge of inquiries. I threw myself into my craft, working up to fifteen hours a day – my first Querent at six, my last at nine. In this way I avoided Jane and any possibility of reflection. I wished not to think upon Magdalene and her fortune. Instead, I trusted that Daniel would send message when he could. Finally on the Friday I was interrupted by a commotion at the front door. Thinking it another bevy of guards sent for my arrest, I hastily gathered my grimoires and was about to leave by way of the garden, when Daniel, dishevelled, his hair unkempt, mud to his shins, barged into the room.

'They have taken her, William! Hopkins' men ambushed us on the road to Basingstoke!'

I crumpled, terror having punched me in the stomach.

'I'm sorry, I could not stop them.' Daniel steadied me with his strong hand.

'Where have they imprisoned her?'

'Essex. There was an oaf of a man – John Stearne – with him, and Mary "Goody" Phillips, a most revolting specimen of a woman who claimed she is the best in the country for seeing the "Witch's marke" upon a person. I did follow them back to Manningtree where Lady de Morriset was examined by the local justice of peace, then handed back to Hopkins for interrogation.'

'When was this?'

'The night before last. I rode as fast as I could back to London.'

'Has she confessed, Daniel?'

'Luckily the guard served in my old regiment. He told me Hopkins has "watched" her these past nights to see whether she's had unholy congress with her "imps". Keep a man from sleeping and he will confess anything. Even I know that.'

'But has she confessed to being a Witch yet?'

'Nay. Not so far. Lady de Morisset is a brave soul. But I know they have used the Witch finder's bodkin upon her.'

Sickened, I picked up my satchel and made to leave.

'Where go thou?' Daniel followed me about the chamber

'To find Nathaniel Bacon; I have a cause to plea with him.'

'Then I shall accompany you as protector,' Daniel argued earnestly. Behind me Solomon sounded his approval.

'I am a dangerous friend – he will take down your name,' I warned Daniel, fearing I had dragged this innocent man into a quagmire he had little understanding of.

The old soldier shrugged. 'I fought for this Parliament. I believed in it. I shall not have it corrupted by the hysteria of ambitious men. Lady de Morisset is no Witch and I will not see her burn.' He gathered up his cloak. 'Come, I know where we can get fresh and fast horses this very day.'

CHAPTER THIRTY-ONE

The fourteenth day of the month of October 1645

The Recorder's House, The Town of Ipswich

The Eleventh House: It doth naturally represent Friends
and Friendships, Hope, Trust, Confidence, the Praise, or
Dispraise of anyone; the Fidelity or falseness of Friends; as
to Fings it personates their favourite, Councillors, Servants,
their Associates or Allyes, their Money, Exchequer or
Treasure; in Warre their Ammunition and Souldiery . . .

Nathaniel Bacon was seated on a carved wooden chair that
resembled a throne, ornate for a man renowned for his intoler-
ance of anything that could be regarded idolatrous, but having
visited the homes of zealots before I have noticed a great hypocrisy in their private choice of décor.

'Master Lilly, you are a long way from London; Ipswich is a
beautiful town but does it merit such dedication?' A man in his
early fifties, Saturnian and morose in demeanour, Nathaniel Bacon
showed little enthusiasm for my appearance – a stark contrast to
our last encounter in which he was most grateful for my counsel.

'I am here on the matter of the arrest of Lady de Morisset.'

'We both know Mr Hopkins is most vigorous in his investigations. He would not arrest the lady without reason. She is a
prodigy of yours, perhaps?' The question was a trap and I knew
it.

'As much as any of my visitors,' I answered sweetly, 'for to call Lady de Morisset a Witch would be to call all my Querents and clients Magicians, Sorcerers and Witches, for she hath exploited my horary, Sigils, and cures to no greater extent than many of these godly and God-fearing Puritans – of which you are amongst.'

At which the same godly Mr Bacon began to fidget like a nervous milkmaid, whilst Daniel, standing as guard, glanced over, faintly smiling. Encouraged, I continued. 'In fact, there are many most powerful and most godfearing Parliament men amongst my most loyal clients. How could it be that such holy men, the very foundation of the Republic, could be considered Demon-lovers and worshippers? Pray illuminate me? For I know both Master Hopkins and yourself boast a most intimate and knowledgeable understanding of Satan. Personally, I have never met the gentleman, so perhaps, in my innocence I have been corrupted?'

Most admirably on cue, Daniel studied the Recorder disapprovingly then rolled his eyes up to Heaven. Poor Mr Bacon now looked close to apoplexy. I paused, wondering if I was pushing the blade in too deep, but loving the rhetoric I could not help myself. 'Indeed, when I think about it, the very same Sigil and spell I used for thee I used for the good Lady, who hath also suffered an unjust burglary. Naturally, thy visit to me is not known publicly, but I do keep records. It would be a great shame if these records would have to be spoken of in court . . .'

'When was Lady de Morisset taken?' All authority was now bled from his voice.

Daniel interrupted before I had a chance to reply. 'Three nights ago on the road to Winchester; she is now in the gaol at Manningtree village.'

'And she hath not confessed?' Bacon asked.

'Nay, there is nothing to confess, despite the torturing the

Witch Finder-General hath inflicted upon her.' I'm afraid, dear Reader, my true sentiment rang boldly here; I could not hide my disgust.

Daniel came to my rescue. 'Mr Hopkins is most admirable in his pursuit of these unholy and corrupting elements who lurk in the most unlikely yet familiar places.'

Bacon looked up. Daniel, gaining courage, stepped forward. 'These unnatural sycophants of evil thrive off innocence and kindness, and are most subtle in their disguise. Thank the good Lord we, in England, have a man of such dedication as Hopkins. However, he is still just a man and capable of error. Trust me, Mr Bacon, Lady de Morisset is no Witch.'

'And you are . . . ?'

'Daniel Jenkins. I fought for Parliament at the battles of both Naseby and Marston Moor, I am a churchgoer – and a stricter Puritan you will not find this side of the North Sea.'

Visibly moved, the Recorder of Ipswich turned back to me. 'I am heartened, William, to see that you keep such pious company. I shall send word tomorrow to Essex.'

'No. Today. Unless you wish me to tell of your last horary request which was of a most unnatural demand – to place a love spell upon one's own wife?'

And within the hour a messenger was sent and the next morning both Daniel and I set off back to London, hope now drying its sticky wings in the sun like a newly emerged butterfly; I dare not even exhale.

It was seven days before Magdalene was returned to London, seven days in which my World disassembled, seven days in which I concealed all emotion but split Time into four simple movements: sleep, pray, eat, work. In this manner I kept my mind empty.

I knew she lived; I knew she had been tortured, and I was filled with the shame of a man who hath been found to be impotent. Should I have saved my sweet Megs somehow? She should have left London months before as I had warned her. But she stayed for me, for us. This was my burden.

A new maid opened the door, a young sprig not more than fourteen years, I wager.

'Where is Rosie?' I asked, surprised not to see her there.

'The last girl, sir, she fled when my mistress was arrested,' the new maid told me as she walked me to the bedchamber. 'Lady de Morisset has not left the room since her return five days ago, nor hath she allowed me to draw the drapes, and she hath barely eaten. Perhaps, sir, you could encourage her? I just got my position and cannot afford her to be corpse by the end of the month.'

The maid paused before the door then pushed it open. The air inside the room thick was with incense and other, more human odours, enveloped me and pulled me in like fingers. When I turned, the maid had gone, a most discreet creature for her years.

'Is that you, William?' Magdalene was a wrapped shadow beneath the coverlet.

I sat beside her. One slender arm extended out beyond the embroidered coverlet, white and thin like the sapling of a silver birch, the wrist ringed by a raw bracelet of bloodied skin. They must have held her in irons, I thought, a slow panic curling my intestines. I took her hand and kissed it. She stank, but I loved her anyway.

''Tis I.'

Slowly, she emerged. Her eyes were sunken and the shaven pale dome of her head was crusted with blood.

'I did not want you to see me so diminished,' she whispered, her voice a thin exhalation through cracked lips.

I had no words, just the taste of fury bitter in my mouth. I gathered her up, bones and skin, her breasts the only weight left upon her.

'You are here now, you're safe.'

'They will come back, William, they will hound people like us until Time ends.' She clutched at my neck. 'But I still did not tell him what he wanted to hear.'

'Shhh . . .' There was no solace for this outrage, this humiliation. Never before had I felt so useless as a man.

'They held me in a dungeon so damp and cold there was water oozing from the walls. They kept a light burning, and a guard who would shout at me if I fell asleep. On the fourth day they did strip me, and shaved all hair from my body. That whorish assistant of his, Mary Philips, searched every inch of my body for a teat by which I was meant to have suckled my familiars, and then . . .' Here she faltered. 'Matthew Hopkins himself brought forth his bodkin – a hideous, needle-sharp instrument which he did prick me in trying to find my Witch's mark.' She pulled up her nightdress, and I thought I would lose my supper in revulsion, so bruised and mottled by pinpricks was her torso, arms and legs. 'He was trying to find a place that did not bleed, nor pain me. He failed – and I did scream, William. I screamed and screamed. But I promise he did not break me.'

'My brave, brave Megs.' If my embrace hurt her she did not show it. 'Where are your herbs? I will make a poultice of camomile and lavender to take the bruising down.'

'You think a poultice will heal me?' Suddenly she was ablaze with contempt. 'You think that will make me whole again? Where were you, William Lilly? When his soldiers came, where were you? You think your lackey was enough to save me?' And then she did beat me upon the chest, until finally she broke into sobbing. But this anger was better than the muted silence of the victim.

When she had fallen back, exhausted, I called the maid and she did lead me to the medicine chest and herbs and I did make the poultice. And later, as Magdalene lay still, I carefully anointed her wounds and it were as if every single burning, execution and torture of those Cunning Folk had made a map upon her body. And as I applied the ointment the faces of these persecuted dead seemed to look up accusingly between my fingers. When I got to the infected pinpricks upon her belly, I noticed she was rounded and heavier than before, despite her ordeal.

Surprised, I sat back. Sitting up, she followed my gaze.

'I see you have guessed – I was fighting for more than just myself.'

Shocked, I couldn't quite believe the meaning of her words.

'You are with child?' The sentence, spoken out loud, was itself a dangerous admission.

'I was frightened I would lose it, but it holds.'

'This cannot be!' To my shame I was, I confess, dear Reader, incredulous. I knew there was no indication of prodigy in my Nativity and this had been a great secret humiliation, one I had finally, in my fiftieth decade, accepted. My work was to be my legacy, and now to be told I will be a father?

I placed my hands on her and read what lay beneath. It was a boy, eight, nine weeks in the womb – a son. In all this chaos, a child that cannot be.

She curled herself around me. 'Are you not pleased, William? A child, an heir to all your wisdom?'

I found my tongue thick in confusion; I would never be able to acknowledge the child as mine, Magdalene would be labelled a whore for having a child out of wedlock, my enemies would charge me as an adulterer. Yet a son! I stepped away from the bed.

'This is a complication I did not calculate.'

Uncertain, she reached for my hand and clung to it. 'We

could to Scotland or France – or even Holland. William, I have family and you have colleagues, reputable Astronomers and Astrologers who could find thee clients. You are still William Lilly and I am still Lady de Morisset, despite this war and the dishonour it brings upon all.'

'This war hath made me my fortune. In these fateful times it is not just Kings and Ministers who look for clarity. I am a married man, a man with enemies who would see me burn. And as for you, they will destroy you for this.' This time I spoke without strategy then felt great chagrin for my tactlessness. She dropped my hand.

'You love me not.'

'I love you, but I love my head upon my shoulders and I love all those I have provided with some illumination of life: the widow's hope, the virgin's dream, the soldier's fortune. This is what sustains me, my Christian service to God. You are asking me to give this all up?'

'But he is *ours*. He will be extraordinary, the sum of all that we both are; he is your son, William!'

'Nay, when he is born we will take him to a good wet nurse who will place him with a childless family. And he will grow up loved and happy.'

'I will not surrender my child!' After which she turned to the wall and spake no more.

In my own house, later that night, I brought out my true Nativity. I do not believe in fixed Fate; I believe that we are able to exceed our astral proclivities and thus armed with fore-knowledge can avoid those casualties our ordained natures or inclinations would run us into.

As I thought, there was nothing that indicated a child. Furthermore, looking upon on the ink-scratched manuscript I was reminded again that in less than two year the possibility of my death still loomed large.

With Copernicus curled at my feet, I sat staring into the light of a candle. It seemed to me in that moment, my household, asleep in blissful ignorance, floated further and further away from me like a ship leaving a remote island. Was this child a punishment or blessing? And I had the fleeting splinter of an image – a floating child who did not seem to touch the earth with either feet nor hands. I thought it ominous, but then did dismiss it from my mind as fancy.

In front of me a moth fluttered frantically about the flame, each odyssey drawing it closer to self-destruction; I tried to save it and could not – was I the moth or Magdalene?

The next morning I cast a horary on the question of this pregnancy. To my dismay, it showed the dragon's tail falling in the fifth house, suggesting a failure of reaching full term. I did not tell Magdalene; instead I stayed away.

CHAPTER THIRTY-TWO

The third day of the month of January 1646

A small lane near the parish of St Antholin's

The Twelfth House: It hath signification of private Enemies,
of Witches, great Cattle, as Horses, Oxen, Elephants,
&c. Sorrow, Tribulation, Imprisonments, all manner of
affliction, self-undoing, &c. and of such men as maliciously
undermine their neighbours, or inform secretly against them.

It were a full six weeks later, on a Sunday and a cruel winter was truly upon London. Ice laced up through glass and lead, ships were marooned in the frozen Thames, dogs and the bodies of beggars were found frozen as stiff as bound faggots in doorway and field, whilst men huddled around fires at every street corner.

Jane and I were just walking back from St Antholin's, Mrs Featherwaite and the two maids following behind in all their Sunday finery, the chatter of the women resounding dully against all that snow, when suddenly, from out of a lane, Magdalene's maid ran forth, face whitened, shivering violently under her worn shawl.

'Master Lilly, Master Lilly! You must come quickly!' She grabbed my arm.

'Who is this, William?' Jane demanded.

'The maid of a patient who doth need my assistance most urgently,' I said, looking over at the maid, prompting her.

'Yes, most urgently!' she exclaimed.

'But on the holy day of rest!' Jane protested.

'Thanatos knows no rest!' I told her curtly. 'I will return when I can.'

As we ran through the streets I questioned the maid but all she would say was her mistress would end up in Bedlam if she continued in her behaviour, and so it was with great trepidation that I pushed open the door to Magdalene's front chamber.

A hunched figure sat before a roaring fire, rocking a wrapped baby in her arms, singing softly to it. She did not look up as I stepped in.

Carefully, I moved toward her; her hair a tangled bush about her gaunt face, the nightdress she sat in much bloodied about the torso and hem.

'So this is he?' I asked gently, indicating the babe.

'I have called him Adam, after the first man. I thought you would like that, it being a good, strong plain name. A Protestant name.'

The babe appeared unnaturally quiet; I had not seen his face yet, but a dread filled me as I moved closer to catch sight of his face. It were tiny, wizened, and blue.

'Let me hold him, Magdalene?' I asked as softly as I could. Instead she drew the tiny corpse closer to her bosom.

'Nay, you did not want him then so you will not have him now.'

It broke me then to see her so wilful in her intent, as if she could rock the child back to life. My child. My dead son. Then the terrible realisation that part of me had wanted this baby burst through my soul. And, I swear, dear Reader, the agony would have killed me then but for the pain of woman before me.

'Magdalene, the babe is dead.'

It was only now that she looked up and seemed to see me.

'No, he is just sleeping. He is so terribly tired, for he came too early, far too early and the birth was difficult, William. So difficult . . . I called out for you but you didn't come, and I tried to stop it, William, I tried . . .'

I knelt before her and placed my hands on her shoulders. 'I know, my love, now give me the babe . . .'

Slowly, she handed me the corpse then a moment later tried to wrestle it from my grasp, but I held him firmly and she gave up weeping. I nodded to the maid, who began helping her mistress to her feet and out of that stained and pungent night-dress. After covering the babe's face, I left the house quietly. It were only then, the tiny stiff body held close to me, I did lift my face to the sky and cry.

I buried him in the back of an abandoned shipyard alongside the River. As I finished patting down the thick black soil over the grave I looked up at the circling seagulls and wondered upon his soul, stillborn before it woke to this Earth, this child who would have been my son.

My grief was private and profound and for a whole month pressed down upon my conscience. It were a bruise upon the heart and I could not afford to think on what might have been. But as time passed I thought of my legacy and in my sorrow this soon possessed me.

The notion of *An Introduction to Astrology* started to draw form like Ariel, the winged Demon, manifesting from my anger. Such a book was longed for by many persons of Quality, and such a book would have the advantage of silencing the malevolent railing of those Presbyterian ministers in their weekly sermons and my critics in Parliament. I *would* be remembered, if not in a child then in what I would leave for the World.

CHAPTER THIRTY-THREE

The Most Difficult Year of 1646

The Corner House, The Strand

Have special regard to the strength and debility of the Moon and it's far better the Lord of the Ascendant be unfortunate than she, for she brings unto us the strength and virtue of all other Planets, and of one Planet to another.

We are all sleepwalkers in this cold, war had sucked all humanity from our hearts. The battles progressed now with great apace as did the new year; the short days revolving in unnatural speed; the dawn, the grey and the night. Truly I feel the apocalypse might be upon us in this year of 1646. Then on the ninth of January Colonel Fairfax and Lieutenant General Cromwell most bravely lead the New Model Army in victory against the Royalists in Devon at Bovey Heath. At last, I thought, here were the first seedlings of Parliament and Cromwell's victory.

Nine days later, when London was blanketed in a miasma of frost and snowflakes, the city of Dartmouth surrendered to General Fairfax and I published my work *Ancient and Modern Prophecies* which I did dedicate to the King and within my preface indicated that if the Pharaoh had listened to Moses, and if Zedekiah to Jeremiah, both their Fates and that of their people would have been happier. If only the King had taken note! The prophesies were from a number of Philomaths and

Occultists I have admired – Mother Shipton and John Dee as well as several ancients. It also contained the Nativities of both Thomas, Earl of Strafford, and Archbishop Laud – their sad Fates explained.

On the third of February the Royalist city of Chester surrendered to Parliament. On my street corner the apprentices celebrated by dancing about a huge bonfire, a pagan rite of drunkenness and licenced brutality. *New England and a new order is within sight!* they sang over and over whilst the Republic crept across the map of England to cover most of her fair flanks.

Thirteen days later it was victory for the New Model Army at Torrington, and the very last of my Cavalier clients began to leave London.

On the tenth of March I did walk to Magdalene's house off Chancery Lane. I had not heard from her for several weeks, and I did fret for her well-being. The spirit of our child sat between us, no matter what our discourse or happiness. I had prescribed herbs for melancholia and womb healing but Magdalene did not have the will to mend. Since losing the child she was greatly diminished in spirit, and the demise of the Royalists' cause had only worsened her condition.

It were a blustery day, and the flags that many had hung in their windows and upon poles in support of the New Model Army and their victories flapped madly in the wind. The flower sellers had already violets and daffodils in their posies, and I watched a young Dragoon court a young washerwoman in mime and humour and laughing she did respond most joyously. I walked on, wishing to catch this hope and youth like a butterfly or bird I could take to my mistress and infect her with the same.

I found Magdalene peering into a Crystal orb. She had taken to much Crystal gazing of late – I suspect it is not the politick she looks for, but the faint trace of the Spirit future of the child that was taken from her. I dared not ask.

'You are finally here, William, I thought thee gone from me. Perhaps for ever?'

'My Querents have been numerous, and then there has been my publications – I did send you the last one.'

'I have it over there, I have not cut the pages.' She pointed. *Ancient and Modern Prophecies* lay discarded upon a table, dust upon the cover.

'There is explanation within for the Royalist surrenders, as well as discourse on other more ancient prophecy; I thought it might distract?' I told her.

At this she did turn. 'Distract from what, Will? The pain now betwixt us?'

Before I had a chance to answer, the maid ran up the stairs shouting, 'The King's army hath surrendered! The King's army hath surrendered!'

Shocked, Magdalene stumbled back and I was awash with a medley of feeling I had not calculated upon; Parliament was now unencumbered and had the chance to make a country where man and Lord might be of equal standing, but now England was without its rightful representative of God at its head, where could that lead but anarchy?

Magdalene looked aghast. 'Can it be true? The end of the monarchy? They will kill him, William, and destroy the likes of me.'

'It is just the army who hath surrendered, no doubt the King will still fight on.' I reassured her, an excitement building within me nevertheless.

'Promise you will not abandon me – promise?'

'Promise.'

And so, both elated and jittery with misgiving, I took my leave, my purpose to find a town crier as soon as possible.

When I finally cornered Jonka he informed me that the commander of the Royalists army – Ralph Hopton – had surrendered the King's army at Tresillian Bridge in Cornwall on the fifteenth of March, but indeed the King still fought on in the North with the few troops he hath about him. And I did fear the King's obstinacy and fatal pride would lead to many thousands more dying before he admitted defeat.

Meanwhile, news of the deadly sweep of Matthew Hopkins' career was reported in pamphlet and verse. He had tried thirty-six women for witchcraft at the Essex assizes, of which nineteen were burnt or hung. He accused a great many hence all over the land – Suffolk, I heard, hath forty tried, and the same in Norfolk, all pricked to the point of confession. This was sin indeed. I was most vigilant, fearing that fatal knock upon the door. There was one Presbyterian rector, a Mr Ralph Farmer, who decried me as a Wizard and openly advocated my death upon the stake through his sermons. Meanwhile Jane railed at me further: she would to New England and daily tried to convince me it would be safer in the colony than in unpredictable England, perhaps she was right.

On the twenty-first of March there was a great and mighty battle at Stow-on-the-Wold: it is, as I had forecast, a victory for Parliament.

Morale was very low with the Royalist army and many had been seen deserting. Now the unravelling of the King quickened, as I had predicted in *The Starry Messenger*. Oh, hapless Monarch.

Then, on the thirteenth of April, Exeter surrendered to Parliament, and on the fifth of May the King finally gave himself up to the Scottish Army, and was imprisoned in Newcastle. I believe he hoped for some leniency.

On the sixth of May Newark fell to Cromwell and finally, on the twenty-ninth of June, the keys of the city of Oxford – the

Royal capital — were handed over to Fairfax, the evacuation of the Royalist garrison having begun the day before. I wondered on the fate of my friends there, Tobias Young, Jane Whorwood, and the courtiers who had helped me. But I was happy, thinking this surrender might lead to some manner of peace.

CHAPTER THIRTY-FOUR

The month of January 1647

The Corner House, The Strand

Behold the condition of Saturn in every Question, he
is naturally ill by his excesses of cold; Mars is of ill
influence, because of his too much heat; in very truth,
neither of them is cold or dry, but signify so much in their
virtue and operation, and therefore in all Questions they
shew tardity and detriment in the Question, unlesse the
Moon and they receive each other in the Signification.

It was now past Christmas and I was most engrossed in my
legacy *Christian Astrology*, an undertaking of great labour in
which I endeavoured, in plain English, to instruct the common
man in the effects and powers of astrology both horary and
natal. Here is an example of how I had advised my students:

*Stand fast, oh Man! To thy God and assured principles, then
consider thy own nobleness, how all created things both present and to
come, were for thy sake created; nay for thy sake God became Man: thou
art that Creature, who being conversant with Christ, livest and reignest
above the heavens, and sets above all power and authority.*

These three volumes would be my greatest labour. Yet I was
finishing them in this year predicted be the most hazardous of
my life. For I knew the Reaper was standing but inches behind
me throughout this dark year of 1647. My Nativity told me my

Clymacterical year of seven was to me troublesome; my Ennertial year perilous and sickly: I was in this year now.

The most profound news was that the Scots have sold the captured King Charles to us, the English, this first week of January, and they were paid, it is said, a hundred thousand pounds for their labour. After, the King travelled south with Pembroke and Denbigh as guard, both acting commissioners for Parliament, but also as old friends of the Monarch.

They said there was still affection for the King on the streets as he rode to Holdenby House in Northamptonshire and, I wager few prisoners boasted such a handsome gaol – but I did wonder if the King truly understood his predicament. I suspected not, such was his belief in his own untouchable God anointed superiority.

I was again at war with Na'worth – George Wharton. In a Royalist newspaper of which he was an editor, a lewd Mercury, a poxy rag circulated under counters and about London in ill-concealed secrecy. He hath called me *that juggling Wizard William Lilly, the states figure-flinger general, a fellow made up of nothing but mischief, tautologies and barbarism.* This pamphlet claims I used trickery to make a fortuitous match between a Mr Howe (a politician of some power) and the daughter of the Earl of Sunderland. And that I had given false advice to the young lady and encouraged her to walk in such a place within she would see her future husband dressed in such a jacket. And that I then instructed the interested party, Mr Howe, to walk in that place in the jacket described. And because I had both parties as clients, my own profit was of motivation, and in doing so I had prevented two other noblemen from pursuing their suit with the same young gentlewoman.

This was a lie, for Mr Howe himself had seen the woman walking *before* he did seek my advice. He then came to me to say he had seen a woman that fitted the description of his wife-to-be and should he pursue the suit? I told him yes, and twice more Mr Howe did come with the same question, and twice more I did encourage him. This was a lesson for all students of the Philomath: you must also use your judgement of character before entering a contract with a Querent. George Wharton's libel was grievous to me, and did mar my reputation. I intended to defend myself in print.

But enough of these petty quarrels. On the Sunday I attended a Mathematicians' Feast at Grisham College, Bishops Gate, that temple of great learning. I was amongst friends, or at least fellow Philomaths, regardless of their politicks (George Wharton was in attendance). I had a particular excitement for this, for I had proposed that my new friend and colleague, a young lawyer of Royalist persuasion who was an admirer of my craft and a reputable Philomath himself, Elias Ashmole, be the patron of the Society of Astrologers of London, a newly formed institute of which I had inspiration. For if we were to survive the onslaught of sceptics and those who married astrology with sorcery a recognised academic body was surely indisputable. The lack of rigorously trained Philomaths, well versed in the nuances and ancient knowledge of the craft, had always pressed upon me. This was one of the reasons I had campaigned for the formation of the Society, and if I am to depart from this world in this year of 1647, I will die happily leaving a legacy for my profession in its highest form. An Astrology Society would promote teaching and knowledge, and although there were some good Astrologers amongst the men that night, many were weak and haphazard in both their judgements and skill. I meant to correct this deficiency and intended both my book *Christian Astrology* and the formation of a society as amends.

I thought Mr Elias Ashmole, despite his youth (he was of twenty-nine years of age at the time) and despite his political sympathies – he was a friend of my nemesis Wharton, and openly Royalist – would make an excellent patron and that I would eventually introduce him to the Grand Council. Ashmole's enthusiasm for astrology, both in the medic and horary, was inspiring indeed. He was the Spring to my Autumn and to hear him speak – nay, to see him listen upon my teachings – enthused me with new-found vigour. I confess, dear Reader, he did save me from this creeping melancholia that crawled through me.

The banquet hall was most handsome and panelled in oak, and I was heartened to see many in attendance, all manner of mathematician, scientist and scholar. There were, as I looked about me, at least five I recognised as Philomaths, apart from Elias Ashmole. I saw Nicolas Culpeper, John Booker, Mr Richard Saunders, a physician I was schooling in astrology, my drinking partner William Pool, Mr Oughtred, a clergyman I had saved from being thrown out of his parsonage in Surrey and my good friend Nicholas Fiske

I had become acquainted with Nicholas Fiske in the year of 1633, and I was much fond of him. He were a person most studious, laborious and, by his own hand, a scholar in astrology, physick, arithmetic, astronomy, geometry and algebra. But Nicholas always lamented the fact that he was no genius in the teaching of his students. The formation of this society would address this deficit of his. And as for Nicholas Culpeper, I did not know a better herbalist or medic in England. Such was the calibre of the men in attendance.

'Master Lilly, 'tis true you have proposed Elias Ashmole for patron?' Culpeper asked. He was wearing a green cravat – an indication he was of Parliamentarian persuasion, and I knew he objected to Ashmole because of his Royalist sympathies. As the discussion of politics was banned from banquets like these, so many choose to indicate their allegiances through quirks of dress – a red feather in the cap meant one sided with the King. I myself was most careful to remain neutral in both dress and speech.

'I think he be excellent in both his presentation and enthusiasm. He also has the gift of youth on his side,' I answered Culpeper.

'I agree, a most exceptional choice, although his politics are not my own.'

'He is still most dedicated to the profession. Will he have your vote?'

Culpeper glanced over to where Elias was holding court with a mathematician and an astronomer, gesturing and talking with most vigour. He was the youngest in the room by a good ten years.

'In him we have a future,' I murmured softly. 'He is an historian by nature and has the most extraordinary library. He is also a man of independent nature. He will make an outstanding custodian.'

'He is certainly much taken with the medic; he talked with me at great length about his health and was most fascinated by my practice of decumbiture,' Nicholas Culpeper replied.

I laughed. The young Elias Ashmole's weakness was hypochondria, and Nicolas Culpeper believed in the taking to a sickbed.

'These are not easy times for men like us,' Nicholas added more seriously.

'And I fear they will grow worse; in fact, I know they will,' I told him.

'Elias will have my vote,' he answered, and I was greatly pleased.

I then went on to the next gathering and started my politicking again. I confess, I was good at this. One of the great skills of a good Astrologer is the capture of a man's persona, and his characteristics are oft visible upon his person. I could, in truth, look at a man or woman and read the carbuncles on their faces like a road map, for warts and lumps upon the scalp are like the pages of the personality. Remember that placement is important; for example, consider what sign the Moon is in and what member of man's body it denotes therein and shall you also find a mark, mole or scar; if Saturn signifies the mark, it's a darkish, obscure, black one; if Mars, then it's usually some scar or cut if he be in a fiery sign. Or else, in any other sign, a red mole; and you must always know that if either the sign or the planet signifying the mole, mark or scar, be much afflicted, the mark or scar is the greater and more eminent. If the sign be masculine, and the planet masculine, the mole or scar is on the right side of the body – the contrary judge if the sign be feminine and the Lord of the chart therefore in a feminine sign. I have found this skill a great advantage in life and medicine, but it is important that the Philomath must perform his art with morality and discretion.

Other questions we did debate on included the physiology of the Lieutenant General and the astrological significance of the two prominent warts upon his visage. I argued that this indicated a great stubbornness and ambition of Cromwell's as well as a weakness in the bowels, whilst others claimed it were a fault in Aries (as Aries ruled the head and Mars, the God of War, Aries) and that there would be two great periods of battle for Oliver Cromwell. We also debated the meaning of a comet sighted over the Netherlands and which Kings might die that year. Much claret was drunk and it was a most satisfying meeting of intellects; I came away greatly enthused and bright in spirit. Suffice to say by the end of the meeting it was confirmed that Elias Ashmole *would* be the patron of the newly formed Society of Astrologers and that night I did dream of Cullum Monroe, that I was a King upon a throne of stars and planets and that he were my son and thereupon he did kiss me upon both my hands. In the morning I was woken by Solomon anxious for his feed, pecking me upon mine hands. But the dream did make me most content.

One windy day a few weeks later an ornate sedan chair with its carriers puffing and most strained with the weight of the man carried within, trotted up to my gate. In great relief they did settle the chair upon the cobbles and a corpulent man in most impressive uniform did disembark and made for my front door, sending Mrs Featherwaite into a spin. It were Sir Thomas Myddleton, a powerful man of the army and a member in Parliament, and to my delight he were visiting me as a querent. I did take careful note of the time – the eleventh of March 1647, as his question was dynamic, a great question, the kind I had aspired to receive so many years before – a query with huge political ramifications – *If Presbytery Shall Stand?*

I shall endeavour to explain to you the significance of this question. There were rumours the King was seeking an alliance to defeat Puritan England with the support of the Scots and in Westminster there was a spilt between the Independents (Puritans who were moderate in their religious zeal and whom had the support of Cromwell) and the Presbyterians (many of whom had Scottish friends). Alas, Cromwell was then retired of the Army, and the Independents could not count on his support. If the King succeeded in this alliance, he could have started another uprising and overthrow the Independents. If there was a successful victory for the King and Scottish Presbyterians, they would rule together and England would become a rigid, fanatical country – a Church State with no joy or freedoms for the common man as the Presbyterian is the most fierce zealot and intolerant of even the Puritans; most pertinently they regard astrology to be the work of the Devil. It was not an England I intended to live in. But there was another important element to the question: the army remained unpaid since its return from the Irish campaign. The great Countryman (as I like to call Cromwell, he being a roughly hewn squire from East Anglia) was now retired from soldiering. Meanwhile discontent with Parliament bubbled in the fields and camps of angry soldiers, like a volcano threatening to erupt.

Examining these quandaries, I considered whether my own opinion would influence the outcome of such an important horary. But my teachings have always held the belief that one should not turn any man away – *expropriate no man, no not an enemy* – and so again I put my own politick to one side and began my figures.

The honorary was cast on the eleventh of March 1647, and it were one of my most important and significant horaries, for within it contained the King's own Fate.

Firstly, I have taken Saturn in Taurus in the ninth house as symbolises Presbytery itself. Saturn in the ninth is of a severe, surly, rigid and harsh temper, so it appeared that the Presbytery shall be too strict and dogged for the English Constitutions. However, I also observed that the enemy of Presbytery also lies with Saturn, for it is Saturn that is afflicting the ninth house and in this I concluded that this was the Countryman himself, Cromwell, and given the position of Mars (the God of War and in this case representing the Army) the Army would reject it. And so I could see that Cromwell would return to lead the Army once again. And why? Because the placement of Jupiter was turning direct in the figure, strongly placed in Cancer but threated by a conjunction of Mars. Jupiter was turning, about to change signs, which would be the Fate of Religion.

In this way Saturn symbolised both Presbytery and Cromwell attacking it. Saturn will begin the change and will not stand or continue. However, if you remove Saturn as well as covetousness, rigidness, and maliciousness, then there might be a hope, yet Presbytery would not survive. However, I saw more in this horary that did disturb me. Three whole years from now shall not pass without Authority itself, or some divine Providence, informing our understanding with a way in discipline or Government, either more near to the former purity of primitive times, or more beloved of the whole kingdom of England. For some time we shall not discover what shall be established, but shall be even as when there was no King in Israel. No King in Israel? I was brave to be so honest in my findings, for this was a dangerous vision – a kingdom without a King.

I delivered the answer to Myddleton, who received it with good grace. But when the news of it reached Parliament it only made me more enemies midst the Presbytery.

The next few months did fly like the whirling arms of a madcap clock. I was oft at my desk writing my manuscript – my cases and notes on my own private horaries and also my many books on the Occult and on Astrology surrounding me like a forest. I confess, sitting many hours there, the lamp burning, it was as if the Almighty himself was directing my quill, that I was writing for the greater good of humanity and I was much pleased. There was honesty and plain truth to those I did describe, and the book began, like the kernel of a seed pushing up through a most fertile soil.

Meanwhile, in the North and in other parts of the land, Matthew Hopkins has grown most confident in his self-declared role as Witch Finder-General and hath published his own pamphlet as means to sway and win public opinion. It has a most pithy title: *The discovery of witches in answer to several queries, lately delivered to the judges of the assize for the county of Norfolk. And now published by Matthew Hopkins, Witch finder, for the benefit of the whole kingdom.* Pedantic and not the least droll, the technique of interrogation he describes is not for the weak-stomached nor any Christian soul, for this is not God's work.

And in these months I did see less of Magdalene; I was coward in this, and hated myself for it.

CHAPTER THIRTY-FIVE

The month of August 1647

The Corner House, The Strand

See the condition of Jupiter and Venus be observed, who naturally are Fortunes and temperate, and never import any malice, unless by accident: where they are Significators without reception, they put forward the matter, but they best performe the matter in question when they apply by Trine or Sextile and to purpose when in Essential Dignities.

By August, as I had predicted in my almanack, we had the pestilence again in London, where in that horrible and devouring plague the dead were few but many were afeard. I was much put upon: the writing of my great work swallowed my nights whilst my clients took the waking hours. I treated many and it was usually the strong and the young who did survive. I treated them with cordials and sweating potions to rid them of the poison – garlic, salt, London treacle, vinegar and saltpetre, as well as home-made plaster to place upon the buboes. It was the most heartbreaking work.

Two days since, one of our maids, a young girl and war orphan, was taken sick. I did isolate her in a back room and gave Mrs Featherwaite all manner of plague recipes and poultice to apply, but the girl worsened. Finally, on the third day, I did step out to go to church to pray for her and also for myself, thinking that clean of soul meant clean of body, and in these days a man is compelled to pray to live another night as plague-fuelled Death is a terrifyingly swift thief.

Outside, in testimony to the dark times into which the pestilence had plunged London, the small green where there would usually be many young boys kicking a ball or playing hoops there were but four youths; a grim reminder of the bills of mortality nailed around the parish (some five thousand dead and counting). And it saddened me to see such creatures, thin and tense, hiding their fear as they knocked about a worn pig's bladder.

As I walked, with my handkerchief held over my nose and clutching a posy, a large moon rose up above the haze of the summer sky and I turned towards the river. The streets were hollowed out, the most able and moneyed having fled the city, and it was just the poor or servants and those engaged by the Parish offices that were compelled to stay and stare the skull down.

But in the back lanes, men desperate and in most part liquor-giddy, openly engaged in acts of debauchery with whores, in frenzied defiance as if copulation itself could ward off disease. I had noted how, in these times, the brothels and whorehouses seemed to spread like the plague itself, some even advertising the notion that congress with a virgin would render immunity – God pity the poor maiden!

A shortage of women had contributed to this desperation as many wives had left to the countryside, their men staying in London to guard property. So the streets were now peopled with humanity at its most base and were, to my mind, a kind of Hell. The red crosses painted on the doors – the signs crying 'Lord have mercy upon us!', the naked corpses piled haphazardly in all manner of macabre embrace, the flies that had descended upon us that summer, harbingers of evils, hell-pests themselves, great black swarms crawling over pus-filled cankers, the glazed dead eyes – orbs of lost hope, emptied of all human endeavour – all added to this illusion.

A strumpet interrupted my journey.

'Good sir, would you like to taste me wares?' Slipping out from a doorway she lifted her skirts to show me her cunty – her thighs silvery above her stockings in the dusk light. To my great shame I was tempted, for I had not seen Magdalene for over a month and there was no wife in my bed. But the whore looked no more than fifteen years, and besides, methinks I saw the mark of the French pox upon her cheek – as a wit would say *a night with Venus, a lifetime with mercury*, the metal providing a cure that was more of an affliction than the disease. So, God save me, I cast my eyes down and walked on.

Death was a miasma so dense it made you forget you were one still living and to smell, touch, and caress was to be reminded that blood still flowed beneath rosy skin; fornication an insolent fist to the sky. But I, like the men spooning to loosen their terror – their white arses pounding a merry jig amid scarlet petticoats – had grown immune to such sights.

I was halfway to church when I came upon a plague pit that was once common land near the river, a chasm filled with the contorted dead, frozen in the very grimace Death found them in. I drew nearer; an acrid smell filled my nose and I could see the columns of black smoke drifting up from the smouldering bodies. So, the gravediggers were burning. I'd heard rumour they were running out of burial sites and this is what they had done: rendered the dead as faggots, I reflected, as my gaze was drawn to the spiralling ashes and it was then that I saw it, the glinting red orb of Mars to the right of the full moon, the War God staring across at the naked beauty of Venus, who had just risen up from the horizon, shimmering like a dancing girl.

The triangular formation was unusual. I had not seen it before and it seemed foreboding – as foreboding as an eclipse or triplet Suns, almost as if Mars and Venus made two eyes and the Moon a howling mouth of the Heavens. Methinks I should have taken heed of the portent and turned back. But I did not, and when I returned from church the young maid had died. There was much sorrow in the house, but I feared the omen suggested future tragedy. My mind sent rattling by both grief and exhaustion I imagined the Presbyterians conspire against me and that I would be again arrested at any moment. It was hard to finish the last section of my book.

As this was said to be the year of my death, I did not trust my luck against the pestilence. There were shutters upon my windows and I consulted Querents through letters they left at an open space within the window. Parts of the city were still quarantined but my own medications and infusions saved both myself and Jane, and, thank the good Lord, Mrs Featherwaite stayed robust.

I dared not see Magdalene, for fear of bringing the scourge to her door but I missed her presence and conversation most sorely; that is, the woman she was before Matthew Hopkins.

Meanwhile the Grand Council of Theurgy hath been disbanded until all signs of the pestilence hath disappeared, but it was rumoured George Wharton was gravely ill with the plague and would not live. Even poor Elias Ashmole was stricken with fever and agues and sometimes I thought I could not breathe the air for fear of dying.

On one of these dark mornings, struggling with my old Demon melancholia, my half-written manuscript before me, I did wonder upon the fate of my *Christian Astrology*. I had chosen a most auspicious date for printing, but would I be able to complete the third volume in time?

Just then Jane entered, announcing that I had a visitor who refused to be barred from the house.

The lady, not young and yet becoming, her hair of russet and her face blessed in Venusian aspects yet peppered with the pits of smallpox, waited in my front chamber. It was Jane Whorwood, who had assisted me in the freeing of the young Lord Pendle from the prison of Oxford castle. As she was close to the King, I knew this was to be a political matter and one most delicate, so did lock the door behind me.

'Mrs Whorwood, it is an honour to see you again.' I kissed her hand.

She looked upon me hard, then began to pace the chamber as she spoke. 'Elias Ashmole vouches for you, as does the Witch Finder-General, Matthew Hopkins.'

I studied her carefully; there was no guile in her face. Encouraged, I spoke frankly. 'A man who will save England from the Devil, if the Devil doth not take him first, Hopkins is no lover of Prince Rupert: he would burn him as a Witch if he had the chance. I am surprised he is a friend of yours?'

'He is a *useful* friend.' She smiled wryly, and I liked her for it.

'And as for Elias Ashmole, he has great understanding of the mystic arts, and is a great prodigy of mine,' I replied carefully, 'but you insisted upon entering my house and I have lost a maid to plague.'

'I fear not the plague but the pox,' she jested, at her own expense, 'but I come on behalf of a great personage.'

'Hampton Court is far from here.' By which I meant to establish she was here for the King who was held there.

'Loyalty knows no distance.' She was neat in her wit, and this made her beauty greater. 'The King fears he will be poisoned and means to escape.' Now I was thankful my house was boarded from all ears and manner of spy. Taking my silence as encouragement she continued. 'He wants to know, Master Lilly, in what quarter of this Nation he might be most safe, and not be discovered until himself is pleased?'

I took note of the time of this question, this being the nub of the horary.

'It will be my great honour to draw up the figure for His Majesty.' At which, dear Reader, you might be surprised, but I thought the King was not without redemption, especially if he now finally fell directly under my guidance.

I did my figures over the next hour whilst Jane Whorwood waited, much taken with Solomon, who, I have noticed, is a veritable flirt with the fairer sex, forever plucking twigs from their hair, and allowing his feathers to be ruffled in a lazy-eyed stupor.

After finishing the horary I informed Jane Whorwood that to avoid further imprisonment the King should stay in Essex, about twenty miles from London. The lady, being of sharp mind herself, remembered a place of that distance where there was an excellent house with all conveniences. She left, well pleased.

The next few days I waited in anticipation, hoping I would hear news of his flight. Instead, I was woken one morning by Jonka crying out in the street, 'The King captured fleeing in the Isle of Wight!'

Alas, if only the King had followed my advice. Instead, weak in self-determination, and undecided whether he should join the Queen in France, he did go to the Isle of Wight and fell under the protection of Colonel Hammond who then betrayed him to the Army Command. In this the King did show himself to be a vacillating man – both England and Charles would have had a very different destiny had he followed my instruction.

A week later we did lose another maid to the plague and the Corner House was much besieged with wailing and grief. I am in the last volume of my works and have found myself smudging ink on my page from the weeping that grips me like a sudden apoplexy. There seems so little meaning to these deaths

– both young women, their futures erased as easily as a late Spring mist. I took the caution of sprinkling the house with Dr Read's perfume against the plague – red rosewater, treacle, cloves and angelica, and also hung garlic to rid it of any further disease. The spectre of Melancholia is only chased away by Industry. I feared the cast of his net almost as much as the Plague and so escaped into my writing and my horary both.

CHAPTER THIRTY-SIX

Summer and Autumn of 1647

Hyde Park

In every Question where Fortunes are Significators,
hope well; but if the Infortunes, then fear the
worst, and accordingly order your business.

Today, heartened by the news that the plague war finally over, I took Solomon upon my shoulder to the Hyde Park for recreation. Wherein I did see the most extraordinary sight, for camped upon the grass plains and between the trees were the tents of the Lieutenant Commander's cavalry and many soldiers loitering and carousing with the local strumpets. Intrigued, I did approach a fine musketeer as he watered and brushed down a stallion tethered to a tree.

'Pray, to what effect are thou in London? Is there to be an invasion? Methinks the King is imprisoned and defeated?'

The youth (for at close quarters I did see he were far younger than I had thought but battle and injury hath scarred his face and pressed a maturity upon his person like a seal in wax) rested the horse brush upon the flanks of the animal.

'Nay, Charles is truly defeated, thank the Good Lord, but our captain, Old Ironsides, has marched to the House of Commons this morn with all of his guards; they say he hath entered as member of Cambridgeshire (as is his right) and hath forced a vote to block the eleven Presbyterian members, those scoundrels who will not pay or hear our soldier grievances with honour. We, the very men who have died and suffered for the cause!'

At which I became most heartened, for it were as I had predicted in the horary I cast for Sir Thomas Myddleton: Cromwell hath returned to lead the army and hath now overthrown the Presbyters.

'Good soldier, I am most glad to hear of this. I warned of such outcomes if the Presbyters continued to ignore the Army's rights . . .'

At which he studied me closer.

'But I know thy face! I have seen thee with the Astrologer John Booker on the battlefields; your predictions were of great encouragement to us soldiers, to know that both God and Fate is on one's side! Thou art William Lilly, thou predicted our victory at Marston Moor.' Excited, he yelled out to his comrades, 'Hey, brothers, this here be Master Lilly! The great Philomath and teller of the soldier's fortune!' And a dozen men turned, fierce in excitement, and were upon me with all manner of questions and would not let me leave until I had blessed them in some manner.

I liked this motley army of ordinary men who had no air or graces. Cromwell hath made officers of bakers, blacksmiths and furriers – all creatures of industry high and low – and had given purpose to the peasant and meaning to the candle maker. There was a great spirit of intent amongst them, for they fight for God and for the betterment of Man or so they believe. I prayed this would be so.

On the way home I did, upon asking on the street, discover that Cromwell hath succeeded in his quest. He hath ousted the eleven members from Parliament but had no love for the demands of the Levellers who wish for one man, one vote. In truth I believed Old Ironsides would have liked to make peace with the King so that there might have been some semblance of normal life and commerce.

I was in Magdalene's bed when she told me of the demise of our nemesis.

'Matthew Hopkins is dead, William, it hath been confirmed both by rumour and written word. The Witch Finder-General died in Manningtree, in his own bed on the twelfth of August.' Magdalene, her face itched by trouble and pain, her body thinner than ever, looked the happiest I had seen her for many a month. She lay back beside me, her hair fallen across my arm, the scent of her drawing me back into all our lovemaking past, present, and future.

I muttered a silent prayer; a death is a death, even if I did loathe the man.

''Tis God's will.'

'Aye, and now he be cradled in the arms of the Devil,' she retorted cheerfully. 'Methinks there might be some redemption in the scheme of things after all, Mr Hopkins' demise is illustration that all tyranny passes.'

'Let's pray you're right,' I replied. I confess, dear Reader, my humours were very dark indeed. The Presbyterians still reign despite the ousting and I now feared fighting and division amongst the Puritans. This poor country hath had enough of this war; the farms were being bled dry and many merchants in London had little or nothing to trade. But here, in my mistress's bed, the world receded and I could be anywhere but in war-torn London.

'It were a natural death?' I asked.

'Some would like to think William Hopkins perished in ducking for being a Wizard, but I have word he died of a disease of the lungs and they buried him very quickly,' she replied.

'Was it dread of pestilence or of desecration of the body by the relatives of those he hath murdered that they feared?' I wondered aloud, then as he were a man finally and all men have souls I added, 'History will judge him, not I. And what of you these past weeks?'

Magdalene sat up then did go from the bed, to make water.

'I have resumed my studies with Sarah Skelhorn, the great skryer of Crystal gazing,' she told me, poised over the chamber pot.

'I thought she were back in service in the Isle of Purbeck? She is good at her gift but she complained that it meant the angels followed her and appeared in every room until she wearied of them. But she is excellent at her craft.' My informants were good, in all my spheres.

Magdalene wiped herself and lowered her nightdress. 'William, she hath shown me the most interesting of spectres trapped in the Crystal. A blackbird carrying a crown in its claws. Death will herald in a new King. But how can that happen?'

I did not answer her – to do so might be considered treason – but I, myself, had seen that England would regain its King; the question was, which one?

'There is something even more wondrous, William.' Magdalene stroked my face. 'Mrs Skelhorn did arrive here because she learnt of my great loss through the Crystal; she is a source of great comfort.'

I sat up, startled. 'But she doth not know who the father was?'

'She believes it to have been a great Royalist, murdered in battle, but William, she did see Adam, grown as a boy with russet hair like myself, staring out. She said there was great confusion around his Spirit.'

I did take her hand and stroke it; poor comfort it seemed to be fed these dreams.

'Magdalene, his soul might be born again to others.'

'How can you be so accepting of Fate! Do you ever fight back?'

'You know I do. But it was written that the child was not to live.'

'If I hadn't been arrested, if I hadn't been interrogated . . .'

'But it happened, and now there is the future to consider. That's what we live for now. Both of us.'

On the sixteenth of August I published my great work *The Christian Astrology*. As I have mentioned, dear Reader, I did cast a horary and chose a printing date to ensure that it would be most auspicious, and so it were proven.

This work took me the better part of twenty months to write, but I believe it to be an important work, perhaps the most important text of astrology this country had ever seen.

The work was in three volumes. The first teaches the reader the fundamentals of Philomacy; it contained all manner of commentary of what a placement of the planets in what house might mean in terms of a man's physique and the workings of his mind; I also gave instruction in the use of an ephemeris and in the drawing of a figure of Heaven.

The second volume I most aptly named *The Resolution of All Manner of Questions and Demands*. It teaches the student how to read and assess the nuance and judgements of a horary figure. And it is here that I drew upon mine own practice – and have cited many of my own horary cases, to great fascination, taken from all parts of my life thus far. In this I meant to portray the many uses and intelligences of the art.

The third volume was a description of how to judge Nativities, and in which I told of my own odyssey, and how I came to be a Philomath.

The works have been received with great interest, and I have received correspondence from all parts of Europe: from Holland, Spain, Sweden, France – all manner of Philomaths have written, most intrigued by the *Christian Astrology*, and have sought my opinion on subjects both astrological and alchemical. I am blessed indeed to be a peer in such august company. Me, a semi-literate clerk from Surrey. I am proof a man can play the advantages of his Nativity and not be doomed by the disadvantages that also hang in the sky at the moment of his birth, and that a man is moulded both by his ambition and his natural attributes. I was also greatly cheered by the fact that this year, 1647, drew to a close, and I had triumphed over the inclination in mine own Nativity. Had I cheated my predicted death?

The King was imprisoned in the Isle of Wight at Carisbrook, but he still dreamt of rescue from the Scots and Irish whilst sections of his army fought on. They say in the castle he hath his loyal servants and was able to smuggle letters to his beloved wife and had use of both a bowling green and miniature golf course within the castle walls. His imprisonment was a luxury not known to most men. If England be a body, the blood hath stopped flowing through the veins.

In this winter both John Booker and myself were called to Windsor, now the headquarters of the Army for they had fallen completely out of love with Parliament – soldier pay being the principal issue. We were transported by coach and four horses such was the esteem General Fairfax held us, and our influence upon his soldiers. Resident in the castle he was most welcoming, telling us that although God had blessed the army with many victories, as yet their work was not done, and he hope God would be with them until His work was done and that they did not seek victory for themselves but for the people and the whole Nation and for that end were resolved to sacrifice both their lives and fortunes. He was grave in his address, his stern visage a veritable torch upon any falsehood or pretence. And here he did fasten his gaze upon myself most ferociously. 'As for the art you good Philomaths study, I hope it is lawful and agreeable to God's word? I don't pretend to understand it, however I do not doubt that you both fear God, and therefore I have formed a good opinion of both thee and thy predictions.'

I looked over at John Booker, but as he appeared stumbling in his reply I did answer for the two of us. 'My Lord, I am glad to see you here at this time; certainly, both the people of God and of all others of this Nation, are very sensible of God's mercy, love and favour unto them, in directing Parliament to nominate and elect you general of their armies, a person so religious, so valiant. The several unexpected victories obtained under your Excellency's command, will eternalise your fame unto all posterity. We are confident God goes along with you and your army, until the great work for which he ordained you both is fully perfected, which we hope will be the conquering and subversion of yours and the Parliament's enemies, and then a quiet settlement and firm peace over all the Nation. As for ourselves, we trust in God and, as Christians, believe in him. We do not study any art, but what is lawful and consonant to Scriptures, Fathers, and Antiquity, which we humbly desire you to believe,' I did conclude most convincingly.

Later we visited my friend, the minister Hugh Peter, who did lodge in the castle at that time. We came upon him reading a pamphlet sent from London that very day. To my dismay, the pamphlet contained a ditty much ridiculing me. It ran thus:

> From the oracles of the sibils so silly,
> The cursed predictions of William Lilly
> And Doctor Sybbalds shoe-lame filly
> Good Lord deliver me.

It was my good fortune that I had already earned Reverend Hugh Peter's respect, and after dismissing the ditty with good cheer and a nipperkin of malt whisky, we three discussed the politick. The Reverend was for the King to be tried and executed, whilst I did argue for leniency. This was yet another issue that divided the people.

CHAPTER THIRTY-SEVEN

The month of February 1648

The Corner House, The Strand

Generally consider the state of the Moon, for if she be
void of course there's no great hope of the Question
propounded, that it shall be effected; yet if she be in Cancer,
Taurus, Sagittarius or Pisces, your fear may be lesse, for
then she is not much impeded by being voyd, of course.

In this month Jane Whorwood did visit the Corner House again
on request of the King, whom, although he liked me not, still
regarded me as the most competent Astrologer in the country.

'His Majesty, imprisoned, believes himself in great danger
either by assassination, execution or poisoning. He intends to
saw through the iron bars of his chamber window at Carisbrooke
Castle. There is a ship arranged nearby that would then take
him onto Kent.'

'Kent? He will be welcome there?' I queried, impressed by
the King's indomitable spirit. But if only he had listened to me
the first time he would not be incarcerated at all.

'The army there would support him and they would then to
London – there are many, William, living in this city, who
would still lift a sword for the King.'

She was right. Magdalene was not the only secret Royalist,
and many still held great love for the Monarch.

'What does he want of me?'

'You must, in your alchemy, have use for Aqua Fortis?'

This was a liquid that could separate silver from gold or copper and could eat through iron. I did use it both in my alchemy and medicine. I nodded reluctantly.

'I would also need a saw with teeth that can cut metal; is this possible, William, for the love of the King?'

'I can do this, providing my name is kept out of the matter?'

'Naturally, and when the King is restored to power he will be most grateful,' she concluded, most happy with my acquiescence. And so I did supply her a large bottle of the Aqua Fortis.

I confess, dear Reader, in most parts I was a sensible man but in times when power swings like a demented pendulum it is useful to have both the opposition and the current elected indebted to oneself. The challenge is to keep those debts well hidden.

Alas Charles did not choose his intimates well. His loyal servant had bribed the guards usually posted beneath the King's window but, after cutting through the bars successfully, His Majesty was most dismayed to see a troop of soldiers below. The guards had betrayed him.

Meanwhile, my reputation continued to sweep through town and village, castle and town hall. I even received a horary question from the imprisoned leader of the Levellers himself, the leader of these revolutionaries who sought to make all men and property equal – Richard Overton. He could not risk visiting me in person; instead he sent a messenger with a letter. His question bemused me as you know I have no love of Levellers. He asked whether the Levellers should join with the private members of the New Model Army and, if they did so, would it serve their cause?

An intriguing question, Cromwell had made much ado over the supporting of this movement, but there was a hidden politick beneath this sentiment.

I knew of Royalists who had fled to Scotland to march with the Scottish Presbyterians to defeat Parliament, whilst Parliament had finally decided not to continue to seek terms with the King for compromise and peace. A second war looked more and more possible.

Therefore I drew up the figure with some trepidation. Richard Overton's Significator was Mercury and it were not placed well in this moment. It was also in retrograde, suggesting a reversal of decision, and despite the Moon being in the Archer's house it was beside the Dragon's tail. This was not auspicious. I looked for the Mars and yes, it were in Aries – and so the Levellers would join with the New Model Army, but Jupiter (the purveyor of fortune) was in the house of betrayal and whispered secret alliances – the twelfth house. Again, my heart sank.

I sent my answer back with the messenger, then steeled myself for further war – by my calculations within two years.

In June of this year John Booker and myself were invited by Ireton, the commander of the camp there, to join the army at Colchester to encourage the troops with our prediction. That city hath been under siege for a good nine weeks to date and much suffering within was rumoured.

It took us a day and a half to ride to the camp. There were a number of Parliament battalions set up in various positions around the great wall that encircled the besieged city. The inhabitants – most of them supporters of the New Model Army and Cromwell – had been caught, like a mouse between pincers, when the Royalists (led by Sir Charles Lucas) retreating from General Fairfax, entered the city, then found themselves trapped within it. The Royalist soldiers had no moral compunction about taking food and supplies from the unsympathetic citizens, and as all gates of the city were blocked by Parliament troops and the army from Suffolk, and General Fairfax hath also blockaded the River Colne, no food nor any provisions had entered the city for a good few weeks.

The castle walls, pockmarked and blackened by cannon fire and artillery, loomed up as we approached by the south road. The cloth tents and makeshift huts of the New Model Army clustered about the surrounding fields and there was one Royalist fortification that lay outside the castle walls.

A massive cannon squatted atop a wall that was beside St Mary's church and looked down at us like a monstrous one-eyed dragon. John Booker noticed me staring up at it.

'A giant, but it will be toppled soon enough. Commander Ireton is no fool, and has full strategy over the idiot Sir Charles Lucas, who along with Lord Norwich and Sir Bernard Gascoigne, seems determined to destroy the people along with the town, to save their own vanity.'

I said nothing, but I knew my old pupil John Humphrys was the Astrologer to Sir Lucas, and had convinced him of a Royalist victory; surely persuasion must be contributing to the truculence of the commander. I had instructed Humphrys in the year of 1640 in the study of astrology and also in what he might discover of his Querent through reading of the moles and marks of his client, but this Humphrys was a laborious person, vainglorious, loquacious, foolhardy and desirous of all secrets, and I did, at the time, refuse to teach him of what he was not capable of, *Artis est celare Artem* (the art is to conceal the real art) as I am always suspicious of those who live not in the fear of God. Such was a person was John Humphrys and I was not surprised to discover him in such an ignoble position.

General Ireton stood waiting for us. ''Tis a great honour and a relief to see you both here.' He told us whilst walking us around the fortifications, 'The Royalist commander, Lord Norwich hath refused to surrender despite being greatly outnumbered – six thousand of the New Model Army to the Royalists three thousand. Instead, he would rather see women and children starve.'

'How can we help?' John Booker asked, whilst I kept my silence, a strategy already forming within my mind.

'Speak to the men, give them hope of victory. They remember well, Master Lilly, your prophecy of victory at Marston Moor; they have been seven weeks sleeping in these miserable ditches, cannon fire reigning down, and they all know there are good Parliamentarian men and women starving within the city walls because of this Royalist vanity.' He pointed to the battlements atop the walls of the city. 'We have spies inside the town: the people have started eating cats and dogs; babies are dying. Yet still Lord Norwich will not surrender. He hath his own puppet Astrologer, a Philomath called John Humphrys, who has him convinced that victory for his troops and for the King is set in Fate by the stars.'

'I know this man,' I told him, at which the General, a pleasant-looking man in his third decade, only months married to the daughter of Oliver Cromwell, studied me most careful.

'So, would his prediction be correct?'

I put out my hand to reassure him. 'My good general, I trained John and I can tell you he was the very epitome of incompetent, an inattentive scholar who lacked discipline and the humility to discern between his own egoistic conclusions and the genuine message carried by good calculation. He is most certainly wrong.'

'Then please, both of you, go amongst the troops, raise their spirits. Morale is low; I have had to shoot a dozen deserters, rations are scarce, and, despite my orders, looting of the local farms rife, regardless of the chastising sermons by the army preacher, and some of these men have family trapped within the city walls. Daily the Royalists throw the bodies of good Puritan men they have executed for "treason" over the walls. We need hope, sir, as much as bread and ale.'

After which he did dismiss us and we were billeted to a small farm close to the makeshift camp, a field scattered with the tents of the higher-ranking soldiers – sergeants and officers of the artillery. The poor infantry often slept under the naked sky, or piles of sticks and canvas, lolling in dirty straw, sometimes sleeping while embracing a pike or a musket as if it were their sweetheart abandoned in some northern city or London slum; the youth of some of them shocking apparent in repose. The more fortunate slept in caravans, or carts of the camp followers – some two hundred wives, widows and whores, a motley parody of a civilisation in miniature, portable in its fashion, petticoats, stained kerchiefs, pewter pots and pans.

One soldier told me the only meat he had eaten for three weeks were the maggots in his oatmeal ration. Others roasted rabbits on campfires, or flouted meat-on-the-hoof – cows, pigs and horses stolen from the nearby fields – on spits.

At dusk, I walked amongst the gatherings, sometimes just listening to snippets of conversation, gauging the spirit and morale of the army, other times helping with my knowledge as physic, – rickets, wounds, apoplexy, fever, how to rid oneself of lice – giving instruction as to what herbs might be gathered and applied. This was how I met a young musketeer called Mercy Stephens, not more than seventeen year of age, who hath a nasty gathering of boils upon his leg. A sharp lad, whose lack of education was made up by a natural intelligence – as I applied a poultice his surliness soon melted into a loquacious grumbling. He pointed to the castle walls, his red jacket frayed and torn from past injuries.

'My cousin and his sister are within and that whoremaster

Fairfax refuses all provisions into the city, yet claims it is the Royalists who are starving the men. Colchester was for Parliament, 'tis not their fault that snivelling coward Norwich with his pet weasel – Lucas – decided to run and hide within the walls. Fairfax should let the women and children leave at least, but no, he means to starve them out.'

'How do you know?'

At which he looked around then pulled so close I could smell the filth and mud ingrained in the leather and cotton of his clothes. 'Can I trust thee? I have no wish to be shot in the morn, nor end up tongueless.'

'Trust me, I am here for the common man and am a servant to his cause.'

'I have been into the city,' the musketeer whispered, his bloodshot eyes (the violence of his life having given him the appearance of a man ten years older) peering into mine. 'I have seen the dying and stretched white belly-drums of infants, women of noble birth whoring themselves for a loaf of bread. Hunger has stripped away all dignity.'

This was the entry I was waiting for, the small crack of light in my plan.

'Can you get me in?'

He touched the green poultice tied to his leg with a strip of rag then spat into the fire, after which he gave me the slightest of nods.

At five, after the army had taken its victuals, a clergyman addressed the gathering of more than three hundred people, preaching his sermon from atop a tower of hay bales, shouting parables from the Gospel that were most dire in their apocalyptic vision. Methinks this thin-humoured cleric meant to frighten the men into battle and it were in this dread-filled aftermath that John Booker and myself did mount that very same tower of hay bales and tell the men that we have done the most careful calculations, indisputable in the eyes of the Almighty, for the fate of men and war is written in the stars and the cosmos was the providence of the Divine, and that we have seen victory for Parliament, not tomorrow, nor indeed for several weeks, but it will *be* and that any other calculation or prediction they might have heard rumoured by other lesser Astrologers was merely poppycock and lies. At these words a great cheer rose up from the men, and truly, dear Reader, I was transported.

Later, when night fell and the camp was a Hellish puppet-play of shadows and silhouettes, Mercy Stephens led me by way of a ditch to the East gate whence a good deal of coin (a valid bribe) ensured our entry into besieged Colchester.

The narrow cobble streets were empty, a curfew having been imposed upon the town. Mercy had changed his musketeer red jacket for the plain smock of a farmer, myself with hat drawn low upon my brow. We half ran, half walked, Mercy, sure-footed and knowing the town, leading me through several small alleys until we reached a dwelling that was little more than a lean-to made of wood and slate built against the castle wall. He lifted the tattered cloth that served as a door.

'John, 'tis Mercy. I have brought turnips and a pigeon, and a friend in need of help,' he called out into the shadows.

In the dim light I could see the outline of a man sitting by a straw pallet on the floor; beside him, a figure lay under a cover, long hair a spidery bleed across the straw.

'Thank God, cousin, not a moment too soon, for I fear Meredith is dying.'

Mercy, squatting down, produced the cooked bird from under his smock, but his cousin, starvation dictating, did grab it and tore the flesh from its bone like an animal. A moment later he gathered his wits and, shamefaced, brought a leg down to his wife's mouth.

'Meredith, 'tis meat, good meat, please my love, eat . . .' The woman, thin as a skeleton, slowly and with great effort rose up to take the morsel, but then did fall back. At which the husband did chew some meat and, after taking it from his own mouth, pushed it into the sunken lips. I turned my face away; this was a siege at its most unforgivable.

'This gentleman here, John, is William Lilly. He's famous for his astrology, you might have heard of him?' Mercy told his cousin.

'Forgive me, sir, I've heard nothing this past two months,' John Stephens said to me, 'and that what I knew now escapes me for the deprivation we suffer. Have you any food, perchance?'

I pulled from my pocket a hunk of bread I had secured for my adventure, thinking it was needed more here.

'Too kind, sir, too kind.'

'Can you help me? I am seeking the lodgings of a Philomath by the name of John Humphrys?'

'He's one of Sir Charles Lucas's lackeys and does live within his property, but I can take you there, for a price?'

And I did give him half a crown, thinking he could not eat it, but perhaps barter. After which Mercy and his cousin John led me to a property where I was admitted by a woman fallen into a dumb stupor wrought from starvation, exhaustion, and anger. This is what struck me most profoundly – the surrender of hope. I had witnessed it in animals much abused by their owners, but never in Man.

I found my old student at the back of the house which had been taken over by Lord Norwich himself. A chicken ran about the room, and there were strings of vegetables and half a hock of ham hanging from the ceiling. No starvation here then, I noted. John Humphrys was at his desk, in the midst of some bogus calculation, and my appearance startled him thoroughly.

'By Jove, 'tis you, Master Lilly, methought I saw a ghost!'

'No ghost, John, but I warrant I should be with the stench of death about this town.' I looked over his shoulder at the figures spread across the oak top, much stained and drawn upon. 'Your calculation is incorrect here; the Mercury didn't fall in that house at that time, I know it for myself, and the Mars was much maligned and not in fortune as you have depicted it here.'

'My craft I learnt from you.'

'You can harness a donkey but you cannot teach it to pull a cart.'

At which he jumped to his feet and did put up his fists. 'How dare you, sir!'

Knowing the man to be a coward, and far too respectful of his old mentor to lay hand upon him, I sat calmly down in his chair.

'I dare because I care. Ours is an ancient craft, John. We carry the weight of prophecy and all the moral responsibility that comes with it. Surely I did teach thee that?'

At which he lowered his fist, and did gruffly reply, 'My calculations are correct, maestro, Colchester will be relieved, and the King's men shall find their support within the month. Fairfax and the Ironsides will be sent running.'

'And it's this prediction which you keep feeding Lord Norwich and Sir Charles Lucas?'

'It is the truth.'

'It is *your* truth that maintains your power here, and that doth set hunger and deprivation upon the hundreds who live within these walls. Their blood will stain your hands for an eternity.'

'I tell you, I have done the calculation!'

'And I tell you *my* maths tells me otherwise. You must encourage Lord Norwich to surrender, for the sake of his men and the good Parliamentarian folk trapped in this city.'

'I have asked the question a dozen times and every time I get the same answer.'

I glanced back at the horary on the table.

'You have chosen the wrong Significator.'

'I tell you, I speak the future. Besides, Lord Norwich hath received a letter from Commander Langdale in the North; he will send Royalists troops to save us and Colchester.'

'He will not.' I made for the door. 'I leave you now, John. You are not a bad man, I know this, but like the King you suffer from hubris – and take note. Hubris, like vainglory, is one of the seven sins.'

I returned to the camp by the breaking of light. Instead of sleeping I turned my back to those condemning walls and did sit upon a hillock gazing upon the sunrise meditating upon the fact it is a confronting thing to be a Man and alive with Death's breath licking at one's shoulder. The terrible noise of cannon fire broke my reverie and I was forced to abandon the outlook.

Later John Booker and I did visit a post armed with cannons pounding St Mary's church and the military position beside it. The pungent odour of gunpowder and the shouting of the men operating the cannons struck me as a strange industry, one that allowed no moral reflection, propelled as one was into the violent instinct of survival. I also noted there were no birds in the trees about us; did Nature smell Death?

Just then the cannoneer observed through his telescope that his position was to be fired upon by the massive cannon I had observed on my first day. The anticipation of seeing this monster in action did momentarily override my fear, but then the cannoneer shouted that we should run, and I did take shelter under an old ash tree. One minute later the cannon ball whistled just over our heads.

'No danger now,' said the gunner, 'but be gone, for there are five more charging.' He was proven right. A good two hours later those cannons had fired and killed that poor man. Later I did see the blood of both the cannoneer and gunner spilt upon the planks. Such is how men's lives end in battle, both profoundly and in the abysmal smallness of a fact.

Whilst as Philomaths we did our utmost to encourage the belief of victory, my secret plea to John Humphrys went unhindered and the siege rolled on in the relentless blaze of a dead-eyed summer. Colchester did not surrender and General Fairfax continued to starve the town, despite pleas from the town council and petitions from outside the besieged city. Soon the heat of August cracked the mud and blistered the lips of soldiers and reports came over the wall of whole families sitting down to meals of soap and candles, of disease and even of cannibalism.

Finally, one afternoon the gates open and I watched a parade of five hundred women led by a woman in her fourth decade, of noble bearing and stoic in appearance. The young and the old, mothers, wives, grandmothers were all in tattered dresses, gaunt and thin, white begrimed ribbons tied to their wrists fluttering in a hopeful breeze. The aged woman leading walked slowly to the tent of the Parliamentarian commander, Colonel Rainsborough, where, I was told, she did attempt to plead with him to allow food at least for the children and the sick.

He did not even answer her, but instead gave the command that the women should be stripped of their clothes, of which the troops did oblige with great merriment. It were a terrible humiliation to see these desperate women, so shamed and huddling, the youngest cowering to protect the collapsed and aged figures of the elder. One had the shape and colouring of my Jane and I was shamed to think this was a humility inflicted on Englishwomen by Englishmen. After they were forced to go back through the city gates without food or relief I did think upon the inhumanity of these soldiers, themselves the sons and husbands of such women.

The next day John Booker and I returned to London and on the twenty-seventh of August Norwich finally surrendered and Colchester was liberated. Later, Sir Charles Lucas and Sir George Lisle were executed. As for John Humphrys, I have no doubt he will receive his reparation either in this life or the next.

The summer passed and then the autumn. I was much taken with my labours and astrology. My marriage had now become a tolerant affection and, as for Magdalene, I felt us receding away from each other as if we were looking into the wrong end of a looking glass. I have become furtive in my dealings with her. Something hath broken between us, yet when I did see her all the threads of our lovemaking and commonality in spirit and mind did net me and pull me closer, and I confess, dear Reader, I would then make all manner of promise to her.

Then, to worsen matters, Parliament began negotiations with the King in Newport on the eighteenth of September, only for the Monarch to declare a few days later that this were a mock treaty and he had only begun such talk to gain time. Oh, the audacity of Kings and politicians! Do they not realise the importance of their words? They are Gods and can't afford to prattle and whore themselves like the ordinary man. Their purpose is of a higher order yet the King betrayed this calling. It appeared he did not believe he was in mortal danger for his life and thought Parliament were playing a game with him. This lack of understanding as to his true position was most unsettling.

Many in the New Model Army were now concerned Charles will escape and begin another war – one that a war-raped England could not afford.

Parliament itself was divided; there were some who supported the notion of a truce with the King and Scotland, whilst others favoured the New Model Army and putting the King on trial. But Westminster itself hath still not honoured the monies and compensations due to the soldiers and thus discontent threatens rebellion.

CHAPTER THIRTY-EIGHT

Winter of the year 1648

The Corner House, The Strand

**A Retrograde Planet, or one in his first station,
Significator in Question, denotes ill in the
Question, discord and much contradiction.**

On the sixth of December a Colonel Pride and his men did set upon Westminster and purge the house of treacherous Parliamentarians (many of them Presbyterian) for refusing Commissary-General Ireton's Remonstrance of the Army. This was a document that, in its essence, argued for the King to be put on trial.

Dear Reader, words were inadequate in their cold brevity to describe how this hath affected London and the country – a man without his head, a child without his father – the sin of executing God's own elect. We, as a people, have only known a God-anointed leader of the nation. We may have been dismayed at the King's incompetency, at his ignorance of the state of his own citizens, at his betrayal of the good Church of England and his choice of bride, but make no mistake: Charles was loved.

To be placed on trial meant the possibility of regicide; many would sooner execute their own grandfather. There were cries for justice, but none wanted the King dead. If only

Charles himself had bent his will to Parliament and the Army! If only!

In truth, the King even imprisoned had been most promiscuous and undignified in seeking support and treaties amid the many factions, flaying about in desperation, bedding himself in with all manner of politick – the Irish confederates, the English constitutionalists, and the Engagers, to name a few. There were also the rumours that Queen Henrietta was still campaigning to raise troops in both Europe and Ireland. All this infuriated the populace and made the common man increasingly believe that the King did not respect Parliament or even his own subjects.

Mrs Featherwaite was most irate. 'He takes us and Cromwell for fools!' she kept repeating. 'What, does the pompous ass believe our boys have been fighting and dying for a joke, a play at power? You mark my words, Master Lilly, this will end badly, both for King and country!'

On Christmas Day, after church and a chastising sermon on the sins of bad governance, and how in Heaven all good men reign equal, I did manage to leave the Corner House on the pretext I was to a tavern to cheer in the New Year with William Pool – a necessity, since Parliament and the good Puritans banned the festival and other Saints' days several years before. But two streets away from the house I did not take the road to the White Hart but instead turned toward Chancery Lane, armed with both a good goose and a cask of port a Querent did give me in lieu of payment.

Snow sprinkled my hat and beard, making all virgin and beautiful. I walked alone, my hat pulled low, relishing being everyman or no-man, my presence pushed into the thinness of negotiating the slippery cobblestones, my breath a billowing mist against the cold. All thought emptied into that minutiae of life. I had left all that I was walking from behind in the Corner House: Jane and her pinched mouth, her grievances buzzing around her like an invisible cloud of muttering Demons, the responsibility of my Querents, my books, the weighty task of championing my profession with my melancholia rumbling on in my chest like a hidden canker. I was interrupted by the stump of an arm thrust before me – an injured soldier begging for alms, a young man not yet twenty, displaying the stump of a leg and an arm. 'Lost at Marston,' he murmured, 'and I was to be a smithy . . .' I gave him coin, and promised to pray for him. He was pathetically grateful and his plight did make me angry.

A moment later I was at Magdalene's door and the new maid answered my knock, flushed and bothered, her unkempt hair pushed roughly beneath her bonnet.

'Good Master Lilly, 'tis a pleasure – and frankly, a relief, to see you on this holy day.'

'And a merry Christmas to you,' I answered, for I confess I was a little intoxicated by this time of the evening. 'How fares thy mistress?' The maidservant checked to see that the street were empty, then let me into the house.

'Badly. Truly, I thought of sending thee a message, such it's been here.' She shut the door, then turned in fierce intent. 'Lady de Morisset hath been in communion with the Angels, and I swear that false Sarah Skelhorn has not helped my mistress's cause. My lady hath not eaten since Tuesday last, refusing all manner of food I have placed before her, telling me eating will turn her body into too dense an element, and that will block the Angels' voices.' The maid leant close and I smelt the lavender she must have washed her hair with. 'She tells me they have told her of the baby, and I fear she is demented with a grief that neither I, nor any Cunning Woman, can cure. But perhaps the great William Lilly can exorcise this pain.' Her words were all sharp irony, and I could not but feel shame.

I found Magdalene in her study, the air thick with burning incense and bay leaf. Chanting, she was bent over the thick pages of a grimoire.

'Ariel, come unto me and speak thy will, Babylon maketh me your vessel and I shall serve thee . . .'

'Magdalene?'

She looked up, her eyes in some far place, so I did repeat, 'Magdalene, 'tis your William.' And then she did see me, her cheeks hollow in a starvation of the spirit as much as the body.

'I am in ceremony and you have broken the circle.'

I sat before her and took her freezing hands unto mine, and then I did see she was barefoot, with the room itself as cold as the winter outside, the fire out in the hearth.

'Where is my Magdalene, where hath she gone?' I asked rubbing her hands.

At which her demeanour did soften and some of her beauty return, inching through her cheeks like a rosy thaw.

'I was with him, William, our child. The Angels took me and I was walking with Adam in a future that might have been.'

In lieu of an answer I pulled her shawl up over her shoulders and called the maid to light the fire and bring some broth.

'Magdalene, you must eat and seize life. Enough of this grieving. You are still young, you might marry again, and then there will be children to fill this house with laughter.'

At which she said nothing. I went to the windows and pulled back the curtains; the bluish winter light filled the room.

'Come, it's snowing, and the church bells are pealing for Midnight Mass to celebrate Christ's birth.'

Magdalene joined me at the window, her body a sliver of curling weight as she leant against me; nought left except the child she once was and the older woman she would become. I did so want to be her protector, her saviour, and, in another life, her husband, but those words were unspeakable.

'It is Christmas, William?'

'It is, and we shall celebrate. I will have it no other way.'

The maid entered with a bowl of broth and placed it on the table. Whilst I did feed Magdalene with a spoon, the maidservant stoked the fire and soon the hearth was burning again. After the maid left us alone, Magdalene regained some of her strength. 'I can see much in the glass, William, it is the world I live in now.'

'Perhaps too much – those of us who are gifted with second sight must learn to close our eyes at times or else risk Bedlam.'

'You think me mad?'

'I think Matthew Hopkins almost broke thy spirit, sweet Megs. I think thee need healing and rest. I can find a cottage for you and your maid, outside of this spinning city. You could go there and I would visit at least once a month.'

'Would you?' She turned to the window, staring out of it at the silvered rooftops and the city skyline in a strange wonder. 'Have they found a truce with the King yet?' she asked, trance-like. 'I fear for His Majesty, I hear his chamber is so dark that it needs candles at midday. His spirit must be low, but he is stubborn, William, and fears he will be poisoned before he has a chance to place his argument before his people.'

'Parliament doesn't want to execute the King . . .'

'Execute him? But they cannot! The King is God's representative on land, this would be the greatest sin!'

'And this is a new world. I do not believe the King has a comprehension of this; he thinks they would not dare to behead a monarch. I also believe he is stalling to create division amongst his enemies. He sees the hatred and discord between Army Officer and MP, between Levellers, Ranters and many others who are only loosely bound for their opposition towards the Royalist. And in this division Charles sees hope.' I tried to keep my words neutral but in truth I was furious at the King for his plotting and his self-destructive stubbornness and angry at Magdalene for destroying herself through grief.

'And you, William, what do you see?'

'What I saw I wrote nine years ago – I observed a solar eclipse in the King's Natal figure that foretold a grim prediction.'

'I remember; the Moon was covering the Sun in the house of Death – the eighth house. And the Sun symbolises the King as he rules in Leo and he is the lord of the tenth house – where all Royals dwelleth. You think he will be executed?'

'I fear the lunar eclipse on his birthday on the nineteenth of November was the last sword to fall. I have concluded that the most material thing signified by this eclipse is a strict questioning, and becoming an even more severe questioning.' I leant forward and whispered, 'Principally to be effected in London and Westminster.'

'They will put him to trial?' Magdalene paled in shock.

'I wrote as directly as I dared in my almanack for 1649 . . . I had seen from the position of the stars that in January there is a perfect trine between Jupiter and Saturn, and we may have strong hopes of being quite cured of our distempers. This will be a fateful time for the King, and I confess, Megs, my astrological opinion hath been sought out by the most powerful Parliamentarians on the matter,' I foolishly told her, for I craved a confidante, so great is the weight of responsibility for such important predictions.

'You have great influence, and this is a big burden indeed.'

'The good Lord Gray, and my old friend, the preacher Hugh Peter, sent for me and I met with them at Denmark House. They wished me to tell them of my observations of this January coming and insisted I read from my two almanacks, which I did.'

And I did recite for my mistress the observations I did share with these men of great influence.

'*I am serious, I beg and expect Justice, either fear or shame begins to question Offenders . . . The lofty Cedars begin to divine a thundering Hurricane is at hand, God elevates men contemptible . . . Our demigods are sensible we begin to dislike their actions very much in London, more in the country . . . Blessed be God who encourages his servants and makes them valiant, and of undaunted spirits to go on with his Decrees.*

Upon a sudden, great expectation arise and men generally believe a quiet and calm time draws near.'

'And what did they do after?'

'They did look most serious and told me that "*If we are not fools and knaves, we shall do Justice,*" in the grimmest of voices. The two of them walked some distance away from me so that I could not hear their whisperings.' All this was true, but I found myself judged in my lover's eyes, and her judgement was not kind. I looked down in shame.

'Oh, William, what hast thou done?'

'I have done nothing except tell of what the stars have told me!' But Magdalene did not look convinced, so I continued my argument, 'Repeatedly I have tried to warn the King of his predilections, and repeatedly he has ignored me. He must make a truce if he is to survive. '

'England without its King . . . this is a new world I want no part of,' she answered quietly, then turned to throw another coal upon the fire.

CHAPTER THIRTY-NINE

The twentieth day of the month of January, 1649

Westminster

The Lord of the Ascendant or the Moon with the
Head or Taile, of the Dragon, brings damage to
the Question propouned, see in what house they
are in, and receive signification from thence.

At this time, I were in the habit of visiting Westminster every
Saturday to see the speakers and to read the atmosphere in the
House. This Saturday was different. As I entered I came across
my friend, the pastor Hugh Peter, who approached me agitated
with a strange excitement.

'Come, Lilly, wilt thou go hear the King tried?'

'When?'

'Now, just now, go with me.'

And so I found myself upon the King's Bench, gazing at the
proceedings, when the King himself did appear. Dressed in the
clothes of one of the Knights of the Garter, he did seem most
majestic and with all his dignities held firm. Curiously, he
spake without his stammer and most effectively. But he did not
doff his hat to the officers nor recognise the legitimacy of the
court.

When he was charged with treason I watched him and saw in
his face incredulity — I do believe he thought Parliament was

bluffing and he did laugh (methinks he regarded many of the ministers, especially those from the mercantile class or farmers' sons, upstarts, and in this had no right to imprison or try himself, he of *Sangre Azul* – the blue blood of the anointed).

The King then claimed this could not be a Parliamentary court for he did not recognise any Lords that he did know. His argument grew most outraged, and when the judge said that the trial was the will of the people, the King did protest that he could not answer to the court for he was a King by blood and not by election, and if he were to answer the charge he would be breaking his oath to serve the people when he were crowned. It were a clever argument that held no sway with his prosecutors – haters as they were of all that smacked of privilege, divine or otherwise.

The judge, a young man named John Bradshaw, became most angered by the King's disrespect of the court. He himself was not cowered by the weighty and until then unimaginable of task of judging a King. A most telling instance was when the King's silver-topped staff did fall by accident to the ground, and Charles, who hath been surrounded by servitude his whole life, waited for a guard to pick it up to give it to him. In that terrible silence, Time and Hatred stretched, but not one person moved to help the Monarch. Instead the whole court stared on in distain until finally the godly John Rushworth picked the staff up and gave it back to the King.

For many, in that moment the King was toppled from Monarch to a simple foolish, arrogant little man – nothing more than Charles Stuart and I was much troubled in both heart and soul. This were the nub of the situation, and until then I truly believe Charles thought he still ruled.

After which his own defence did rumble on until Judge Bradshaw again did warn the King that he doth interrogate the power of the court which did not become one in his condition, as he were the one standing in the dock and not the people of England. A most grim caution and I wasn't the only man in that chamber that prayed the King heeded it.

The trial lasted seven long days and was most tragic and frustrating as ever I did witness.

On the Sunday, my good friend the preacher Hugh Peter conducted a prayer meeting in Parliament in which he did argue a case to separate *salus populi* from the *vox populi* – to make distinct the good of the people from the voice of the people. This was clever, for Hugh Peter was suggesting to the King that he might accept the legitimacy of the court for the *good* of the people and not because of the *voice* of the people – a dignified compromise, and one that would allow the Monarch to keep his head.

King Charles did not exploit the suggestion. Again, stubbornly, he refused to answer all charges in the afternoon session. My spirits sank lower.

The next day – Monday the twenty-second – again the King refused to answer all charges. Instead he stood up in the dock, a frail, short stature yet emulating utter unquestioning superiority in his stance and manner and began to read a document he had written explaining his refusal in a thin, stuttering voice, again claiming the Parliament before him was not properly constituted.

About me some had their heads in their hands, others were openly muttering in anger and frustration, all were exasperated and much infuriated by this truculence, and I could see that if the King continued in this way he was in great danger indeed, and yet he still appeared most ignorant of the mood of both court and judge.

On the twenty-third and the twenty-fourth January there were three more sessions, and still King Charles did not acquiesce. Desperation and resignation now filled the chamber like a terrible weight whilst the Monarch, oblivious, remained upon the podium in the middle of the hall, now reduced to an island of incomprehension and suicidal stubbornness.

On Thursday the twenty-fifth in a private session between the Parliamentarians it was decided that the King was guilty and they now debated whether his punishment should be death. The situation appeared hopeless and I could not see any stability in an England without a King and I confess I did wonder at the King's own strategy. He would have been aware of his own martyrdom, if executed, and how this would play in the game of history. Was this his long game?

The court next met on Saturday the twenty-seventh. Again, Charles refused to answer the charges; instead he did request conferences with the Two Houses, the Lords and the Commons, but his request was rejected. He was then given two more opportunities to plea, but again he refused to answer. I am most pedantic in the telling of this, but it is important to comprehend the great, spiralling tension of such a trial. England's security was held in the balance and in the taverns, the hearths, fields and farms, nothing else was talked of and many were afeard. For great numbers still saw the King as God's representative and to execute him would surely bring God's wrath upon both England and its people. Would his death herald in the End of Days? There were some who believed so. Cromwell was no fool: he could not afford another revolt if the King faced the axeman and no one wanted the unholy and unprecedented task of regicide staining their soul . . . yet there were those in that chamber who did want the *man* Charles Stuart dead. Yet when we as one did lean forward in our seats, willing the King to grasp the chance to live and adopt humility, he gave us no hope.

Finally, most exasperated and with no other choice, Judge

Bradshaw officially declared the King guilty of treason and passed his sentence as death.

Immediately disbelief rolled through the chamber, followed by shock, the intellectual possibility far removed from the reality of hearing those fatal words. Only then, I believe, did King Charles understand the gravity of his situation, tragically too late, and only then did he try to argue the charges, but Judge Bradshaw cut him short. Suddenly the King was a frightened man, shaking his head in incredulity, all pomp and rank expelled like air from a balloon.

On the Sunday I heard that they were having trouble finding enough brave MPs to sign the death warrant. This did not surprise me: no man wants to be immortalised in history for such an office. The Parliament was frantic and did spend both the Sunday and Monday waking important folk from their beds and pulling them from their churches in the search for anyone who would put their names upon on the fatal warrant.

On Monday the twenty-ninth of January, the day before the planned execution, I did attend a secret meeting with Hugh Peter, John Rushworth and a couple of other powerful men. After hours in heated debate discussing ways of reaching the King and persuading him to both repent and accept the justice of the court, we came to no conclusion. Besides, we had no way of reaching the King alone without his guards, and so I returned to the Corner House with heavy heart. I thought to visit Magdalene, but could not face her distress, may the Lord forgive me for this weakness.

Next day, on Tuesday the thirtieth of January, 1649, I had decided to stay in my chambers in the Corner House, as I had woken with a great remorse of the spirit. I opened my eyes at four in the morning, the window cloudy with an evil, creeping frost, the fire in my grate nothing but smouldering embers.

I got up, the floor freezing against my naked feet, and walked to the window. Outside the moon had tinted the fog into a landscape of failed dreams and spectres. Today, I thought, the King will die, and something indivisible but profound will evaporate from the morality of the English Soul and there is absolutely nothing I can do to prevent it. Suddenly I felt old.

'William?' Jane called from the chamber beside mine. She appeared in the doorway, dwarfed by her nightdress, her small skull cupped in a knitted sleeping cap. 'You cannot sleep either?' In bare feet she padded across to me. 'He will die, won't he?'

At which I did draw her to me, the warmth of her rotund figure an uncommon truce in our warring marriage.

'I will go to see the beheading, Jane. I thought I would not, but the King needs men like me there. We are the witnesses to this barbarity, and we have nothing but our courage to feed his own in this darkest of moments.'

'Then I will join you, William.' And, finally, I recognised the silent valour of my wife.

A pall hung across London in expectant horror – even the dogs had stopped barking, the grey sky already in mourning. The scaffold had been erected before the banqueting hall at Whitehall Palace and Jane and I and Mrs Featherwaite, both women dressed in the most decorous and sombre black, had left at dawn to secure a good position in the crowd. The streets were silent, the shops, taverns, and markets all closed in respect; some windows hung with black crêpe in sombre reverence.

Around Whitehall a huge crowd waited in the glacial cold, with some on roofs to watch, others upon carts and all manner of ladder. All in a reverent whispering, as if they were about to witness a miracle or some great holy event; the usual merriment and jostling at executions absent.

Some were weeping and tearful, some still disbelieving, thinking perhaps a chariot of Angels might descend and rescue Charles or that Parliament might reverse the judgement at the last moment, but all were tense in a kind of dread (for both their souls and for England, I warrant).

On the edge of the crowd several self-proclaimed prophets preached in graphic illustration the oncoming doomsday after the King falls headless upon the block whilst there were many I did recognise in the crowd, both Querents and supporters. We had pushed close to the front, close enough to be able to hear and see the King, the desire to etch the terrible consequence of this unnatural death upon my memory paramount.

Finally, at two in the afternoon they led the King out of one of the windows of the banqueting hall, directly onto the scaffold. Charles was dressed simply; bareheaded, he stood with such dignity, his hair flowing to his neck. And he did not appear frightened but quite calm, flanked by executioner and the Bishop.

A great hush swept across the crowd as he stepped forward, broken only by the bawling of a baby, and he spake thus, directing his speech chiefly to Colonel Thomlinson who had the charge of him:

'For the people . . . truly I desire their Liberty and Freedom as much as any Body whomsoever. But I must tell you, that their Liberty and Freedom, consists in having of government; those Laws by which their Life and their Gods may be most their own. It is not for having share in government, sir; that is nothing pertaining to them. A subject and a sovereign are clean different things, and therefore until they do that, I mean that you do put the people in that liberty as I say, certainly they will never enjoy themselves.

'Sirs, it was for this that now I am come here. If I would have given way to an Arbitrary way, for to have all Laws changed according to the power of the Sword, I needed not to have come here; and therefore, I tell you (and I pray God it be not laid to your charge) That I am the martyr of the People.'

Then the King, speaking to the Executioner, said, 'I shall say but very short Prayers, and when I thrust out my hands . . .'

And the King did demonstrate, his small white hands pathetic against the black of the scaffold. But the executioner, taking note, did know the sign, and my own heart squeezed in painful anticipation whilst the pressing crowd about me seemed to not dare to breathe. Then the King asked Bishop Juxon for his night cap, after which he did neatly placed upon his own head and then again turned to the executioner.

'Does my hair trouble you?' at which the executioner told him it did, so with the help of the Bishop and the Executioner the King tucked all of his hair beneath his cap. And, dear Reader, how ordinary was this King now, how like a bareheaded servant of God who stood simply before his Maker. And now I could see that he did have fear, and that there were many in that audience that wished their courage out like a swelling wave to carry him forth.

'I have a good Cause, and a gracious God on my side,' the King told Bishop Juxon, as if to reassure himself.

The good bishop did gently reply, 'There is but one stage more. This Stage is turbulent and troublesome, it is a very short one: But You may consider it will soon carry You a very great way; it will carry You from Earth to Heaven; and there you shall find a great deal of Cordial, Joy, and Comfort.'

Around me women broke into sobbing at these words, and those who before did jeer, were silent.

Listening, Charles answered, 'I go from a corruptible, to an incorruptible Crown; where no disturbance can be, no disturbance in the World.'

'You are exchanged from a Temporal to an eternal Crown – a good exchange,' the bishop replied, clasping the King's hands for a moment.

Then, after asking the executioner whether his hair was well, the King took off his cloak and the pendant of the Order of the Garter and did hand it to the Bishop, then took off his doublet and placed his cloak back over his waistcoat.

After several short words to the executioner and a murmured prayer, for they had made the block so low he had to lay down flat, the King knelt and stretched out his hands in the gesture he had shown the executioner. In seconds, and in one single blow, his head was cut from his body. In that moment the people watching all gave a huge groan, as if part of England itself had been severed and a great pain did grip my heart.

The executioner then did hold the head up high by the hair for all to see, and the crowd surged forward, for some wished to soak their handkerchiefs in his blood, believing the King were now a martyr and that all that was once his body holy properties. Next to me, Jane fell in a dead faint.

As Mrs Featherwaite and I struggled to lift her back to her feet I caught sight of Magdalene, standing at the back of the crowd. She was white as the snow, her eyes fixed straight ahead at the sight of poor Charles' ashen head, her maid pulling at her arm as the crowd jostled, threatening to dash her to the ground.

The sound of Mrs Featherwaite calling brought me to my senses and I was compelled to carry my wife home.

After we had put Jane to bed, Mrs Featherwaite lifted her apron and wiped the tears from her face. 'I will never be the same, and me a Puritan.' She blew her nose loudly. 'What have we done? What is England now?'

'Anarchy, bloodshed, betrayal of neighbour by neighbour,' I answered flatly, devoid of hope and tired of humanity.

"'Tis the apocalypse, sir?'

'Nay, in time all will right itself and there will be a crown again at the head of England.'

At which Mrs Featherwaite bustled off to the kitchen, a little comforted, and I could turn to the hearth, free at last to weep.

I was interrupted by the sound of a tapping upon the window. At first I ignored it but then I saw a messenger pigeon upon the sill, the plumage of which I did recognise.

The scroll unfurled was no longer than my finger, the calligraphy shaky in its emotion.

Forgive me this transgression, my sweet Philomath . . . my world has ended and I now seek solace in another.
   I will love you always, Magdalene.

I cannot remember how I travelled so swiftly to her dwelling – perhaps it were Angels who carried me, or Fear that gave me winged sandals. But I remember her young maid, innocent in her unknowing, surprised to see me banging upon the door.

I remember how we had to break the lock on the bedchamber.

I remember the coldness of Magdalene's body lying upon the bed, her lips stained dark with hemlock, her eyes staring out upon a sky I could no longer share.

❧

Epilogue

My life naturally continued, my reputation and my publication of pamphlets of much knowledge both astrological and medical for the poor and working man did grow accordingly.

I stayed married to Jane and bought (for I was a man of no little wealth) a cottage in Hersham in 1652 and in February of 1653 Jane did die and I shed no tears, for all affection by then had ceased between us.

In October 1654 I married Ruth Needham, a woman a number of years younger than myself. This was the most happy marriage and union: she was signified in my Nativity by Jupiter in Libra (the most generous placement for bountiful companionship) and we did live most content the rest of my years – twenty-six in total – together.

In 1665, as I had predicted, plague raged terribly in the City of London. And I treated very many poor people for the disease. And I can tell you, people were most civil as to when they brought the urine of infected people to the house – standing at a distance to make sure neither I or my household were infected. I ordered cordials for those infected and not likely to die that caused them to sweat, and many recovered. My landlord at the time was frightened of my visitors and ordered I should be gone. He had four children, and when I did escape to the country with my wife and my household, I did take them with me and provided for them. Six weeks after I left this dwelling the landlord, his wife, and many servants died of the pestilence.

A year later I was summoned before Parliament to explain how, some fifteen years before, I had predicted both the plague and the Great Fire of London that raged from Sunday the second of September until Wednesday the fifth of September, in the pamphlet entitled *Monarch or no Monarch* in the illustration of both a great fire with the Gemini twins of London being fed into the flames and the depiction of gravediggers, coffins and great pestilence. Some claimed I did set the fire myself, others claimed I was a Sorcerer. I argued I were totally innocent of any designs upon burning the city and that it was only the finger of God. I argued exceedingly well and the committee was satisfied. Such are the great dangers of prophecy!

And so, from my cottage in Hersham, I did continue my work as both medic and Astrologer with the very poor. Later in my life, having no natural heirs, I did cultivate one John Gadbury, both as an Astrologer and Heir, but he did turn upon me and did much in the press and in pamphlets to discredit both my predictions past and present and my cures. This was a source of great pain and disappointment to me, but I continued my practice, surviving the second civil war and the purging by Charles II of those he perceived murdered his father. Indeed, I was even called upon on more than one occasion to give this new King my astrological advice. And as the century drew to a close the advance of Nova Scientia did, indeed, erode the influence of the Philomath but Elias Ashmole's great friendship did save me as did the irrefutable reputation of my *Christian Astrology* increasingly adopted by therugy students across the globe.

Finally, having lived a good long life, and in great happiness with my third wife, I passed into the arms of my Lord in the year of 1681 in the month of June. And I thank thee, dear Reader, for thy patience and sympathetic ear in hearing my story and beseech thee to take courage both from the stars and from thy own will.

'*God suffers no sin unpunished, no lie unrevenged.*'
William Lilly.

Acknowledgements

I would like to thank the following: the astrologers Peter Stockinger and Sue Ward for their generous insights into William Lilly, astrologer and close friend Yasmin Boland, astrologer and historian Kim Farnell for her editorial input and sharp eye, my UK agent Julian Alexander, my Australian agent Rick Raftos, my commissioning editors at Little Brown UK – Antonia Hodgson and Maddie West – and my desk editor Thalia Proctor.

strong sense of humour, I felt I could give him this vulnerability and pleasure as a way of taking you, the reader, into his psyche and under his skin. Magdalene spoke through me, a blending of many of the female seers, prophets, double-spies and Wicca-folk who existed in those war-filled years, and took her own vivid shape. Profound, brave and ultimately tragic, she was a character I grew to love, and I hope you ended up loving her too.

The wind was making a mockery of her red hair, the grace of her movement catching at my senses . . . We made an odd couple, her in her blue and scarlet court finery and myself in the plain cloak, jerkin and shirt. But there was a pleasing symmetry to our intelligence that did bind us as a natural match. Desire is a terrible burden for the moral man.

It would be great to know whether you too were moved by their great love story. How did you find the story of Hector Able, the Cunning Folk wizard? Did you enjoy the maverick actor Tobias Young? William's dangerous trip into Royalist Oxford? How real were the streets of civil war London for you?

It's hard to bring up reviews – even as a seasoned writer! But they are our life-blood and the only way we know if we are reaching our readers. So I'd love it if you could leave a review – it really takes away the loneliness of writing and brings me to you.

Finally, I'm also contactable through my website and my blog – and if you liked this book do read my other historical fiction and thrillers.

Info: www.tobsha.com
Love Tobsha x

Dear Reader, hello . . .

My heartfelt thanks for reading *The Magick Of Master Lilly* and taking the time to immerse yourself into the extraordinary world of William Lilly, one of the most amazing astrologer–wizards of his era. Writing this book has been an intense and long journey for me, both thrilling and, at times, yes, magical, as some of the synchronicities I've experienced along the way have been too extraordinary to rationalise away. More than many of my other books I have felt like a conduit; a mere voice to a story with its own power. For example: I sent away for a second hand book of grimoires I knew William Lilly must have had on his bookshelf. When it arrived, I discovered written in the book the owner's name and his address – which happened to be in Manningtree, the very town in which William Lilly met Matthew Hopkins!

I have always been fascinated by those pivotal years in the seventeenth century where many things considered magical and wondrous were superseded by science then finally Enlightenment. And, as some of you will know, I have always had an interest in mysticism and astrology and that dangerous dance between pre-determinism and free will – nature versus nurture. All of which ultimately lead me to Maestro Lilly, magus and horary astrologer extraordinaire. Even more exciting was to read about how his career and life had been set against a tense London in the grip of civil war. This was an amazing man who ended up influencing both political events and the politicians themselves. How much of his horary was Time-Magick? How much of it was genuine prediction or powerful planting of suggestion?

And then there is the character of Magdalene . . . fictional, I confess, but knowing that William had an unhappy second marriage, and knowing he was a earthy sensual man with a

~❧~

Bibliography

William Lilly, The Last Magician: Astrologer and Adept by Peter Stockinger and Sue Ward, Mandrake 2014

Christian Astrology: Book One and Two by William Lilly, Cosimo Classics 2005

William Lilly's History of His Life and Times: From the year 1602 to 1681 (illustrated edition) by William Lilly edited by Elias Ashmole, Dodo Press 2009

A Biography of William Lilly: The Man Who Saw The Future by Catherine Blackledge, Watkins Media Ltd 2015

Familiar to all – William Lilly and Astrology in the 17th Century by Derek Parker, Jonathan Cape 1975

The Moment of Astrology – Origins in Divination by Geoffrey Cornelius, The Wessex Astrologer 2003

The Grimoire of Arthur Gauntlet – A 17th century London Cunning-man's book of charms, conjurations and prayers edited by David Rankine, Avalonia 2011

Religion and the Decline of Magic: Studies in Popular Beliefs in 16th and 17th Century England by Keith Thomas, Peregrine 1973

The Fated Sky: Astrology in History by Benson Bobrick, Simon and Schuster 2005

Astrology and the Popular Press: English Almanacs 1500-1800 by Bernard Capp, Faber and Faber 2011

Memoirs of the life of that learned antiquary, Elias Ashmole, Esq;

drawn up by himself by way of diary with appendix of original letters by Elias Ashmole, Ecco print editions 2010

Elias Ashmole: His Autobiographical and Historical Notes, his Correspondence, and Other Contemporary Sources Relating to his Life and Work, Vol 2: Texts 1617–1660 ed: C.H. Josten, Oxford University Press 1966

The English Civil War: A People's History by Diane Purkiss, Harper Perennial 2006

Cromwell, Our Chief of Men by Antonia Fraser, Weidenfeld & Nicholson 1973

The King's Peace 1637–1641 by C.V Wedgewood, Penguin 1983

The World Turned Upside Down – Radical Ideas During the English Revolution by Christopher Hill, Penguin 1972, 1975

God's Fury, England's Fire – a new history of the English Civil Wars by Michael Braddick, Penguin 2008

The Weaker Vessel – Woman's Lot in 17th England Part One by Antonia Fraser, Weidenfeld & Nicholson 1984

Her Own Life – Autobiographical Writings by Seventeenth-Century Englishwomen edited by Elspeth Graham, Hilary Hinds, Elaine Hobby and Helen Wilcox, Routledge 1989

Susanna's Sisters: Early Quaker Women and the Sects of 17th England by Patricia Brown and Simon Webb, Langley Press

Drama and Politics in the English Civil War by Susan Wiseman, Cambridge University Press 1998

A Jovial Crew (17th century play) by Richard Brome. Editor: Ann Haaker, pub Edward Arnold 2013.